Readers' praise for THE UNQUIET BONES

Thoughtful and curious, surgeon Hugh is an engaging character who feels totally real. – Rikki B. USA

Absolutely loved the book and cannot wait for the next one. One of the best medieval genre novels I've read in years. More of the same please – soon! – David C. UK

I enjoyed the setting, the period, the very realistic characters and the dry wit. – Donna B. USA

I enjoyed the story, and the insight into life in 14th century Britain. A lovely way to learn history – I'm looking forward to the sequel. – John H. UK

I read all of it in one go; it's quite the best medieval mystery I've read in a while. I teach medieval history, so it's always nice to read something by someone who actually knows what they're talking about. Can't wait for the next one! – Sarah T. USA

The first chronicle of Hugh de Singleton is a great read. – Richard A. UK

I found your novel a most enjoyable read and a rewarding venture into the history of Bampton in the company of real and entertaining characters. Should I find myself in the UK again I will definitely stop for a peek at St Beornwald's. – Anne Marie C. Ireland

A wonderful story, which could have been ghost-written by a true 14th century surgeon. I'm looking forward to reading more of his work. – Jill M. USA

A great read – appreciate the detail – and the glossary. I hope you have more to follow! – Ross D. Australia

As a retired nurse I enjoy reading the history of medicine. This book fed my hunger and left me wanting more. I am sending a donation to help save the beautiful old church in the story. – Patricia N. USA

This is an outstanding book and I found it impossible to put down. I shall look forward to the next chronicle with eager anticipation. – Roger F. UK

The first chronicle of Hugh de Singleton was first rate all the way. Amusing, educational, interesting, clever, and realistic all rolled into one fantastic piece of work. I am eagerly awaiting the second.
– Annie E. USA

Just a few lines to say how much I have enjoyed reading *The Unquiet Bones*. It is going on my 'keeper shelf' with my other favourite medieval mysteries. I hope this book is the first of many. – Sue G. UK

An excellent first novel. The plot is well thought out and moves along nicely, with enough in the way of twists, turns, and red herrings to keep the reader interested. – Gary M. USA

What an outstanding first novel! Great plot, easy to read ... I've read all the Cadfael books and *The Unquiet Bones* exceeds them all. Can't wait for the next book in the series. – Peter S. UK

Excellent debut of a fine new protagonist ... the author shows a firm grasp of history. We can cheerfully hope that this will be the first of many. – Suzanne C. USA

I have never written to an author before but I really feel I must thank you for *The Unquiet Bones*. I have so enjoyed this book. I am a great fan of medieval whodunits and this must rank as one of the best. – Roger G. France

All in all this was a great first novel and I will purchase any others forthcoming from this author. – Ruth I. USA

The book contains fascinating insights into medieval surgery. *The Unquiet Bones* is a delight to read and I'm looking forward to the next installment. – Chris P. USA

I have just finished *The Unquiet Bones* and I loved it – a breath of fresh medieval air. – Annie C. USA

You've created a real sense of place, coupled with characters a reader can like and be interested in. Hugh is a great hero and I look forward to more of his adventures. – Maria H. USA

It was a wonderful read; I can't wait to see where Master Hugh's adventures will take him. – Travis B. USA

A Corpse at St Andrew's Chapel

The second chronicle of

Hugh de Singleton, surgeon

MEL STARR

MONARCH
BOOKS

Oxford, UK & Grand Rapids, Michigan, USA

First published in the UK in 2009 by Monarch Books
(a publishing imprint of Lion Hudson plc),
Wilkinson House, Jordan Hill Road, Oxford OX2 8DR.
Tel: +44 (0)1865 302750   Fax: +44 (0)1865 302757
Email: monarch@lionhudson.com
www.lionhudson.com

Reprinted 2010 (twice), 2011.
First electronic format 2010.

ISBN: 978-1-85424-954-8 (print)
ISBN: 978-0-85721-040-1 (e-pub)
ISBN 978-0-85721-039-5 (Kindle)

Distributed by:
UK: Marston Book Services Ltd, PO Box 269, Abingdon, Oxon OX14 4YN;
USA: Kregel Publications, PO Box 2607, Grand Rapids, Michigan 49501.

British Library Cataloguing Data
A catalogue record for this book is available from the British Library.

Printed and bound in the UK by MPG Books Ltd.

For Amy and Pastor Jen

"Many daughters have done well, but you exceed them all."

Proverbs 32:29 (NKJV)

Acknowledgments

On a June afternoon in 1990 my wife and I found a delightful B&B in the tiny village of Mavesyn Ridware. Tony and Lis Page, the proprietors, became good friends. Nearly a decade later Tony and Lis moved to Bampton, where Susan and I were able to visit them in 2001. I saw immediately the town's potential for the novels I intended to write. Tony and Lis have been a great resource for the history of Bampton, for which I am very grateful.

Dr. John Blair, of Queen's College, Oxford, has written several papers illuminating the history of Bampton. These have been a great help, especially in understanding the odd situation of a medieval parish church staffed by three vicars.

When he learned that I had written an as yet unpublished novel, Dan Runyon, of Spring Arbor University, invited me to speak to his classes about the trials of a rookie writer. Dan sent some sample chapters of *The Unquiet Bones* to his friend, Tony Collins, Editorial Director of Monarch books at Lion Hudson plc. Thanks, Dan.

And thanks to Tony Collins, my editor, Jan Greenough, and all the people at Lion Hudson for their willingness to publish a new author with no track record.

To our many friends in the UK: your hospitality over the years has been a blessing. Thanks especially to Peter and Muriel Horrocks, Ron and Joan Taylor, George and Sally Kelsall, Frank and Jean Mitchell, and John and Jane Leech.

Mel Starr

Glossary

Angelus Bell: Rung three times each day – dawn, noon, and dusk – to announce the Angelus devotional.

Ascension Day: Forty days after Easter. In 1365: May 22.

Avignon: A city now in southern France where the popes resided from 1305 to 1378.

Bailiff: A lord's chief manorial representative. He oversaw all operations. Collected rents and fines, and enforced labor service. Not a popular fellow.

Beadle: A manor officer in charge of fences, hedges, enclosures, and curfew. He served under the reeve. Also called a hayward.

Buttery: A room for beverages, stored in "butts", or barrels.

Candlemas: Marked the purification of Mary after the birth of Christ. Women traditionally paraded to church carrying lighted candles. Tillage of fields resumed on this day.

Chasuble: A sleeveless outer garment worn by a priest during the mass.

Compost: A vegetable and fruit casserole, often including cabbage, parsnips, carrots, turnips, pears, and currants, flavoured with spices, wine, and honey.

Compostella: A city in northwestern Spain thought to be the burial place of the apostle James. A popular pilgrimage goal.

Coney: Rabbit.

Coppicing: To cut a tree back hard to the base to stimulate the growth of young shoots.

Corpus Christi: The Thursday after Trinity. In 1365: June 12.

Crenel: Open space between the merlons of a battlement.

Donatist: One who holds that sanctity in a priest is necessary for the administration of sacraments.

Dredge: Mixed grains planted together in a field; often barley and oats.

Ember Day: A day of fasting, prayer, and requesting forgiveness of sins. Observed four times per year on successive Wednesdays, Fridays, and Saturdays.

Easter Sepulcher: A niche in the wall of church or chapel where the host and a cross were placed on Good Friday and removed on Easter Sunday morning.

Farthing: One-fourth of a penny – the smallest silver coin.

Feast of St. Edward: March 18.

Fewterer: The keeper of a lord's hunting dogs.

Ganging: A Rogation Day procession around the boundary of a village.

Gathering: Eight leaves of parchment, made by folding the prepared hide three times.

Haberdasher: Merchant who sold household items such as pins, buckles, buttons, hats, and purses.

Hallmote: The manorial court. Royal courts judged free tenants accused of murder or felony, otherwise manorial courts had jurisdiction over legal matters concerning villagers. Villeins accused of murder might also be tried at hallmote.

Hayward: See "beadle."

Heriot: An inheritance tax (called a fine) paid to the lord of the manor – usually the heir's best animal.

Hocktide: The Sunday after Easter; a time for paying rents and taxes. Therefore, getting out of hock.

Hue and cry: Alarm call raised by the person who discovered a crime. All who heard it were expected to go to the scene of the crime and, if possible, pursue the criminal.

Hurdle: A panel woven from willow or other pliable wood, used for fencing in animals.

King's Eyre: A royal circuit court, presided over by a traveling judge.

Kirtle: The basic medieval undergarment.

Lammas Day: August 1, when thanks was given for a successful wheat harvest.

Leirwite: A fine for sexual relations out of wedlock.

Liripipe: A fashionably long tail attached to a man's cap.

Lombardy custard: A custard made with the addition of dried fruit.

Lych gate: A roofed gate in a churchyard wall under which the deceased rest during the initial part of a burial service.

Malmsey: the sweetest variety of madeira wine, originally from Greece.

Marcher country: Border lands between England and Wales, and England and Scotland.

Marshalsea: The stables and associated accoutrements.

Maslin: bread made from mixed grains, usually wheat and a coarser grain such as rye or barley.

Merlon: A solid portion of wall between the open crenels of a battlement.

Michaelmas: September 29. The feast signaled the end of the harvest. Last rents and tithes were due.

Pannage: a fee paid to a lord for permission to allow pigs to forage in the forest.

Parapet: The upper level of a castle wall.

Paschal moon: The first full moon after March 21.

Pax board: An object, frequently painted with sacred scenes, which was passed through the medieval church during service for all to kiss.

Pence: A penny – the most common medieval English coin. Like the half-penny and farthing (one-fourth penny), made of silver. Twelve pennies made a shilling and twenty shillings a pound. There was no one-pound coin.

Pottage: anything cooked in one pot, from soups and stews to simple porridge.

Poulterer: The lord's servant in charge of chickens, ducks, and geese.

Reeve: The most important manor official, although he did not outrank the bailiff. Elected by tenants from among themselves, often the best husbandman. He had responsibility for fields, buildings, and enforcing labor service.

Rogation Days: The Monday, Tuesday, and Wednesday before Ascension Day. Also called "gang days."

St Crispin's Day: October 25.

St David's Day: March 1.

St Scholastica Day Riot: February 10, 1355. Several townsmen and students were killed in the riot.

St Swithin's Day: July 15.

Soapwort: A perennial herb with pink or white flowers which emits a pleasant odor when bruised.

Surcoat: An over-garment.

Toft: Land surrounding a home. In the medieval period often used for growing vegetables.

Treaty of Bretigny: Cemented the English victory over France at Poitiers in 1356.

Verderer: In charge of the lord's forest lands.

Villein: A non-free peasant. He could not leave his land or service to his lord, or sell animals without permission. But if he could escape his manor for a year and a day he was free.

Vyaund cyprys: A chicken and rice pottage, often tinted with blue coloring.

Whitsunday: Pentecost; seven weeks after Easter Sunday. In 1365: June 1.

Woodbine: A shrub often found twining about a tree – a variety of honeysuckle.

Yardland: Thirty acres. Also called a virgate. In northern England also called an oxgang.

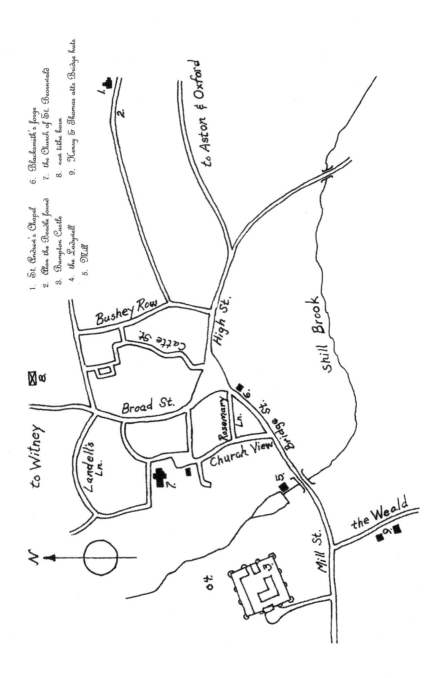

1. St. Andrew's Chapel
2. Glen the Beadle found
3. Bampton Castle
4. the Ladywell
5. Mill
6. Blacksmith's forge
7. the Church of St. Beornwald
8. new tithe barn
9. Henry & Thomas atte Bridge huts

to Witney

Bushey Row

Castle St.

High St.

Broad St.

Landell's Ln.

Rosemary Ln.

Church View

Bridge St.

Mill St.

Shill Brook

to Aston & Oxford

the Weald

N

Chapter 1

I awoke at dawn on the ninth day of April, 1365. Unlike Malmsey, the day did not improve with age.

There have been many days when I have awoken at dawn but have remembered not the circumstances three weeks hence. I remember this day not because of when I awoke, but why, and what I was compelled to do after. Odd, is it not, how one extraordinary event will burn even the mundane surrounding it into a man's memory.

I have seen other memorable days in my twenty-five years. I recall the day my brother Henry died of plague. I was a child, but I remember well Father Aymer administering extreme unction. Father Aymer wore a spice bag about his neck to protect him from the malady. It did not, and he also succumbed within a fortnight. I can see the pouch yet, in my mind's eye, swinging from the priest's neck on a hempen cord as he bent over my stricken brother.

I remember clearly the day in 1361 when William of Garstang died. William and I and two others shared a room on St Michael's Street, Oxford, while we studied at Baliol College. I comforted William as the returning plague covered his body with erupting buboes. For my small service he gave me, with his last breaths, his three books. One of these volumes was *Surgery* by Henry de Mondeville. How William came by this book I know not. But I see now in this gift the hand of God, for I read de Mondeville's work and changed my vocation.

Was it then God's will that William die a miserable death so that I might find God's vision for my life? This I cannot accept, for I saw William's body covered with oozing pustules. I will not believe such a death is God's choice for any man. Here I must admit a disagreement with Master Wyclif, who believes that all is foreordained. But out of evil God may draw good, as I believe He did when he introduced me to the practice of surgery. Perhaps the good I have done with my skills balances the torment William suffered in his death. But not for William.

I remember well the day I met Lord Gilbert Talbot. I stitched him up after his leg was opened by a kick from a groom's horse on Oxford High Street. This needlework opened my life to service to Lord Gilbert and the townsmen of Bampton, and brought me also the post of bailiff on Lord Gilbert's manor at Bampton.

Other days return to my mind with less pleasure. I will not soon forget Christmas Day 1363, and the feast that day at Lord Gilbert's Goodrich Castle hall. I had traveled there from Bampton to attend Lord Gilbert's sister, the Lady Joan. The fair Joan had broken a wrist in a fall from a horse. I was summoned to set the break. It was foolish of me to think I might win this lady, but love has hoped more foolishness than that. A few days before Christmas a guest, Sir Charles de Burgh, arrived at Goodrich. Lord Gilbert invited him knowing well he might be a thief. Indeed, he stole Lady Joan's heart. Between the second and third removes of the Christmas feast he stood and, for all in the hall to see, offered Lady Joan a clove-studded pear. She took the fruit and with a smile delicately drew a clove from the pear with her teeth. They married in September, a few days before Michaelmas, last year.

I digress. I awoke at dawn to thumping on my chamber door. I blinked sleep from my eyes, crawled from my bed, and stumbled to the door. I opened it as Wilfred the porter was about to rap on it again.

"It's Alan... the beadle. He's found."

Alan had left his home to seek those who would violate curfew two days earlier. He never returned. His young wife came to me in alarm the morning of the next day. I sent John Holcutt, the reeve, to gather a party of searchers, but they found no trace of the man. John was not pleased to lose a day of work from six men. Plowing of fallow fields was not yet finished. Before I retired on Wednesday evening, John sought me out and begged not to resume the search the next day. I agreed. If Alan could not be found with the entire town aware of his absence, another day of poking into haymows and barns seemed likely also to be fruitless. It was not necessary.

"Has he come home?" I asked.

"Nay. An' not likely to, but on a hurdle."

"He's dead?"

"Aye."

"Where was he found?"

"Aside the way near to St Andrew's Chapel."

It was no wonder the searchers had not found him. St Andrew's Chapel was near half a mile to the east. What, I wondered, drew him away from the town on his duties?

"Hubert Shillside has been told. He would have you accompany him to the place."

"Send word I will see him straight away."

I suppose I was suspicious already that this death was not natural. I believe it to be a character flaw if a man be too mistrustful. But there are occasions in my professions – surgery and bailiff – when it is good to doubt a first impression. Alan was not yet thirty years old. He had a half-yardland of Lord Gilbert Talbot and was so well thought of that despite his youth, Lord Gilbert's tenants had at hallmote chosen him beadle these three years. He worked diligently, and bragged all winter that his four acres of oats had brought him nearly five bushels for every bushel of seed. A remarkable accomplishment, for his land was no better than any other surrounding Bampton. This success brought also some envy, I think, and perhaps there were wives who contrasted his achievement to the work of their husbands. But this, I thought, was no reason to kill a man.

I suppose a man may have enemies which even his friends know not of. I did consider Alan a friend, as did most others of the town. On my walk from Bampton Castle to Hubert Shillside's shop and house on Church View Street, I persuaded myself that this must be a natural death. Of course, when a corpse is found in open country, the hue and cry must be raised even if the body be stiff and cold. So Hubert, the town coroner, and I, bailiff and surgeon, must do our work.

Alan was found but a few minutes from the town. Down Rosemary Lane to the High Street, then left on Bushey Row to the path to St Andrew's Chapel. We saw – Hubert and I, and John Holcutt, who came also – where the body lay while we were yet far off. As we passed the last house on the lane east from Bampton to the chapel, we saw a group of men standing in the track at a place where last year's fallow was being plowed for spring planting. They saw us approach, and stepped back respectfully as we reached them.

A hedgerow had grown up among rocks between the lane and the field. New leaves of pale green decorated stalks of nettles, thistles and wild roses. Had the foliage matured for another fortnight Alan might have gone undiscovered. But two plowmen, getting an early start on their day's labor, found the corpse as they turned the oxen at the end of their first furrow. It had been barely light enough to see the white foot protruding from the hedgerow. The plowman who goaded the team saw it as he prodded the lead beasts to turn.

Alan's body was invisible from the road, but by pushing back nettles and thorns – carefully – we could see him curled as if asleep amongst the brambles. I directed two onlookers to retrieve the body. Rank has its privileges. Better they be nettle-stung than we. A few minutes later Alan the beadle lay stretched out on the path.

Lying in the open, on the road, the beadle did not seem so at peace as in the hedgerow. Deep scratches lacerated his face, hands and forearms. His clothes were torn, his feet bare, and a great wound bloodied his neck where flesh had been torn away. The coroner bent to examine this injury more closely.

"Some beast has done this, I think," he muttered as he stood. "See how his surcoat is torn at the arms, as if he tried to defend himself from fangs."

I knelt on the opposite side of the corpse to view in my turn the wound which took the life of Alan the beadle. It seemed as Hubert Shillside said. Puncture wounds spread across neck and arms, and rips on surcoat and flesh indicated where claws and fangs had made their mark. I sent the reeve back to Bampton Castle for a horse on which to transport Alan back to the town and to his wife. The others who stood in the path began to drift away. The plowmen who found him returned to their team. Soon only the coroner and I remained to guard the corpse. It needed guarding. Already a flock of carrion crows flapped high above the path.

I could not put my unease into words, so spoke nothing of my suspicion to Shillside. But I was not satisfied that some wild beast had done this thing. I believe the coroner was apprehensive of this explanation as well, for it was he who broke the silence.

"There have been no wolves hereabouts in my lifetime," he mused, "nor wild dogs, I think."

"I have heard," I replied, "Lord Gilbert speak of wolves near Goodrich. And Pembroke. Those castles are near to the Forest of Dean and the Welsh mountains. But even there, in such wild country, they are seldom seen."

Shillside was silent again as we studied the body at our feet. My eyes wandered to the path where Alan lay. When I did not find what I sought, I walked a few paces toward the town, then reversed my path and inspected the track in the direction of St Andrew's Chapel. My search was fruitless.

Hubert watched my movements with growing interest. "What do you seek?" he finally asked. It was clear to him I looked for something in the road.

"Tracks. If an animal did this, there should be some sign, I think. The mud is soft."

"Perhaps," the coroner replied. "But we and many others have stood about near an hour. Any marks a beast might have made have surely been trampled underfoot."

I agreed that might be. But another thought also troubled me. "There should be much blood," I said, "but

I see little."

"Why so?" Shillside asked.

"When a man's neck is torn as Alan's is, there is much blood lost. It is the cause of death. Do you see much blood hereabouts?"

"Perhaps the ground absorbed it?"

"Perhaps... let us look in the hedgerow, where we found him."

We did, carefully prying the nettles apart. The foliage was depressed where Alan lay, but only a trace of blood could be seen on the occasional new leaf or rock or blade of grass.

"There is blood here," I announced, "but not much. Not enough."

"Enough for what?" the coroner asked with furrowed brow.

"Enough that the loss of blood would kill a man."

Shillside was silent for a moment. "Your words trouble me," he said finally. "If this wound" – he looked to Alan's neck – "did not kill him, what did?"

"'Tis a puzzle," I agreed.

"And see how we found him amongst the nettles. Perhaps he dragged himself there to escape the beasts, if more than one set upon him."

"Or perhaps the animal dragged him there," I added. But I did not believe this, for reasons I could not explain.

It was the coroner's turn to cast his eyes about. "His shoes and staff," Shillside mused. "I wonder where they might be?"

I remembered the staff. Whenever the beadle went out of an evening to watch and warn, he carried with him a yew pole taller than himself and thick as a man's forearm. I spoke to him of this weapon once. A whack from it, he said, would convince the most unruly drunk to leave the streets and seek his bed.

"He was proud of that cudgel," Hubert remarked as we combed the hedgerow in search of it. "He carved an 'A' on it so all would know 'twas his."

"I didn't know he could write."

"Oh, he could not," Shillside explained. "Father Thomas showed him the mark and Alan inscribed it. Right proud of it, he was."

We found the staff far off the path, where some wasteland verged on to a wood just behind St Andrew's Chapel. It lay thirty paces or more from the place where Alan's body had lain in the hedgerow. But our search yielded no shoes.

"How did it come to be here?" Shillside asked. As if I would know. He examined the club. "There is his mark – see?" He pointed to the "A" inscribed with some artistry into the tough wood.

As the coroner held the staff before me, I inspected it closely and was troubled. Shillside saw my frown.

"What perplexes you, Hugh?"

"The staff is unmarked. Were I carrying such a weapon and a wolf set upon me, I would flail it about to defend myself; perhaps hold it before me so the beast caught it in his teeth rather than my arm."

Shillside peered at the pole and turned it to view all sides. Its surface was smooth and unmarred. "Perhaps," he said thoughtfully, "Alan swung it at the beast and lost his grip. See how polished smooth it is… and it flew from his grasp to land here."

"That might be how it was," I agreed, for I had no better explanation.

As we returned to the path we saw the reeve approach with Bruce, the old horse who saw me about the countryside when I found it necessary to travel. He would be a calm and dignified platform on which to transport a corpse.

We bent to lift Alan to Bruce's back, John at the feet and Shillside and me at the shoulders. As we swung him up, Alan's head fell back. So much of his neck was shredded that it provided little support. I reached out a hand to steady the head and felt a thing which made my hackles rise.

"Wait," I said, rather sharply, for my companions started and gazed in wonder at me. "Set him back on the road."

I turned the beadle's head and felt the place on the skull which had startled me. There was a soft depression on the skull, just behind Alan's right ear. This cavity was invisible for the thick shock of hair which covered it. I spread the thatch and inspected Alan's scalp, then showed my discovery to reeve and coroner.

John Holcutt was silent, but Shillside, after running his fingers across the dent, looked at me and asked, "How could a wolf do this?"

We stood and pondered this new discovery. The coroner moved first to offer an explanation. "See there, amongst the nettles in the hedgerow. There are many rocks, tossed there from the field. Mayhap Alan sought escape in the brambles but fell back and struck his head. That would account for where we found him. And unconscious, he could not defend himself as the beast tore his throat."

I admit this made a neat explanation for what we had discovered. But I was yet troubled. "Would a man, a strong young man like Alan, fall back so violently that striking his head would kill him?"

"'Twould not have to kill him," Shillside countered. "If he was knocked senseless the wolf could do its work an' he would not be able to defend himself."

"Then where is the blood?"

"Blood?" The coroner was puzzled.

"A living man, even knocked senseless, will bleed much from such a hurt as Alan has suffered. It is only the dead who will not bleed."

"Then Alan died when his head struck the rock, you think?"

"I do," I agreed. "Or when a rock struck Alan."

"But... wolves do not attack a man with rocks," Shillside said softly. "I think you are skeptical that he died from an attack by beasts. Why so?"

"Have you heard any report of wolves in the shire?" I asked him. "John, have you?"

The reeve shook his head. "Nor have I. I think no man alive in Bampton has ever heard a wolf howl."

"Some other beast, then?" Shillside offered.

"What? A bear? Even in Scotland they are unknown. Wild dogs? What other ravages have been done? Hounds would take a sheep and leave the remains to mark their work, as would a wolf, I think. No such loss has been reported to me, or on the bishop's lands either, or I should have heard of it."

Another matter had troubled me. Alan's feet were bare. "We found Alan's staff, but where are his shoes? Would a man," I asked my companions, "go out of a night to enforce curfew unshod?"

The reeve and coroner looked down to Alan's feet. Shillside sucked on his lower lip, but neither man spoke. We all knew the answer to that question: not likely.

We bent again to the task of lifting Alan to Bruce's broad back. The old horse shuffled when he realized what he was asked to bear. But the animal had borne Lord Gilbert in battle at Poitiers and had smelled blood and death. He did not flinch from his task. John took the halter and, at Bruce's slow pace, our cortege moved to the town and Alan's house on Catte Street.

The beadle's home was like its neighbors. Built of timbers, wattle and daub, with a roof perhaps better thatched than most. A wisp of smoke drifted from the gable vent. We found Matilda planting onions in the toft behind the house. There is work which must be done even when a spouse has disappeared. No one had sought her out with the news that her husband was found. No one wanted to be the source of bad tidings or have the responsibility of comforting the disconsolate. So I did it. Hubert Shillside stood beside me as I spoke the words Matilda had feared for twenty-four hours. The knees of her surcoat were stained with earth, as were the hands which first dropped, then came up to cover the sobs which broke from a face new twisted in grief.

I saw a bench at the rear of the house and brought it to the woman. She sat, or rather, collapsed, gratefully upon it. Her sobs must have penetrated the house. Matilda had no sooner sat than an echoing wail arose from within. She had been trying to get work done before her son awoke.

The child's cries brought Matilda's to an end. She rose, brushed past me and the coroner, and ran to comfort her babe. She reappeared with the sobbing lad a moment later. The child blinked in the sunlight under sleep-tangled hair and peered suspiciously at me from the safety of his mother's arms.

Matilda knew grief. She had renewed its acquaintance four months earlier, just before Christmas, when a newborn daughter died before ever seeing the light of day. The midwife, Katherine Pecham, was known by all to be competent. There was no fault in her work. Rare indeed the mother who sees all her children past the graveyard to maturity.

The woman stood in the doorway, then leaned heavily against the jamb. I felt compassion for her, but knew her sorrow would not endure long. There were in Bampton and the Weald five men under thirty-five or so years who were widowers or who had not yet taken a wife. One had lost a wife in childbirth. After a decent interval for her mourning, some would call. And as they cast jealous eyes on each other, the period allotted for Matilda's mourning might become indecent. Well, she would have something to say about that.

Matilda was no more than twenty-five years old and prettier than most tenants' wives who, by that age, are already worn with work and worry. And she would bring to a new marriage a half-yardland. She would be required to pay a heriot, and an entry fee for her son and heir when he was old enough to assume his father's land. But these would not be burdensome. I knew this because, in the absence of Lord Gilbert and his steward, Geoffrey Thirwall, I would determine these fines.

"Where was he found?" Matilda asked.

The coroner told her, and explained that Alan's death seemed likely caused by an attack of some wild beast, perhaps a wolf. Her eyes grew wide at this revelation.

I asked if she knew of any reason why her husband would leave the town on his rounds.

"Perhaps," she whispered, "he saw the wolf and tried to drive it away."

If indeed a wolf killed the man, that explanation was as good as any I and Hubert Shillside had contrived. I asked if I could see Alan's shoes. Matilda was no fool.

"'E wore 'em, din't he," she retorted. "'E wan't daft... t'go 'bout at night w'out shoes. 'Oo knows what a man might step on in the dark?"

I was properly silenced. But that was the answer I sought and expected. I traded a glance with the coroner. We exchanged raised eyebrows. At such moments I often try to raise but one eyebrow, as does Lord Gilbert Talbot. But I have been unable to master the pose. I am convinced it is an ability to which only the gentry are born.

"What 'appened to 'im?" she asked.

There followed a pause as Shillside and I each waited for the other to speak. The coroner looked away, as if he found some unusual event down Catte Street which required his attention. So I told her.

"We have brought him to you," I concluded. "He is at your door, in the street. John Holcutt waits there with him. You may make arrangements with Thomas de Bowlegh to bury him tomorrow."

The next day was Good Friday, but it would never again be good for Matilda, wife of the beadle. Each year at the remembrance of our Lord's death she would recall her own loss and the day would be doubly distressing. I recall my own loss each time I see a pear or smell cloves or eat a Christmas feast.

"I will see him," she said with some firmness, and turned to walk from the rear to the front of her small house. 'Twas but a few paces. The coroner and I followed.

John Holcutt stiffened when he heard the front door squeal open on winter-rusted hinges and saw Matilda and the child approach. Matilda stopped, staring at the horse and its burden for long minutes. None dared break the silence. Passers-by averted their eyes, crossed themselves, and silenced their steps.

Matilda stepped softly to her husband, shifted the

child to her hip, and reached out a hand to sweep unruly hair from Alan's cold forehead. She caressed her senseless husband and bent to whisper in the unhearing ear. I made it my business not to listen.

The spring sun was now well up over Bampton's rooftops, shedding bright golden light on the scene. In this brilliance, as she stroked her dark-haired husband, something caught Matilda's eye. I thought at first she had discovered the dent at the back of Alan's skull, but this was not so. She parted his locks and drew forth a blue thread.

"What's this, then?" she asked, and held the object forth.

Alan wore nothing blue. His surcoat was brown, his cotehardie yellow and his chauces grey. And no doubt his kirtle was as white as Matilda could make it.

I took the thread from her. It was a faded blue length of coarse woolen yarn, about as long as a finger. Matilda had plucked it from her husband's scalp near the place where his head was bruised.

"Have you a garment of this color?" I asked.

"Nay... though 'tis common enough."

I turned to Hubert Shillside. "Did any of those who found Alan this morning wear blue? I think not, but 'twas not full light yet, and my mind was otherwise occupied."

The coroner thought back on the discovery and pursed his lips in concentration. "The plowman who remained in the field with the oxen, did he not wear a blue cotehardie?"

"I paid him no attention," I admitted. "If you saw this I will take your word for it."

Matilda looked from me to the coroner during this conversation. She held the thread before us between two fingers. "I think, Master Hugh, that all is not as you wish," she said quietly.

Shillside gave me a look that said, "Now see what you've done!" I could not help it. I am not as those who can dissemble easily and hide their thoughts from others.

"Some things puzzle me," I admitted. "His shoes..."

I nodded toward the bare feet stiff at Bruce's flank. "Where are they?"

"I think," Shillside observed, "they will be discovered on the feet of one of those who found him this morning."

"Mayhap, but they should not be a reward for the discovery. They are Matilda's, to dispose of as she will."

"Will you seek them?" the widow asked. "Cobbler could cut 'em down for me, I think."

"I will," I promised, and so began a journey in which I sought one thing and found another. Much of my life has been like that. I have seldom found what I most urgently sought, and only rarely sought what I found. Since much of what I enjoy is then the result of a good fortune which I knew not to seek, I attribute the laudable in my life to the will of God, who, it is written, knows what we need before we ask. He knows, for I have told him often, that I need a good wife, but no matter how I seek such a woman, she will not be found. I must not entertain these thoughts, else my mind will turn to Lady Joan Talbot, now the Lady de Burgh. Such meditations are bittersweet. I prefer to avoid them, but I cannot. Memories of Lady Joan are an itch which from time to time must be scratched.

John, Hubert and I took Alan from Bruce's back and laid him on the bed he had shared with Matilda. He was stiffening in death, so that the corpse wished to retain the bend it had assumed while slung over the horse. Inducing him to lay straight and flat on the bed was an awkward business, especially in the presence of his weeping wife.

Shillside told Matilda that he would return in the afternoon with a jury, for any unexplained death must be examined and pronounced accidental or murder. The coroner had carried Alan's stave all this time. He propped it in a corner of the house as we prepared to leave.

I asked the grieving widow for the blue thread. The death troubled me, but at that moment the stolen shoes annoyed most. My sense of justice was violated. It seems a small thing, now. But I was determined to find the plundered shoes this day and return them to Matilda before nightfall. I knew not if the blue thread might lead me to the thief, but if I found a garment matching the thread I might also find a man who knew more than I of this death.

Chapter 2

Dinner at Bampton Castle was a simple affair while Lord Gilbert resided elsewhere. He permitted the serving of three meats – other than fast days, of course – in his absence. Lord Gilbert was more frugal than most of his class.

I had had no breakfast, so stuffed myself on a roasted chicken, a coney pie, and cold venison. Some might think it strange that I had such an appetite after dealing with the dead all morning. My stomach is seldom discomfited. I would then sooner have had a nap, but a sense of injustice swept somnolence from my head.

I determined to visit the plowmen first, so walked left on Mill Street when I left the castle yard. I found it necessary to pause at the bridge over Shill Brook. I have seldom been able to pass a stream without gazing at the moving water. I attribute this to my childhood along the Wyre at the manor of Little Singleton. The two streams are not alike. The Wyre is slow and muddy and tidal and home mostly to eels. Shill Brook dances between narrow banks, its water pure and clear, a home to trout.

The plowmen were yet at work, their six oxen moving ponderously from one end of the strip to the other. I waited for them near the path, where they would turn for another pass down the field. In the bright light of a warm April day I saw as they approached that neither man wore a garment matching the blue thread in my pouch.

The beadle, they insisted, was shoeless when they found him. I showed them the blue thread. This was a mistake, I realized later. But that is the nature of our errors. We recognize our blunders after we have committed them. If we could see our errors as they approached, we might avoid them.

Neither of the plowmen could identify a garment of that shade. While this fruitless conversation was taking place I saw one of the men peer over my shoulder. I turned to see in the distance Hubert Shillside and eleven others of the coroner's jury come to inspect the place where Alan lay and question those who discovered him.

I lingered to hear the plowmen answer as Shillside asked much the same questions I had asked. Their responses were the same. I was convinced they spoke the truth. And I was convinced neither had taken Alan's shoes. The wooden-soled footwear which protected their feet was old and the leather which fixed the shoes to their feet was tattered. The beadle wore similar shoes, as did most who toil in the soil, but he would not wear shoes so worn as these. He was more prosperous than these plowmen.

Shillside and his jurymen turned back along the path to town and I followed behind, uncertain of further measures I might take. I had come to Bushey Row, fifty paces behind the coroner's men, when it occurred to me that I might speak to the priest at St Andrew's Chapel. This cleric was probably closest of all men to the scene of Alan's death. Perhaps he had heard some disturbance in the night – the cry of a man or the snarl of a beast. I turned and retraced my steps.

I had returned to the place where Alan was found when in the distance I heard my name called. I turned and saw John Holcutt waving vigorously and striding purposefully in my direction. He was but a hundred paces away, just turned from Bushey Row on to the path to the chapel. He came puffing up to me a moment later.

"You are needed, Master Hugh," he panted. "The miller was openin' the sluice gate this mornin' when he slipped. Stones there be mossy from the damp. Wheel began to turn and caught 'is arm as he reached to steady himself."

"The arm is broken?" I asked.

"Prob'ly... an' near wrenched from 'is shoulder. He's in great pain."

"Was he just now beginning his day? 'Tis well past noon."

"Nay. The injury happened early. He asked 'is wife to arrange a sling and thought to continue 'is work. But he cannot, and so wishes you to attend him."

I turned to walk back to town with the reeve. The priest at St Andrew's Chapel would have to wait.

Andrew the miller had suffered a grievous injury. His right arm was drawn from the socket at his shoulder, and his forearm was broken. I was confused as to what steps I must take to treat the man, or more to the point, in what order I must take those steps. Had his arm been whole I would have put his dislocated shoulder right, but to do so requires leverage and tugging on the arm. This I could not do, broken as his was.

But if I should wait for the broken arm to mend, his displaced shoulder might then be so long out of joint that it could not be put right.

I explained this to the miller. I could spare him more pain, leave the shoulder as it was, and set the broken arm. Or, I could attend to the dislocated shoulder, causing him great pain in the break for a few minutes. He could suffer now, and perhaps regain the proper use of his arm, or he could avoid agony now and live his life with the affliction of a useless arm.

"'Ow can I work the mill with but one arm?" he asked.

"You may have two good arms by St Swithin's Day if you choose to have me make your shoulder right this day. Otherwise I think you will be burdened with a crippled arm from this day on.

"I will set the break first, splint it strongly, and put a heavy layer of stiffened linen all about. Then I will see to your shoulder... but I will tell you now, the hurt will be great. I will make a potion, but it will not suffice to free you of all distress."

The miller was not a man of strong character. He avoided affliction when at all possible. Come to think on it, so do I. So do most men. I watched the miller's eyes as they flickered about the dusty room, as if he sought some deliverance from his condition. But there was no escape.

Gradually his eyes steadied on me.

"This must be done, an' I'm to have two good arms?"

I nodded.

"You will make the potion strong?"

"I will… but it will be of but small relief."

Andrew looked at his arm, resting in a makeshift sling on his ample paunch, and stretched a finger as if to test whether or not his situation was really so desperate. His grimace told us both that it was.

"You will do this today?" the miller whispered.

"As soon as I can procure tools from the castle and return."

The miller nodded, too choked with apprehension to speak. As the mill was adjacent to the castle, I returned promptly with my supplies. In that time Andrew had grown pale with anxiety.

I secured a cup of ale from the miller's well-fed wife and mixed a large portion of ground hemp seeds and willow bark into the drink. Andrew watched with enlarged eyes as I did this, but took the cup and drank the potion down when I offered it to him.

It is my experience that, when a potion is administered to deaden pain, it will achieve its effect an hour or two after it is consumed. I told the miller to sit quietly and wait for the palliative to do its work. I would return when the time had come to proceed with my task.

As it was less than half a mile to St Andrew's Chapel, I set my feet in that direction when I left the mill. I could see the priest there, ask what I might, and return to the mill before the ninth hour. This time I did not linger at the bridge across Shill Brook.

The priest at St Andrew's Chapel of Beme is a slovenly, unlettered man. He holds his position there only, I suspect, because he will perform the duties of the tiny parish – if parish it could truly be called – for the minimum remittance of one third of the revenues – a requirement laid down by Pope Alexander III 200 years ago. One third of the revenues from a parish so small as that which attended mass at St Andrew's Chapel was not enough to attract a man who could do better, and any educated cleric could.

Father John Kellet, clerk and priest of St Andrew's Chapel, had not, I believe, ever been more than ten miles from Bampton, the place of his birth. He had been heard boasting that he had never set foot in Oxford, although I must admit that, in the few conversations I had with the priest, this subject did not arise, and most residents of Bampton and the Weald might make the same claim.

Father Simon Osbern, of the Church of St Beornwald in Bampton, trained John in the priestly duties. But the course of study was too brief for anything but the rudiments. Kellet had no Latin. He merely spoke the words of the mass, extreme unction, and other sacraments by rote. Why, I wonder, must this be so? Can it be that God cannot understand English? Must men worship in a language they do not understand, led by a priest who speaks what he does not comprehend?

Men will say that I spent too much time while a student at Oxford listening to Master John Wyclif. Perhaps this is so. But his arguments made sense to me then and do yet, though I am a peaceful man and chose not to challenge the bishops over the issue.

St Andrew's Chapel is an ancient structure. It was old when the Conqueror came from Normandy to wrest the kingdom from King Harold. The wall about the churchyard is now tumbled down in places, so that pigs may wander in and root amongst the graves. The absentee rector should see to the mending, but like many in his position, he cares more for his purse and his living than he does for keeping a small chapel in good repair.

Those parts of the wall which yet stand firm are covered in ivy and nettles. Soon this foliage will topple more stones, unless it is uprooted. The rector will not pay to have this done, and John Kellet will do no work which may be avoided. The future of the walls of St Andrew's Chapel yard seems bleak.

I scanned the building as I approached. It was not

so disordered as the wall, but there were slates missing from the roof. I suspected that the worshipers got wet on rainy Sundays.

The chapel is small; no more than twelve paces long and perhaps seven paces wide. So the tower at the west end of the structure is also small, but it is within the tower that John Kellet lives. The room is convenient, I suppose, as well as cheap. When the priest wishes to call his small flock to mass, he has but to walk to the center of his chamber, where the bell rope passes through from floor to ceiling.

Slate shingles on the porch were in poor repair, also, and I noted that the door was beginning to rot at the base as I pushed it open and entered the dim interior of the chapel.

Sunlight slanting through the narrow south windows illuminated dust motes floating like down in the still air. The dust would eventually join the layer of grime which covered the flat surfaces inside the chapel. I ran a finger across a windowsill and left a dark streak in the accumulated dust of many years.

I turned to the stairway which led to the vicar's room and was about to ascend when I heard the door at the head of the stairs creak open on corroded hinges. The priest had heard me open the door from the porch and was descending to discover who had entered his seldom-visited demesne.

I was again astonished at the girth of John Kellet. I do not understand how a priest who tends such a meager garden can grow so fat. I had apparently interrupted his dinner, for I saw a grease stain on his long tunic and he licked his fingers as he came into view at the foot of the stairs.

The tunic was black, as befits a priest. As he approached I saw that it was made of a soft, fine wool. It was wrinkled and food-stained, but of better quality than the tunic that Thomas de Bowlegh, vicar of a larger church, wore.

"Ah, Master Hugh," Kellet's voice echoed off the

grey stones of floor and walls. "What... what brings you here this day?"

I wished to return quickly to the miller's broken arm, so did not squander time with niceties.

"A man died along the path to Bampton yesterday... or perhaps the night before."

The priest started, and his sleepy, heavy-lidded eyes grew wide.

"Alan, the beadle," I continued. "Did you know him?"

"Uh... aye, I believe so. Along the path, you say?"

"Aye. Just the other side of the wood beyond the churchyard. Plowmen found him this morning."

"Did he have lands there?" the priest asked.

"No. He'd gone out to watch and warn Tuesday eve, and never returned."

The priest pursed his lips. "Tsk," he muttered. "Such a young man... but death takes us all."

"Did you hear any strange, unnatural sound Tuesday eve?"

"Why, no. This death, does it trouble you?"

"I think, perhaps. The man's throat was torn, as if a wild beast had attacked him. His head was broken, I know not how, and his shoes are taken, which no beast would do."

"A beast, you say?" The priest frowned, and his mouth dropped open for a moment.

"Perhaps. His throat was torn. Fangs or claws might be the cause. Do you know of any wild hounds ranging in this parish?"

Kellet scratched the back of his shaggy head. "I've heard of nothin' like that. 'Course, there is much waste land between here an' Aston, since the great death. Beasts could prowl there an' none the wiser."

"Have any cotters hereabout lost animals recently? Sheep, or even fowl?"

"Oh, a duck or two goes missing every month or so, but I think a fox would do no harm to the beadle."

"If you learn of evidence that savage beasts have

been seen or heard, you must send word to me. It is my duty to keep Lord Gilbert's lands free of such marauders... if such there be."

"Mayhap," the priest said, scratching his scalp again, "wolves have come down from Wales. The winter past was cruel. I have heard that wolves still prowl those untamed lands."

"Perhaps," I agreed. Actually, I did not agree. But having no better theory myself, I saw no reason to challenge the point. Certainly there is now, since plague has struck twice, in England much wasteland, where wolves could live and travel unmolested. But would a wolf make his presence in the shire first known by an attack on a man? I have heard tales of wolves, that they travel in packs and are seldom solitary. And they howl. Wolves are not silent creatures. It seemed to me a wolf would announce his presence with the taking of a sheep, or perhaps a pig rooting for last autumn's acorns in the forest.

"I must return to Bampton. The miller awaits, with a broken arm. But before I go, there is also the matter of the missing shoes. Should you see a man wearing good shoes when he has owned recently only poor ones, send for me. This," I held out the blue yarn, "was found at the scene of Alan's death. Does anyone hereabouts wear a garment of this hue?"

Kellet stared at the strand and, I thought, seemed ill at ease. He shifted from one foot to another before he made answer.

"Wold is grown in most every toft," he commented. "'Twould make a color much like this. But no, I know of no one of this parish who owns a cotehardie or surcoat of this pale blue."

"Should you see such a garment, call for me at the castle."

"I will... I will, indeed. And I'll keep me eye peeled for shoes, as well."

I thanked him for this, and set off for the town and the injured miller.

The miller had not moved from his bench. I found

him sagging against a beam, his eyes gratifyingly heavy. The hemp and willow had done their work. Although the bruise made by the wheel was now growing fiercely purple, the break in Andrew's forearm was clean and simple to treat. I took several thin canes I had cut along Shill Brook and bound them tightly about the forearm when I was satisfied that it was straight. I directed the miller's wife to bring a bowl of water from the pond. Into this I poured a pouch of quicklime. All that remained was to soak linen strips in the plaster and wind these about the canes and the miller's arm until it was well encased. I continued the stiffened linen past the miller's elbow, to provide as much support as possible for the business of putting his shoulder right.

While the plaster dried and hardened I explored the shoulder with my fingers to see how badly out of joint it was. I felt the ball of the miller's upper arm, and pressed firmly through his fleshy shoulder to find the empty socket. When I had found both ball and socket I manipulated the arm gently to see what work I had before me to put these parts together. I was shocked when I heard a muffled "click" and felt the arm spring back to its place under my touch.

Andrew twitched and yelped in a brief moment of pain, then relaxed as I dropped my hands and stepped back.

"Ah... you warned me. I shall try not to jerk about so as you work. How... how long will you be at putting my shoulder right?"

"I am done," I replied, with rather more pride than was meet.

"Done?" The miller's eyes widened. He moved his shoulder experimentally. "But I thought... you warned me of great pain. 'Twas but a prick. The potion, it must have been strong, indeed."

"Indeed," I agreed.

The miller stretched his shoulder again. "'Tis a wondrous thing, how with but a shift of your fingers you set me right."

I did not tell Andrew that I was as amazed as he at the ease with which his shoulder was made whole. If he chooses to believe my skill extraordinary and tells his customers – and that would be all who live on Lord Gilbert's lands, villein or free – that Master Hugh is gifted at his work, must I be distressed?

I told the miller that I would call on him in a few days to see how he got on, and that before St Swithin's Day I would remove the stiffened linen and splints.

The miller was known as a parsimonious man. He was known also, like most of his trade, for defrauding on return of flour if he could do so without detection. He asked my fee. I expected an argument, but he paid without rancor. He fished six pence from a small chest which stood on a dusty table under the single dusty window which lighted the dusty mill.

The evening sun was well down in the west when I left the mill and turned toward Mill Street. I was just in time to see John Kellet waddle across the bridge over Shill Brook. The priest's tunic billowed before his belly like a sail full of wind. Immediately across the bridge, he turned and took the path to the cottages in the Weald. Something to do with one of the bishop's tenants, I assumed, and made my way to the castle.

I had made no progress in finding Alan's missing shoes. This vexed me, but no matter how I considered the situation, I could see no path leading to their discovery. Unless someone reported new footgear on another, Matilda was not likely to get her husband's shoes back.

Next day was Good Friday, beginning the commemoration of our Lord's death and resurrection. I decided on a bath, both to clean myself for the holy days and, while I soaked, to devise some way I might track the missing shoes.

The kitchen was busy preparing supper, but not too busy. Lord Gilbert was in residence at Pembroke Castle, keeping the peace in Wales. So the evening meal would be simple. I told the cook that I required six buckets of hot water, delivered to my chamber after the meal.

For supper this day there was parsley bread, a pea soup, and cabbage with marrow. This was not a meal which would have satisfied Lord Gilbert Talbot, who at Pembroke at this hour would likely be dining on such as venison and salmon, and enjoying a subtlety with each remove. But compared to the fare at the Stag and Hounds, on the High Street in Oxford, where I dined until Lord Gilbert brought me to Bampton, this repast was a feast.

When the simple meal was done I returned to my chamber – which did not take long, as the room opened on to the great hall. I busied myself with knives, scalpels and sharpening stone from my implements box until a light rapping sounded on my door. I opened it to see the child Alice atte Bridge standing before me, a bucket in each hand. "Hot water, sir," she smiled, and curtsied.

As she did so some of the water slopped out of the buckets to the flagging. Two buckets full of water were a significant weight for her slender shoulders. "Sorry, sir. I'll bring somethin' t'mop it up."

"Never mind. It'll dry. Just pour the water in the barrel and fetch four more buckets."

Alice dumped the water, glanced briefly at my instruments where I had spread them on my table, then scurried off for more. A year and a half had passed since I first met the girl. She had come to me seeking help for her father. He had slipped on icy cobbles and broken a hip. I could do nothing for him but administer potions which would relieve his pain and ease him to the next world.

The child had two half-brothers who would have despoiled her of anything she possessed from her father, could they have done so. But at her father's death I advised her to remove all goods from the hut she shared with her father and take them to the castle. She was put to work in the scullery. Apparently this labor agreed with her. She was no longer the scrawny waif I had aided. She was taller, and no longer looked to be constructed of splinters and coppiced beech poles. I noted as she brought the next buckets that there were now pleasing bulges under her plain cotehardie. These curves were set off remarkably well by the simple belt she wore about her waist, a part of her which remained gratifyingly slender.

When she had delivered the last of the hot water and had curtsied her way out – no one having told her that she need not curtsy to a mere bailiff – I bolted the door, stripped off my clothing, and submerged so much of myself as was possible into the cask. This cask the carpenter had sawn in half for me.

I scrubbed myself clean with a much-shrunken woolen cloth which I keep for the purpose. I had had no bath since Ash Wednesday, which was more recent than most, as I am one of the few foolish enough to risk illness by bathing in winter. So it was pleasant to renew acquaintance with hot water and soak in the barrel until the water cooled. But I admit that no insight occurred while I squatted immersed in my barrel. Alan the beadle's shoes were as lost after my bath as before.

I went from barrel to bed, taking time only to dry myself. I thought I should fall to sleep quickly; I had a full stomach and was warmed from my bath. But slumber would not come. I might as well have attended Alan's wake, and sat with the corpse all night.

I reviewed the day and its events. The monotony of repetition did not quiet my mind. When I saw the glow of the waning paschal moon in my window, I rose from my bed, dressed, and quietly left my chamber. The porter's assistant slumbered at the gatehouse. His duty was to keep watch over the castle through the night, but there was peace in the land and few brigands would dare Bampton Castle. His duty was tedious and conducive to slumber.

I coughed and scuffed my feet until my approach roused him. I did not wish the derelict watchman to awaken and find a shadowy stranger atop the castle wall. I bid the fellow "good evening" and climbed the gatehouse steps to the parapet.

I circled the castle wall indolently, stopping often to gaze through the merlons over the sleeping village to the east, and Lord Gilbert's fields and forest to the west. Most of the village slept. Occasionally from the town I heard voices. Someone at Alan's wake, I think, had too much ale and could be heard from Catte Street.

This echo of distant voices caused me at first to ignore another sound which came faintly to my ears. I know not how long I may have heard the howls before the indistinct sound finally registered in my mind. Off to the east, beyond St Andrew's Chapel, I heard a yapping and howling soft in the distance.

I made my way to the tower at the southeast corner of the castle wall. This seemed to be the closest point to the direction from which the sound came. There was silence for a time, then the howls began again. As I listened the origin of the keening seemed to move to the south of the town, until after an hour or so of intermittent howls and silence, the source seemed to move directly south of the Weald. And then I heard it no more.

I had never before heard a wolf howl, but it seemed to me I had done so this night. Tomorrow, Good Friday or not, I would need to track and dispatch the animal which made these howls in the night. I did not know if this was the beast which slew Alan, but it seemed to me a reasonable suspicion. Perhaps Alan, as his wife had guessed, in his patrol had heard the wolf while Bampton slept and followed the sound to investigate. This would explain why he was found away from the town. But it would not explain his absent shoes.

I returned to my bed and slept fitfully until I heard in the distance the Angelus Bell sound from the tower of the Church of St Beornwald. I desired to organize a party immediately to seek out the wolf, but at the third hour Alan the beadle would be buried. I would not show disrespect to the dead by taking away those who would mourn and walk in his procession.

Chapter 3

I broke my fast with half a loaf of good maslin and a pint of ale, then made my way to Catte Street. Because of my position I would be among the chief mourners and, with Hubert Shillside, John Holcutt, Matilda, and a few other small burghers, would lead the procession to the church.

I was surprised to see that Matilda had provided a coffin. Most of the tenant class rest on their bier encased only in a black linen shroud. Alan's brother and three others from the town took their places at the poles. When Thomas de Bowlegh arrived to lead the procession, they lifted the coffin and we in the cortege fell in behind the priest.

Matilda and most of the others began wailing in grief as the coffin left the ground, but I walked silently beside Hubert Shillside as we passed from Catte Street to the High Street and turned right up the Broad Street. As the procession entered Church Street I spoke: "I heard the beast last night," I whispered.

"Beast?" Shillside questioned.

"Aye. The wolf which may have slain poor Alan. Sleep escaped me, so I rose to walk the castle parapet. 'Twas then I heard it, howling."

"A wolf?"

"Perhaps. I know little of wolves but that they are said to howl of a moonlit night. 'Twas no hound, of this I feel certain."

"Where away?"

"To the east at first, beyond St Andrew's Chapel. Then, as the hour grew late, it moved to the south beyond the Weald."

"Think you Alan heard it while we slept, and died following the sound?"

"I suspect it. But I would have his shoes. A wolf may have taken his life, but 'twas a man took his shoes."

"Aye," the coroner agreed, and we fell into a companionable silence for the remainder of the walk to the church.

Our conversation was not overheard by any other in the procession for the lamentation which accompanied our steps. Matilda and her sisters and cousins wailed loudly. Others in the procession behind them added to the din. The clamor did not subside until the bearers lowered the coffin at the lych gate.

Father Thomas is a good priest, and sends a man to meet God with dignity, even a bit of elegance – which some might think more than Alan's station required. But if a poor man cannot receive consideration while on his bier, I know not where he may find it.

The bearers lifted the coffin again and took it to the church. Father Thomas spoke the Mourning Office in a clear, strong voice, then removed his chausable. A cloud of incense floated over poor Alan as the vicar swung the censor. He sprinkled holy water on the body, then began our Lord's prayer, which all followed. There were the usual prayers of forgiveness and deliverance from judgment, then the bier was lifted once again and all followed it out through the porch to the churchyard.

Father Thomas led us to a shaded corner near the wall, made the sign of the cross, and sprinkled holy water on the gravesite. The gravediggers, who had remained well back in the cortege, now came forward and set their spades to work at the chosen earth. The priest read psalms while these two were at their work.

When the grave was ready Alan's brother lifted the coffin lid and he and the other bearers drew Alan in his shroud from the coffin and lowered him into the grave. As I suspected, Matilda could not afford to bury her husband in a coffin, but wished to show respect for her mate, so had rented a box from the carpenter – who stood in the group of mourners and watched as the gravediggers filled in the hole while Father Thomas spoke the final collect for forgiveness.

As the last dirt was shoveled on to the grave I caught a movement from the corner of my eye. Richard Hatcher, one of Lord Gilbert's tenants, was motioning to John Holcutt from the churchyard wall. I gave no more attention to this, but went to offer sympathy to the widow. Matilda stood silent, staring at the fresh earth, her child clinging to her skirts, as the group of mourners began to break apart.

I do not now recall what I said to her. 'Twas probably trite. I thought to say to her that a funeral is not a time when the living mourn the dead, but rather a time when the dying remember those who are now alive in Christ, if their faith was whole.

Perhaps I should have spoken these words but I was uncertain how she would receive them. I may say this to her at some later time. I have learned that it is easier to say later what one should have said before, than to unsay what should not have been said at all.

Some may accuse me of forgetting purgatory. I have not. While a student at Oxford I rented from another scholar a Gospel of St John and copied it. These pages I have read many times, so that I remember many of the passages. Jesus said of himself, "Therefore if the Son makes you free, you shall be free indeed."

If our Lord has made a man free, how can he then be imprisoned in purgatory? And how is a man made free? The scriptures speak plainly: through faith in Christ, the Son of God, who takes away the sins of the world. If Christ has taken away Alan's sins, why must he be punished for them in purgatory?

I will again be accused of listening overmuch to Master John Wyclif, who has taught similar views. And purgatory has been a part of church tradition for many centuries. But again, I hold with Master Wyclif that a tradition must be supported by scripture to be valid. I find no place for purgatory in holy writ. But I am no smasher of temple idols, howso they might need to be toppled. Let others challenge the bishops; I wish only to heal men's broken bodies. Perhaps I am a coward.

Alan the beadle left no funds with which his widow might endow an oratory where monks could pray him out of purgatory. When it comes Lord Gilbert's time to die, Petronilla will certainly furnish a chapel in some monastery where prayers will be said for his soul forever. Will Lord Gilbert win release from purgatory before Alan? Our Lord said 'twas easier for a camel to pass through the needle's eye than for a rich man to enter heaven. Then what of purgatory and endowed chapels and perpetual prayers? Although Lord Gilbert is generous to the poor, it seems to me his soul would be the better if he gave more to them now, while he yet lives, and less to the monks when he is dead. If he gives enough to the poor, he might not need to give even a penny to the monks.

Well, these are matters for theologians and scholars. My mind was arrested and returned to the churchyard when John Holcutt tapped me on the shoulder and brought me from my musing.

"Richard Hatcher," he said, "has found a dead lamb this morning."

There is nothing unusual about a dead lamb in springtime, but something in the reeve's tone told me that, in this case, there was. I turned to John as he spoke.

"Dead an' half eaten, 'twas. Throat tore out an' guts spread about... what wasn't ate up. You think 'twas the beast which attacked Alan?" John asked.

"I know of no other cause," I admitted. "And late last night I walked the castle wall and heard some beast howl. We must seek Father Thomas' absolution, for I think we must forsake our Good Friday obligations and hunt the beast while its track may be found."

I sent the reeve to the castle to organize the hunt while I sought the vicar. I found him in the church, preparing for the Good Friday mass which would soon begin. Father Thomas scurried from images to crucifix, adjusting veils and seeing to the good order of his church. Townsmen and villeins were beginning to arrive. Most wore the grey and brown cotehardies they donned every day, but those who could afford it wore black, or sometimes yellow, to honor the day.

I awaited the vicar at the Easter Sepulcher, where shortly the unveiled cross would be placed for the allotted time, to be withdrawn with much rejoicing Easter morn. Some churches have a small room reserved for this rite, but at the Church of St Beornwald a niche in the chancel wall, boarded up with thick oak planks, serves this duty.

Satisfied that all was in readiness, Thomas withdrew from the niche to find me standing behind him. "Ah... Master Hugh. You startle me."

I apologized, and explained the need which would draw a dozen of us from the mass this day. A marauding beast is a serious matter, and the priest knew it. The loss of a lamb was bad enough. What of the calves new born which would soon be put out with their mothers in the meadows and fallow land? Father Thomas gave his blessing to our pursuit, and I made my way out through the porch as others entered.

Shillside had got wind of the chase and was at the castle with his son, William, a reedy lad of seventeen years, who was twitching with enthusiasm. John and Richard had gathered several more villeins and tenants and the fewterer, with two old hounds Lord Gilbert had left behind in his kennel at Bampton when he removed to Pembroke before St Crispin's Day last autumn.

We followed Richard Hatcher to the meadow. Crows and circling buzzards had already taken note of the carcass. The field was west of the town. I had heard no beast howl from that quarter, but I know little of wolves. Perhaps, I thought, they are silent when at the hunt.

The early spring grass was not grown long enough to be beaten down, so no path leading to or from the lamb was visible. And while the sod was soft from spring rains, it was not so pliant as to leave behind the track of a wolf or any other creature.

The castle fewterer brought the hounds to the slain

lamb and led them around it in a circle. The dogs sniffed bemusedly at the lamb and the turf around it.

"'Tis odd," the fewterer muttered. "They seem not interested. When Squire was young," he motioned toward the white and black hound, "he'd a' been off in a flash... an' Tawny, too, though she was never the hunter as Squire was."

He led the hounds in a circle once again, larger this time, and noted a place where both animals took some time snuffling about the meadow grass. When the circle was completed, with no other sign that the dogs had found an interesting trail, he returned to the spot, unleashed them, and ordered them off on the scent.

The hounds obeyed with scant enthusiasm. "Squire be ten years old," the fewterer remarked, as if to excuse the animal's lack of zeal.

The hounds followed their noses to the edge of the fallow ground, then turned south along a hedgerow which separated the meadow from a newly plowed field to the east. The dogs followed this barrier, with the hunting party close behind, to the edge of a wood. No coppicing had been done in this grove, so there was little to hinder the advance of our company. Ancient trees so blotted the summer sun here that little vegetation grew on the forest floor.

We kept the hounds in view readily enough, for they proceeded at a leisurely pace, though there was little undergrowth to impede them. Two archers in the party notched arrows, unwilling to be caught unready should a wolf suddenly appear from behind an oak. They need not have been so cautious.

The forest gave way to meadow again, and we entered bright sunlight on the Bishop of Exeter's lands. We followed the hounds to another hedgerow, beyond which was a field that the bishop's villeins had newly plowed.

The track then turned north, as the hounds followed the wall. I began to wonder if the beast we trailed was old, or injured, that it did not leap a hedgerow or fence to continue its path, but instead went round.

We had come near to the place where the beast would have been when I heard it last in the night. But the track seemed wrong. Unless the hounds were backtracking, following the path the animal made as it sought a meal, rather than the trail it left after it slew the lamb.

The track plunged once again into the forest, and we followed until, 200 paces beyond, the wood ended on the banks of Shill Brook, a quarter-mile downstream from Mill Street Bridge.

"This is a waste," I told the fewterer. "The dogs are backtracking. We go where the beast was, not where it now is."

"'Twas the only scent the hounds found," he replied defensively. "An', even if 'tis so, we may come upon the beast's lair, where it lays in the day before seeking prey at night."

I agreed that might be so, knowing little of wolfish habits, and predicted that when we waded across the brook, the hounds would soon turn east. I must cease making prophetic statements. They seem usually to be wrong. When we crossed the stream, the track did not lead east. It led nowhere.

We splashed across to the north side of the brook (for here it flowed east, having turned from its southerly path through the town) and waited for the hounds to find the scent. They could not.

After much fruitless trotting about, their noses pressed to the ground, the fewterer called them to us. "Strange they cannot recover the trail. Squire can't see so well in 'is old age, I think, but I never see 'im lose a scent."

"Perhaps," I suggested, "the animal passed through the brook for a few paces. If we follow downstream the dogs may find their way again."

The fewterer leashed his hounds and led them along the north bank of the stream. Occasionally they frightened a trout from under the bank, but they gave no sign that they had recovered the scent.

We followed the brook for 200 paces or more, until

the fewterer pulled at the leashes and turned to me. "Mayhap the beast left the brook on the other bank. If we find no track here we might return on the other side."

I agreed, but was not ready to do so yet. We fought our way through brambles and undergrowth until we were nearly to Aston. The party did not complain, but as we continued east they more and more often peered at me with questioning eyes.

Perhaps the wolf had been this far east when I first heard it howl, but if so the dogs had found no trace of its presence. I spoke the words all were eager to hear, and we waded back across the brook to retrace our steps on the south bank.

The hounds seemed to enjoy this sport. They occasionally flushed a rabbit or a hedgehog. But when we arrived back where the trail had emerged from the wood to cross, as we thought, the brook, they had found no spoor to interest them. We had been three hours at our work, and were nearly back where we began.

The only course remaining was to seek the track upstream, toward the town. I directed that the hounds be separated, one dog on either side of the brook. As we set out I heard the bell from the Church of St Beornwald ring the ninth hour.

The dogs followed their noses up the brook all the way to Mill Street Bridge. They did not recover a scent. Tenants and villeins of Lord Gilbert Talbot and the Bishop of Exeter gazed in wonder as we clambered up the banks of the brook to the bridge. We made a rare spectacle. A dozen tired, mud-caked men, scratched and bloodied, and two weary old hounds. I was going to need another bath.

Hubert Shillside turned to me as we stood perplexed on the bridge. "I think," he complained, "we must find better hounds. These are too old… they have missed the trail somewhere."

This thought had occurred to me, but before I could reply the fewterer leaped to defend his charges.

"Nothin' wrong wi' the dogs. They're not so young as t'run down a stag, maybe, but if there was a wolf left a trail they'd find it."

"So you say, after Master Hugh heard the beast, and after the slain lamb, that there must be no wolf because your hounds cannot find it?" Shillside remarked sarcastically.

"'At's what I'm sayin'. Master Hugh may've heard a wolf... no offense," the fewterer looked at me and tugged his forelock. "But there be no trail or the dogs would'a found it."

"But they did," I said.

"Maybe," the fewterer muttered.

"What is your meaning?" I challenged the old man.

"Oh, they found a scent. But t'were it a wolf they'd a been more eager to be off."

"You are sure of this?"

"Nay. Can't be certain. But I've worked Squire an' Tawny since they was pups. I know 'em... an' old or not, they didn't act like they was on a trail of no wild beast."

"Well, wolf or no, they are fatigued from the day's labor, as are we all. Return them to their kennel and feed them well."

"Will you be wantin' 'em tomorrow?"

"No . . . unless there is better reason than we have found today."

"What is to be done, then?" John Holcutt asked. "Must we hope the beast will travel on to curse some other place?"

"No. There may yet be a way to take this marauder. Take two or three others back to the meadow where the lamb lies. Build a screen downwind of the lamb. Tonight we will watch the meadow. Perhaps the wolf will return to its kill. You two," I said to the archers, "will accompany the reeve and me tonight."

Chapter 4

Our company broke apart, its dispirited members making their weary way to their homes, or, in John Holcutt's case, to the meadow. Tomorrow there would be an all-night vigil at the church, awaiting Easter dawn and the removal of the cross from the Easter Sepulcher. Tonight we four would keep a vigil as well.

The two archers were known to me. They were tenants on Lord Gilbert's land, and I had seen each put a dozen arrows into the butt end of a barrel at 200 paces. Unless John Holcutt built the screen well away from where the lamb lay, if the wolf returned this night he would find an unwelcome surprise. This thought reminded me that the time had come to renew the archery competitions Lord Gilbert sponsored on Sunday afternoons. Such contests were suspended for the winter, but 'twas time to renew the practice.

I ate a light supper, then made my way to the meadow where the reeve and his assistants were completing the screen. John had built a framework of saplings and fallen branches from the nearby wood. Into this he wove tall grasses which had withstood the winter, and ivy and foliage from the hedgerow. The blind was but two paces from the thistles and nettles of the hedgerow. No beast would come upon it from behind. The dead lamb lay forty paces west. No wolf who fed there this night would need another meal.

I sent the reeve and one archer to the castle for supper, and kept the other archer with me. It was not yet dark, but I did not wish both archers absent should the wolf return before they finished their meal. I would send the unfed archer to his supper later.

I might have sent them both with John, and kept a bow and arrows with me as I watched alone. But this would have been a mistake had the animal chosen that moment to return to its kill. If wolves laugh, the beast would surely have done so as any arrows I loosed fell wide of their mark.

John and the first archer returned, well satisfied, and I sent the other to his meal as the twilight faded. Only the outline of bare tree limbs was visible to the west, where the setting sun still gave illumination to the sky. By the time the second archer stumbled up to the blind from his supper, the meadow lay tenebrous under a starlit sky.

If a wolf had chosen to return then silently to finish its meal, we should never have seen it. But two hours later a waning moon rose over the greenwood to the east and the pale white carcass of the lamb became visible. It was undisturbed. I was uncertain whether to be pleased or regretful that we had not been visited in the dark.

We were not visited in the moonlight, either. One by one my companions fell asleep. Their steady, measured breathing was the only sound to break the silence of the night. I let them sleep. Unless they snored, as one of the archers was wont to do. A gentle kick usually brought him awake and stopped his rumbling. And the reeve woke from his slumber several times to watch with me. He may as well have slept, for no beast visited the meadow that night.

I sent my companions to their homes as the sun rose over the fields and forest to the east toward Aston. I required of each man that he rejoin me at the screen at sunset. I was unwilling to accept failure. There would be many others awake all this night in the church, keeping the Easter Vigil. We four would honor God by doing our duty to Lord Gilbert and the tenants and villeins of his manor.

I returned to my chamber in the castle and lay on my bed for a fitful sleep until dinner. I dreamed of pale blue yarn and wooden-soled shoes and slavering wolves.

The castle cook revived my body and spirit. A good

meal almost always performs that miracle. There was this day a leg of mutton, a coney pie and a ham, with mushroom tarts, a compost and cooked, spiced apples.

Thus refreshed, I went about manor business for the afternoon. It was my duty to inspect Lord Gilbert's manor each day. This day there was plowing to oversee and the manuring of a field ready to be planted to barley. As dusk settled on the town, I joined the stream of residents walking to the Church of St Beornwald for the lighting of the great Paschal Candle and the commencement of the Easter Vigil. My soul was drawn to remain, but duty demanded otherwise. I stood at the rear of the nave while the great candle was lit, then quietly made my way out through the porch into the darkening churchyard.

The two archers were at the blind before me, and John Holcutt appeared soon after. This night was colder, and the waning moon appeared in the east an hour later. We shivered in the cold and waited for the moon to rise. When it did it was often obscured as a thickening body of clouds drifted from north to south across the town and meadow.

At dawn the clouds thickened more, and in the growing light I could see what only the touch on my face had told me 'til then: snowflakes drifted across the meadow. But the lamb lay as it had been for two days.

My knees were stiff with cold and it was with some discomfort that I stood and stretched. I remember my father, who rarely complained of anything, lamenting aching joints when winter came. Was I become my father already?

We four peered over the screen at the undisturbed lamb, stamping our feet to drive out the cold. This exercise was not successful.

Neither was the watch over the dead lamb, so I called it off. I told John and the archers that, unless the wolf gave more sign, we would no longer seek it, but hope that it had traveled to some far county.

I walked, stiffly at first, like an old man, back to the castle and my chamber. I wished to clean myself before Easter Mass, so asked for a bucket of hot water to be brought. I would not eat. It is my custom to fast before mass, as was once customary, but now seems an uncommon privation.

I had laid the blue yarn found in Alan's scalp on my table. My eyes fell upon it as I awaited my bucket of hot water. I picked it up, sat on my bench, and twirled it mindlessly. I had contemplated that thread many times but was no nearer to its significance, if it had any, to the beadle's death and his missing shoes.

While I toyed with the yarn I heard a soft rapping on my door. I bid the maker enter, and Alice atte Bridge pushed open the door. Her right shoulder sagged under the weight of a bucket of steaming water.

So it was that the girl saw me twisting the blue yarn about a finger. She stood watching, awaiting instructions.

"Any place will do, Alice," I nodded at the bucket. She took me at my word and dropped her burden in the middle of my chamber, still watching the blue yarn. The girl turned slowly to leave, obviously curious about the yarn. I found myself eager to explain to her – to anyone – its importance. So I told her of finding Alan the beadle, which news she had surely heard already, and of the pale blue yarn found in his hair, and his missing shoes. I did not ask her if she knew of a garment of that shade. I should have. Alice seems incapable of falsehood. I might have been spared a brawl in a darkened road and a thump across my skull.

I dismissed her and went to scrubbing myself, attempting to wash away cobwebs of sleep as well as dirt, so as to prepare my soul and body for the celebration of our Lord's resurrection. I was more successful with body than with spirit, for had I not been standing for the mass I should have fallen asleep during Thomas de Bowlegh's homily. This message, I thought, was not one of his best. But perhaps his discourse lost its power at my ear rather than at his lips.

By tradition Lord Gilbert's servants, tenants, and

villeins would receive a feast this day at the castle. Most Lords fed only their servants an Easter dinner, but Lord Gilbert, though parsimonious on other occasions, was lavish when it came to sharing his board at Easter. Perhaps he is more charitable than most nobles. Or perhaps he likes to display his wealth.

Although Lord Gilbert was absent at Pembroke, he instructed me to continue the custom. The great hall at Bampton Castle is small, so I ordered tables set up in the castle yard for the villeins, while tenants would dine in the hall. The day was cool, but there was no more snow, so those who ate in the yard were not much discomfited.

Tenants and villeins who dined at Lord Gilbert's table this day brought eggs, which was also customary. We who fed at the castle board would see our fill of custards and poached eggs for the next fortnight.

There was, as is traditional, no work done for the next week. I chafed to see such idleness, but I suppose 'tis well for men to have some relief from their labors. Especially since, when Hocktide was past, the work of summer would truly begin.

The week was cold, not lending itself to celebration. The clouds which appeared on Easter eve remained over Bampton 'til Thursday, bringing Scotland's weather with them. Better both the Scots and their clime remain to the north.

On Hocktide Sunday I set up a table in the castle yard – the weather being much improved – and collected rents and fees due Lord Gilbert. Harvests had been good the previous two years, so there were few unable to pay. These, as Lord Gilbert instructed, were granted extra time, but their arrearages were carefully noted. In times past a tenant unable to pay his rent might be cast out and his land leased to another. But since the great death there were few workers and much unused land. A tenant dismissed could not be replaced. And tenants knew this. I was pleased that most paid without complaint. Lord Gilbert would surely have been unhappy to return to Bampton to discover that rents were uncollected. But he would have been equally unhappy should I dismiss a tenant who could not be replaced.

On the Monday and Tuesday after Hocktide Sunday the residents of Bampton indulged in a curious spectacle, unknown to me before I came to the town. On Monday the wives of Bampton whipped their husbands through the streets. On Tuesday husbands got revenge and whipped their screeching wives through the town. I suppose no harm was done. I saw few who took advantage of the custom to lay on strong blows. Certainly wives, whatever disagreements they might have with their husbands, did not thrash them, for they knew they would receive similar blows next day. And husbands who scourged their wives too strongly knew they would eat cold pottage 'til Whitsunday for their vigor.

It was St George's Day, ten days after Easter, before life in Bampton resumed its normal routine. I called for hallmote to meet that day. Lord Gilbert's tenants and villeins selected John Prudhomme to replace Alan. John held a half-yardland of Lord Gilbert, and seemed not to fear his new duties. As there had been no wolf's howl heard for nearly a fortnight, why should he?

I awoke from my slumber next morning itching from bites I had received while at my rest. Hallmote had met in the great hall the previous day, and some tenant or villein had brought with him to the assembly some unwanted guests. As my chamber opened directly off the hall, and in the night I was the nearest warm body available, the pests sought me out.

In my chest there remained several bundles of fleabane I had gathered the previous summer. I took a bundle and broke the dried stems, leaves and faded flowers to small bits. These I placed in an earthen bowl, along with a coal from my faded fire. Then I closed the door and retreated to the hall.

Shortly after I was gratified to see a wisp of smoke curl from under my door. Satisfied that the fleabane was smoldering well, I was about to seek the kitchen for a loaf when Alice atte Bridge appeared at the buttery and saw my smoking door.

"Oh, sir!" she yelped, and turned to run for aid.

With some difficulty I arrested her flight. She returned to the hall, gazing suspiciously at the fumes now pouring copiously from under my door. I thought some explanation in order.

"'Tis fleabane. I was visited in the night, and am now driving off my callers."

Alice peered at me, uncomprehending.

"Fleas," I explained. "Some unwashed villein introduced them into the hall yesterday. They found a home in my chamber last night."

"Oh, sir… may I have some?"

"Fleas?"

"Nay, sir. Of them I have plenty. I sleep in a closet off the scullery, and they vex me now an' then."

"I have more fleabane, but 'tis in the chamber and I must not disturb the fumes while they do their work. Return at the ninth hour and I will give you some."

"Thank you, sir." The girl curtsied and ran gracefully off down the passage past the buttery door. I watched her scurry away. It was a rewarding experience. But I immediately felt sheepish for permitting my thoughts to wander so, with Alice but a child of fifteen years or so. Well, some tenant or servant to Lord Gilbert would have a fine wife in a few more years.

I left my chamber to the smoke and set off to find breakfast. I warned the servants at the kitchen to take no notice of the vapors rising into the great hall from under my door, then went to my daily rounds.

John Holcutt was busy seeing to the marling of a field and needed no advice on the matter from me. I walked to the meadow where the lamb was slain, but found only a few wisps of wool where the animal had lain. It was Richard Hatcher's lamb. Doubtless what remained of it had become his dinner.

I was returning to the castle for my own dinner when the sound of shouting and agitated voices reached me across the meadow. Above the distant cacophony I heard my name. What now, I wondered? Life in Bampton was returning to its settled, peaceful ways after Alan the beadle's death. I wished for no interruption of that tranquility.

I trotted across the meadow and walked rapidly down Mill Street past the castle toward town and the din. As I crossed the bridge over Shill Brook I saw a crowd milling before the blacksmith's shop, where Church View Street entered Bridge Street. Some in the throng saw me approach and I was immediately hailed and urged to make haste. I did.

The knot of onlookers parted as I approached and in their shadow I saw a man lying in the street in a great pool of blood. One hand twitched at his side, the other was clasped to his neck. Between the fingers clutching his throat blood flowed in a copious stream. I knelt in the dirt and saw the man's eyes follow me as I examined the wound under his fingers. Something, or someone, had slashed through the great vein. He had only minutes to live unless I could staunch the flow of blood.

"A cloth," I shouted. "A clean cloth – quickly!"

A housewife in the crowd presented her apron. It was flour-dusted but clean enough. I pried the fellow's hand from his wound and pressed the folded cloth tight against the gash.

I required my instruments, but could not leave my patient to fetch them. From the corner of my eye I saw a youth who had won a footrace last autumn at Michaelmas. I called to him.

"Run to the castle and fetch my instruments." The youth gazed at me blankly. "Find Alice, the scullery maid. She knows the box where they are kept. My chamber will be clouded with smoke... pay that no mind. Run! Be off!"

The mob parted and the youth sprinted away toward the castle. I returned my attention to the pale form at my knees. Blood seeped from under the folded apron, but not so profusely as before.

"Who is this?" I asked. "What befell him?"

A dozen voices related the news. I could make no sense of their words. By shouting louder than they I managed to quiet my informers. I searched for a face I knew and saw Hubert Shillside's adolescent son. He was a stolid youth, and perhaps lacked imagination. But in this matter I did not seek invention, but fact.

"William... what has happened here?"

The crowd was restive, and one or two would have answered for the youth, but I silenced them and bid the lad continue.

"There was an argument... many heard." Heads nodded in agreement. "Philip accused Edmund of something."

Then it was that I recognized the bloody figure over whom I knelt: Philip, the town baker. And standing before his forge, his arms pinioned to his side, was Edmund, the smith. The smith's eyes were wide in fright, or amazement, at what he had done. He made no move to escape the grasp of those who clutched his arms.

"Philip picked up Edmund's hammer, as he'd laid it down when the dispute began," William continued. "But he swung wide, not bein' accustomed to swingin' hammers. Edmund swung back with a piece of hot iron in his tongs. Philip ducked but the edge caught 'im by the throat... an' there he lays."

"What was their dispute about?" I asked.

"Dunno," William offered. "Wasn't close enough t'hear plain. Just saw when Philip swung the hammer."

The matter in dispute was of little importance at the moment. I did not press the matter, but rather concerned myself with Philip's seeping neck. The man began to moan, but in his mouth I saw no blood. I was relieved. If the stroke had penetrated his throat he must die, for the bleeding would continue no matter what I did for his external wound.

I kept the sopping apron pressed close against the laceration and wondered when the runner would return with my instruments. The lad arrived soon enough, and I saw from the corner of my eye the mob part to allow him through. Alice had followed, and pressed in behind him.

I called for a bystander to take my place at the

wound while I readied the instruments I would need. The crowd hesitated, and in that moment Alice knelt at my side. "Wha... what must I do?" she stammered.

"Keep this cloth pressed tight against the wound until I tell you to release it. Then be ready to apply it again should I need it."

She nodded understanding and did not hesitate but took the red, sodden apron in both hands and forced it against the cut.

I opened my kit and prepared needle and thread. As I worked I asked the curious who hovered above me for an egg. A crone lurched wordlessly off down the High Street in response.

I would have liked to repair the torn vein first but knew of no way to do that without releasing a great flow of blood once again. So with needle and thread in my right hand, I held my left above the wound and told Alice to release the apron.

When she did, blood flowed again from the torn flesh, but not so much as before. A clot was beginning to form at the edge of the cut.

I gripped the lips of the wound with the fingers of my left hand. As I did so Philip groaned and twisted in pain. I spoke rather more sharply than I ought, I fear, and told him to be still, else I could not patch his cut. I should be more generous in such situations, but sometimes I lack sympathy for those who need my care because of their own foolishness. Certainly if Philip had not first picked up the hammer he would not now be producing a stream of blood in the street.

One hand was not enough to close the wound. As I pinched one end shut the other opened and poured forth more blood. I needed a third hand. Alice saw my dilemma and provided the extra appendage. She reached red fingers past my hand and pinched the other end of the laceration closed. No words passed between us, but she smiled, then looked back to her work.

With two sets of fingers closing the wound I could work quickly, and in but a few moments was able to stitch shut the laceration. Alice used her free hand to squeeze blood from the dripping apron, then dabbed at the fresh effusions as I worked.

The old woman who had set off for an egg returned as I pulled the last suture tight. I broke her egg in a cup from my instrument box and removed the yolk. The albumen I spread over the stitched wound.

Normally I follow the practice of Henry de Mondeville, who taught that wounds heal best when dry. Therefore I apply few salves to a cut such as Philip received, preferring only to wash the wound in wine. But I thought in this case a poultice might serve, for a few days. I bound Philip's neck in strips of linen, then assisted him to a sitting position.

Philip's eyes wandered and I thought he might swoon. His face was white and his lips pale blue. I had thought to ask some of the gawkers to assist him to his feet and see him down the High Street to his home and bakery on Broad Street. This could not be done. Philip had lost too much blood.

I sent Will Shillside to the carpenter's shop for a plank and two poles. When he returned I instructed two men to lift the baker onto the plank, his feet and arms dangling on either side, and with a pole crosswise at each end four spectators bore him home. I told Philip I would visit him on the morrow and that he must rest 'til then.

As the bearers moved off with Philip I heard another commotion and looked up to see the baker's wife come panting up to her husband. She had been tardily informed of her husband's hurt.

I stood aside while three women competed with one another to tell the lurid details, including some particulars of which I was unaware.

When they had done I spoke, and told her to see that her husband did not rise from his bed until the morrow, when I would call. The woman nodded understanding, shook flour from her apron, and wordlessly followed her husband toward Broad Street. She took the news well, I thought. Too well, as it happened.

I turned to Edmund, still standing at his forge. "Release him," I told his captors, who were holding his arms but loosely anyway.

"What have you to say of this matter?" I asked the smith. He did not reply, but looked to his feet and with a toe began rearranging clinkers on the floor of his forge.

"What did you argue about with Philip that came to this?" I pressed, and nodded to the bloodstains soaked now into the dirt of the street but yet visible.

"Ask Philip," the smith replied. "'Twas he come to me."

"What about?"

The smith was silent, and went to stirring ashes with a toe again.

"If he complains of you to the manor court you will be compelled to speak."

"He'll not, I think."

"Why? Because he brought the first blow?"

"Aye... there's that," Edmund agreed.

"And there is more?" I waited, but received no reply.

I was sure there was more to this tale but could not get it from the smith. I gave up, waved his captors off, and set out for the castle with my instrument box tucked under my arm. Alice was waiting for me at the bridge, gazing down into the brook. Her hands were free of the baker's blood. She must have washed them in the stream.

"You did well," I told her, and joined her at the rail.

"Will the baker live?" she asked.

"Aye. Unless he attacks the smith again before his wound heals."

"Would 'e 'ave died had you not sewed 'im up?"

"Probably."

Alice was silent for a moment, staring upstream at the mill and its wheel. I was about to suggest that she would be needed at the castle when she spoke.

"Did you see me brother?"

"Your brother? Where?"

"In the crowd, watchin' as you sewed up the baker."

"I paid little attention. Which brother?"

"Henry."

Alice had two half-brothers, born of her father's first marriage. These two were angered when their father married a second time, fearing loss of patrimony. What they expected to gain from their father, a poor cotter with a quarter yardland and a scrawny pig, I cannot tell.

Henry, I presume, gained his father's quarter yardland, the hut, and anything Alice left in it. He is a tenant of the Bishop of Exeter. I am not informed of the business of that manor in the Weald, though the property be but across Mill Street from the castle.

"I was anxious for Philip," I said. "I remember Will Shillside looking on, and a few others. I did not notice your brother."

"He was at the edge of the crowd. I saw 'im when I came up wi' the lad you sent t'fetch the box."

She looked down at my instrument case. I could not tell where this conversation was going. Perhaps nowhere, for Alice became silent again. I am a patient man. The girl had, I thought, more to say. I listened to the mill wheel creaking as it turned, and to the splash of water through the sluice. We were so still and silent that a small trout ventured out from the shadow of the bridge and positioned itself below us, waiting for the current to bring a meal its way.

"I saw 'em when I was kneelin'… when you asked for help."

"Saw what?"

"The shoes. I was down close to the ground, like, an' you notice things down there you don't when standin' up."

"Your brother's shoes?" I guessed. I had a feeling I now knew what the girl wanted to say, and why she found it difficult.

"Aye. Him as hardly ever owned any, as I remember. Least, not like them 'e wore today."

"Did he never wear shoes, even in winter?"

"Oh, aye… but made 'em hisself. Never paid cobbler for shoes."

"And what of the shoes he wore today?"

"Wood soles. Thick, like they was new, an' leather t'bind 'em to 'is feet. Soft leather, 'twas. Tanned."

"Like those missing from the feet of Alan the beadle?"

Alice nodded her head and gazed back toward the mill. For all the mistreatment she had endured at her brother's hands, she no doubt felt disloyal for bringing me this report. And, perhaps, apprehensive that her brother might learn of her disclosure.

The girl remained silent, her eyes on the turning mill wheel but not, I think, seeing it.

"The blue yarn," she whispered. "Henry once had a cotehardie of blue. 'Twas old and faded last I saw it."

"Threadbare?" I asked.

"Aye... tattered, like."

"So that loose threads might fall from, say, a ragged sleeve?"

"Aye."

"When did you last see your brother wear such a garment?"

"Before I came t'live in castle, sir. I see little of Henry now, so what he owns I know not, but 'twas before father died I last saw 'im wi' the old blue cotehardie."

"You have performed two good services this day," I told her. "I will see to this business of your brother's new shoes and old blue cotehardie. Rest easy. He will not learn how my suspicion was aroused."

A look of relief brightened her face.

"Run back to the castle and explain my absence at dinner to the cook. Ask him to send a meal to my chamber. I will be there straightaway."

"Aye, sir," she chirped, and set off as I directed. I watched with pleasure as she hastened away. Well, there was nothing much else to look at; I had already viewed the mill and stream.

Chapter 5

After a cold dinner in my reeking chamber I made my way across Mill Street to the path leading along Shill Brook and the cottages in the Weald. These were the bishop's tenants. I had not had cause to venture down this lane since I treated Alice's father, unsuccessfully, for his broken hip.

His hut lay in disrepair, the toft overgrown and the door fallen from its leather hinges. Whatever of the man's possessions his sons thought valuable enough to keep from Alice, this dwelling was not among them.

I did not know which of the next two huts belonged to Henry atte Bridge. I rapped on the door of the first, which was ajar, and was rewarded for my efforts by the appearance of a disheveled woman of indeterminate age carrying a basin on one hip and a runny-nosed child on the other. Both mother and child appeared to have taken seriously the maxim that winter bathing might cause serious health issues.

Henry, the woman said, lived in the next hut. She was the wife of his brother, Thomas. The wife of a quarter yardland tenant cannot lead an easy life, I reflected, as I gave her thanks and left her to her pot and child.

The next dwelling gave a better first impression. The roof was newly thatched, and freshly oiled skins stretched across the windows. I thumped on the door to no result but sore knuckles. In the silence between my assaults on the door I heard distant voices. After a third attempt at the door I gave up and circled the house to the garden toft in the rear.

A woman was there, spading manure into her vegetable beds. It was her voice I had heard, directing children who were assisting in the work by breaking the clods she turned over. The woman used an iron spade. This surprised me. Most cotters can afford only wooden tools with which to work their land.

This woman was as robust as her sister-in-law was frail. And also the children appeared well fed. She rested a foot on the shovel and eyed me suspiciously as I approached. The appearance of a lord's bailiff seems often to create that expression on the faces of the commons.

"Good day," I greeted her in my most cordial tone.

The woman remained silent, as if there was no need to reply if she had no argument about the quality of the day.

"Is your husband at home?"

"Nay," she finally spoke. "Workin' on the bishop's new tithe barn."

I knew of that project. The Bishop of Exeter, in a fit of abundance, had ordered his old tithe barn at Bampton demolished and a new and greater structure raised in its place.

Beams had been hewed over the winter, and now the framework was rising on the bishop's land north of the town. I remember Master John Wyclif speaking of a passage in the Gospel of St Luke where our Lord spoke to his disciples about a wealthy man who pulled down an old barn and built a greater one, but died before he could enjoy the wealth he had stored there. I tactfully avoided mentioning this scripture when discussing the new barn with Thomas de Bowlegh, whose duty it is to oversee construction for the bishop.

Master John, I think, would not be so considerate, for I often heard him condemn prelates for their venality. The criticism of an Oxford master, however, is of little consequence to those in Avignon.

I told the woman I would return in the evening to speak to her husband and made my way around the house to return to the castle. As I passed the gable end a gust of wind brought the scent of roasting meat to my nostrils. I looked up to the gable vent. Wisps of smoke, common enough from such a hut, drifted from the opening.

At the front of the house, out of sight of the toft, I stopped at a window and tested the oiled skin which covered the opening. I found a loose corner and lifted it to peer inside.

The hut was dark and my eyes were accustomed to the bright afternoon sun. But eventually I saw in the smoky interior a small child turning a spit over the central hearth. A low fire glowed there on the stones, and an occasional drop of fat from the haunch on the spit sizzled on the coals. The child stared blankly back at me as he turned the spit. I dropped the skin and, guiltily, I confess, hastened to the path and back to Mill Street.

Perhaps, I thought, it was mutton the child was turning. But where would a quarter-yardlander – well, half-yardlander if he now possessed his father's meager estate – get a roast of mutton? I believed I knew the smell of roasting mutton, and this was not it. And the haunch on the spit was large, larger than a sheep, more closely the size of a deer. A small deer, perhaps, but yet larger than any ewe or even a ram. I knew where a joint of venison would come from: poaching.

From the appearance of Henry atte Bridge's wife and children, they had eaten well for many months. Most cotters would think themselves fortunate to feed their children an egg, much less a joint. Even if the roast was not venison, I wondered where he got it. As he was the bishop's tenant, it was not my business to ask, unless the slaughtered animal belonged to Lord Gilbert's demesne or to one of his tenants in my bailiwick.

I told the cook to keep a supper warm for me, then made my way back to the Weald as the sun dipped behind the leafless oaks and beeches in Lord Gilbert's wood to the west of the town.

Tendrils of smoke still drifted from the gable vent as I approached Henry atte Bridge's hut, but I could detect no scent of roasted meat for the family supper. Henry must have been forewarned that I would call, for the door opened before I could rap a second time on it. The man stared at me with unconcealed hostility. I had dealt firmly with the fellow at the time of his father's death eighteen months before, berating him for his lack of filial observance. He had not forgotten.

The man stood squarely in the door, silent, as if

daring me to either speak or enter. I looked from his scowling brow to his feet. He wore wooden-soled shoes with softly tanned leather binding them to his feet. I inspected his footgear for a long moment, then returned my gaze to his face. He blinked. I saw alarm in his eyes, but the look passed quickly.

"You was 'ere t'day seekin' me," he challenged. "'Ere I am... what d'you want o'me?"

I decided to brazen my way through the interview, so pushed past him through the door as I said, "I wish to discuss your shoes."

The interior of the hut was now near dark, lit only by the coals glowing on the hearth and the fading light of the setting sun which managed to penetrate the window skins.

Soon the embers would be covered and the family would retire to bed. As I entered the hut Henry's wife and three children looked up at me from the table, spoons in hand. Before them sat bowls of pottage. I peered through the smoke into the corners of the darkening dwelling. My eyes could find no roasted meat. But my nose detected yet the faint scent of... what, venison?

I turned to Henry atte Bridge, who stood silent, silhouetted in the door. "Have you owned those shoes long?"

"Not long," he bristled. "A fortnight."

"They seem of fine workmanship. Did you buy them of Adam, the cobbler?"

"Nay... he wants too much. Bought 'em in Witney."

"Witney? Surely a long way to walk to purchase shoes. And the price is controlled... unless the cobbler at Witney is selling at a lower price in violation of the law."

"They was used," atte Bridge growled. "Fella bought 'em died. 'Is wife sold 'em back to the cobbler."

"Oh. And how did you learn of this bargain?"

"Father Thomas sent me an' two others to Witney with a cart an' team to get beams for the new tithe barn."

"And you took enough money on this journey to buy shoes?"

"They was cheap, I tol' you."

"Aye, so you did… from a dead man's feet. How much did you pay for these, uh, used shoes?"

"Thruppence."

"A bargain, indeed, as they appear little worn."

Henry made no answer, but stood sullenly, outlined in the door. No doubt he would have liked to throw me bodily out of his house, and was certainly strong enough to do so, as I am of slender build and Henry was short and thickset. There are advantages as well as trials to serving as bailiff to a powerful lord.

I wrinkled my nose and tested the air. "You have enjoyed a joint for your first remove," I asserted.

"Ha… where would I find meat this time of year? The hog me an' me brother butchered last autumn is gone, but for a fletch o' bacon."

"Hmm. My nose misleads me, then," I shrugged.

Henry atte Bridge made no answer but to fold his arms and glare. I looked over my shoulder at his wife and children. They sat frozen on a bench, spoons of cooling pottage hovering between bowl and lips.

He was lying about the roasted meat, although I could gain little by pressing him on the matter. Was he lying about his shoes also? I thought it likely. And whereas I had no way to prove his deceit about the mutton or venison or whatever it was his lad had been turning on the spit, I could discover the truth of his shoes. I had but to travel to Witney.

The sun was well down behind the western forest when I returned to Bampton Castle and the gatehouse. The cool spring evening was without a breeze, and the sky, bright blue and cloudless as the afternoon wore on, was now black in the east and a faint golden gray through the leafless trees to the west. Brilliant stars speckled the night, like flecks of snow on a parson's robe.

Alice was waiting for me in the great hall, sitting on the cold flags, her back against the wall. She must have guessed what I was about that evening, but spoke instead of fleabane. She rose, sleepy-eyed, as I approached. It was this movement which told me she was there, for the hall, lit only by a single cresset, was so dark I did not see her sitting near my chamber door.

"Please, sir... you said this mornin' as I might 'ave some of the flower what drives fleas away?"

"Ah, yes... you may. I will prepare some of the herb. In exchange you go to the kitchen and get me some supper. I told the cook to keep a meal ready for my return."

"Thank you, sir." The girl curtsied and scuttled off toward the buttery door, becoming invisible in that shadowed part of the hall.

My chamber still held the scent of burned fleabane. I hoped that the stink would be more objectionable to vermin than to me. If so, I should sleep unmolested this night. I gathered the remainder of the fleabane from my chest and broke a handful into the bowl I had left smoldering on my floor that morning. I spread another handful of broken stems, leaves and purple flowers across my mattress. I was left with but little of the herb should fleas reappear before summer brought another harvest of the tiny flowers. I resolved this summer to gather more than in the past. Just in case.

Alice returned with my supper – cold mutton, cheese, and a loaf of fine wheat bread.

Mutton is not my favorite dish when served hot. Cold, it leaves a thick coating of grease on the tongue to mark its passage. The bread and cheese did little to scour the taste away.

I gave Alice the bowl of fleabane and instructed her in its use: burn half, then strew the other half on her mattress. She should wait, I told her, until the morrow, so that the fumes might have the day to permeate the closet where she slept.

The girl took the bowl, curtsied again, and turned with the fleabane pressed to her breast as if I had given her a pouch of silver pennies. Well, when one is assaulted by fleas, their elimination might be worth a sack of pennies to him who could afford it.

I had business on the manor next day, so could not

start for Witney until the morning's work was done. John Holcutt was to oversee the planting of dredge on one of Lord Gilbert's fields and I wished to observe the planting of peas on another of the demesne fields. If peas are planted too closely together, rather than increase the yield per acre, the plants will choke each other and produce a poor crop. But if the peas be planted too sparsely, weeds will spring up and produce the same untoward result.

I set the planters to work with their dibble sticks, and instructed them to sow at three bushels per acre, no more and no less. I waited until the work was well begun, then made my way back to the castle for my dinner. I had told the marshalsea to have Bruce ready at noon. The old horse knew he was to travel, saddled and bridled as he was, and was stamping and blowing with impatience when I reached the stables. I did not make the beast wait.

At the north edge of Bampton I passed the place where the bishop's men were erecting his new barn. Eager for a break from their work, they leaned on their tools and watched as Bruce ambled past. Among the upturned faces was that of Henry atte Bridge. When he was certain I looked his way he spat upon the ground, then returned to cutting a mortise with hammer and chisel.

Aside from Henry atte Bridge and his salivary salutation, I quite enjoyed the ride through sunlit, spring countryside. Low shrubs and plants on the forest floor were popping into greenery. Taller trees had yet few leaves, so the road was not shaded and Bruce and I were warmed with the sun at our backs. Meadows along the way bustled with life. Jackdaws and wrens chirped and flitted about, seeking seeds and the early hatch of unwary insects.

I had ridden this way before. Less than a mile from town I passed the coppiced wood where, eighteen months past, I had watched as pigs, rooting for acorns, uncovered a blue cotehardie. The discovery of that garment led to the identification of bones found in Lord Gilbert's castle cesspit, and eventually revealed a killer. Now I had another body, and a blue thread taken from it. I began to dislike the color blue.

A few hundred paces beyond the coppiced wood where the pigs and I made our discovery the road split, the left fork leading to Shilton and Burford. Bruce knew that way, and would have followed it had I not pulled on the reins to guide him to the right.

Two miles later we crested the hill southwest of Witney and dropped down into the valley of the Windrush.

I pointed Bruce down the High Street, past the impressive spire of St Mary's Church, to the Buttercross at the market square. The square was busy of a Saturday, even though Thursday was market day in the town. I was about to ask a scurrying citizen for the location of the cobbler's shop when I saw on the north side of the market square a house with a shoe painted on a wooden plank which swung from a beam above the door.

The shoemaker had not ended his work yet this day. I heard a light tapping as I paused at his door before rapping my knuckles upon it. The tapping ceased immediately and moments later a face with a quizzical expression on it peered at me through the partly opened door. The cobbler had not, I think, been expecting either trade or a strange visitor.

I asked if he was the town shoemaker. His response was to glance with rolling eyes above my head at his sign, as if to signal my ignorance to some onlooker.

"Aye," he finally said. The man looked down at my serviceable – although hardly new – footwear, then asked, "You need shoes?"

I explained that I needed not shoes but rather a few minutes of his time to inquire of a previous customer. This information did not seem to fill the man with joy, but he turned and nodded me into his shop.

To the right, behind the door, was the cobbler's bench, set before a south window. On it I saw a pair of shoes much like those Henry atte Bridge wore. These shoes were nearly complete. I had interrupted the cobbler as he nailed the finished leather to the thick wooden soles. No doubt he wished me soon gone, so he could complete his work before the light faded from his window and his labor must, by statute, cease for the day. Indeed, I wished to conclude my business quickly also. I did not want to find myself on the road alone at night. Free companies have not been seen in this shire for many years – we are not so cursed as is France by these brigands – but 'tis well nevertheless for the man who travels alone to reach his destination before dark.

The shoes on the cobbler's bench were so like those on Henry atte Bridge's feet that I thought myself on a fool's errand. Of course, they were like the shoes on the feet of most of the commons, but this thought did not register at the moment.

Along the wall beyond the bench was a shelf. On it I saw five pairs of shoes awaiting buyers. Three pairs were like the unfinished set awaiting completion on the bench. A fourth pair was more delicate, made of softer leather, and with leather soles. The fifth pair seemed much out of place. They were of fine leather, with the outlandishly long, curled toes now favored by nobles. Whoever wore these shoes would have to walk up stairs backwards and tie the toes to his calves or he would be forever tripping over them. I wondered who in this town would buy such shoes. Perhaps the Bishop of Winchester, or one of his minions.

"What is your price for shoes such as these?" I asked, nodding toward the pair on his bench.

The cobbler's eyes narrowed as he tried to guess the reason for my question. "Six pence, for such as these." He pointed to the bench. "As the law allows."

I knew what the law allowed. The Statute of Laborers has been renewed twice in the decade since Parliament first saw fit to save us all from the avarice of those who eke out a living with their hands.

"Do you sell for less... if the shoes be old and worn?"

The cobbler gazed at me from under furrowed brows. "Why would I make shoes old and worn?"

"Shoes you might have made new, for one who then

died. Do you buy and repair such shoes?"

The cobbler's visage cleared. "Ah, I see. I might do, did any seek such of me."

"You have not done this recently?"

"Nay. Oh, I repair worn shoes often enough. But not of the dead to sell again."

"A fortnight and more ago did you not resell the shoes of a dead man?"

"Nay. I've sold but new for the past year an' more." The cobbler glanced at his shelf. "An' not so many new, either."

"A man... not of Witney; did such a one buy new shoes like those?" I pointed to his bench.

"A fortnight ago, you say?" The man's brows narrowed again. "Why do you ask me of this?"

It was a fair question. "I am Hugh de Singleton, bailiff of Lord Gilbert Talbot's manor at Bampton. There is a question of law... regarding ownership of shoes, which has recently arisen there. One says he has shoes purchased in Witney while here on the Bishop of Exeter's business."

"A fortnight ago? Nay, no man not of this town bought shoes of me then."

"Of another? Is there another cobbler in the town?"

"Ha! Enough trade here to keep me an' me family alive, no more."

The cobbler was a thickset man, thick of neck, wrists and fingers. Thick in the belly as well. I thought his business not so thin as he professed. A man's stomach often reflects his success in trade.

"Of this you are certain?" I pressed. "If a man from Bampton says he bought shoes of you in the days before Easter, you say he lies?"

"Aye... he does."

I gave the man two farthings for his trouble, retrieved Bruce from the shrub where I had tied him, and set out for home. Meadows were quiet now. Birds sought roosts for the night, and the sun, casting long and twisted shadows across my way, provided little warmth.

Bruce is an old horse – he carried Lord Gilbert at Poitiers – and does not like to be hurried. So it was that darkness overtook me before I reached Bampton. And the sliver of new moon resting in the treetops did little to break the gathering gloom.

I was yet half a mile from town when the attack came. Bruce sensed it first, and 'twas well he did. I was drowsing upon his back when he twitched and shied to the left. This motion brought me back from the edge of sleep, yet I was not so alert that I could sense a blow coming or fend it off. But Bruce's shudder threw off the assailant's aim, so that the club he would have laid aside my skull struck a glancing blow on my right shoulder instead.

The blow unhorsed me and I landed in the mud upon my left shoulder. The next morning I awoke equally sore on each side. I wonder now that I had the presence of mind to immediately roll to the verge. Had I not, the next blow would have succeeded where the first failed.

I saw as I scrambled away from my attacker a silhouette against the darkening sky. This figure had a club raised in both hands and brought it down viciously on the place in the mud where I had toppled an instant earlier. As the ground was darker than the sky, I had the advantage of my foe. I could see but little of his form, but he could see none of me against the darkened earth. My brown cloak blended with the mire to make me, but for face and hands, invisible.

The cudgel which might have broken my head cracked and snapped when it struck the earth at my side. The odds were evened a bit.

A boy who grows to manhood with three older brothers, as I did, learns to defend himself in a scrap. Once, when I was twelve or perhaps thirteen, I became embroiled in a dispute with my next older brother. Nicholas was two years older, a stone heavier, and a hand taller. It was his height, I think, which caused a blow of mine to miss its mark, which was his chin, and strike instead his throat, upon his adam's apple.

I learned two things from this misguided stroke.

The first is that a man's throat is a much softer target than his teeth. A blow against a foe's neck will not result in split knuckles as will a fist against a man's jaw.

And secondly, I learned that the adam's apple is a tender part of human anatomy. No sooner had I struck my brother than he fell to his knees gagging and retching, both hands to his injured throat. He did not recover from this agony quickly. And all the while he gasped and suffered, I begged his forgiveness and pleaded mischance – which it was, although I admit that he had antagonized me so that at the moment I cocked my arm I intended to do him some harm. But not so much as I did.

This event returned to me as I scrambled to my feet. My attacker threw the broken remains of his cudgel at me, and missed, as he could not see me clearly. This was good, for although I saw his arm swing forward above me as I struggled to my feet, I could not see the broken club to duck as it whistled past my ear.

With a grunt of rage the man charged. I stepped back and allowed him to stumble into the darkened ditch at the edge of the road. Combat with my brothers came back to me again. As they were older and larger, it was always their goal to seize me in close struggle and wrestle me to their will. I learned to keep my distance and not be drawn into a grappling contest.

My attacker had fallen to his knees in the ditch, and was now below me. I was the one who was upright and silhouetted against the evening sky. So when the man charged at me again from the verge, on his knees, I did not see him coming until he was upon me.

His shoulder struck me in the hip and together we rolled in the muddy road. We came to a stop, with my assailant on top. I knew I was in trouble. Although I could not see either his face or form, I knew he must be heavier than me, for I am a slender man.

Bruce, as this battle raged, stood as he was when I was dislodged from his back. He had seen enough of combat to be unsurprised when the men about him fell into strife. The horse waited patiently for the outcome.

But he did not like it when my foe and I rolled close behind him, panting and grunting. Bruce aimed a gentle kick from a massive rear hoof just as my mysterious attacker propped himself over my fallen form and bent to seize my throat. The kick struck the fellow on his back and sent him tumbling over my head into a roadside hedgerow as if he were some child's discarded plaything.

I silently thanked Bruce for his aid and scrambled to my feet to prepare for another rush. It came, but not soon. I heard, from the brambles of the ditch, my assailant gasping for the breath Bruce's blow had knocked from him. Had I my wits fully about me then, I would have mounted Bruce and sent him galloping for home. It is always easier to think later what should have been done in such moments. Usually what should have been done, and what was done, are different things. Rarely have I looked back on the calamitous events of my life and found my conduct at those times to be what I later determined it should have been. Surely I am not alone in this.

I girded myself for the fellow's next attack, which I assumed would come when he could gather his wits. Come it did, although had he any wits he would not have plotted this attack at all. So I waited. But not, perhaps, for returning wits.

This time I thought to crouch low so as to hide my shape in the shadows of the forest across the road. I watched as the dim form slowly extricated itself from the brambles of the verge, stood, and cast about seeking me. At last the man's face settled in my direction and with a howl of fury he threw himself at me.

I stepped to my left, the better to position my right fist. It was too dark for my assailant to see this movement clearly, so he plunged ahead where he thought I was. His face, which I could not recognize in the brief moments it was dimly visible, was a pale orb reflecting the nearly vanished twilight. For as he lunged he faced the west, and I, toward the east.

I cocked my arm, clenched my fist, and when he drew near I aimed a blow to strike just below that waxen visage. I put all my inadequate weight behind the stroke. As the man was lurching toward me, the combined effect was of some consequence. And as I hoped, my fist caught him just below the chin, directly upon his adam's apple.

He fell, bellowing, to his knees, tried to stand, then dropped to the mud again. This, combined with the direction of his final lunge toward me, brought him again close to Bruce's hindquarters. The animal seemed not to mind men's quarrels overmuch, so long as they did not include him. But when it seemed the disputes might embrace him as well, he did what any worried horse might do.

This kick was, I think, delivered with more force than the first, as if Bruce wished to say, "I warned you... now pay the price."

It was too dark to see where the kick landed, but I heard it well enough, and I heard the wind go out of my foe like air forced from a blacksmith's bellows. I heard him roll, gasping and choking once again, to the darkened hedgerow. I could see nothing of him there, but there was much to hear. The fellow tossed himself about and groaned in agony, so that had I been a hundred paces from the place I could have heard him clearly. Someone, perhaps closer than that, did hear this thrashing and moaning. Perhaps they thought the sufferer was me. I am sure they hoped 'twas so.

Again I had opportunity to mount Bruce and be off, but again I did not. Perhaps it was curiosity which fastened me to the spot. I wondered what might come next, when I should have rather escaped, for when the man recovered from his hurt I might learn a thing I did not wish to know.

But I was fortunate. The scuffling and retching by the hedgerow ceased, replaced by deep and labored breathing. I sensed, rather than saw, that my attacker was risen to his feet, and braced myself for another charge. It did not come.

Instead I heard the man's uneven footfalls as he stumbled through the mud and into the forest which bounded the western edge of the road. I heard him plunge into the wood, then above the crackle of breaking twigs and crushed leaves I heard a voice. 'Twas barely more than a whisper, due to stealth, or perhaps the blow I gave his throat. I know not which. And because he created such a racket as he dove into the copse I did not hear clearly all that was said. But three words I heard well enough to not mistake them: "Begone... he lives."

It was me spoken of, I am sure. And no sooner had these words come to me from the woods than I heard other feet making hasty departure, stumbling over the winter's fallen branches not yet gleaned for firewood.

Then the forest grew quickly silent and I was left standing alone in the darkened road. There had been two who awaited me this night, but only one saw fit to attack. Why was this so? Two might have overpowered me. Perhaps they thought that one assailant was enough. My slender physique would not strike fear in the heart of a sturdily made man. Whatever the reason, but one had fallen upon me and with Bruce's aid he had been driven off. I felt fortunate. The words hissed from the forest but a moment before came back to me. "He lives." It was clear to me that I was not attacked for my purse. I was intended to die in the mud of the road.

I thought I knew who my assailant was, and why he wished me dead. But to kill a man because of a pair of shoes? Who would do such a thing? Perhaps, I reflected, there is more to this matter than shoes.

Such thoughts occupied my mind as I stretched my aching shoulders, climbed to Bruce's broad back, and settled myself for the last half-mile to Bampton and the castle. Certainly Henry atte Bridge despised me for interfering in his life. I had demanded his presence and homage at his father's funeral. I had helped his half-sister escape with what few possessions she could gather from her father's hut. I had discovered his falsity about his shoes. He could not know this yet, but perhaps suspected it, for he saw me ride north earlier that day.

Wilfred had left the gate open and the portcullis

drawn awaiting my return. I gave Bruce over to him with a charge that the horse was to receive an extra measure of oats this night. He assured me that the marshalsea would be so instructed and led the animal to the stables while his assistant swung the doors closed and cranked down the portcullis.

I did not wish to show myself to the castle residents in my soiled state. Dark as it was in the castle yard, Wilfred was unaware of the mud which covered me, but the light of a single candle would make my condition clear.

So I was relieved to gain entrance to the great hall, and my chamber, without being seen. There remained some water in a bucket from my morning ablution. I removed my soiled clothes and mopped my grimy face and arms before donning clean chauces, kirtle and cotehardie. When I felt presentable I made my way to the kitchen and procured for myself another cold supper. This was becoming a habit I had no wish to continue. I fell asleep that night pondering how I might confront Henry atte Bridge. I might have saved myself the worry. Someone else confronted him first.

Chapter 6

Sunday dawned bright and clear. There was in the yellow tint of the sun's slanting beams a promise of warmth before the day was old.

I admit that I find it disagreeable to rise for matins on the Lord's Day. This is especially so when winter holds a dark curtain over all so early in the morning. But this day glistened with the promise of spring. And I was alive. It was clear to me that two men wished it otherwise. I had Bruce to thank for my life, but God also. If he could be diverted from more important matters to see my life prolonged, I would be ungrateful to ignore an opportunity to thank Him for His trouble.

I left the church after matins to await the mass in the churchyard. Many centuries of burials have left the grounds around the Church of St Beornwald lifted above the paths which lead from the church to the graves and the lych gate in the churchyard wall. In this way the church at Bampton is like that of my home in Little Singleton, and every other churchyard in the kingdom. Should Christ delay his return, these burial hummocks will someday, I think, rise to block the sun from the church windows.

I climbed one of these low mounds and sat, my back to the rising sun, to wait for the bells which would announce the next service. No sound but the soft piping of a bullfinch disturbed my reverie. The bird left his oaken perch at the edge of the churchyard and darted, a small orange and black comet, past the church tower and into the wood to the north of the churchyard. A bullfinch! I hoped this fellow had not many brothers hereabouts, for if so, they would soon be feasting on the buds of Lord Gilbert's apple trees.

Beyond the wood where the bullfinch vanished I saw other birds. In the high, distant sky four buzzards circled in the calm morning air, black against the blue heavens.

St Beornwald's bell jolted me from my wool-gathering and I joined the flow of worshippers making their way to the porch. The stone building was cold, so when Father Thomas concluded his sermon all present were pleased that they would soon be released to return to the sun, now well up above the town rooftops and making the church windows a blaze of color.

The vicars greeted parishioners at the porch as we filed eagerly from the building. Not that all were impatient to be released from their worship, although surely some were of such a mind. After a long winter a pleasant spring day is much welcome and not to be wasted.

As I walked the path from porch to churchyard I noticed Thomas de Bowlegh in conversation with a woman. Her back was to me, but Father Thomas' features were visible, and creased with concern. His brow was furrowed, and his lips pursed. Then the woman, in great agitation, turned to point to the east and I saw it was Emma, the wife of Henry atte Bridge. Perhaps, I thought, he came home last night in ill humor and beat her to make up for his loss elsewhere. And now she complained to the Bishop of Exeter's representative of her husband's cruelty.

I walked on toward the castle and my dinner but had gone but a few paces down Church View Street when I heard my name called. Thomas de Bowlegh had ended his conversation in the churchyard and was now panting after me. "Master Hugh... a word," the vicar puffed as he approached. "Henry atte Bridge... you know him?"

I nodded.

"Henry has disappeared. His wife came to me this morning after mass."

"Is he a reliable man?" I asked. I thought I knew the answer to that question, but perhaps others saw the man differently than I.

The vicar hesitated. "No less than others. He's not

run off before, and does his week work for the bishop with no more prodding than most."

"Ah, yes, the new tithe barn. I saw him at work on it yesterday as I passed."

I saw a quizzical expression pass briefly across de Bowlegh's face, so I explained my mission, the reason for it, and what I had learned. I also told him of the attack. I saw the vicar's jaw grow tight and his lips draw into a thin line as I completed the tale.

"Think you he has fled… to escape judgment for his misdeeds?"

"What does his wife think?" I replied.

"Does she know of his transgression? She did not speak of such. But she wouldn't, would she. No, she fears some harm has come to him."

"Did she say why he was out past curfew?"

"He had returned from working on the new barn, then told his wife he was off to seek wood in the forest. 'Tis a right the common folk have on the bishop's lands, as with Lord Gilbert's estate, I think."

I nodded, for I know well the ancient liberties. "And he did not return?" I asked, "even with the dawn?"

"Nay. The woman is anxious that he be found. She fears he has suffered some hurt and lays injured in the forest."

"You wish me to search Lord Gilbert's woodlands hereabouts?"

"Aye. He should not have been gathering wood on m'lord's land, if gathering wood was his business, but such as he might seek where they will, rather than where they ought."

"Did he tell his wife where he might seek wood?"

"Aye. Said as he'd seen many limbs down in the wood near where the tithe barn is new built."

"And near where I was assailed last night," I added.

"You think Henry atte Bridge the man who lay in wait for you?"

"What other man wishes me ill?"

"Perhaps 'twas a thief."

"Perhaps. But as the miscreant plunged into the wood I heard him say to another, 'He lives.'"

"Hmmm." The priest pulled at his chin, an action which reminded me of Lord Gilbert Talbot, who does likewise when puzzled. "Perhaps we should begin our search at the place you were attacked. There may be a trail we might follow. Do you think your blow, or the horse's kick, might have injured the fellow so he could not continue his flight... if 'twas Henry who did this thing?"

"I think he was not so badly harmed as that."

And then the circling buzzards caught my eye again. They drifted on the wind north of the town, near where I had fought for my life the night before. I watched them silently, and as I did the vicar turned to see what so absorbed my attention.

We stared at the great birds, contemplating their possible significance. The vicar spoke first. "I will gather some clerks. Will you come and show us where we must begin our search? I think," he sighed, "'twill not be far from where those buzzards now soar."

"Aye... not far."

Father Thomas and I returned to the church, where we found Simon Osbern and three clerks preparing for evensong. The priest explained our mission, tactfully omitting any word of the altercation wherein I had found myself.

"Master Hugh," he asserted, "believes he may have seen a man in the north woods, near to the new barn... is that not so, Master Hugh?"

"Aye, though 'twas near dark. I can show you the place."

The four men needed no urging to leave their duties and join the hunt. When a man has heard the beginning of such a tale he is not content until he knows the end of it.

I led our party north on the Broad Street, past the bishop's new barn now standing completed to its frame and thatching. Truth to tell, I was not sure of the exact place along the road where I was waylaid. It was near dark, and I was not concerned at the time with the scenery.

I slowed my pace when we were well past the new barn. The others kept in step, the clerks behind as fitted their station, Thomas de Bowlegh and Simon Osbern at either hand. The priests' gaze swung between me and the road. They studied me intently while I studied the path.

There had been few travelers on the road that day. No one was about his trade on a Sunday. So I followed the track of a well-shod horse as we made our way north. The animal had been going south, and not so long before. I was sure the horse was Bruce.

It was. We came upon a place where the horse had halted for some time. The drying mud of the road was patterned with the marks of the animal's great hooves. At the side of the track I saw the verge disturbed where first I, then my attacker, had scrambled in the mire. I stopped.

"This is the place?" Father Thomas asked. "Whereabouts in the wood must we begin our search?"

I pointed to the grove, where the night before I had heard two men scrambling through the dark. Above my upraised finger the buzzards circled over the forest, a hundred paces west of the road. I glanced in their direction. Father Thomas followed my gaze and divined its meaning.

"Come," he commanded, and plunged into the wood. Simon Osbern, the clerks and I followed.

Father Thomas is a fine priest, but his skills are not related to either strength or endurance. In but a few moments the priest was winded and staggering from the exertion of pushing through brambles and fallen branches. He is not a young man. After a few stumbles over ground ivy and limbs he tired, so that when his foot caught the next tendril he fell heavily. This did him no great harm. The forest floor was deep in rotting leaves.

I pulled the priest to his feet and, together with Simon Osbern, I cleaned his robe of debris.

"We should," I advised, "be more prudent in our search. Let us return to the road and spread ourselves a few paces apart, then re-enter the forest at a more careful pace."

The others agreed, having no better plan. Our company covered a space perhaps thirty paces in breadth, and we had gone but a few steps beyond the vine which snared Father Thomas when a clerk called out in a high-pitched yelp.

The urgency in his voice drew us scrambling to him. He stood near a tall beech, and as we gathered about him he pointed to the leaves at his feet. There, nearly obscured in rotting vegetation, lay a shoe. The sole was of wood, and the leather which would bind it to a man's foot was new and little worn. It was much like the shoes I had seen on the feet of Henry atte Bridge. Of course, it was much like the shoes on the feet of any man who could afford to go shod of a spring day.

Because the beech tree was not yet in leaf a pattern of dappled sunlight penetrated the naked branches and left bright patterns on the forest floor. The partly visible shoe lay in one of these illuminated places, else its colors would have blended with the leaves so that, had it been in shadow, it might have gone undetected.

We stood in a circle and stared at the shoe as if it came from the foot of a leper. No other made a move to retrieve it, so I did. There was nothing to be gained from inspecting the shoe. As I have said, it was much like others worn by the commons. Father Thomas broke the silence.

"A man making his way in haste through a dark wood might lose a shoe." He peered unblinking at me as he spoke.

"Had he reason enough for haste, he might not wish to turn and seek a lost shoe in the dark, when 'twould not be easy to recover," I replied.

"The shoe points deeper into the grove," I continued. "Let us resume our places and see what else may be found."

We did not go far before the issue was resolved. It was Simon Osbern who made the discovery. A man lay face down in the mould. His arms were thrown forward and extended above his head, with palms flat upon the forest floor. He wore but one shoe, and his chauces and cotehardie were stained with mud. Above the bare limbs of the forest the buzzards circled silently on broad wings. We crossed ourselves.

I knew who this must be before we turned him to his back. My conjecture was correct, for when we rolled him over it was the face of Henry atte Bridge which stared unseeing at the buzzards.

The vicars and clerks lifted their eyes to me. I felt my cheeks flush, for I was sure this death was my doing, even though I could plead self-defense. Only Father Thomas knew of my struggle with the dead man, but in my guilt I felt all must suspect.

Thomas de Bowlegh broke the silence. "What has caused this death, Master Hugh?"

Without a close inspection of the corpse I could not tell, and told him so. I could see no wound or other mark likely to bring death to one so young and strong. The injury must be, I thought, internal and invisible; a blow to the neck, or perhaps the kick of a horse.

"We must raise the hue and cry," said Father Simon, "and Hubert Shillside must gather a jury and bring them to this place."

That was done, and before the ninth hour Shillside and his coroner's jury stood about the corpse. The coroner bent to examine the dead man more closely. I thought he gave special attention to the neck, but perhaps this was my imagination. Shillside stood and turned to me.

"Master Hugh, have you examined this man?"

"No. We awaited your arrival."

Shillside scratched his head. "I find nothing amiss. He was gathering wood, you say?"

"'Tis what he told his wife," Father Thomas replied.

The coroner peered about into the lengthening shadows. "I see no bundle hereabouts… and why is he so muddied? A man would not be so filthy from falling headlong into last year's leaves."

Muttered agreement followed this assertion.

"How did you find him?" Shillside asked.

"Face down," I said. "Arms outstretched."

"As if he was struck down while running," one of the clerks added.

"Then let's turn him and see what may be invisible to us now."

Henry atte Bridge was rolled face down again, and I placed his stiffened arms above his head as they were when we discovered him. The coroner knelt beside the body and motioned for me to join him on my knees on the forest floor.

"I see no cause for death. There is much about this I do not like," Shillside said softly as we examined Henry's broad back.

These words were barely spoken when I saw, as I scrutinized the prone form, a mark on atte Bridge's back which caught my attention. This had escaped me when I first saw the corpse, for the man's cotehardie was old, frayed, torn in many places, and stained with age and mud.

I touched the edges of a small tear in the cotehardie. This break in the fabric seemed clean, unlike other rips, the fringes of which were raveled and uneven. I brushed dirt from this opening and saw, obscured by soil and debris, a dim russet oval, a nearly invisible stain against the weathered brown of the garment.

Shillside saw my interest and bent to examine the torn fabric. "What have you found?" he asked.

"Perhaps nothing," I replied, but as I spoke I pulled up the hem of the cotehardie and reached a hand under the kirtle and across the dead man's back. I felt there what I suspected. When I withdrew my hand the fingertips were dark with congealed, drying blood.

"He has been stabbed," Father Thomas said softly.

"I fear so," I agreed. Had the vicar not suggested a cause of death I might have been more thorough in my examination. If a similar matter should arise in the future I must not allow others to plant suggestions in my mind, for I am too willing to allow them to take root.

I turned the body onto its back again, and with the aid of a clerk I stripped off the cotehardie and kirtle. We turned the hairy fellow to his stomach once again, and the wound was plain.

There had been little bleeding. I believe this was so because the injury penetrated to the lungs and heart, and so atte Bridge died quickly. The blade which struck him down was not large. The wound in his back was the size of my little finger. Perhaps this limited the flow of blood. The wound was just to the left of the man's spine. Perhaps he tried to run from this attack, but his hurt was too great and he fell headlong where we found him.

The clerks found several fallen branches, broke them to appropriate lengths, and created a litter upon which we transported the body from the wood. Worshippers had gathered before the porch of St Beornwald's Church, awaiting evensong. They watched in open-mouthed silence as our company passed. Simon Osbern and two of the clerks left us at the gate to the churchyard, and several members of the coroner's jury, their duty completed for the moment, dropped away as we made our way down Church View Street and turned on to Bridge Street.

As our somber cortege approached the bridge over Shill Brook I remembered the shoe I still carried. Its mate was yet fixed to the left foot of the corpse, bobbing in step with the rhythm of those who carried Henry atte Bridge home. I increased my pace, stepped behind the corpse, and slipped the other shoe from the cold, pale foot. Hubert Shillside walked beside me and watched me do this, but said nothing.

The six men who carried Henry atte Bridge home deposited their burden at the door of his hut in the Weald. Our approach was silent. None of the inhabitants heard us draw near and no face appeared at the door, which was open to the warm spring afternoon. To be truthful, I felt a chill as I stood in the shadow formed by the house as the sun sank low in the western sky. Father Thomas rapped on the doorpost. The knock brought a pale, frowning woman to the door.

Henry atte Bridge's widow – though as yet she did not know her condition – was a worried woman. After a long winter we were all a bit waxy, but she was ashen, with dark shadows under her eyes from a sleepless night. There would, I thought, be more nights like that in the woman's future.

Hubert Shillside stood beside the vicar at the door. Neither man held aloof from a dinner table, so Emma did not at first see the object of our visit lying in the dirt behind them.

Father Thomas came quickly to the point of our call. When his words were complete he stepped back so the woman could see clearly the lifeless form of her husband. She choked out a brief wail, which brought her children to the door, but then became silent. She raised one hand to her mouth, and with the other restrained her eldest son, who would have pushed past her to better view his father.

Thomas de Bowlegh remained with the woman to arrange her husband's burial while Shillside and I and the others but for one clerk drifted away toward Mill Street and the town.

"'Tis a murder the bishop must deal with," the coroner said as we approached the bridge.

"Aye, which means the vicars of St Beornwald's will have added duties," I agreed. I was relieved. Searching out Henry atte Bridge's slayer would not be my obligation, for he was the bishop's man.

I parted from Hubert Shillside, and those of the coroner's jury who remained, at the Mill Street and headed for the castle. I had eaten nothing this day, and hunger burned my belly. But I had another task first, before I could consume a cold dinner.

I sought Alice in the scullery, and found her finishing her work for the day. She looked up enquiringly from under a stray wisp of hair, which she swept aside with the back of her wrist.

"Were you told that your brother was missing?"

The girl shook her head. "Nay... which one? Henry or Thomas?"

"Henry. He has been found."

Perhaps it was the tone of my voice, or the manner of my speaking, but the girl stopped her scrubbing at a pot, wiped her hands on her apron, and watched me intently, waiting for an explanation.

I told her what had happened, or so much of what had happened as I knew, omitting only the fight along the road the night before.

"So 'e was murdered, then," she concluded. This was a statement, not a question, as if the manner of her brother's death was not a shock to her.

Although he was not Lord Gilbert's man and was no concern of mine, I had many questions about this death, and thought I might assist the vicars in their search for a killer. It did not seem to me at the time unnatural to be curious about the fate of one who had tried to do me harm.

"Had your brother enemies?" I asked. I thought I knew the answer to that question.

"Had better ask had 'e any friends," she replied.

"There were many, you think, who wished him ill?"

"More'n would've wished 'im well, I think." The girl looked away and silently focused on the scullery window, now glowing bright from the setting sun. "'E learned young 'e was stronger'n most an' could 'ave 'is way of weaker men... so I've 'eard."

"Even a weak man is strong enough to plunge a knife into another," I said.

"A weak woman, also," the girl added, and returned to her pot.

Her assertion got my attention. "Think you there are women who wished your brother dead?"

"Ask Emma," the girl sighed.

"He beat his wife?"

"Aye. More'n most. When I was with me father, livin' at the Weald, before you brought me 'ere, I heard 'er yellin' an' gettin' smacked about."

"Often?"

"Reg'lar, like... 'specially when 'e was drunk."

"He was drunk often?"

"Ev'ry Saturday, reg'lar like. None in the Weald could sleep 'til 'e had done knockin' Emma about an' she stopped screechin'."

The killer of a man who has made many enemies may successfully elude apprehension. It is the killer of a man with few enemies who, it seems to me, is most likely to be caught. The vicars faced a daunting task.

Alice curtsied and smiled thinly as I turned to go. The girl really had grown quite fetching, though far beneath my station. Well, whether a woman is beautiful or not has little to do with her rank. Consider the number of gentlemen who take a mistress from the commons while wed to some ill-favored lady whose attractions of land and dowry could not for long make up for her appearance or demeanor.

I called next door at the kitchen and requested a meal from the unhappy cook, who until my appearance had thought his work complete for the day.

Alice was sent with my meal. As I ate I thought of shoes and blue yarn and murder. And, yes, of the child Alice also, who, quite disconcertingly, was no longer a child.

Hubert Shillside called for his coroner's jury to meet Monday morning in the church. As I had no pressing business, I attended. All there had seen the puncture in Henry atte Bridge's hairy back. No other cause of death was apparent. The jury soon decided that the death was murder, though none who voted so seemed much grieved at the loss. As I left the church I saw Hubert Shillside enter into a solemn conversation with two of the three vicars of St Beornwald's Church, while a flock of clerks circled nearby.

I had brought with me to the church the shoes from Henry atte Bridge's feet. I was confident they had once protected the feet of Alan the beadle. As I walked from the churchyard I heard from a distance a thin keening. I stopped and turned to my right where, at the corner where Church View joins Bridge Street, I saw a funeral procession come into view. There were few mourners. A dozen men and women and a scattering of children followed Simon Osbern and the bier.

I made my way down Church Street to the High Street, then walked left on Catte Street until I came to the house of Alan the beadle. Matilda was pleased to see me, or pleased to see the shoes, I know not which. She did not ask how I recovered them, and I did not venture to tell her. We made small talk for a time; she was getting on well, thank you; her son missed his father, did not sleep well for many nights after the funeral. Neither did she. But wasn't it fine weather we enjoyed? And the early onions and cabbages were sprouting nicely.

I departed Catte Street in a better mood than I had entered. Certainly the warming sun at my face had something to do with my good humor, but a light conversation with an attractive woman had some small part in my rising spirits. I am not well versed in such things, but I believe Matilda might have been flirting with me. Either that, or she had some speck in her eye which caused her to blink uncommonly often.

I intended to return to the castle and seek my dinner, then be about Lord Gilbert's business for the afternoon. But as I reached Church View while making my way down Bridge Street, I glanced north and saw a clot of mourners just inside the churchyard wall. I turned and walked to the church.

The gravediggers had nearly completed their work as I reached the lych gate. Henry atte Bridge would rest just within the southeast corner of the churchyard, a few paces from Alan the beadle. I entered and watched as Father Simon spoke the final collect and Henry was lifted in his shroud from the plank which formed his bier. The shroud was black, as befits such occasions, but ill made and poorly stitched.

As his brother and another lifted Henry from the plank, the seam of the shroud split, spilling the dead man's arm from its place. The arm lay in an old, tattered sleeve of faded blue.

I pushed my way to the front of the mourners, a thing easy to do as there were so few of them. And of those in the group I believe few mourned. Thomas atte Bridge and his assistant set Henry down beside the open grave to repair the shroud and replace the drooping arm. Before they could take him up again I reached between them and seized the badly frayed cuff of the blue cotehardie in which Emma had chosen to bury him.

This act caused raised eyebrows, but one advantage of being bailiff to a powerful lord is that one may do such things without feeling a necessity to explain. And I didn't. Although I did later make plain my motive to Simon Osbern.

My action at the grave produced two threads from the frayed blue sleeve. The tint was familiar. I was eager to compare this find with the blue yarn taken from Alan's corpse. I turned from the bewildered assembly and hastened back to the castle. The blue wool from Henry atte Bridge's burial garment matched perfectly the yarn drawn from Alan's scalp seventeen days before.

I compared the woolen fragments and thought that I knew what had happened to Alan the beadle on the path to St Andrew's Chapel. He had left the town to investigate the howl of a strange beast; a beast I also had heard. Alan had died at the jaws of that animal, or more likely trying to escape its jaws, along the dark lane. Henry atte Bridge had found him there, wearing nearly new shoes for which the beadle could have no further use. Henry had taken the shoes, then perhaps dragged the body into the hedgerow to... to what purpose? That I could not explain. Who can know the mind of a thief who will plunder the dead?

I thought little more of the matter as I went about my business that day. Lord Gilbert's sheep were to be moved to a new field, so that the fallow field they had grazed and manured could be plowed. This business took most of the afternoon, for Lord Gilbert has a large flock, and sheep are wont to go in every direction but that which they should. My father thought them the stupidest of God's creation. When the afternoon was done I found myself in renewed agreement with him.

I could not sleep that night. My mind wandered back to its earlier conclusions regarding the death of Alan the beadle and Henry atte Bridge's role in that sorry event. Although my bed was warm and the night cool I rose past midnight to walk the parapet and consider that which caused me such unease.

If Alan died on the road, and the beast attacked him there, why the dent in the back of his head? There were no rocks in the path. But if he fell into the hedgerow while fighting a wolf, and lay hidden there in death, how was it that Henry atte Bridge found him? Alan's corpse was drawn so far into the nettles that he was discovered by a plowman in the field which lay inside the hedgerow. Those who passed by on the road for the day he lay dead did not discover him. And why was Henry atte Bridge walking that path? His work at the new barn would take him north out of Bampton, not east toward St Andrew's Chapel.

I circled the walls of Bampton Castle twice but my perambulation brought me no nearer a solution to the riddles my mind created. I understood how a thread of blue yarn might fall from the raveled sleeve of Henry atte Bridge and become lodged in the beadle's dark locks. This find indicated that Henry had grasped Alan by the shoulders and neck at some time. But why? To haul him into the hedgerow? If so, Alan died along the path. Then why the blow to the back of his skull? Perhaps after dragging the corpse into the bushes Henry let the body fall so that it struck the stones hidden there with great force.

No. A fall of two or three feet would not do the damage to Alan's skull I had found. And there was the blood. Or not enough of it. Henry atte Bridge surely had something to do with the death of Alan the beadle, but what that was I could not determine.

I expected, or perhaps I hoped, to hear a wolf howl that night as I circled the walls of Bampton Castle. I heard no such beast, nor any other sound. The castle and town slept peacefully, although there may have been those who turned uneasy in their beds, unknown to me. I know now there were several who had cause to rest uneasy.

I returned to my own bed, now grown cold, and thought how agreeable it would be to find a wife for such a moment as this. I fell asleep reflecting on the pleasures of such a search and its successful culmination.

Chapter 7

I awoke with grainy eyes as dawn lightened the window of my chamber. I could not sleep longer, but had no wish to leave my bed and plant my feet on the cold flags. I did so anyway. I decided as I lay abed that I would this day visit Emma atte Bridge. My questions might easily be resolved. Surely the woman knew something of her husband's business. Her response to a few questions might permit me to sleep more soundly.

They had rather the opposite effect. I broke my fast with wheat bread and ale, then walked across Mill Street to the Weald. No morning sun warmed this day. Thick clouds had swept in from the north during the night. I wrapped my cloak tight about me and shivered as if December had returned, without the glow of Christmas to warm my soul. The blossoms newly forming on Lord Gilbert's apple trees would think better of opening further this day.

No door in the Weald was open to spring air this day. I knocked vigorously a second time before Henry atte Bridge's widow cracked her door to see who disturbed her morning. Her expression did not speak joy at the discovery.

I invited myself into the dim, smoky interior of the hut. The fire on the hearth was weak and produced little heat, so that there was no draft to draw the fumes up to the gable vents. Three children gazed unblinking at me from a bench, bowls of yesterday's cold pottage balanced precariously on their laps, their fingers clotted with the coagulated meal.

I introduced myself, though I am sure the woman remembered who I was. It does no harm to remind people from time to time that I serve as bailiff to Lord Gilbert Talbot. Emma pushed the door shut behind me and waited, jaw set, to learn the reason for my visit.

I would gladly have given her a reason, had I known it myself. It would be foolish to say that I chose to visit her this morning because I could not sleep the night before, but that was the truth of it. I decided to ask first about the blue cotehardie in which she had buried her husband.

"'Twas old... an' could be spared," she answered. "Henry said as 'twas too worn to be of use any more. He'd not worn it for a time."

"How long? Since Easter?"

Emma was startled at this question, for she looked up at me abruptly. I saw her brow furrow and guessed that she was uncertain whether or not she should tell the truth. She evidently could discover no reason to lie, so after a moment's hesitation nodded, "Aye, 'bout then."

As we spoke I watched over her shoulder while her children went back to their bowls. They paid me no more attention, but returned to their meal with enthusiasm, licking sticky fingers as they shoveled food into their mouths. The oldest finished his breakfast as I watched. He reached into his bowl and drew forth a chunk of meat which he proceeded to stuff into his mouth until his cheeks bulged. He chewed contentedly, and turned his gaze back to me and his mother.

In the spring of the year those tenants and villeins who had a pig to slaughter in the autumn have usually consumed the last morsel of the animal. I was surprised that this hut was yet able to flavor its pottage with meat. Perhaps this was the last of the fletch of bacon Henry atte Bridge had spoken of. Or perhaps it was from the haunch I'd seen roasting on a spit.

"The shoes your husband wore when last I called... he did not buy them in Witney."

Emma gazed steadily at me, as if assuming she had heard but a portion of what I wished to say and that I would shortly continue. She was correct, but I hoped to build my inquiry on her responses. This was not to be.

The woman knew when to be silent. Perhaps living with Henry atte Bridge taught her that skill.

"I traveled there and saw the cobbler. He sold no shoes to a man of Bampton."

The woman remained silent for a time, but finally spoke. "May be there be two shoemakers in Witney. The town is grown larger now than Bampton... so I hear."

"No. Larger it may be, but it supports but one cobbler. Shall I tell you where your husband found his shoes, or would you tell me?"

"They was gone when the coroner's men brought 'im to me. Who so struck 'im down made off with 'em... one o' Lord Gilbert's men, an' likely. It be your work to find 'em an' return 'em t'me."

Emma spoke this accusation with some heat. Either she knew not where her husband came by his shoes, or she was a skilled dissembler.

"The shoes have been returned to their rightful owner," I replied.

"Nay! No man brought Henry's shoes to me."

"He was not the rightful owner, nor are you. Do you tell me how he came by them, or must I tell you?"

"Dunno what you be talkin' of. My man is dead an' murdered an' had 'is shoes stole an' you come to me talkin' foolishness."

The woman's voice had increased in both pitch and volume, so that her children looked up from their bowls – which were now near empty anyway – with large and frightened eyes. I think they had heard such conversations before, and knew a fight might follow.

"Very well," I shrugged. "The shoes your husband wore were first on the feet of Alan the beadle. Your husband took them from him."

Emma knew well the truth of my assertion. Her mouth opened twice, as if she was about to speak denial, but closed again, like a fish gulping water in Shill Brook.

"I have returned them to the beadle's wife."

"'Tain't right. They was Henry's shoes," Emma muttered. But the heat was gone from her voice. She was giving up the fight. I pressed for final victory and withdrew my purse from under my cloak. The woman watched with curiosity as I withdrew from it the blue thread found in Alan's hair.

"Does the color strike you? Have you seen such before?" I asked.

"Nay... 'tis blue... what of it?"

"This fragment was found in Alan's scalp, when his body was found."

Next I withdrew the threads I had pulled from the cotehardie now buried with her husband. "These came from the garment you buried Henry in yesterday." I held the threads before her eyes. Even dark as it was in the hut, the similarities were clear.

"Henry wouldn't kill nobody for 'is shoes," she protested.

"Perhaps not. But he had no objection to taking them from the dead."

The woman looked again at the threads, her brow furrowed, as if considering whether or not she was in a fight worth waging. Her eyes fell to the dirt at her feet. That was her answer.

"What was your husband doing on the road to St Andrew's Chapel? His work on the bishop's new barn would not take him that way."

Emma curled bare toes into the packed earth of the floor of her hut, and finally replied.

"My Henry was a Christian man. Went to confession reg'lar... not like as them who confess but once a year for Lent."

"He went to the priest at St Andrew's Chapel to confess? Not to the vicars at St Beornwald's Church?"

"Nay... would only seek absolution from Father John, none other."

"Why so?"

The woman was silent again for a time, then replied, "Said as 'ow John Kellet was not so harsh in penance as was them of St Beornwald's."

I had heard Thomas de Bowlegh speak of penance

and the judgment a priest must use in dispensing it. If the penance was too harsh, the sinner might forgo its completion and doom his soul to hell. But if the penance be too light, it may not absolve the sin, and so condemn the man to thousands more years in purgatory. Unless, of course, the sinner was a gentleman and could endow a chapel or chantry. Then a lighter penance might be called for. But for Henry atte Bridge such a consideration would not apply. He would earn his way out of purgatory by deeds, not money, for of that he had none.

"A question asked in confession," I replied, "is, have you found anything and kept it? I wonder how your husband made answer?"

Emma considered my remark rhetorical. She made no reply. Her arguments were defeated, but there was yet some fire in her eye. I spoke next a concern which had troubled me since I rose that morning and set off to visit the Weald.

"You are not to vex the beadle's widow. She is Lord Gilbert's tenant and so comes under my bailiwick. She dwells on Catte Street, as you may know. I think you will have little business on that lane, so I would not like to discover that you have been seen there."

I tried to impart my most stern expression, but the woman scoffed and turned to her children. A bailiff should be known for potential, if not real, severity (as well as avarice, which is their most widely remarked trait). I had not yet developed that reputation. I am uncertain whether this made my office more or less tedious. A bailiff may succeed in his work if he is feared, or perhaps if he be admired. I noticed neither dread nor veneration from those I governed for Lord Gilbert Talbot. I thought as I left Emma and her hut in the Weald that my tenancy in the office of bailiff might not be long, and that soon I would again be only Master Hugh, surgeon.

A cold, misty rain began to fall as I approached the castle. John Holcutt would see little work done this day. In the meadow west of the castle Lord Gilbert's cattle bunched together as if the compact herd might drive off the chill and wet. As I passed under the portcullis Wilfred the porter saw me pass his post and called after me.

"Master Hugh! Father Thomas' clerk was here but a short time ago. The vicar wishes for you to attend him… when you have leisure."

I thanked the porter for this announcement and turned from the gatehouse to make my way to the town. The truth was, I had much leisure on such a day, although it was also true I would prefer to spend it in my chamber. I might call for a fire to be laid in my hearth. Perhaps, with good fortune, the comely Alice might be sent to perform the task.

I thought on that agreeable scene while I crossed the bridge over Shill Brook – I did not pause to examine the current this day – and into the town. The vicarage, that occupied by Thomas de Bowlegh, was north of St Beornwald's Church on Laundell's Lane, so I wrapped my cloak snug about me to ward off the wet and chill and hurried up Church View. I saw no other soul about. Such a day would be expected and considered mild in February. But April is not to deal so with men, and we take such weather as a kind of betrayal. Smoke drifted heavily in the cold mist from chimneys and gable vents. The burghers and townsmen of Bampton had no wish to leave their firesides this day. Nor did I.

After much thumping on the vicarage door that heavy oaken portal finally opened. The vicar's hearing grew weaker each year. Soon, I think, he must give up hearing confession, or, in order to be heard the penitents will need to shout so that the whole town will know of their misdeeds.

"Ah… Master Hugh. I am sorry to bring you out on such a day, but we – Father Simon and Father Ralph and I – are in agreement that the business of Henry atte Bridge must be speedily resolved."

I tried to make my face blank while the vicar spoke. I knew where this statement might lead and had no wish to go there. Father Thomas surely suspected this, and was prepared.

A great fire burned on the vicarage hearth. He drew me to it and bid me be seated on a bench placed close before the blaze.

"John!" the vicar thundered through an open doorway to a servant. "Bring wine."

Wine, not ale. Surely the vicars of the Church of St Beornwald wished something important of me. Thomas spoke of the intemperate weather while the servant filled our cups with malmsey, but when the man departed – to listen behind the door, I'm sure – he came readily to the point.

"The bishop of Exeter has no bailiff for his lands in Bampton... as you know."

I did.

"Edwin Crank serves as reeve, and serves well, but the bishop expects us, the vicars, to do the work of bailiff. As there be three attached to one church [An unusual practice. I was much surprised to learn of it when I first came to serve Lord Gilbert.], he assumes we will find time among us to deal with manor business."

I made no reply. The vicar had asked no question of me yet, and I was not eager to discover what was desired of me. Rather, I knew what was wanted, but had no wish to hear my suspicion confirmed or ease the vicar's task.

Father Thomas was silent, sipping his wine and watching me over the rim of his cup. He hoped, I think, for my sympathy for his overworked state. I savored the wine and held my tongue. I did not intend to make this easy for him. I regretted this attitude later. It is not seemly for a Christian man to interpose impediments to those who seek his aid.

"There is some business," he continued, "for which we three are unsuited." Bowlegh peered at me over his cup, searching for agreement. I sipped my wine and offered none.

"The murder of Henry atte Bridge... one or more of us must forsake his duties to God and the Church of St Beornwald to seek a killer. This will put great burdens on the other and the clerks to maintain church offices, do you not agree?"

"I think seeking a murderer might be considered by God as duty to him," I replied.

"Ah… yes… surely. But all men have duties to God, and those obligations differ according to our station and competence."

Father Thomas had laid his snare well. I could not disagree.

"You have displayed much competence," he continued, "in discovering miscreants. The matter of the bones found in Lord Gilbert's cesspit, and the disappearance of Sir Robert Mallory and his squire. You found the truth of that business."

"After I nearly caused an innocent man to hang from the gibbet at Oxford Castle," I reminded him.

"But you corrected the error and discovered the truth. We – Father Simon and Father Ralph and I – wish your aid in this matter of Henry atte Bridge."

The vicar continued quickly, before I had time to object. "We thought to send a clerk to Lord Gilbert at Pembroke, seeking his permission for you to employ your time in this matter, but wished to sound you out first."

So the vicars were prepared to go over my head, and Father Thomas was tactfully advising me so.

"It may be that the killer is one of Lord Gilbert's men," Father Thomas continued, "in which case the investigation would be your bailiwick. As Lord Gilbert's lands hereabouts are more extensive than the bishop's properties, and his villeins and tenants more numerous, it seems likely to us that this may be so. Do you not agree?"

I did agree. His logic was good, and he knew Lord Gilbert would see the matter as he did. And the malmsey was very good; dark and red and not near to being vinegar. But I did try to press a hard bargain.

"You must permit me to seek answers where I will," I demanded. "The bishop's men must know they are to cooperate."

"They will be so instructed," he nodded.

"And if this inquiry takes too much time from my

duties for Lord Gilbert you must permit me to relinquish it."

But Father Thomas can drive a hard bargain, as well.

"I would be sorry if you gave up the charge. Should it become known that you struggled with Henry atte Bridge on the road, and, but for his killer, of course, was the last man to see him alive…"

I saw his point, which foolishly I had not before. Circumstances made me suspect in the death – to those who might learn of my fight along the Witney road. I had told only Thomas de Bowlegh of this incident. Perhaps he told the other vicars. Regardless, his point was well made and I took it readily.

"So to exonerate myself I must find him who did that for which otherwise I might be blamed?"

The vicar nodded. "I know you, Master Hugh, and your skills. You have saved men's lives and freed them from pain in the months since Lord Gilbert brought you here. I do not believe you capable of chasing a man down and plunging a dagger into his back."

"Not even a man who attacked me?"

"Not even such a man. But others may not think so… so rationally, should your brawl with Henry atte Bridge become known."

"No one knows of it but you… and Henry's killer."

"There are others… a few."

In answer to my scowl he continued quickly, "I spoke of the attack to Father Ralph and Father Simon when we discussed what must be done."

"Will they hold their tongues?

"Father Simon will, I think. I am not so sure of Father Ralph."

"Then you must speak to him, and soon. If knowledge is abroad that I fought with Henry atte Bridge, then even if I discover his murderer there will be men who believe I have accused another to free myself of guilt. Justice would be charged as injustice."

The vicar's face fell. He had not thought of this. He

looked to the fire and rearranged coals with a poker before he spoke again.

"I should have kept silent," he agreed finally. "But I thought you might resist my request."

"And wished to apply some gentle pressure to see that I would not?" I completed his thought.

"Aye. I wished confirmation from Father Simon and Father Ralph that my path was a wise one."

"Did they agree?"

"They did."

"You must speak to them this day, without delay, and warn them to be silent. Else I am undone. Bampton may lose a bailiff and a surgeon and I may lose my life."

"Surely not," the vicar objected. "You are known and respected in the town."

"I am an outsider, newly come to this place. When the commons are heated and a hanging is offered they will cheer the death of any man and consider him guilty, be he so or not. Remember Thomas Shilton? He was of this place, or near so. But when I found against him, wrongly, none rose to defend him. They were ready to jeer as he swung from the beam with purple face and swollen tongue."

Father Thomas looked from the fire to the window to me. "It is near time for canonical hours. I will urge Simon and Ralph to silence."

I left the vicarage with cluttered mind and burdened heart. By the time I reached the castle the mist had ceased, and when dinner was served in the hall I saw broken sunlight begin to penetrate the south windows. I cannot recall what was served that day. Other thoughts occupied my mind. When the meal was done I set out from the castle to seek a murderer, but found two. Eventually.

The afternoon sky above Oxfordshire cleared, and inhabitants of the town ventured out upon muddy streets. The cooper had opened his shutters and from his shop issued the smell of fresh-shaved wood and the regular cadence of his draw knife as he plied it against new staves. The sun appeared occasionally between banks of clouds, but not enough to dry the streets. My shoes were caked with mud before I passed the bishop's new barn and found the place where Henry atte Bridge and I had rolled on the verge in our struggle.

I thought to retrace the path the searchers had followed into the wood, to see if any object or clue might have gone unnoticed. The seekers that day were watching for a man. Any other thing foreign to a forest might have gone unremarked. So I plunged into the undergrowth and was soon wet to the skin. The new foliage was dewy from the morning rain.

I found the place where Henry atte Bridge lay in death. 'Twas easy to do, for the searchers and then the coroner's jury had beaten down the shrubs of the forest floor for many paces in a circle about the place where the corpse lay. I found a fallen branch and went round the spot, overturning the trampled leaves with the stick. I found nothing but what is common to a wet wood in April.

I enlarged my search and with the stick I turned over matted leaves and prodded at the vines and scrub between the place where Henry was found and the road. Shortly after the Bell of St Beornwald's Church announced the ninth hour I found, midway between the road and the trampled ground, the shaft of an arrow.

This arrow was incomplete. There was no point affixed to the shaft. Where the point once was I could see a splintered end and the hole where a pin had held point to shaft. The arrow was clean and unmarked by the rot which soon overtakes wood in such a damp, shaded place. The arrow was carefully notched, and the goose feathers set into the shaft were skillfully split and placed.

I searched the forest for another hour, until shadows were long across the grove, but detected no other object there by the hand of man. The iron point of the arrow was not to be found.

There was no reason for an arrow to be in Lord Gilbert's forest. Henry atte Bridge was struck down by a small dagger. I saw the wound. And the place was too close to the town for a poacher to feel safe taking one of Lord Gilbert's deer. I discarded the stick as I pushed my way from the forest fringe to the road, and re-examined the arrow as I walked back to the castle.

Bampton had but one fletcher, and since the Treaty of Bretigny the town could not supply him with enough business to keep his children fed. What does a man need arrows for if he cannot discharge them at another? Some were needed for practice – which reminded me again that I needed to resume Sunday afternoon archery trials in the castle forecourt – but arrows loosed at targets may be retrieved and reused. So I did not expect Martin the fletcher to be at his craft when I approached his house on the Broad Street. He was not. His wife directed me to the south of town where, near Shill Brook, I found him finishing the seeding of a bean field.

The fletcher swung his dibble stick to his shoulder and studied me as I approached. I was careful to step between his planted rows, but my appearance did not seem to bring the man any pleasure for all my caution. The approach of a lord's bailiff has generally that effect. Tenants and villeins know that if a reeve or bailiff seek them out it will concern some trouble which will require their assistance. So I was not surprised when the fletcher observed me across his field with narrowed, cautious eyes and lips drawn thin.

I held the broken arrow before me for the fletcher's inspection and asked if the object was his work. His response was quick.

"Nay... not of mine."

"You are certain?"

"Aye. 'Tis well made, but not my work. See here," he took the arrow from my hand and held it up before my eyes, "the feathers be from a goose. A wild goose, I think. I use feathers from Lord Gilbert's tame geese. The poulterer saves 'em for me. They be mostly white, not grey, as these." He tapped the fletching. "But 'tis good work. I'd be proud to call it my own."

I thanked the fletcher for his answer and saw relief

soften the lines of his broad face. His mouth moved as if he would speak, but as quickly clamped shut. Much curiosity may bring distress, as the commons know. The man held his tongue.

Another question came to me as I turned to leave the bean field. "This arrow is well done, you say. Do you know the work?"

The fletcher took the shaft from me once again and studied it intently. I think he pondered the effect of his answer as well as the workmanship. After a close inspection he raised his eyes to mine.

"Nay... 'tis not possible to tell. 'Tis much like the arrows foresters and yeomen make for their own use. 'Tis of alder, not ash, so 'twas made, I think, for practice. Ash would not have broken so."

"A skillful yeoman?"

"Aye. Whoso made this has much practice. 'Tis nearly as good as mine. See how straight is the shaft." He held the arrow to his eye and peered down its length. "And the fletching is neatly done. This arrow will fly true."

A well-made arrow, broken, lying in the leaves of Lord Gilbert's forest close by the town and near to the place a lifeless body was found. I puzzled over this as I left the fletcher to his bean field and made my way back to the town.

The sun was low over the rooftops and bright in my eyes as I walked down Bridge Street toward the mill and castle. Before I had reached the bridge over Shill Brook I determined to resume archery competition the next Sunday. I would, at that event, make close inspection of arrows loosed at the butts to see if any resembled the shaft in my hand. This resolution cleared my mind, as did the flowing waters of the brook. I stopped on the bridge to watch the stream flow below me. The world might be a baffling place, full of wonder and discouragement, but the brook flowed on unchanging and predictable. God's constant in a mutable world. But for my growling stomach warning me that I might miss my supper, I would have remained longer at the bridge, enjoying the calming brook.

The weather had much improved this day. There was yet light when the evening meal was done, so while grooms dismounted tables and moved benches aside in the hall I walked the parapet. Circumnavigating Lord Gilbert's castle would not find for me evidence of a murderer, but might provide time to order what I knew already – which was little enough.

The castle shadow stretched long to the east. Indeed, the mill was now shaded and the shadow of the southeast tower darkened Shill Brook and the bridge. Beyond the bridge I watched a figure approach. It was Hubert Shillside's gangly son, all knees and elbows and splayed feet as he strode resolutely toward the castle. I paid him no mind, but continued my stroll to the northeast tower, then to the northwest. From that elevated corner I could look south along the west wall and the gatehouse.

I saw there the Shillside youth again, lounging against a small tree some twenty paces from the portcullis. As I watched his attention was drawn to the gatehouse and he stood stiffly from the sapling.

The object of his attention slipped through the gatehouse door toward the darkness under the tree. Alice. I watched the two stand in shadowed conversation, then Alice turned back to the gatehouse. Wilfred was about to close the gate and drop the portcullis. She turned back to the youth for another word, then flitted from tree to castle and was gone from sight. I remained atop the northwest tower and watched the coroner's boy lope happily back to Mill Street and off to the darkened town.

There were yet four days before Sunday to announce another season of archery competition. I told as many as I met, advised castle servants to do likewise, and for those few who could read I posted a notice at the door of St Beornwald's Church.

Thursday of that week was May Day and as always it was celebrated with joy and foolishness. I heard castle residents awake and about before dawn, and before the third hour these youth, Alice atte Bridge among them, returned to the castle laden with blossoms from flowering trees and green sprigs of hawthorn – but without the flowers, for all know it courts misfortune to bring the blossom of the holy thorn into a house.

They erected a maypole before the castle gatehouse and maidens of the town danced around it. Alice, in grace and comeliness, put the others to shame. No doubt Will Shillside thought the same.

On Saturday I purchased a cask of fresh ale from the baker's wife and drew from the castle storeroom three targets used the previous year. From the castle strongbox, which in the absence of Lord Gilbert I kept in my chamber, I took five silver pennies for prizes and was ready for the competition.

There is joy in resuming a pleasurable activity which one has been compelled to abandon. Add to that sentiment the delights of a warm spring afternoon and you will understand why the resumption of archery competition was a success – for all of Bampton but me.

Men stood contemplating the butts with bow in one hand and a mug of Lord Gilbert's ale in the other. One might think these fellows would become most accurate as the afternoon wore on and practice brought back skills grown stale over the winter. But not so. Most loosed their best arrows in early practice, before I announced the competition. 'Twas much ale, I think, which rattled their aim.

Women and children stood along the castle wall where they could cheer or heckle the archers as they chose. The sun warmed the stones and soon small children lay dozing at the base of the wall while their mothers, losing interest in the volleys of arrows, knotted together to discuss events of the winter past, both real and imagined.

Older children – but for the boys who neared the age when they also might possess a bow – also lost interest and were soon chasing each other and being caught with joyous shrieks. 'Twas a good day to be alive.

I had dual motives in resuming archery competition. Should war with France resume, I did not wish King Edward to find Lord Gilbert negligent in the training of his archers. And I wanted to find arrows like the broken one I had found in the wood.

I succeeded; to such effect that the success did my investigation no good at all. Most of those who loosed arrows at the butts possessed arrows like the one I found. Grey feathers from wild geese fletched half and more of the shafts I saw that day. And those seemed as well made as the found arrow which Martin the fletcher had so praised. I think that skill in making arrows is not so rare a knack as the fletcher led me to believe. Any one of a dozen and more men at the competition might have made or loosed the arrow I found. I could see no way of determining what, if anything, that man might have to do with the death of Henry atte Bridge.

Alice atte Bridge was among those who watched the archers, when her duties in the castle kitchen were done. She took a place along the castle wall among the other women, but as she was of the castle, not the town, and unmarried, she had little discourse with her companions.

Soon, however, one of the competitors walked near her and the two were promptly lost in conversation. Will Shillside was old enough to pull a man's bow, and for the first time in his life took part in the practice. I do not remember him showing any great skill. This is to be expected. Surely many years and thousands of arrows are necessary for proficiency.

His competence with a bow might be in doubt, but as he leaned upon it he seemed more the man than the boy he was without it. Alice appeared to note the transformation as well, for her eyes were bright and her conversation animated. Will found this diversion more interesting than the competition, for I did not see him again take his place at the mark. Why this conversation should trouble me I cannot tell, for I knew the girl, howso winsome she was becoming, was beneath my station. No bailiff could wed a scullery maid and expect his lord to retain him in his position. Odd; when Lord Gilbert first approached me about the position I did not want to be bailiff of Bampton Manor. Now that I am bailiff I do not want to lose the post.

The ale was gone and the last arrows of the competition loosed when the Angelus Bell rang from St Beornwald's tower across the town. I awarded the prizes to the winners; the best was Gerard the forester's son, Richard, from Alvescot, who put five of six arrows firmly in the center of the butt from 200 paces. I think if this youth desires Lord Gilbert's venison as a greater reward for his skill he will have it, and perhaps he already has.

I slept well that night, to my surprise. I feared I would lay in my bed and think of corpses and arrows, or perhaps Alice atte Bridge. But my thoughts proved amenable to slumber and I awoke the next morning much refreshed in body and spirit.

My breakfast was a loaf warm from the castle oven and a pint of ale. I consumed this in my chamber while I pondered what I might do to discover the murderer of a man no one liked. If a likeable man be done to death, his killer will surely be one less admired, and so those who suspect him of the deed have little hesitation to tell of what they know. But when a man held in low regard is slain, the mortal stroke is likely to come from one held in greater esteem than the victim. Who, then, will inform the bailiff and send a friend to the gallows? I swallowed the last of my ale, spit out the dregs, and wished myself free of the task.

A knock on my chamber door drew me from these black thoughts. The porter's assistant was there with a message. An elderly widow of the town wished to speak to me. I followed him to the gatehouse where I found the woman waiting, bent over her stick. She was known to me. She complained of an ache in her shoulders and indeed she suffered much from the disease of the bones. I had treated her for this malady several times but not, I fear, with much success.

"Ah... Master Hugh," she greeted me from under her bent brow.

"Good morning, Sarah. Are you well?" A foolish

question. Who seeks the surgeon when they are well?

"Nay. 'Tis me shoulders again. I'm terrible distressed. Do ye have more of the oil such as you gave me at Candlemas?"

"Did the oil help?"

"Oh, aye, it did. But 'tis gone for a fortnight."

I told her to wait at the gatehouse and I returned to my chamber. The oil Sarah sought was produced from bay leaves and monk's hood, and when rubbed vigorously upon a bruise or aching joint will relieve the hurt. I was startled to see how little of the oil remained in my pharmacy. I poured it all into a vial, stopped the vessel with a wooden plug, and carried it to the sufferer.

I gave Sarah the vial with strict instructions that, after rubbing the oil on her aching shoulders, she must not touch her hand to her lips until all trace of the oil was washed clean of her fingers.

The widow accepted my remedy, fished in her purse for the farthing fee, then tottered off toward Mill Street clutching the vial to her shrunken breast. I knew what I must now do this day, and the thought pleased me, for while I gathered bay leaves and the root of monk's hood I would not have to consider the murder of Henry atte Bridge.

Had I discovered my shortage a month sooner, I would have had an easier time gathering more bay leaves. Sweet laurel is green all winter through and easily identified in a bleak winter wood. But now all the low plants were bursting out in color, from fragile pale yellow-green to darker hues of full summer. These herbs, many having uses of their own, disguised the plant I sought. But some months before I had discovered a thick patch of sweet laurel at the fringe of the wood behind St Andrew's Chapel, very near the place where the coroner and I had found the beadle's cudgel. I threw a sack across my shoulder and set off for the chapel.

My route took me past the place where, nearly four weeks before, the plowman found Alan's corpse. 'Twas well the man was found when he was, for now the place was dense with new growth of nettles and hawthorn. A body lying there now would not be found until autumn.

The wood behind St Andrew's Chapel was thick with sweet laurel, as on my previous visit. I filled my sack with leaves and had yet enough time to seek the monk's hood to complete the physic.

I had seen what I thought to be monk's hood when following the hounds as we tracked the beast which must have attacked Alan and howled in the night. The patch lay south of Shill Brook where the stream turned east toward Aston. I crossed a fallow field to the brook, waded it at a shallow place where the water flowed swiftly over a gravel bed, then set off to the west where I remembered the monk's hood to be.

It was too early for the purple flowers to be in bloom, so I had to search carefully for the narrow, multi-pointed leaves before I found what I sought. I dug up several plants, washed the roots free of dirt in the brook, then placed them in the bag with the bay leaves.

I was careful as I returned to the castle not to put my fingers to my mouth. The root of monk's hood is a powerful poison. I do not know if the small amount of the oil from the root left on my fingers could cause death, but have no desire to discover so in experiment. Monk's hood is like many good things God has given to man. Used wrongly, it becomes a curse.

After dinner – a fine meal of game pie, pork in spiced syrup, and tarts made from mushrooms new found in the forest – I went to my chamber to prepare a fresh batch of salve for Sarah and others afflicted in their old age.

I used flax-seed oil as a base, and set a pot to simmering on a charcoal brazier while I turned my attention to the leaves and roots I had gathered in the morning. With mortar and pestle I crushed the bay leaves fine and poured the fragments into the warm flax-seed oil. Next I mashed the monk's hood root to a pulpy mass and stirred that into the thickening oil as well. There are some who believe that the oil of bay and monk's hood serve best when pure, but I hold with the view that flax-seed oil also relieves affliction, and makes a fine carrier for the oils of bay leaf and wolfsbane root. I finished this work shortly after St Beornwald's bell rang the ninth hour. I was sorry to be done with the task, for now I had no excuse to ignore the search for a murderer. I left the oil, leaves, and roots to bubbling and departed my chamber. I had no destination for my feet, but it is sure I would not find a killer while sitting upon a bench in my chamber watching a steaming pot.

I walked Bampton's streets with no goal in mind and after several turns found myself drawn to the north in the direction of the bishop's new tithe barn. I heard the sound of industry as I approached; a hammer on a chisel cutting a tenon; an adze smoothing a beam; a draw knife shaping a treenail. I stopped to watch this activity from the road and as I did several questions occurred to me which might, I thought, be answered by the workmen.

I approached the builder with the adze, who stood bent over his work in a pile of sweet-smelling shavings. He did not see me approach, so I coughed so as to advise him of my presence. I did not wish to startle him as the adze came down for another strike, for fear I might deflect his aim. I had no desire to employ my surgical skills on the fellow's ankle.

"Good day," I offered.

"Aye... 'tis." The man leaned on his adze and with a calloused hand brushed a stray wisp of hair back under his cap. He seemed pleased to have a reason to cease his labor.

"You must have heavier work, since Henry atte Bridge is no more among you."

"Aye," the man spat into the pile of shavings. "But the vicar says he'll send us another, so we'll be four again, soon."

"Does the work go well, without a man as you are?"

"Same as always. Henry were no worker. Least, no carpenter. Can't see why reeve put 'im with us for his week work. Should'a had 'im plowin', where 'e'd do some good."

"He lacked skill?"

"Aye. An' had little wish t'learn."

"He must have owned some competence. He seemed prosperous enough for a man with but a half yardland."

"Aye," the adze-man scowled. "'E fed well for a man wot shirked."

Here before me was a man who disliked Henry atte Bridge. Did the other two laborers, casting sidelong glances at me while they worked, feel the same? Was their dislike intense enough to distill into hatred? Surely an objection to a man's work would not lead another to plunge a dagger into his back. Would it?

The man shaping treenails finished another fastener and sauntered over to join the conversation. Then the tenon cutter decided he was not to be left out, and followed him. I was soon surrounded by three men redolent of sawdust and oak shavings. The scent was a significant improvement over their natural odor.

"Have you ever seen," I pointed to the forest across the road, "an archer in that wood?"

The three men peered at each other for a moment, as if to get their stories aligned. But perhaps I am too mistrustful. The tenon cutter answered.

"What would an archer be doin' in Lord Gilbert's wood?"

All knew the answer to that.

"Are there deer to be seen in that wood, so close to the town?"

"Never seen any," the adze-man replied. He looked at the others and they shook their heads in agreement.

I was about to tell them of the broken arrow I had found there, but thought better of it. I am learning to keep my own counsel and trust no man until he prove himself. I cannot say that this is a good thing – to mistrust all. And surely I do not. There are many I trust to speak truth: Master Wyclif, Lord Gilbert Talbot, Thomas de Bowlegh, Hubert Shillside, even Alice atte Bridge. But rather than trust a stranger until he prove faithless, I was becoming one who mistrusts another until he might prove to me his veracity. Perhaps this is safe for a bailiff, to pass his life suspicious of all men and their motives, but it is not enjoyable.

"Did Henry speak of enemies?"

The barn builders gave sidelong glances to each other before the adze-man, who seemed to be nominated their leader, spoke.

"'At's 'bout all 'e'd speak of, them as done 'im wrong an' 'ow 'e was like t'get even w'them as harmed 'im."

"Had you ever done him harm?"

The tenon cutter snorted. "Ev'ry man of the bishop's has, I think, an' most o' Lord Gilbert's, too."

I could agree with that, being Lord Gilbert's man and having offended Henry atte Bridge more than once.

"He took offence quickly, then?"

"Aye," the tenon cutter muttered. "Thought the whole shire was out t'do 'im mischief."

"I am told that he attended confession often... at St Andrew's Chapel."

At this revelation the adze-man laughed heartily and the others grinned. "Henry? Confession?" The man chuckled again. I waited to be apprized of the cause for this mirth. An explanation was not long in coming.

"'E 'ad much t'confess, that I'll agree," the tenon cutter said finally.

"An oath on 'is lips whene'r 'e was wrathful."

"And was this often... that he was wrathful?"

"Most ev'ry day. An' more'n once in a day, too," the treenail shaper added.

"You are not sorry to be rid of him, then, I think?"

"Nay. Well, not in... in that way." The tenon cutter spoke, then hesitated as he understood what I might think. "I'd not wish any man struck down," he continued. The others nodded agreement. "But 'tis a truth we're pleased as not to 'ave 'Enry atte Bridge to deal with."

"Should you see a man prowling Lord Gilbert's wood," I nodded toward the copse where Henry atte Bridge was found dead, "tell me of it straight away. Especially so if he carries a bow and arrows." I thought it unlikely I would hear from the builders, but 'tis true, I've heard, that a miscreant will return to the scene of his crime.

Perhaps it is also true that a bewildered bailiff will also seek out again the scene of the crime he is bound to solve. I left the workmen and was drawn to the forest. To find what? I knew not: some thing which did not belong that might direct my steps toward a killer.

I found the stick I had used and discarded the week before. It was branched at the end, so I could stir through the leaves with it as with a pitchfork. I spent the next hour churning the forest floor. The Angelus Bell rang while I searched, and the shadows grew long. It would soon be too dark to see any object alien to the forest. I resolved to make one more pass between the road and the beaten place where Henry's body had lain.

There was, between the road and the place we found Henry, a patch of brambles perhaps three or four paces across which had grown up where an opening in the wood permitted sunlight to strike the forest floor. Young nettles grew thickly among and through them. No man, be he ever so hurried, would willingly plunge through these brambles. But when Henry ran through the forest it was near dark. Perhaps he or his pursuer got into the patch.

I have enough experience of nettles that I made no attempt to penetrate the brambles. I contented myself with poking about the fringe, using my stick to push the stems apart so as to peer into the center of the brambles. It was enough.

A close inspection showed several places where the stems of the stinging vegetation were broken, the new leaves on these stalks wilting toward the ground. I pushed my stick under some of these and lifted the broken canes to the late afternoon light. On one of these stalks I saw a wisp of black. I flailed away with the stick until the stem I sought broke free of the soil and I could pull it to me.

At first I could not determine what it was I saw fixed to the bramble thorn. But when I drew it close I found myself inspecting a tuft of black wool. Henry atte Bridge, when he was found, wore brown and grey. No black. I had found, I was sure, some remnant of his killer. But perhaps not. There was a man in the wood that evening when Henry attacked me. He called out to him. Did this bit of wool come from that man; a friend and cohort perhaps? Or did another run headlong through these nettles and brambles and leave this mark of his passing? Were there two men in the wood that night, or three?

Before I left the wood I set myself another task. The new leaves of the nettle are a pleasing addition to a soup or stew. I plucked from the fringe of the patch enough to fill my pouch. The castle cook, I knew, would appreciate the gift.

After supper I retired to my chamber to ponder three scraps of wool; two of blue and one of black. I knew the origin of the blue fragments. Black wool is most often found draping priests and clerks and those who take holy orders. Why would such a one leave part of his robe stuck to a thorn in the forest? The color of a man's garb has little to do with where he may be found. A man may stumble into a patch of nettles no matter what he wears. So had I a clue to the death of Henry atte Bridge or not? I could not tell. All I knew of a certainty was that I had found three woolen fragments. If they spoke, they whispered so softly I could not hear their message.

Chapter 8

Walking the parapet of Bampton Castle became a common evening pastime. The exercise settled my mind for rest. And as I walked I might puzzle out a solution to the mystery of Henry atte Bridge's death, although, truth be told, compassing a pile of stone brought me no nearer an explanation of that business. I was but going round in circles, mentally and physically. If walking was to direct me to a murderer, I would need to choose a path outside the castle walls.

I questioned Thomas atte Bridge. The man could offer no reason for his brother's death. Or would offer no reason, if he could. The man seemed resentful of his dead brother. A glance about at Thomas' hovel while we spoke explained that sentiment. Why two brothers of similar circumstance should live so differently did not then occur to me.

I attended mass on Sunday no closer to discovering a killer than when Thomas de Bowlegh assigned me the task. I did not wish to explain my failures to the vicar, so hastened from the church when Father Thomas had recited the final prayers and Simon Osbern pronounced the blessing.

I was too slow. Thomas de Bowlegh hailed me from the porch as I walked through the lych gate. I had hoped to leave the churchyard unseen in the press of the retiring congregation.

"What news, Master Hugh?" the vicar panted as he hastened across the churchyard. I told him of the wisp of black wool I'd found in the nettles and watched his lip curl as I did. I wondered at this.

As I completed the tale Simon Osbern appeared

at the porch, watching his departing congregation and basking in the spring sun. Father Thomas saw him there and called him to us.

"Simon... your cook flavored his soup with nettle leaves Monday when we supped together, did he not?"

"Aye, he did so."

"Whereaway did he find them?"

"Oh, I sent him to the wood where we found poor Henry atte Bridge. There is a patch there, growing up through blackberry brambles. I saw it when we searched last week and thought then 'twould be worth gathering a sack full of the leaves for the table."

"What does your cook wear?" Father Thomas then asked – a question which was surely not expected and brought a look of surprise to Simon Osbern's rotund face.

"Why... an old robe of mine, cut down as a surcoat."

"Black, is it not?"

"Aye. Why do you ask this?"

Father Thomas turned to me. He expected me to provide the explanation to Father Simon, so I did.

"I found a tuft of black wool caught on thorns in the wood you spoke of. And the nettle stems were somewhat broken and disordered. I thought it was a thing which might lead to a killer, but I see now 'twas but preparation for your dinner."

"There is no other progress to report?" Father Simon frowned.

"None, I fear. Wait... there is the arrow."

"Arrow?" the vicars chorused.

"Nothing to do with the crime, I think. I found a new-broken arrow in the wood last week, near where Henry's body lay. Some poacher escaped the verderer's watch and took a deer, is my guess."

"So near the town?" Father Simon asked skeptically.

"What better place?" Father Thomas replied. "The verderer would not expect a poacher in such a wood."

"And I can find no better explanation," I agreed. "An arrow plays no part in this business, and I can discover no other reason for one to be found lying broken on the forest floor."

The discovery of that would come sooner than I might have guessed.

Father Ralph sauntered up as I took leave of the vicars. I saw them standing by the lych gate, deep in conversation, as I turned from the churchyard to make my way down Church View Street. Father Simon glanced up in my direction as I turned the corner, met my eyes, then turned again to his companions. I was too far from them to hear their conversation but I suspect my failure to find a killer was significant in their discussion.

The castle cook provided a dinner worth remembering that day. The parsley bread was filled with currants, there was duck with milk and honey, pork in spiced syrup, and a cherry pottage made from the last of the cherries dried after the harvest last year. I lingered over the meal and so was nearly late for archery practice.

There were fewer competitors this day than the week earlier. The novelty of renewed shooting wore off quickly, I think, and as the Treaty of Bretigny had brought war with France to an end – temporarily, I am sure – many saw no need to perfect a skill which might go unused.

The archers who needed practice least were most numerous this day. They enjoyed showing off their skill and besting others equally talented. Those who performed poorly the previous Sunday, and were most in need of drill, were less likely to appear this day. I understood. No one likes to be seen as incompetent before wives, children and neighbors.

A tenant of the Bishop of Exeter appeared this day, alert and eager for competition. He was a large, strong fellow, with forearms as large as my bicep. Strictly speaking he should not have been allowed to participate; the vicars of St Beornwald's Church should have scheduled their own contest. But I saw Lord Gilbert's men welcome the fellow warmly, so I ignored his imposition and allowed him to participate. And, indeed, he drank little of Lord Gilbert's ale, contenting himself with the flight of his arrows.

This beefy tenant of the bishop's was, I learned, named Andrew. The bow he strung was longer than any other at the mark by half a forearm, and thicker as well. Many men could not have drawn it, and few could hold it on target without quaking from the strain. I watched as several tried.

Practice began this day with the mark at 100 paces from the butts. Most arrows rose from the mark, then curved gently down to the targets, but not Andrew's missiles. His arrows, loosed from that great bow, hardly lifted above the height of a man's head before slamming into the butt with a resounding thwack.

Andrew's arrows struck the target with such force that they were difficult to dislodge from the wooden butts. It was after the second volley that Andrew, attempting to draw an arrow, snapped the shaft while wrenching it from the target. He threw the broken arrow aside with a muttered curse, then returned to the business of withdrawing the point from the butt. The arrow was ruined, but the iron arrowhead could be reused, fitted to a new shaft.

I saw then how it might have been with Henry atte Bridge. An iron arrowhead might leave a wound similar to that of a slender dagger. And if the shaft broke off inside the wound the result might seem to be the work of a blade rather than an arrow. The iron arrowhead might remain, invisible, in Henry's back, while the broken shaft lay on the forest floor to be discovered.

But how to determine if this befell Henry atte Bridge? His grave would need to be opened, the injury inspected. I berated myself and Hubert Shillside and the coroner's jury for sloppy work. I have learned from this; what seems to be must be shown to be. A supposition, while usually accurate, is not always so, and must be proved before acceptance.

Uprooting a man from his rest in the churchyard is not a thing approved by most, for they expect to go there themselves eventually and prefer their slumber be undisturbed. I wished to exhume Henry quietly, inspect the wound in his back, and rebury him as quickly as might be. The fewer who knew of this, the better. If my intentions were known before I put spade to earth there might be those who would prevent me. Emma might see objection as a duty to her husband's memory.

The more who knew of my plan, the more likely it was that some would object. At first I thought to approach the vicars of St Beornwald's Church with my request.

The churchyard was their bailiwick, and Lord Gilbert's lands were mine. But there would be three then who knew of my intention. None could be sure that the secret would be preserved. And what if one of the three forbid the excavation as sacrilege? Better to proceed without permission and on my own. If the exhumation provided no new information no one need know of it. If I discovered the point of an arrow embedded in Henry atte Bridge's broad back, the find and my insight in seeking it would go far to forgive any insult to the dead, to the churchyard, to the vicars.

But could I dig up Henry atte Bridge without aid? The soil of his grave was yet soft and would be easy to remove. The grave itself would be easy to find, even in the dark, when I proposed to do the work. I resolved to invite the assistance of John Prudhomme, the new beadle. If I was discovered digging in the churchyard it would be John most likely to detect my midnight labor. Better he know of my intentions than stumble upon me, spade in hand, as he made his rounds after curfew. And another shovel at the work would speed the deed.

The new beadle was one of those who stood at the mark, bow in hand, as this scheme tumbled through my mind. Prudhomme was not a winner this day, nor had he ever taken a silver penny for his skill. Yet his arrows struck the target with regular accuracy, and he made the winners struggle for their prize. Perhaps one Sunday his skill might combine with luck and he would win. But not this day.

The ale was gone, the pennies awarded, and the sun

resting on the upper branches of the west forest. I watched from the gatehouse as grooms carried the butts to the storehouse and participants and spectators drifted off to Mill Street and their homes. John Prudhomme and his wife and three children walked among them. I followed the throng, at a leisurely pace, then waited at the bridge until the streets were empty.

Shadows were long and only treetops glowed with a golden light when I approached the beadle's house. I heard children's voices within, and laughter. This family had enjoyed their day together and were now preparing with easy hearts for the night and slumber. I wonder if ever I might have such an experience? The thought so arrested my mind that I hesitated before the house, unwilling to intrude upon the scene.

Laughter ended abruptly with my first knock upon the beadle's door. A late caller at any house is unlikely to bring good news. All the more so at the house of the beadle. John opened the door expecting, I think, some trouble, although certainly not the trouble he got.

I invited John to walk with me, an invitation he might have refused from another, but not Lord Gilbert's bailiff. I wished to be out of earshot of all others, even his family, when I explained what I needed of him this night.

The beadle's jaw fell when I explained that which I intended to do, and the part he was to play. But after I gave him the reason, and told him my suspicion, he agreed reluctantly to the role I asked of him. Most men like to see the resolution of a mystery, even if so doing seems to toy with peril.

So it was that in the middle of the night I procured a shovel and a length of rope from the marshalsea storeroom and took a stub of a candle from the hall. Bruce nickered softly as I passed his stall, expecting, perhaps, an outing. But he did not wake the marshalsea and I was able to climb to the parapet undisturbed.

I crept silently to the north wall, as far away as I could get from Mill Street and the castle gatehouse. I could see, in the glow of a waning moon just up over Bampton rooftops, the Ladywell. Hermits and pilgrims sometimes spend the night at the well, in prayer and meditation. I hoped, be there any such at the well this night, they were either asleep or entranced.

I leaned as far over through a crenel as I could and let the shovel fall. The earth below was soft from recent rain and shadowed from the sun. The shovel hit the sod softly and I was reassured.

I tied knots in the rope to aid my ascent, then tied the rope about a merlon before throwing the loose end to the ground. I slid down the line, retrieved the shovel, and walked quickly to Mill Street and the bridge. I was without concealment while on the bridge, so hastened to cross the brook. I would gaze into its dark waters another time.

John Prudhomme awaited me at the churchyard. He sat in shadow, his back against the wall, so I was startled when he spoke.

"Whereaway is this grave, then?" he whispered.

I motioned for him to follow through the lych gate and led him to the corner of the churchyard where soft dirt underfoot and a pale, sandy reflection of the rising moon indicated a new grave.

We set to our work, attempting to achieve two uncomplementary goals: speed and silence. John whispered as we began the work that he had been careful to see that the town streets were empty before he went to the church to await me. So we gave ourselves over to speed and were less stealthy in the work than we might otherwise have been.

Beads of sweat soon popped out on my forehead and dripped in my eyes. 'Twas not warm. Anxiety was the more likely cause, I think.

St Beornwald's Churchyard is a place of many burials. It has been hallowed ground since before the Conqueror crossed from France to take the throne of England. Now, when a grave is dug, those who do the work are likely to come upon another before they have excavated any great depth. So it must have been for those who buried

Henry atte Bridge. We were barely past waist deep when my shovel struck something soft yet unyielding. John detected the change in the pattern of my work, and soon he also motioned that his spade had met resistance.

At that moment a movement along the church wall caught the corner of my eye. My heart stopped, then tried to rise through my throat. We were discovered. I motioned John to silence and studied the place where I was sure I had seen some stirring along the wall. The beadle followed my gaze. I thought I could hear his heart beat, but perhaps 'twas only my own. We must have made an apparition to any who prowled the wall; two men standing waist-deep in an open grave. Then I saw the motion again. A cat! The animal crept along the top of the wall, seeking mice who made their home in the chinks. I was doubly relieved, for 'twas not a black cat, which would surely have meant trouble for my work. John saw also, and I heard him chuckle in relief. I joined him.

I drew the candle and tinder from my pouch and struck flint against steel until I managed to catch a spark on the tinder to light the wick. The candle sputtered to life and I bent to lower it into the grave. There, partly obscured by unexcavated dirt, I saw a pale blue tunic.

It was the work of but a few moments to clear away enough earth that we could turn the body. What I sought was on the back of the corpse. And I did not relish gazing longer on Henry atte Bridge's swollen face and dirt-encrusted eyes, even in the dim light of a single candle.

I had brought with me in my bag a blade and forceps. These I made ready while the beadle reached into the grave and pulled the tattered cotehardie up to the corpse's shoulders. There was much dirt and discoloration across Henry's back. I had to hold the candle close to see the wound, even though I knew very well where to find it. I pressed the scalpel into the wound and enlarged it. I did this hurriedly, without craft. Henry would not mind. Nor any other, I hoped.

I pushed a finger into the enlarged wound and found what I sought, what I should have found earlier had my work then been more thorough. The iron point of a broken arrow lay deep beneath the putrid flesh and clotted blood. I pushed the forceps into the wound, pressed firmly, and with a tug began to draw the point from Henry atte Bridge's corpse. But before I could extract the arrowhead it caught, perhaps against a rib, and my forceps slipped from the point. I had to twist the arrowhead so that the point might pass between the bones.

The iron point, I believe, had passed through his heart and lungs and embedded itself in his sternum, or perhaps a rib. This caused it to so fix itself in the man that the arrow broke rather than came free when he fell, or perhaps when he staggered against a tree.

Perhaps. There would be time for reflection later. I extinguished the candle and motioned to the beadle to refill the hole. We left Henry atte Bridge face down in his grave. He will not mind, I think, and at the resurrection – from what I know of his life – he is unlikely to rise to see the return of our Lord in the eastern sky. Sweat again beaded my brow before the grave was refilled. We smoothed the soil so the place would look, as much as possible, undisturbed, and leaned heavily on our shovels when the work was done.

I bid John "Good night" at the lych gate and stole quietly down Church View to Bridge Street while the beadle made one more circuit of the town before seeking his bed.

The north wall of the castle was reassuringly dark in shadow when I arrived. I found the knotted rope where I left it, tied the shovel to the end, then clambered up the wall, my feet walking their way up the stones while with the knotted rope I pulled myself through the crenel. I pulled up the shovel, undid the knots, and coiled the rope while crouched along the parapet. It was becoming known in the castle that I might occasionally be seen prowling the parapet at night. Still, I preferred not to be seen. 'Twould be one thing to explain my own presence atop the wall, quite another to account for a rope and shovel. Only later did I consider that I am Lord Gilbert's bailiff. In his absence I need explain my behavior to no one. Still, people will talk.

Next morning, after a loaf, some cheese, and a cup of ale, I inspected my discovery. The broken arrow found in the forest fit the point drawn from Henry atte Bridge's back. I knew this would be so. The cotter was not stabbed as he fled through the wood. He was shot. In the dark. By someone with much skill, or excellent vision, or both.

A deer, struck by an arrow, will not fall where it stands, but will run in panic until it collapses in death. Will a man also run from the place he is struck, until vitality drains from him and he falls? I have never seen a man so smitten, so cannot answer of a surety, but I think it must be so. Somewhere between the road and the place we found him lying in the mould Henry atte Bridge was struck down.

I had new knowledge of this murder, but what to make of it? I could tell no one of the discovery, else I must relate how I came by the information. As it happened, this was for the best. I was to learn that knowledge is a strong weapon, especially so when an adversary knows not of its possession – like an unseen dagger hidden under a belt.

With awl and mallet I drove out the pin which held the point to the broken shaft, then pried the iron tip from the arrow remnant which had remained with the point. This arrowhead was not like most others seen at the butts of a Sunday afternoon. It was the length and thickness of my thumb, and had not the broad "Y" shape of the hunter's arrow. It was a bodkin, made for penetrating a knight's armor. I had seen others like it. It was useless now that the realm was at peace. The metalwork seemed so usual that I despaired of learning anything from it. Nevertheless I placed it in my pouch and set off to consult the castle blacksmith.

I did not assume the arrowhead to be his but wanted an untainted opinion. I thought he might recognize the workmanship. If Edmund, the town smith, made the point he might not wish to identify his craft. A bailiff asking questions of the maker of an arrowhead could mean no good thing for the creator.

Edwin, Bampton Castle's farrier and blacksmith, pursed his lips as he turned the bodkin in his thick fingers. 'Tis Edmund's, I think. 'Tis not so long as mine. Tries to save on iron, does Edmund. But a bodkin needs weight t'punch through armor."

"Do other smiths make points in this manner?"

"Might be… I know only of Edmund."

I left the castle and crossed the bridge to the town and Edmund's forge. His shutter was up, smoke rose from his chimney, and charcoal glowed under the draft of his bellows. I heard his hammer ring rhythmically as I approached.

I don't know what I expected to learn from the fellow. He readily owned the arrowhead as his work. Had made hundreds like it. But none recently, as such points as this were useful only at time of war. Sold such as this to any who had a farthing to buy it. Nay, could not tell from the point when he'd made it, or for whom.

'Twas a fool's errand I had set myself to. I stuffed the point back in my pouch and set off in exasperation for the castle. On the way I met Thomas de Bowlegh puffing down Church View Street.

"Ah," he gasped. "We are well met… I must speak privily to you."

I led him aside and we walked from the road down to the verge of Shill Brook. No passerby on the bridge could hear us there, as the splash of water over the mill wheel obscured even the sound of our voices, moreso the words we spoke.

The vicar glanced up to the bridge to see if we were observed, then, satisfied of our privacy, reached into his pouch and drew forth a candle. My candle. I had forgotten it in haste to leave the churchyard.

"Father Simon found this," the vicar whispered, "atop Henry atte Bridge's grave."

My heart pounded so vigorously I was sure Father Thomas would remark upon it. He did not, but continued. "As he entered the churchyard this morning for matins he noted a strange thing. Two recent graves, near to each other, but their color was different. The grave of Alan the beadle was light, the soil dry, but the grave of Henry atte Bridge was dark. He approached and found the earth atop the grave damp, as if there had been rain upon it in the night. Then he found this stub of a candle. As you are charged with finding Henry's killer we thought to consult you on the matter. What think you, Master Hugh? Have grave robbers profaned St Beornwald's churchyard?... or those who would worship the devil?"

During the vicar's tale I found my wits and calmed myself so I was able to make answer.

"What would be buried with Henry atte Bridge to lure grave robbers? They did not molest Alan's grave?"

"Nay. Just the one... it appears."

"Let us go see," I suggested. "Perhaps some explanation will present itself."

I fervently hoped this would be so. At least the walk to the church would give me time to devise an explanation. I did not wish to speak the truth to the vicars of St Beornwald's Church, at least, not yet, but neither would I lie. I resolved to tell the truth if I must, but misdirect Father Thomas to some other resolution if I could. As we entered the churchyard such an opportunity presented itself.

"There," Father Thomas exclaimed as we passed through the lych gate. "You can see from here what Father Simon saw. Though the soil of the cotter's grave is some drier now."

The vicar was correct, and Simon Osbern was to be commended for his perception. The two graves, those of Alan and Henry, were some twenty paces apart. Alan's lay just under the spreading canopy of an elm, a giant tree which grew up long centuries ago just outside the churchyard wall. Indeed, the wall was askew where the tree had grown up under it and lifted the stones. Henry atte Bridge's grave lay well away from this or any other tree, in the open.

I stood quietly between the two graves and lifted

my head to study the elm. New leaves were beginning to appear on its spreading branches. Thomas de Bowlegh studied me, the candle yet in his hand, as I considered the tree.

I walked first to Alan's grave, knelt, and sifted the dry surface soil through my fingers, then did the same at Henry's grave. The soil here was yet moist from being disturbed. There was no denying it, or suggesting the discovery but a product of an over active imagination. I felt the grass around the grave, inspected my fingers, then peered up at the elm again.

"You found the candle here?" I asked as I stood to my feet.

"Father Simon did."

"Perhaps the damp earth and the candle may be unrelated."

The vicar's eyebrows lifted in question at this. I continued.

"There was a heavy dew last night... see how the turf is yet beaded with it here, about the cotter's grave. But there," I pointed toward the beadle's grave and the old elm, "there is little wet, for the tree shielded the ground and dew collected on the new leaves rather than the grass."

The vicar inspected the wet grass beneath his feet, then Alan's grave, and then his eyes turned skyward to examine the elm.

"What of this candle?" he asked.

"'Tis but a stub," I observed. "Most likely it came from castle or church." This was no lie. "Perhaps it came from the church, in the cloak of some townsman who saw it was near gone and found opportunity to take it for use in his home." This very nearly was a lie, for surely I wished Father Thomas to believe a thing I knew to be false. I apologized later and the vicar was quick to absolve me. My conscience rested the better for it.

"Surely it must be as you have said," the vicar agreed. "There could be nothing buried with Henry atte Bridge worth the digging to retrieve."

The priest was wrong, but did not know it. This seems usually the case with error. If a man knows he is wrong about a thing he will usually amend his thoughts so they may harmonize with truth. Usually. There are, I think, those who would rather hold to error, whatever the evidence, than be forced to change their thoughts of a matter.

I left Father Thomas satisfied that his churchyard had not been violated. I needed to see to Philip and had intended to do so for several days. As I was in the town and near the bakery, I walked to his home to perform my duty.

The baker's shutters were open and the fragrance of new loaves poured from his shop. This odor was not the only thing the bakery produced. A woman's shrill voice, shouting curses and imprecations, flowed also into the street. I was uneasy for eavesdropping, yet all who walked the street that day with me heard the same. The woman's last words were plain: "And a plague on that meddling surgeon!" she screeched. "Better you should've died like a dog in the street!"

A door slammed, and all was silent. I made for the shop entrance, thought better of it, and hastened on down the High Street a hundred paces or so before I turned and reapproached the bakery. I hoped Philip would believe my appearance was tardy enough that I had not heard his wife's fulminations.

Baking was near done for the day. Philip was drawing the last loaves from the oven as I entered. The bakery was pleasantly warm; even so, I thought Philip perspired more than would be produced by a warm oven on a mild spring day. Sweat beaded his forehead and upper lip. He wiped it away with a sleeve as he saw me enter, and bid me "G'day" in a voice both harsh and low. I returned the greeting, but reflected that, from the sounds I had heard earlier, this was not a good day for the baker, nor was it likely he enjoyed many good days at all. Solomon the wise wrote that a nagging wife was like water dripping endlessly. A shrieking wife must be a never-ending torrent. I had a brief thought that perhaps a wife was not an untarnished blessing after all, but the notion soon passed.

"I have come to inspect your wound," I said lightly. The baker lifted his hand to the bandage on his neck.

"It causes me no pain," Philip muttered. What pain he felt came from another source, I think.

"I will unwrap the dressing and see how it knits. Here... be seated on this bench."

Philip obeyed and I went to my work. I was pleased to see a clean wound. The stitches held well. There had been some bleeding and pus issue onto the wrapping, but not for some days. The residue was dry and hard. The egg poultice had done its work. And perhaps the hot iron which caused the injury had cauterized it as it sliced through flesh.

A door opened as I inspected the wound. No doubt the man's wife had re-entered the bakery. Shortly after I heard footfalls on the steps leading to the living quarters on the upper floor. Philip said nothing, but his eyes swung wildly, as if he expected to be impaled upon a bread knife at any moment.

"We may leave off the dressing now. The hurt heals well. Whatever," I asked casually, "did Edmund do to cause you to swing a hammer at him? That's a poor contest for any man to enter against a smith."

I waited, but there was no answer. Philip moved a hand cautiously to his neck, and said finally, "No dressing? You will not dress my hurt?"

I explained, as I find myself obliged often to do, that I follow the practice of Henry de Mondeville. That learned surgeon taught that wounds heal best when left dry, open to the air. I had wrapped Philip's wound only to retain the poultice, and to protect the cut from further injury. Healing had progressed so that there was no longer a need. But Philip's injury was ugly and left a red streak down his neck, from jaw to kirtle. I think he wished it covered for appearance as much as healing. All who saw the wound would remember that Edmund had bested him.

When I finished my explanation of his treatment

I ventured again to the cause. "Do you wish to charge Edmund with assault at hallmote?"

Philip hesitated. "Nay... 'twould do no good."

"What good will be done should no charge be brought?"

"No good," he muttered, "but perhaps less harm." And with that he turned to deal with his loaves, a sign of dismissal. But I was not to be put off so easily.

"My fee for saving your neck is four pence."

The baker shrugged, left the room for a moment through a passage next to his oven, and shortly returned. He held out a hand to me, and when I raised my own he dropped four silver pennies into it. Silently.

I cannot now explain why I did not feel sympathy for Philip. He deserved it, heaven knows, although at the moment, 'tis true, only heaven knew why. I did not, but might have guessed. Then, had I been more gentle with the baker I might not have learned the truth. At least, that part of the truth he knew.

I placed the coins in my pouch and moved to the door but did not leave. I turned back to the baker and said, "Your wife seemed much aggrieved but a little time past."

Philip stiffened as if a dagger had pricked him between the shoulders. My remark was not a question, so Philip did not answer. I continued.

"It seems you have angered both smith and wife."

"Edmund is known for 'is temper," the baker mumbled, "an' no man lives who has not sometime offended 'is wife."

As he spoke his shoulders drooped, like a scarecrow with the support pole removed. "Then why," I countered, "swing a hammer at a strong man known for his rage?"

"'Twas done in heat," the baker replied softly, but would say no more.

I left him, crestfallen, toying with the scar on his neck. There was a matter here I did not know. Perhaps I had no need to know of it. But I am Lord Gilbert's bailiff. Any business which might lead to blows exchanged on his demesne becomes my business. So I must concern myself with the dispute between baker and smith as well as search out a murderer. The death of Alan the beadle, how so it may have happened, was receding from my thoughts. It should not have, for these three incidents were entwined, although I had no clue yet that this was so.

Chapter 9

Many hours that week I spent prowling the darkened parapet of Bampton Castle. This perambulation helped order my mind, but no matter how I sorted and arranged what I knew, I was no closer to identifying a killer. Few in Bampton or the Weald seemed much disturbed by my failure. Even Thomas de Bowlegh mentioned the matter but as a passing comment when we met on the street on Thursday.

And the normal work of May occupied my thoughts so that with little effort I was able to forget Henry atte Bridge. Until Sunday. No sooner had I passed from porch to church than I saw the three vicars and their clerks preparing for matins. I imagined that Simon Osbern peered reproachfully at me. Perhaps it was not my imagination.

Then during the mass Father Thomas read from the Epistle to the Romans: "Christ died for us while we were yet sinners." He lifted his eyes while he read and seemed to gaze at me. This passage I knew well. Perhaps I needed to be reminded that the Lord Christ died for Henry atte Bridge as well as for me. And to take his life was as great a sin as to murder King Edward. Perhaps not in the eyes of men, but if I wished to be weighed in God's balance and not be found wanting I must amend my ways and see men as God sees them.

These thoughts tumbled through my mind at dinner and into the afternoon, when once again archers, their families, and spectators, lined the castle wall to practice their skills and drink Lord Gilbert's ale.

Onlookers came and went as the sun sank toward Lord Gilbert's forest to the west of the castle. One of the late arrivals had not attended the previous competitions. John Kellet made his way to the cask and drew a mug of ale, then stood in conversation with others who had temporarily put bows aside to quench a thirst.

I paid the newcomer scant attention until I noted from the corner of my eye a figure being pushed to the mark. It was the rotund, black-clad form of John Kellet.

Others at the mark made room as the priest was thrust, with much laughter and jesting, to the mark. One took his empty cup, another placed a bow into his hands, and a third brought forth a quiver of arrows and a glove.

The priest of St Andrew's Chapel held the bow comfortably, notched an arrow, grinned at his audience, then drew the bowstrung across his expansive belly. I watched in amazement as the parson took careful aim and loosed the arrow. He missed.

Much hooting and laughter followed. Kellet grew red in the face. He drew another arrow from the quiver, notched it and drew the bow. No smile played about his lips; they were drawn tight across his teeth. His audience grew silent, awaiting the arrow's release. When it came all heads turned to follow its flight. The arrow struck the center of the butt with a solid "thwack."

Cheers and merry exclamations followed, subsiding only upon the release of the third arrow, which also found its mark. The priest launched twelve arrows at the target that day and missed but twice. He left the mark, the quiver empty, with many clapping him on the back and complimenting his eye.

Hubert Shillside had attended the competition this day, perhaps to inspire his son, whose competency surely needed encouragement. I saw the man leaning against the castle wall, watching with his son, as John Kellet sent arrow after arrow thudding into the butt.

I sauntered through the crowd to where Shillside and his son were propped against the wall. "A surprising performance," I said.

But the haberdasher did not seemed over-surprised, although he did agree with me. "Aye… he missed twice.

Lack of practice, surely. And a strange bow."

I was taken aback by this remark until I understood that the astonishing thing about Kellet's performance was not that he had hit the target ten times, but that he had missed twice.

"Before he took holy orders he'd not have missed once at twice the distance," Shillside remarked by way of explanation.

"He was skillful as a younger man?"

"Few could best him."

"I have not seen him at the mark, or even in attendance, before this day."

"'Tis said he was warned away. The vicars of St Beornwald's Church thought it unseemly for a man who chose a vocation to disport himself so of a Sunday afternoon."

"They will not be pleased, then, to learn of his lapse this day."

"If they are told," Shillside winked. "All here know the tale, but I think none would see poor John come to grief for a few arrows on a pleasant afternoon."

"Poor John?"

"Aye. He has but a thin living from that chapel, and no kin since his mother died… and that many years past."

"How did he come to be at the chapel?"

"He was left an orphan. Father Simon was new at St Beornwald's Church, from Exeter. He took 'im in as servant an' made place for 'im. John was quick an' soon learned the words of holy office, though he could not read, of course. A great mimic, 'e was. When St Andrew's Chapel fell vacant the rector could find none willing to accept so slender a living. Kellet volunteered. Was made clerk one day and ordained the next."

"He seems adequately rewarded for his exile there," I commented. "He has missed few meals of late."

"Aye," Shillside agreed. "There is that. Does well from confessions, 'tis said."

"I have heard he does not assign a rigorous penance."

"So 'tis said. An' there be those willing to pay a priest well for his… uh, understanding."

"And the vicars of St Beornwald's? They are not troubled?"

"Who can say? If they saw him removed, who could be sent to replace him? An' as 'tis, he lives without taking much of the bishop's purse. I think our vicars know they would not have the good bishop's ear should they complain. 'Tis a sleeping dog best left to lay as is."

"It was while he served Father Simon that he learned to handle a bow?"

"Nay. As a tyke he'd follow his father of a Sunday afternoon. Odo Kellet was skilled. He was at Crecy. John practiced with a bow 'is father made for 'im when he was but a wee lad."

"And when he went to Father Simon he was allowed to continue his practice?"

"Aye. War with France meant all who could must learn the use of the longbow. 'Twas not 'til he went to the chapel he was pressed to give it up."

"He has kept his skill."

"Aye. An' he enjoyed that bit of showin' off, I'd say."

I had not noticed that during my conversation with Hubert Shillside his son had wandered off. But as I turned to survey the departing archers and spectators (there was practice only this day, no competition; I did not wish to be too free with Lord Gilbert's purse), I saw the youth approach the gatehouse. Alice atte Bridge stood there, her back against the sun-warmed stones, smiling shyly at his approach.

She could do worse. Much worse. The youth had two sisters only. He would inherit his father's business as Bampton town's haberdasher. And I knew Alice well enough to know that Will Shillside could do worse, also. Although whether or not the coroner would agree to his son's choice was another matter. Alice could bring nothing but herself to such a union. That, for most men of means – and their sons – was not enough.

I supped that evening on cold beef and wheaten

bread, then walked the parapet until the last gleam of twilight faded beyond the Ladywell and the forest. I reflected on the day, and whether or not I had learned a thing important to the mysterious death of Henry atte Bridge. Only a man of suspicious nature would think so. John Kellet was skilled with a bow and wore black wool. Was this enough to cause me to suspect him a murderer? And he knew the dead man, for Henry had often, it seems, used his confessional.

But would the fat priest hide along a dark road in company with a man who wished me harm? I had no quarrel with John Kellet. Would he then kill Henry atte Bridge for his failure? This seemed not credible. I put it out of my mind and sought my chamber and bed.

Before he departed Bampton for Goodrich and Pembroke, Lord Gilbert had given instructions for the enlargement of the marshalsea. While he resided at another place the stables at Bampton were quite large enough. But like most of his class he thought himself a connoisseur of horses and never seemed to have enough palfreys for his wife and son, coursers for the hunt, or dexters for the list and war.

Lord Gilbert went to Goodrich for Christmas, as was his custom, then on to Pembroke for St David's Day. This holy day is observed only in Wales, and Lord Gilbert desires to be present should Welsh enthusiasm get out of hand. He planned to return to Bampton by Lammas Day and expected the enlarged marshalsea to be ready for his return. In early November I had sent to Alvescot for the verderer and told him of the beams I would require. He and his sons were to cut and hew them over the winter and bring them, with sufficient coppiced shoots for wattle, to the castle before Whitsuntide. As Lammas Day was but nine weeks hence I thought it wise to seek the man and assure myself that timbers were cut and shaped and ready for transport to the castle.

Anxiety overtook me as I mounted Bruce and set off through the forest for Alvescot and the forester's hut. It was not the forest which caused my unease, although the last time I rode Bruce through a wood I was attacked. Rather, I worried that Gerard had been lax and had not prepared the beams, or was just now doing so. I had directed the fellow to cut the trees in the autumn and winter, when they would be dry of sap. If he was just now toppling them he might have the beams hewn and ready by Whitsuntide but they would be green. As they dried they would twist. Lord Gilbert's new stable wall would not be plumb, nor the roof tree true. Lord Gilbert is a particular man. Even his marshalsea must be orderly though none but horses and grooms dwell therein.

'Twas Rogation Day when I rode out to Alvescot. I knew well the limits of Lord Gilbert's manor, and saw little need to walk the countryside beating the bounds of Bampton with willow branches. As I approached the hamlet I heard its residents a ganging, marching about the limits of the village behind Walter de Notyngham, the priest. A bell rang incessantly, and small boys yelped as they were bounced off trees and posts and rocks to help them memorize the village limits.

As I entered the village from the east I heard the marchers to the north and saw their banners beyond St Peter's Church as they trailed priest and cross. A shriek then punctuated the general commotion and as I drew near I saw a youth pulled dripping from the chilly waters of Shill Brook. Doubtless he would not forget that the stream, much reduced here upstream from Bampton, formed the northern boundary of the village.

I tied Bruce to a post of the lych gate and waited by the churchyard wall until the marchers completed the circuit of the village. This did not take long. Alvescot was small before plague struck. Now there were barely a dozen families to serve this forlorn forested fragment of Lord Gilbert's manor of Bampton.

Alvescot's inhabitants completed their march around the hamlet and broke apart to attend to their own business. Gerard possessed a cottage near the churchyard and soon I saw him approach, limping slightly, favoring his left leg and foot.

The verderer had walked in such manner since I put his head together nearly two years earlier. He and his sons had been felling an oak in the forest between Alvescot and Bampton. A limb of the tree smashed his pate when he failed to move quickly enough from under the falling tree. He complained also of feebleness in his left arm. Why this should be so I cannot tell, for it was the right side of his skull, just above his ear, which suffered the blow.

I greeted the man, and he smiled warmly, as a man might to another who has saved his life. He guessed the reason for my visit. "You've come about beams, eh?"

"Aye. Will they be ready to transport to the castle by Whitsuntide?

"Ready now. Hewed, stacked, an' dryin' since Candlemas."

"Excellent. And how does your head? Are you troubled yet with headaches?"

"Oh, not so much. 'Tis not me head that gives trouble... 'tis the weakness in me arm an' leg."

"This does not improve?"

"Nay. Same as has been since you patched me up."

This condition puzzles me. Mondeville wrote nothing about such a phenomenon, nor has any other surgeon so far as I know. That a man might lose some function of his body from a thump on the head is well known, but why the loss would be opposite to the place of injury I cannot guess.

"I'll send carts to haul the timbers to the castle. How goes Lord Gilbert's woodland? Did many trees fall over winter?"

"Nay... no but one, an old beech come down just after Twelfth Night. 'Twas too bitter to do aught 'bout it then. But after the Feast o' St Edward we hewed it to timbers. They be stacked along wi' the oak, if Lord Gilbert needs more than planned for 'is new stables."

As we talked we walked across the muddy lane to Gerard's hut. He led the way to the toft, where in a wood yard behind the house he showed me the pile of oak and beech awaiting transport to Bampton. All was done as required. No fault could be found with the forester's work, although for the frailty of his left hand and leg I assumed his sons and assistants had done most of the work under his direction.

Beside the beams was a rack of pollarded poles drying under a thatched shelter. Gerard followed my gaze.

"Rafters... got to cut 'em when they're the right size, or there'll be no use for 'em. Wait 'til they be needed an' they'll be grown too large. I'll send a stack w' the beams. No use for 'em here, since plague."

At the rear of his hut, between the building and the wood yard, I saw a heap of wattles ready also for the new stables. Gerard saw my eyes move to the pile, and spoke. "Cut 'em just three days past, so they'll be green-like an' bend easy. Poplar. They's best for wattle."

As I walked past the pile of wattle sticks I absently grasped a wand and flexed it, as if to try the forester's opinion. The twig bent readily, indeed. I replaced it and strolled on.

The door to the rear of Gerard's cottage stood open to the warm spring day and I glanced in as I walked past. A bench occupied the doorway, placed so as to catch the sun. On it were a dozen or so of the straightest poplar shafts, a knife, and a scattering of goose feathers.

Gerard again noted the direction of my gaze and spoke. "Can't shoot arrows now, since me eyes is gone cloudy an' me arm's too weak to hold a bow steady, but nobody makes a truer shaft. All say so."

"You use poplar?" I enquired as I picked up one of the unfinished arrows.

"An' alder... for practice, like. Was we t'be at war wi' the Frenchies again I'd use ash. Poplar be good enough for practice."

"And hunting?"

"Hunting?" The verderer stepped back in shock. "Lord Gilbert hunts wi' hawks an' hounds an' none other may hunt in this wood... 'Tis my job t'see t'that." He concluded this remark with some vehemence.

"You've seen no sign of poachers in Lord Gilbert's forest? No unburied bones or entrails?"

"Nay! Me an' me lads keep a sharp eye for such practice... well, Richard an' Walter do. Me eyes, you know... 'Twould be worth me position to allow thieves to take Lord Gilbert's deer."

"Do you make arrows to sell, or are they for your sons' use? I saw Richard two weeks past, I think, at the castle of a Sunday afternoon."

"I make 'em, mostly to keep me 'and in practice, like. Not much use for arrows now't we ain't got Frenchies t'shoot at. 'Spect that'll change. Usually does."

I agreed. Peace is too valuable to use overmuch. It must be parceled out in small quantities, interspersed between large amounts of war. King Edward would soon find reason enough to resume war in France, I was sure. Or the French king would find cause to attack English possessions. Gerard knew this as well as did every Englishman, and Frenchman too.

The beams, ready or not, could not be taken to Bampton until Friday, for Tuesday and Wednesday were also Rogation Days, and Thursday was Ascension Day.

I awoke early on Ascension Day and after a breakfast of maslin loaf and ale went to the castle parapet to watch the dressing of the Ladywell. This well is ancient, its water said to bring miraculous cures to the ill who seek relief in faith. Even beasts are said to recover health if brought to drink water from the well.

Devout men of centuries past had built a small grotto about the well. Even before I mounted the parapet faithful men and women had begun to bedeck the stones with flowers. Before St Beornwald's bell rang for matins the Ladywell – so named as sacred to the mother of Christ – was covered in blooms.

I left the parapet and castle and joined others in procession to the church. Many carried new willow shoots in honor of the day, bundled with blue ribbons of linen or woolen strips.

Ascension Day mass is, to me, a joyous event. I am

reminded that Christ said He would one day return in like manner as He departed. Such a day will indeed be a joy, for after it there will be no more pestilence or famine. Princes will no longer war upon each other and the commons. I might almost wish Christ may return tomorrow.

But should He do so I will never hold a dear wife close, nor shall I watch children and grandchildren play about my feet. Much sorrow will be ended when the Lord Christ returns, but some joy also. Considering all, it is my wish that our Lord delay His return awhile yet. Perhaps when I am bent with age and stumble upon my way with rheumy eyes and unsure step, then perhaps, when I have seen sons grow to honorable manhood, then I might be pleased to see Christ appear in the eastern sky. Well, I think our Lord will appear when He is ready, which time neither I nor any man can know. So it will behoove me to be ready when He is. Although I do pray He will tarry until I find a good wife.

Early Friday morning I sent six men, six horses, and three carts to Alvescot to haul the beams to the castle. I thought two trips from each would complete the work. It was near the twelfth hour, the sun hanging low above the west forest, when the heavily laden carts appeared a second time through the trees bearing their burdens.

The carts and their tired horses and villeins passed through the gatehouse and made their way toward the southeast corner of the castle yard, where the marshalsea was to be extended. I watched as the beams were unloaded, having nothing better to do until the evening meal, when from the corner of my eye I saw John Holcutt standing under the gatehouse in conversation with a woman.

I perceived nothing unusual in this conversation so paid it no mind. But a few moments later the reeve approached, smiling, holding a spade in one hand and some obscured object in the other.

"You seem pleased with yourself, John."

"Aye. I have done Lord Gilbert good service this day."

"How so?"

The reeve held forth the spade. It was iron, and well made. "I have added this to the castle tools… for two pence. And," he continued, "two nails, for a farthing."

John lifted the object in his left hand and presented it for my examination. It was a block of wood – beech, I think – about the length of a man's hand, half as broad, and two fingers in thickness. Driven through this wooden fragment were two iron nails, each as long as a man's fingers.

"What do you suppose it may be?" the reeve asked as I took the object and inspected it. "I see no useful purpose for such a tool. Seems a waste of two nails to me."

"Well, the nails will be useful for the new stables. And tuppence for a good shovel is money well spent. Who sold these for such a price?"

"A woman… she brought the shovel to the gatehouse an' asked Wilfred was anyone about who might buy from her. He sent for me. She would have three pence, she said, an' 'twould have been a good price. But I got her to take two."

"Do you know this woman?"

"Nay. Said as she was a poor widow what needed to feed 'er younguns. Seemed well enough fed to me."

"Come," I nodded toward the gatehouse. "Perhaps Wilfred will know who 'twas."

John peered at me beneath a furrowed brow. "Is it important?"

"Probably not, yet I am uneasy about this bargain."

"You think I did wrong in spending Lord Gilbert's money so?"

"No. You spent wisely. But who sold these, and why, and what this," I lifted the wooden block with its nails, "may be is a puzzle to me."

Wilfred watched us approach from his post at the gatehouse. He sat on a bench, his back against stones warmed by the afternoon sun, but stood, as well he might, when reeve and bailiff both approach.

"The woman who sold these to John… do you know her?"

"Aye," the porter replied. "Emma, her whose man got buried a month past."

I studied the spade John Holcutt carried. No doubt it was the tool I'd seen the woman plying the day I sought her husband and found her in the toft. Whatever Henry atte Bridge's source of income was which allowed him to purchase an iron spade, both he and it were now gone. Doubtless the woman needed two pence more than an iron spade.

I sent the reeve to the castle storeroom with the spade, but kept the wooden block with its embedded nails. The device intrigued me. I placed it in my chamber while I supped, but my mind was not on the meal. Until the second remove, when was served a favorite dish of mine – pork in spiced syrup. I cut a substantial piece from the roast as a groom placed it before me.

While I enjoyed the pork I noted that much of the syrup soaked into the trencher. If I wished to enjoy the flavor of the malmsey and spices in the syrup I must eat of the stale bread. I admit I considered this, but decided it might appear gluttonous to those who dined with me.

So I finished my pork and observed the brown stain made in the trencher by the cook's savory syrup. It was at this moment a disquieting thought seized me. The alarm I felt so possessed me that I could hardly bear to finish the third remove before hastening to my chamber and the wooden block.

This block was partly discolored, as if with age. Its appearance was a mottled brown, much like the hue of the cook's syrup. But the wood was not of uniform color. Some places on the block's surface were stained more darkly than others. The side which held the nail heads was hardly discolored at all.

I put a fingernail to one of the darkened areas, between the two nails, and scraped it across the surface. A brown, powdery residue appeared under my fingernail. I took a scalpel from my instrument box to repeat the experiment, and scraped a small pile of powder onto my table. It was grown too dark to inspect this material closely, so I lighted a cresset and brought it close to the scrapings. I had seen such a color before, many times. Before me, on my table, was a tiny mound of dried blood, or something much like it.

Tomorrow I would need to visit the Weald again and seek Emma atte Bridge. I would rather face a thousand ravens, each trying to pluck out my eye. But I needed knowledge of these nails and knew of no other place to find it. I foresaw another night pacing the parapet.

I found Emma in her toft next morning, weeding amongst her onions and screeching at her children. The urchins were apparently being instructed in the proper method of extracting weeds from a row of onions. If volume indicated the success of their education, they were being well taught.

The woman saw my feet appear at the corner of her hut, stood, and with the back of a wrist swept hair from her eyes. She stared silently at me from under her hood, which she wore open and turned back. The locks she brushed into place were showing streaks of grey, and deep furrows creased the corners of her eyes and mouth. Her children noted the sudden silence and stared from their knees at their mother and the visitor they had seen before.

Emma glared at me, but refused to speak a greeting, even an unwelcome one. So I fished the wooden block and nails from my pouch and held it before her. "You sold this to Lord Gilbert's reeve yesterday."

The woman remained silent, her eyes flicking from me to the block in my hand.

"What is it?" I asked. "To what use is it put?"

"Dunno," the woman finally said.

"It was your husband's?"

"Aye... found it in 'is pouch."

"You never saw him use it?"

"Nay. Never seen it 'til I was goin' through the pouch an' found it. Thought the castle might want nails. I seen the carts goin' in with timbers. Figured you was buildin' somethin'."

"Indeed, the nails will find good service. You do not know to what work your husband put them?"

"Nay."

I decided to change the subject. "The spade... did Henry buy it from Edmund?"

The woman shrugged. "Suppose. 'E din't say."

"'Tis a better tool than most might own," I remarked.

Emma looked past me to the corner of her house. "'E were a good provider, was my Henry."

"So you sold the spade to provide for your children, now Henry's buried?"

"Aye. You an' the vicars might find who 'tis murdered 'im, but that'll not feed us."

I thought as how Emma was now placed in competition with Matilda for the eligible bachelors and widowers of the town. I knew who would win that contest. But Emma would probably be content with second place.

I bid the woman good day and heard her again bellowing admonitions to her offspring before I had got thirty paces.

I turned at Mill Street to enter the town – after my customary halt on the bridge to observe the brook. While I leaned on the paling I heard sharp words issue from the open door of the mill. A moment later the miller's wife appeared, dragging a sack. This she stacked beside another like it, muttered something through the open door, then stalked after her words back into the mill.

Here is a woman, I thought, who will be glad in three more weeks when her husband's broken arm be mended.

Edmund looked up from his hammer and anvil as I approached. His brow creased to a frown. I have noticed that my appearance unannounced does that to foreheads more often since I became bailiff to Lord Gilbert Talbot's manor at Bampton. I almost never caused a scowl when I was but Master Hugh, surgeon. Edmund might yet worry that the baker would charge him at hallmote. So I thought.

I smiled at the smith but his rutted brow remained unchanged. I withdrew the block and nails from my pouch and presented it to him.

"Good day, Edmund. For what purpose was this made?" I held the object out for his inspection.

The smith turned the block in his thick fingers, felt of the nails, then spoke. "I know not... nothin' I've seen before."

"You did not make it?"

"Nay. Might've made the nails. Look like my work."

"Did you sell nails to Henry atte Bridge?"

"Might've. Sold 'im hinges two years an' more past. 'E wanted nails too, I remember."

"How many nails, for two hinges?"

The smith hesitated, then replied, "Twelve... for the hinges 'e wanted."

"How much did that cost him?"

"Thruppence each for hinges... an' tuppence for nails."

"Henry atte Bridge spent... what, eight pence to swing his door?"

"Aye. 'Bout that," Edmund agreed.

I did not ask the smith where Henry would find eight pence for hinges. Certainly he would not know. Leather hinges served most cotters and probably had sufficed for Henry, until he found enough money to install iron hinges. But were there no other things a man in Henry atte Bridge's place could find to spend eight pence on which would serve him better? He might have purchased a dozen and more hens and fed his children eggs. Well, there is no explaining how some men, both rich and poor, spend their treasure.

I did not return to the castle, though it was near time for dinner. Once across the bridge I turned again into the Weald and walked to Emma atte Bridge's iron-hinged door.

The toft – indeed, the entire hut – was silent as I approached. The only sign of life was a curl of smoke which eddied from under the gable vent. The family, like others, were at their noon meal.

Surely the woman did not expect my return, nor any other visitor, I think. I knocked on the door, and in response a bench upset in the hut as the one who sat upon it sprang up.

"'Oose there?" Emma called through the oiled skin of the window.

"'Tis Master Hugh. I am sorry to disturb your dinner. I have but one more question."

I heard the latch lifted and the hinges in question squealed softly as Emma opened the door and peered at me. Again the woman was silent, staring at me under lowered brows, her mouth pursed. She did not invite me to enter. I am Lord Gilbert's bailiff. I need no invitation.

"I should like to examine the hinges Henry installed on this door."

The woman stepped back grudgingly and allowed me to open the door enough that I could enter the dim, smoky room. With the door open to daylight I could see the hinges plainly. Only two nails held each hinge to the door-post. There was, in each hinge, a hole for a third nail which might at one time have been driven home like the others, but was now missing. Each hinge was held in place, to door and jamb, by five nails, not six.

I took the block from my pouch and held it close to the upper hinge. The heads of the nails fixing the hinge in place were the same as the nails piercing the block.

"The nails you sold came from these hinges," I told Emma. "When did your husband remove them?"

"Don't know," the woman shrugged and chewed on her lower lip. "Din't know as 'e did."

"You did not see him draw them?"

"Nay."

The woman said no more. I apologized for disturbing her dinner and made my way back to the castle in time for my own meal.

My thoughts were not on the castle cook's culinary creations that day. I puzzled over the wood and nails as I ate. Perhaps, I thought, the tool served for dealing with animals in some new way. The blood – or what I took to be blood – seemed to point to such a use. But John Holcutt, whose duties with demesne livestock made him knowledgeable of all instruments needful for working with beasts, recognized no purpose for this thing.

I was near to giving up study of the strange tool, knocking the nails from it, and forgetting the puzzle. But in my chamber after dinner I examined the thing again.

My previous study had concentrated on the nails. It seemed to me that whatever this tool was designed to accomplish, it was the nails which were to do the work. The wooden block served but to hold them in place, and as a handle.

I have told of the size of the piece. As I examined it again I noticed that the block was not symmetrically shaped. The block was slightly narrower at one end than at the other, and the sides were beveled. I recognized then what it was and berated myself for my lack of imagination. I set off immediately for the town and the Broad Street where I might find Ralph the cooper.

He was at his vise, drawknife in hand, shaping a stave. He stood in a pile of sweet-smelling shavings which, as at the new tithe barn, helped obscure the fact that their maker was overdue for his spring bath.

The cooper looked up from his work, recognized me, and smiled. As well he might, for my previous business with him had always involved a purchase for the castle storeroom or buttery. He saw a lucrative sale in his future.

Then his eyes fell to the wooden block and its captive nails and the grin on his face melted like butter in July. Here, I thought, may be found another mystery.

"Good day, Ralph," I smiled broadly. I wished the fellow at ease; I thought I might learn more from him than if he was anxious. And from his new-fallen countenance I felt certain he had some reason for worry. And it had to do with the block.

"I have a tool here which no man can explain."

The cooper's eyes darted from my face to my outstretched hand and back again.

"Henry atte Bridge, who was struck down in the forest, you may remember, made this. See how the wood is shaped like a length of barrel stave." I handed the piece to Ralph, who took it gingerly, as if the nails were yet hot from Edmund's forge.

"How long ago," I asked, "did Henry come to you seeking wood?"

I might have asked if Henry had sought wood of him, but then the cooper might deny the source and I might never get the answer I needed. Better he thought I knew the origin of the block for a certainty.

"'Twas but a scrap," Ralph offered. "A stave was split an' discarded. Henry asked for a piece."

"Beech, is it not?"

"Aye."

"Did Henry say his purpose? Did he show you the nails as they are now?"

"Nay... 'e had no nails. Just asked for the wood."

"Did you ask a price?"

"Nay. 'Twas no good to me but for the fire. I cut off a hand's length an' Henry were satisfied."

"When did he ask for this?"

The cooper made much of his struggle to remember. His brow looked like a new-plowed field and he scratched at his chin.

"Weeks ago now, 'twas."

"How many weeks?"

"Before Easter. Aye... before Easter 'twas."

"How long before?" I pressed.

"A week, p'rhaps more. Aye, 'bout a week."

"And he carried the wood away without telling of his need, or driving nails through it in your sight?"

"Aye. That's 'ow 'twas, Master Hugh."

The cooper wished fervently for me to believe this. But did he desire this because the tale was true, or because it was false? A man might wish to be believed for either reason. And why should it matter to him whether I believed him or not? I was inclined to believe the man, and as it came to pass, the tale was true.

I studied the man and chewed my lip, trying to invent some other questions which might illuminate the purpose for the block and nails. Ralph saw this, and said, "'E come back day before Easter."

"Saturday?

"Aye. Said I was to tell none of 'is need an' the wood I gave 'im."

"He did not say why?"

"No. With Henry like as 'e could be, I din't ask. But 'e din't want any to know of it, I think. Couldn't figure why. Do you know why?"

"This is why you seemed distressed when I came to you today with the block?"

"Aye. Don't know as what Henry wanted with it, but seems to me 'twas to no good... or why'd 'e care who knew of 'im 'avin' it?"

I walked the castle parapet again that night, twirling the piece of stave and nails as I did. I felt certain now I knew its use. But I could not prove it. And I did not know why it was used as it was. I did know that I was deep into a mystery which included much I did not know. I resolved then to keep a record of these events, so as to order all things in my mind, and as a register should I in the future decide to write a chronicle of this affair.

There was an obstacle to this decision. I had in my chamber but six sheets of parchment and a pot of ink nearly dry. If I was to put my thoughts to parchment I must travel to Oxford to renew my supply. A journey to Oxford through the spring countryside seemed a pleasant distraction and, perhaps while swaying along on Bruce's broad back at his stolid pace, some new notion explaining events since Easter might occur to me.

Chapter 10

I planted my feet on the cold flags of my chamber as soon as dawn lightened my window. The cook was surprised to see me, as I am not usually early from my bed. There was a warm wheaten loaf fresh from the oven, and cheese and ale, for my breakfast.

I searched out John Holcutt while the marshalsea prepared Bruce, and told him of my journey. He would serve as Lord Gilbert's agent in my absence, which I planned to take but two days. A trip to Oxford and back might be completed in one day, on a younger horse, by a competent rider, who did not mind arriving home after dark. But Bruce was aged, and my skills at horsemanship are meager, and I remembered clearly the last time I rode at night alone. And there was more I wished to do in Oxford than purchase ink and parchment.

There is much profit in a springtime journey to Oxford. It was indeed a pleasant occupation to observe the countryside as Bruce ambled upon his way. Villagers were mostly at work in their tofts, as by this day in May the fields were all plowed and sown.

Birds darted from meadow to forest, completing nests. Even the oaks, last of the trees to achieve full foliage, seemed sure enough of the season to bring forth leaves.

The journey brought me nearer to Oxford, but no nearer to assembling the events of the past months into some coherent pattern. I gave up the attempt and turned myself to observing the approaching town as Bruce's great hooves clattered across the Oxpen's Road Bridge.

Some of my most agreeable memories involve Oxford. But some unpleasant memories of the place are yet green in my mind as well. The St Scholastica Day Riot, of which I took no part, but which drove me and many other students from the town, remains vivid in my mind's eye. And as Bruce ambled past the castle and the old keep I thought back to the testimony I gave there before the king's eyre which came near to sending an innocent man to the gallows. It is, perhaps, good to remember our errors. But perhaps not. Men seem to repeat their mistakes with some frequency. Is it forgetfulness or foolishness which is to blame?

I guided Bruce to the High Street, where I stabled the grateful beast at the Stag and Hounds. I relieved my hunger with a half capon. It is often comforting to note that the world continues day after day with little change. But the unimproved character of the food and ale at the Stag and Hounds did little to reassure me of the permanent nature of things. Capons are to be fat. Mine this day was stringy as an old rooster, which I suspect it was.

I was not much distressed to leave off gnawing at my meal and set my feet toward my first object in the town. I dodged illegal vendors and students on Cornmarket Street, turned east on Broad Street, and presented myself to the porter at Baliol College. He was new, and did not remember me. Not that this made any difference, for the scholar I sought, he informed me, was no longer there.

Master John Wyclif had another position, the porter told me, as Warden of New Canterbury Hall. So I retraced my steps down Cornmarket Street, past the High Street, to St Aldates and Master John's new home.

The porter at New Canterbury Hall admitted me with little hesitation, this being a time of peace between the town and its university. I followed his pointed finger across a cloister and thumped on the door he indicated. I was unsure if Master John would be within, for the day begged to be enjoyed out of doors. Or the scholar might be about his duties, which are always heavy when dealing with young men full of sap and conceit.

But my old (well, not so old; he is only ten years older than me, but has grown a beard to distinguish himself from his pupils) teacher was in his chamber, and greeted me at his door.

"Master Hugh! Welcome. You have found me." The warden of New Canterbury Hall swept his arm about the cloister. "What do you think of my new position?"

"Baliol College has the worst of the bargain, I think."

"Hmmm. I would agree, but 'twould be unseemly. Come in... come in, and tell me how that business turned out which drew us together last."

"'Tis a long story. Better told on such a day while we stroll the water meadow."

Wyclif peered up at the sky from under his hood. "You speak truth, Master Hugh. I devote too much time to study. It is well you have come to draw me from my books for a time."

We crossed the meadow toward the Cherwell, and I told Master John of Hamo Tanner, his daughter, and Sir Robert Mallory. I told only so much of Lady Joan as was necessary to the tale, but Master John is a quick man and saw there was a part of the story I had neglected.

"What of Lady Joan?" he asked.

"Married. To Sir Charles de Burgh... and with child, I am told."

Master John stopped and faced me there in the tall meadow grass. "I hear melancholy in your voice, Hugh. Did you wish to win the lady for yourself?"

"She was above my station. I gave the matter no thought."

"If you would share conversation with me, Hugh, I wish you would be truthful."

I protested, but Master John turned and resumed his path toward the Cherwell. The meadow grass was tall, ready to be cut, and brushed my knees as I strode after him.

"So, you find me out," I laughed. "'Tis true, if the lady would have had me I would have been her slave for life."

"But you never offered that service?"

"Nay. To do so would have placed a gulf between us, for she could not have accepted."

"Aye. You are correct, I'm sure. Is there another lass to consider?"

I admit that a fleeting vision of Alice atte Bridge darted through my mind as I answered, "No."

"You have given up the pursuit, then?"

"Not so. I pray daily that God may send me a good wife."

"But thus far He has refused? What do you to aid His work?"

I did not reply, for in truth I did nothing to alter my estate. We walked on in companionable silence until we came to the river.

"You might consider yourself fortunate," Wyclif said.

"How so?"

Master John picked up a fallen willow branch and cast it into Cherwell stream. "Consider… had you married the Lady Joan Talbot and brought her to your bed, could you have provided for her the wealth to which she was accustomed? Surely not. Might she not soon regret her poverty and rue her life with you? And even did she not, you would see in every frown, in every disapproving word, a hint that she resented her state."

"So you advise me to seek a poor lass for a wife?"

"Perhaps. But not if such a woman thinks you, a prosperous man, be her path to a life of ease."

"So I must not marry either rich or poor? What of beauty? Lady Joan was… is a great beauty."

"Aye. I believe I saw her once in company with her brother. I'll not debate the issue. She is indeed a great beauty. But consider, then, her husband," Master John continued, seating himself on a log and gazing out at the willow-banked Cherwell. "Men gaze lustfully at his wife. Must he not consider that some of these be more handsome, or more wealthy, or better spoken than he? Perhaps there are men who are all three. Will he not fret that his lovely wife's affection be stolen from him? Women are the ficklest of all God's creation, so say the sages."

"Lady Joan would not betray her pledge," I

remonstrated. "You do not know the lady."

"Ah, but will not Sir Thomas worry anyway, each time his comely wife holds a gentleman's eye? I do not know the lady, but I do know men."

"So I should seek an ugly wife?"

"You put words in my mouth, Hugh. Can a man find happiness married to a woman no other man wants?"

"You vex me, sir. A wife must be neither rich nor poor, neither beautiful nor ugly."

"Ah... there you have it, Hugh. 'Tis Aristotle's Golden Mean. Moderation in all things. Find yourself a wife who is beautiful, but not extravagantly so. A lass who comes of a father with some money, but not so much that he has indulged her. A woman who is quick of tongue and mind for good conversation, but not so witty that she may become a shrew."

"You have my future well in hand. Where do I find such a woman? And mind you, I still prefer beauty, regardless of your logic."

"That," he chuckled, "I leave to you. And to God. I am at an end to my advice."

An end to his advice, perhaps, but he knew well where I might find such a lass as he described and was about to set me in her direction.

We sat upon the log in collegial silence, watching the flowing stream and listening to the hum of the town across the water meadow. I was loath to disturb the moment, but finally spoke.

"There is another matter I would seek your views upon."

Master John raised his eyes from the river to meet my gaze. "I thought as much. Few men seek me for marital advice."

I thought to remark that I was not surprised, but held my tongue.

The sun was low across the meadow, washing Oxford's steeples and towers in golden hues, when I completed my account of Alan the beadle, Henry atte Bridge, the beast, the shoes, the blue yarn, a dead lamb, and the nail-studded block. When I finished I drew the block from my pouch and placed it before Master John.

The scholar held it aloft to catch a ray of the setting sun angling through the willows.

"'Tis indeed an unusual instrument. But you have divined its purpose, or I mistake the set to your jaw."

"Aye, I have a theory."

"As do I," Wyclif replied. "I would hear yours."

"Such a tool could tear a man's throat and none the wiser. And should a wolf howl in the night, the injury would seem to be done by the beast, not a man."

"Such are my thoughts," Wyclif agreed. "But the man who did this is dead, you say?"

"Aye, and I know not why he would kill the beadle. Surely a man will not kill another for his shoes?"

"Some men might," Master John scowled, "but I am of the same mind. There is more to this matter than shoes. So now you seek one who killed a murderer?"

"Aye. But did such a one kill for revenge? Or, perhaps 'twas in error. Or did Henry atte Bridge die so as to silence him? Mayhap Henry had a partner in this business of Alan the beadle."

Master John plucked a blade of grass and twisted it round his finger. "All these are possible... but I lean to silence."

"As do I," I agreed. "If Henry atte Bridge was shot down in error, the mistake was grievous, for I must be the only other target, and I was standing in the road, opposite the flight of the arrow. If revenge, then three must have been in the wood that night – Henry, the one he called to, who could have been no enemy seeking vengeance, and one unknown who struck him down."

Wyclif unwound the grass from his fingers. "Doubtful, for if so it would mean there is another who knew of his attack on your beadle. Unless this Henry was so unloved there were others who wished him ill."

"He was not admired, but I think none sought his life."

"Someone did, and when you learn why Henry atte

Bridge slew the beadle you will, perchance, discover who had reason to shed his blood.

"'Tis near time for supper," Master John stood and stretched. "Will you dine with me this evening? New Canterbury Hall is of the new scheme... students make their abode in the college, and take their meals there also. There are merchants and landlords who dislike this new way, but the method prevents much trouble in the town."

"I would have taken my supper at the Stag and Hounds."

"Hah. So you will accept my invitation. I know the place well. Do you sleep there this night?"

"Aye."

"There are empty cells at the college. Sleep here. You will awaken lousy at the Stag and Hounds."

Master John did not need to beg me. I changed my lodging willingly.

Supper was but barley pottage and maslin, but the students partook enthusiastically. The conversation fell to a debate concerning the late king of France, John II, who had died a hostage in English custody the year before. He had been captured at Poitiers, and held for a great ransom, but was released so as to return to France and raise the funds. His son was to remain hostage in his place, but fled.

When King John learned of this he considered it a breach of honor and so placed himself in English hands again. King Edward's brother kept him at the Savoy Palace, in London, where he died some months after his return. No Englishman had a hand in this death. Only living kings are worth a ransom.

Some students argued that the French king was foolish to return, others held that chivalry demanded it. I took no part in the dispute, but watched as Master John goaded his charges with questions or demolished ill-considered remarks with a word. Such conversation would not be a part of the discourse at the Stag and Hounds. Conversation there generally centered on the appearance and habits of the newest wench.

The long glow of a near-summer evening illuminated and warmed the west-facing wall of the cloister at Master John's door. We sat, after supper, on a bench with our backs to the warm stones and spoke of various things. Our conversation had no special theme. It ranged from the weather, which we agreed was agreeable, to the old king and his new keeper of the privy seal, William of Wykeham.

Said William is an able man. This is good, for Edward is not remarked for wisdom even among those who defend his many virtues. There are nobles who despise William. They detest a peasant's son at the king's right hand. As darkness fell and the stones at our backs cooled we agreed that William's counsel could be no worse than that of the barons and bishops. This conclusion was probably subversive and heretical, but the wall had no ears so our judgment carried with it no penalty.

I bid Master John farewell next morning after we shared a loaf warm from the college bakehouse.

"I trust," he remarked, "you have found what you sought at Oxford."

"Nearly so. I need to seek but one more thing before I leave the town."

"Indeed; what is that?"

"When ended the business of the bones in Lord Gilbert's cesspit I set my hand to write down the tale. Some day long hence perhaps a man will read of the affair while I wait in the churchyard for the Lord's return. Now I am persuaded that this new matter of Alan the beadle must be recorded as well." Master John nodded. "So I am come to Oxford to seek parchment and ink of Aelfred."

"Ah… my pride is well rebuked. 'Twas my opinion brought you here, so I thought."

"Your views mean much to me, but I admit, 'twas the parchment brought me to Oxford. Now I must go and beg Aelfred to sell me some of his precious supply."

Aelfred the stationer had long been the bane of Baliol's scholars and students. His shop was nearest to the college, on the High Street. If he disliked a master's teaching, or the cut of a student's gown, he would refuse to sell to him. Neither parchment nor vellum nor the ink to write upon them could be pried from his flinty grasp did he dislike the buyer. Those he displeased must purchase from another vendor. He seemed to like me well enough. He did not withhold when I offered to buy.

"Hah… you speak of Aelfred," Wyclif chuckled. "He is not so particular now. He has a competitor."

"Another stationer does business on the High Street?"

"Aye. Near enough. From Cambridge, 'tis said, although we do not hold that against him."

"From Cambridge? What has brought him hither?"

"His father is a stationer there. And as Cambridge is not so great with students as Oxford, there is not enough custom for him to set up on his own, nor did he wish to steal his living from his father. So here he is, and has found good business, I think, for he sells to all with a smile."

"That would indeed be a novelty."

"If you seek his shop you will find it readily enough. 'Tis on the Holywell Street, but a short way from Baliol College. You will know the place from afar off for the students passing to and fro."

"This new fellow has attracted much business, then?"

"Ah… well… I would not say he or his business is the attraction," Wyclif smiled.

"You speak in riddles. I feel myself taken back to a lecture where you challenged us students with conjectures that would choke a bishop."

"Choking bishops is a talent of mine. But fare you well, and may God grant you success in your endeavors."

"May He, indeed," I replied, and set off up Cornmarket Street for Baliol College and Holywell Street.

It was as Master John predicted. I was but a few steps past the gate to Baliol College when Broad Street straightened enough that I could see past Catte Street into the curve of Holywell Street. Two hundred paces or so before me I saw three black-gowned students milling about before a shop. As I watched and walked they took counsel of each other, threw back their adolescent shoulders, and disappeared inside the shop.

When I first entered the stationer's shop I did not understand the reason for their manly display. The interior was dark, as the establishment was on the south side of the street and the shutters opened to the north. The slanting morning sun did not penetrate to the shaded corners of the business.

I envisioned the proprietor as a young man, setting out on business on his own, but the man who waited on the youths was middle-aged, and carried himself with the stiffness of old age. There was another figure in a dark corner of the shop, arranging bundles of parchment and vellum on a shelf. When this person turned toward me Master John's words and the behavior of the students became clear.

My eyes beheld a lovely young woman of perhaps twenty years. She looked up from her duties and smiled, and my heart was captured. My heart does not do battle well against attractive females who possess a fetching smile. Truth to tell, I had surrendered it several times before, but those who seized it in the past always found some way of returning it, wounded and scarred, to me.

The girl turned and addressed me, asking might she be of service. Two of the students turned to her, hoping, I think, that she spoke to them, then watched, subdued, as she approached me.

The girl was of average height – perhaps on the tall side of average – and slender. Her neck was long and flawlessly white. Fair hair, not quite blonde, framed her face from under a turned-back hood. Her eyes were brown, and seemed to dance with laughter, though what she found amusing I could not tell. I hoped 'twas not me.

I was smitten. As I have written, this was not a new experience for me. I was become accustomed to the blows.

She wore a long cotehardie of deepest red, which swayed delightfully as she left the corner where she had been employed and walked toward me. The bodice of this garment was cut fashionably low, and thus gave more than a hint of an ample bosom, made more fetching by the belt she wore about a slender waist.

It is customary at this point in describing a beautiful woman to make some point regarding her flawless face and complexion. In all truth I cannot do so, for the girl's nose was somewhat over-large – although, unlike my own, it pointed out straight and true, whereas my own has a decided turn to the right. And an unfortunate pimple marred her left cheek.

But when she smiled these flaws faded. The girl possessed straight teeth, and these shown through red lips in a smile which seemed to bring light to the dim recesses of the shop.

The girl stopped before me and waited until I remembered that I had been addressed and had made no answer. Her large eyes remained fixed on mine, and the corners of her eyes crinkled to duplicate the laugh lines creasing the corners of her mouth. I believe she knew her effect on men, and enjoyed their bewilderment.

"Parchment… uh… I would like some parchment. And a pot of ink," I stammered.

The girl turned to the shelf where I had first seen her. "How much?"

I had intended to purchase three gatherings, but had I done so I would not need to visit Oxford to replenish my supply for many months. I thought quickly – which surprises me even now when I think back on it, for beautiful women usually leave me dazed – and replied, "One gathering."

The girl began to count, leafing through the sheets with nimble fingers. She spoke and counted at the same time. I was amazed. I could not do it, nor could any other, I think.

"You do not appear a copyist," she remarked.

I suppose I did not. I wore no robe or gown, but chauces cut tight to show a good leg, and a short cotehardie. My hood ended in a liripipe of fashionable length, which I had wrapped around my head, as young men now do.

"Indeed, you observe correctly. I do not earn my bread with goose quill in hand."

"I have not seen you here before," the girl continued.

"I am from Bampton."

This information the girl received blankly. I think she had not heard of the place, being new in Oxford.

"'Tis a short way to the west, fifteen or so miles. Most of the town is in the manor of Lord Gilbert Talbot. I am his bailiff, and also a surgeon."

"A surgeon?" The girl looked toward her father as she spoke.

"Aye."

"My father suffers much. A complaint physicians cannot cure. Perhaps you might have a treatment...?"

I turned to view the stationer. He stood erect and tall and seemed well enough to me. He and the young scholar had apparently agreed on the price of the book, and coins were exchanged as I watched.

The three students cast wistful glances toward the girl, then passed from the dim shop to the sun-bright street. They seemed morose. I believe my appearance interfered with their goal, which was not, I think, literary. Well, the day was bright with spring, the term was near done, and they were young. They would soon forget their disappointment.

The girl spoke as the students reached the door. "Father, this is... uh..." She turned helplessly to me.

"I am Hugh de Singleton," I bowed.

"A surgeon," the girl added quickly. "Perhaps he might help you."

"I am done with physicians," the stationer snorted, and the smile faded from his lips. "My money is gone; the ailment remains."

The girl looked helplessly to me. "He has suffered near a year," she explained.

"I am not a physician. I make no judgments of unbalanced humors, nor can I diagnose a man's illness with a sniff of his piss."

166

The young woman blushed, but I wished to make clear that some things I could not do. And furthermore, saw no need for another to do them, either.

"'Tis not a complaint suited to a surgeon," the stationer said. "The best physicians in Cambridge and Oxford cannot help me."

"The best?"

"Aye, must be… they charged enough."

I was now curious of the man's disorder, and, I admit, eager to see if I might succeed where some arrogant physician had failed. I know, not all physicians are arrogant, but most are.

"What is the malady which besets you?" I asked. "I will tell you plainly if I can cure it or not."

The man peered at his daughter, sighed with exasperation, then spoke. "'Tis a fistula… just there." He reached an arm stiffly behind his back and poked gently about his ribs, just above the kidneys.

"The physicians, they have treated it with salves and egg albumin?" I guessed.

"Aye. But 'tis no better."

"This fistula – how did it first appear?"

"Near a year ago. I fell from a ladder… struck my back. There was a stick laying on the ground where I fell, a bit of broken plank. A sharp end drove into my back. 'Twas a nasty wound, and will not heal no matter what is applied."

"Nor will it," I told him.

"Never?" The girl gasped.

"Not so long as poultices and salves be the remedy."

"Is there another?" the stationer asked.

"Aye."

"You are sure of this?"

"More so than of ointments."

"What is it you would do?" the girl asked.

"The fistula oozes blood and pus, does it not?"

"Aye," the sufferer agreed.

"At its root there will be an abscess. This must be

removed. No salve can do so."

"What must be done?" The stationer was now interested, but hesitantly so.

"The putrid flesh must be excised."

"You mean, cut away?" He frowned.

"Aye. The wound is putrefied and will never heal as it now is. A new cut must be made, to trim away the decay. A clean wound may then heal. A corrupt wound such as you describe never will."

"You can do this?"

"Aye. Well, not now… my instruments are in Bampton."

"Master Hugh is come to Oxford for parchment and ink," the girl said. "He is bailiff in Bampton for…"

"Lord Gilbert Talbot," I assisted the girl.

I saw the man's nose wrinkle in distaste, though he tried to hide it. Given the avaricious reputation of most bailiffs, 'twas understandable. "Lord Gilbert Talbot? He who married Petronilla Boutillier?"

"Aye, the same."

"Great grand-daughter of the first King Edward," the man explained to his daughter.

I could see the girl's mind churning over this information. "She's cousin once removed to t'king, then?" she deduced.

"Aye," the stationer agreed.

"You know Lady Petronilla?" I asked.

"Nay. Heard of her, that's all. Folks like to talk 'bout the gentry, you know."

This is surely so. There are those of the gentry who provide much for the commons to talk about. Lady Petronilla was not such a one to furnish a fertile plot for imaginings to grow, but gossip is a vigorous weed and can take root and prosper in the thinnest soil. I did not ask what the stationer had heard of Lady Petronilla, nor did he volunteer the information.

"You have done such surgery before?" The man asked.

"Many times."

"And was't successful?"

"Not always. A good result depends on what has caused the fistula. If the abscess be too deep, or the product of a cancer, the surgery will not answer."

"But such as mine?"

"I must examine the fistula before I can say if success is likely. But for injuries such as you describe, good fortune often accompanies the work."

The stationer shrugged, looked to his daughter and spoke. "Kate, mind the shop while Master... Hugh, is it?" I nodded. "While Master Hugh has a look at my back."

Kate! The girl's name was Katherine.

The stationer led me to stairs which climbed to the living quarters above the shop. He grimaced once as he twisted to free himself from his cotehardie, and again as he drew up his kirtle. A linen belt wrapped around his body obscured the fistula, but a stain on the cloth showed clearly where it lay.

The stationer unwrapped the linen girdle, the turned his back to me. "'Tis a great trial. What think you? Can you deal with it, or will this be the end of me? I don't like to talk so before Kate, but I know a thing like this can take a man to his grave."

"It could," I agreed. "A stick of wood did this, you say?"

"Aye. Broken it was, and sharp. Punched through cotehardie and kirtle like a blade."

"You fell a great distance?"

"Aye. The ladder broke when I would have repaired the sign above my father's shop in Cambridge. The sign came down in a storm, whence came the splinter as well. Pitched me into the street on my back."

"Did any fragments of the broken limb work out of the wound?"

"After Kate drew the splinter from my back? Not that I recall."

"You suffer pain when you twist your body, is this not so?"

"Aye."

I pulled the skin of the stationer's back apart the better to see the fistula, then squeezed the flesh together. The man gasped, and yellowish pus oozed from the injury.

"Can you do aught for me?" he asked through clenched teeth.

"I can. 'Tis my belief that a fragment of the stick you fell on may be lodged in your back."

"You can remove it?"

"Aye, but not today. My instruments are in Bampton."

"When? Tomorrow?"

"You are eager to see this done," I smiled.

"Was it your back and your wound, you would be also." He chuckled in spite of his discomfort.

"'Tis so, I'm sure. I have business for Lord Gilbert tomorrow, but next day I will return to deal with this. You should have ready then a jug of wine, and some ale."

"You wish me drunk for this surgery?"

"No," I laughed. "I will put powdered herbs into the ale. They will help you deal with the pain. The wine is to wash the wound when I am done."

"Day after tomorrow, you say?"

"Aye. And now I must return to Bampton. I have purchased a gathering of parchment and a pot of ink. What is your charge?"

"Ah… if you can relieve me of this affliction I will supply all the parchments and ink you wish until the Lord's return."

As he spoke the man wrapped himself in the stained linen belt and donned his kirtle and cotehardie.

"You have the better of me," I said. "You know my name, I do not know yours."

"I am remiss," he frowned. "My injury often drives other thoughts from my mind. I am Robert Caxton. My daughter, Katherine, you have met."

"Indeed. A most lovely young woman."

I feared I had misspoke myself, for the stationer made no reply, nor even gave me a glance. No doubt he had heard such appraisals before.

Caxton was on his way down the stairs to the shop before he spoke again. "Favors her mother," he said softly.

As he had vowed, the stationer would take no pay for his ink and parchments. I clutched the bundle under an arm, promised to return two days hence, and walked through the clamor of Oxford's streets to the Stag and Hounds and the patient Bruce.

Chapter 11

There is much to be said for Oxford's bustle and energy, but after nearly two years in bucolic Bampton I was not sorry to cross the river and leave the din behind. I arrived at Bampton Castle too late for dinner, which was become my custom since Easter. I spent the afternoon at my duties for Lord Gilbert, chief of which was seeing to the construction of new stables for the marshalsea. John Holcutt had the work well in hand, but was pleased to relinquish the business to me and seek his occupation in Lord Gilbert's fields. John is better suited to beasts and grain than adze and hammer.

The builders needed little advice from me. Corner posts were set true and tenons and crossbeams fit tightly. Of course the workmen knew that I or John would observe their work, so I cannot say whether the labor would have been done so well due to pride alone.

I advised the marshalsea that, after a day of rest, I would require Bruce again, and on the Thursday before Whitsunday I slung a pack full of herbs and instruments over his rump and set off again for Oxford.

This day was not so pleasant as that of the journey three days earlier. Thickening clouds blew in from Wales and before I was past Cote a cold mist began to fall. I saw no sign of life in the villages I passed, but for the occasional wisp of smoke from a gable vent which hung thick and low in the air 'til it mingled with the drizzle.

The mist became a steady rain before I reached the Thames Bridge. Bruce and I were soaked through before we reached the Stag and Hounds. I left instructions for the old horse to be dried thoroughly and fed, washed down a dinner of coney pie with a mug of watery ale, and set off for Holywell Street and my patient.

I was expected. The shop was shuttered against the weather, but my knuckles made contact with the door but once before it swung open. I stood, dripping, with my fist ready to strike the door again. A distant observer might have thought I had it in mind to rap on the nose the one who greeted me. This was assuredly not so, for Kate peered around the door as she opened it, and smiled when she saw 'twas me. I melted. And not because of my sodden condition.

The shop was equipped with fireplace and chimney, as befits a prosperous merchant. The girl drew me to the fire and pulled a bench close. She took my cloak and hung it beside the fire. I sat, steaming and dripping, as she called up the stairs to her father.

The shop was dark, lit only by the fire. Even were the shutters open there was not enough light on such a day to see my work. And with rain yet falling I could not proceed even in the toft. I had no choice but to delay the surgery.

I told Caxton this as he took a place on another bench opposite me. I could not see in the darkened room whether his face reflected relief at the postponement, or dismay that the deliverance he sought would not soon appear.

The stationer sat stiffly on his bench. One who knew not of his affliction might think him a hard, rigid man. But I had seen him deal with young customers and knew his posture was more likely due to his discomfort than a measure of his character.

Kate had busied herself in the room behind the shop when her father appeared. I saw her approach through the corner of my eye carrying two leather tankards which she offered to me and her father.

"Ale," she advised, "fresh-brewed."

"I have in my sack some herbs to add to your father's ale. 'Twill make a potion to relieve the pain of surgery. Should the sky clear we may then proceed without delay."

I had dropped my bag on a table when I entered the shop. I went to it and fished about in its damp recesses until I found the stoppered bottles I sought. One contained ground willow bark, the other the pounded seeds of hemp. I poured a generous amount from each into one of the tankards and gave it to the stationer.

"These herbs will make the pain of surgery less severe," I told the man as he drank. "But you will be afflicted, even so."

Caxton peered at me over his tankard, then tipped it and swallowed more.

"The potion will take effect in an hour or two," I told him. "Let us hope God will clear the sky so we may proceed with our business."

"Amen," the stationer agreed, and finished his potion.

The benches upon which we sat were of unequal length. The stationer's was short. Kate had directed me to the longer of the two. I resumed my place and there lifted my untouched tankard to drink when the girl reappeared from the hidden room behind the shop. She carried a smaller cup. I saw her glance at the two benches, divined her intent, and slid to the end of mine so she might sit. I wondered if she might think this invitation too forward. She did not, and sat primly next to me without a look in my direction. Her father, however, scrutinized us intently. I saw in the firelight his eyes flicker from me to his daughter and back again.

"Have you lived long in Bampton?" he asked.

"Two years come Michaelmas. I thought to practice surgery here in Oxford, and set up for a time on the High Street. But Lord Gilbert Talbot invited me to Bampton after I was of service to him."

"You hale from Oxford, then?"

"Nay... Lancashire. My father held the manor of Little Singleton of Sir Robert de Sandford, but as I am the youngest of four sons I was sent to Oxford to study and make my own way in the world."

"Hmmm," he mused. "Most scholars who do

business here intend to serve at law, or in holy orders. I know of none who studies surgery."

"That was my intent as well... to be a lawyer and advise kings. But a friend gave me a book. 'Twas about surgical practice. I read it through three times and when I completed the course of study at Baliol College I set off for Paris and the university there, where the book's author, Henry de Mondeville, had once taught."

"You were welcomed there?" Kate asked with some surprise.

"Aye. Even though we held the French king, a student paying his way was accepted though he came from England. And I did not brag of the English victory at Poitiers."

"A good friend," the stationer observed, "to give away a book."

"'Twas a dying bequest. Four years ago, when the plague returned, he was stricken. I did what I could to ease him. For that service he gave me his three books."

As I spoke I noted a sudden gleam appear between wall and shutter. But it quickly faded. Then the opening to the room at the rear of the shop lightened as a brief flash of sunlight came through a skin-covered window in the rear of the house.

The stationer looked toward the floor beams above his head. We were silent for a moment, then he spoke: "The rain has stopped."

Kate rose from the bench, walked silently to the door, and pulled it open. A few drops yet fell from the thatching. The sky was mostly grey, but dotted with tiny swift-moving patches of blue where the cloud cover was beginning to break.

I stood in the doorway the better to observe the weather and felt Kate close behind me. Unlike some young women – and older, too – whose presence can be detected by the scent of their unwashed bodies, the girl exuded the pleasant fragrance of soapwort and woodbine with which she had recently freshened her clothes. Crones say that if honeysuckle be brought into a home there will soon be a wedding. I regarded the sky and wondered if the girl had a husband in mind.

The stationer rose slowly from his seat and glanced between us at the broken clouds. "Think you to proceed?" he asked.

"Aye. If the table is placed in the toft there will be light enough to see my work."

Kate helped me drag the heavy table into the space behind the shop. The door from the small back room into the toft was barely wide enough to serve. Caxton tried to assist, but the exertion caused him to catch his breath and turn red in the face.

I instructed the stationer to remove his cotehardie and kirtle while I returned to the shop for my instruments. When I returned he was standing beside the table shivering. 'Twas not a warm day. Still, I expect his quaking had more to do with uncertainty about my skill than the chilly air.

I sent Kate for the wine, then assisted Caxton on to the table. I had him stretched face-first on the planks when the girl returned.

It is my practice to bathe in wine the place where I intend to make an incision. There is no tradition which calls for this, but it seems to me that if washing a wound in wine after the cut is made will aid healing, then perhaps doing so before applying the knife may be beneficial also.

So I poured wine over the exposed fistula and wiped the liquid about with a scrap of clean linen. Caxton winced as the wine touched his sore, but otherwise lay quietly while I set out my instruments. Kate stood in the doorway, uncertain whether or not to stay. She saw me glance in her direction, and spoke: "Must I go?"

"No. Observers do not trouble me. But there will be blood, and your father may cry out in pain. Should you swoon, I will be too busy to assist you."

"May I help?"

"I think not. This surgery will not require three hands."

I scraped pus and crusted ooze from the fistula, then

probed the putrid flesh with a lancet. I hoped to feel some resistance just under the skin which might tell me that the wood fragment I suspected was not lodged deep. But I felt nothing though I thoroughly probed the area between two ribs where the fistula lay.

While I poked at Caxton's ribs his daughter left her place at the door and stood by her father's head. She took his outstretched hands in hers and waited, her eyes fixed on me as I laid the lancet aside and selected a scalpel.

With this blade I enlarged the fistula in a line parallel to the ribs. I took three separate strokes to deepen the cut until I thought it had reached to the ribs, but no deeper. I wished to avoid entering the abdominal cavity, unless such trespass be unavoidable.

The laceration I thus made was longer than a man's finger; longer, perhaps, than needful, but I wished no interference with my inspection of the abscess. With the blade I pushed aside flesh and fat to the depth of my incision. There was pus there, and corrupt flesh about the fistula, but no foreign object.

I stood upright and wiped sweat and a stray lock of hair from my eyes. The day remained cloudy and cool, but I perspired. There was nothing to do but enlarge the incision and continue the search for the root of the fistula.

A few strokes of the blade added a knuckle's length to the cut. The stationer, who aside from an occasional gasp through clenched teeth, had been quiet, now twitched and writhed under my knife. Kate stood silent, her hands tight to her father's. Not once did she look away from the bloody wound I had made in her father's back.

I separated flesh from rib with my scalpel in this extended incision and there glimpsed the cause of Caxton's distress. It was indeed a fragment of broken oak, driven so deep into the fellow's back it had lodged under a rib, between the bone and abdominal wall, just above a kidney.

I tried to tease the offending fragment from under the rib with the point of my scalpel but could not. Some hard, white gristle with which I was not familiar had nearly encapsulated the wood and held it firmly in place.

With the blade in my left hand to open the wound I took forceps in my right hand and found the end of the embedded splinter. The first tug was unsuccessful. The forceps slipped from the gristle. I found the fragment again, grasped the thing more tightly, and pulled.

A sliver near the size of my little finger came out from under the stationer's rib. He gasped and his legs jerked, but he did not cry out. He is a person of great fortitude, as is his daughter. She watched the process from beginning to end without blanching.

I took the offending fragment, still held tight in my forceps, to the end of the table and held it before the stationer's watering eyes. "This was lodged beneath a rib," I explained.

Caxton raised his head to inspect the fragment. "Much thanks," he whispered.

"I will stitch the wound and you will soon be good as new."

I requested more wine from Kate, and threaded a needle while she ran to fetch it. I closed the wound with fourteen stitches, bathed the cut in wine, and when I was done assisted Caxton to a sitting position on the table.

"'Tis improved already," he exclaimed. "Will you dress it now?"

I was again required to explain that I follow the practice of Henry de Mondeville, who taught that wounds heal best when dry and uncovered. Aside from the occasional poultice of egg albumin, a wound left open mends most readily. I know that this practice contradicts the ancients and the university physicians, but de Mondeville saw his method work in practice. I am a Baliol man, so I should not write this; perhaps the books are wrong.

Caxton seemed unconvinced of this, but as I had been successful thus far in dealing with his affliction he made no objection. His daughter helped him into kirtle and cotehardie, we dragged the table back into the workroom, and we were done. And just in time. The sky was clearing as evening drew near, and the sun was dropping behind the rooftops to the west of the toft as I completed the needlework on the stationer's back.

I made my way through darkening streets to New Canterbury Hall. I hoped Master John might invite me to occupy the empty room which had been my home two nights earlier. The porter recognized me, for it was not yet dark enough that my features were obscured, and sent me unaccompanied to Master John's chamber.

A dim glow through the window told me that the scholar was within. I rapped upon his door and heard from the other side a bench scrape across the flags. Wyclif drew open the door, his brow furrowed. Behind him a book lay open on a table, under a sputtering cresset. He was clearly annoyed at being disturbed in his study. But then he recognized me in the gloom and a smile washed the frown from his face. Well, I assume it did. Master John's beard obscured his mouth quite thoroughly, but his knitted brow relaxed and he greeted me warmly.

"Master Hugh?"

"Aye... my profession called me to return to Oxford."

"Surgery? Come in and tell me of it."

Wyclif shoved the heavy door closed and drew me to the table where he pulled up a second bench and motioned for me to sit. He took his former place, and studied me across the cresset.

"Now then," he said, "what work have you done this day?"

"I took heed of your advice when we last parted, and sought parchment and ink of the new stationer on the Holywell Street."

"Ah, did you so?" The scholar's eyes crinkled. "Did you find the wares agreeable?"

"Indeed. There is much agreeable about the place."

"I thought you might find it so."

"The stationer was ill disposed," I told him.

"Oh? He seems congenial enough when I call."

"Aye. His affliction distressed him but did not cause him to distress others."

"And what of this affliction?"

I told Master John of the stationer's injury and the surgery I had performed that day. His eyes glowed in the cresset as I related the tale. There are some who dislike hearing of wounds and blood. Wyclif is not such a one. He listened intently, and questioned me twice about the procedure.

"And Caxton's daughter stood at his head the while?" he asked.

"She did... held firm to her father's hands as I worked."

"A remarkable lass," Master John observed. "Do you not agree?"

"Aye. And others find it so, as well. It was as you suggested, I should find the stationer's shop by the students at his door. There were three as I entered Tuesday."

"She does no harm to her father's business, I think," Wyclif observed.

"You suggest that parchment and ink are not enough to attract an Oxford youth?"

"Enough? What is ever enough?"

"A good meal taken in a hall with pleasant companions," I asserted. "Is that not enough for a man?"

"Hmmm," Wyclif shrugged and pursed his lips. "For a time... but you would not refuse such a feast were it offered again next day."

"Then the labors of the mind; are they not enough for a man?"

"For some, perhaps."

"For you?" I probed.

"Ha. You think me immune to the charms of the stationer's daughter?"

"Kate... Katherine?"

"Yes. I heard her name spoken once. I will tell you, Hugh, were I married I would yet enjoy my books. Now I am wed to books... can I not enjoy the sight of a pretty maid?"

"Do not carry the parallel too far, Master John."

"Nay," he laughed. "All analogies eventually break down, useful as they may be."

"Do not your books grow tiresome?"

"Sometimes... as I suppose a beautiful woman may also grow tiresome be she of an ill-favored character."

"What of the stationer's daughter?" I asked.

"Kate?" He smiled. "She seems a pleasant lass... not only to the eye, I mean."

"So I think, although I've met her only twice." I laughed then, which Master John must have thought out of place, for he pursed his lips and his brow lowered. "Here we sit," I explained, "talking of a comely maid as if we sat in the din of the Stag and Hounds. Surely this is a topic in the air of that establishment as we speak."

"No doubt," he smiled, "and perhaps the same lass be under consideration."

I could not say why at that moment, but the thought of Kate Caxton as a subject for discussion in the Stag and Hounds caused me some unease.

"Perhaps," I agreed. "'Tis safer to speak of a lass than politics or religion."

"Aye. Few have lost their heads for commenting on a lady's face or form."

"Unless a noble husband or father be near and take offence," I offered.

"Just so," the scholar smiled.

Wyclif had pushed his book aside to clear the table before us. I glanced at the volume, still open, and saw that it was a book of Old Testament prophets. Master John followed my gaze and answered my unspoken question.

"Habakkuk... a minor prophet not often studied. But I find all scripture profitable. It speaks to those who will listen."

"I have never read this prophet," I admitted. "What does he say?"

"He lived in troublous times... much like our own. Listen as he speaks to God." Wyclif bent over his book, turned back a page, and ran a finger down the lines. "Why do you show me iniquity, and cause me to see trouble? For plundering and violence are before me; there is strife, and contention arises. Therefore the law is powerless, and justice never goes forth. For the wicked surround the righteous; therefore perverse judgment proceeds."

The scholar raised his eyes to mine. "God speaks to me in this passage. Does He not to you?"

"Aye. Iniquity, trouble, plundering, violence, strife, contention... such is the world. My position requires me to deal with these ills. Does God supply a remedy for the prophet? Has he a word from God?"

"He does, though not what a man might expect." Master John turned a page and squinted at the script through narrowed eyes. "Ah... here... 'Behold the proud, his soul is not upright in him; but the just shall live by his faith.'"

"Is this the antidote to evils? That a just man live by his faith?" My bewilderment was evident in my voice.

"Ah, Hugh, do you not see? All these evils perplexed the world then as they do now. How can a just man fight them? Can a man reform the world?"

"Unlikely, what I've seen of it."

"True. Yet a man must do battle against wrong when and where he can, if God grants him courage for the struggle, as He has you, I think."

"But I will not win that fight, will I? See all those of the past who fought valiantly against wickedness, but evil yet grips the world and shows no sign of letting go."

"It does," Wyclif agreed, "and will until God sends His Son to return."

"What, then? Must a man strive and yet know he will face defeat in the end?"

"What is defeat? When a man comes to his grave, having done all he can to serve God and man, will he not inherit an eternal place with God? Is that not victory?"

"Aye," I agreed, "but long delayed."

"Well," Wyclif laughed, "most men hope 'twill be long delayed."

"So until that final victory a virtuous man must live

in an earthly struggle he will surely lose?"

"Not so, Hugh. Do not be so melancholy. 'The just shall live by faith.' The apostle Paul says much the same thing in his letter to the Ephesians. Though the devil and his minions do their worst, the just man will live because of his faith."

"Even should one of satan's minions slay him?"

"Even so. His faith will grant him life on earth, and in the world to come."

"What of a man's deeds?"

"The prophets all speak of righteous living. 'Tis expected of a man."

"Will a man then live also by his deeds?"

"Perhaps," Wyclif mused. "But actions seldom bring a man to faith."

"Whereas faith will spur a man to act," I completed his thought.

"Aye."

"'Tis my faith in you has brought me to your door," I added. "I have faith you will provide me a place to sleep this night, as you did two days past."

"Your faith will be rewarded. Have you supped?"

"No. I thought to seek an inn before I retire."

"The streets are dark. Best I send you to the kitchen. The cook will have something for you."

He did, and a loaf for my breakfast, as well.

I slept well, and in the morning retrieved Bruce from the stable behind the Stag and Hounds. I had set out for Bampton when a thought caused me to pull on the reins and turn the old horse toward Holywell Street. I should visit my patient before I depart. This duty was made more satisfying with the knowledge that the stationer's daughter might be present. She was, and greeted me when I entered the shop. Her father was not at hand.

"I have come to see your father before I return to Bampton," I announced. I looked about the empty shop, worried that the man was suffering ill effects from the surgery. "Is he yet in his bed this morning?"

The girl laughed. "Nay. Come and see."

I followed her through the door to the workroom, and from there could see through the open door into the toft. The stationer was there, plying a spade.

"He awoke this morning and decided 'twas not too late to plant vegetables. He has been at the work for an hour already."

The stationer saw us standing in the door and ceased his labor. He brushed a lock of his thinning hair from his sweating forehead, leaned on the spade, and grinned at me. "I thought I would never sow a garden again."

"The wound does not trouble you?" I asked. I was startled to see him so employed less than a day after I had sliced into his ribs.

"'Tis a bit sore, and I was stiff when I rose from my bed. But this," he looked about him at the earth he had turned, "has worked out much of the ache."

Caxton must have seen the surprise in my eyes and mistook it for concern. His countenance fell, and he added, "Have I done wrong, to engage in this work so soon?"

The stationer had stripped off his cotehardie and worked in his kirtle. I looked to his back to see if the linen was stained but no discharge from the wound was evident on the fabric.

"If there is little pain I think you do well. But you must not exert yourself so that the stitches tear. As I said yesterday, I will return in a fortnight to remove the sutures. Even after that there is some danger that the wound may reopen."

"So I should lay down my shovel, then?"

"No. But do the work with care. Do not strain to lift a heavy clod."

"I will heed your advice. You finished the work and departed yesterday before I thought to pay you. What is your fee?"

"I thought we had a bargain," I smiled.

"Ah," Caxton laughed. "parchment and ink for surgery. Do you write much? This back of mine may cost me dear."

"I am well supplied. But when I return to remove

the stitches I may have need of another gathering."

"You shall have it, and gladly."

Kate stood silent between us as the conversation unfolded, but now she spoke. "If you fix a day for your return to deal with the stitches I will prepare a meal for you."

I thought of the day, and the stationer's healing, and made reply. "Your father is not a young man. His wound will take longer to mend. Perhaps a fortnight is too little time. Let us say the Wednesday after Corpus Christi? The wound will have six more days to knit."

Caxton looked from me to his daughter during this exchange. There was a somber smile on his face, as if he witnessed a thing which caused him both pleasure and distress.

The day set for removal of the stitches was agreeable, so we then parted; I to mount Bruce and set him for Bampton, Caxton to return to his spade, and Kate to her work in the shop.

Oxford began the day under mixed clouds and sun, but as I crossed the Castle Mill Stream Bridge the clouds thickened and lowered. I rode through a gloomy countryside, which did nothing to lift my spirit. By the time I saw the spire of St Beornwald's Church poking above the trees my soul was in deep melancholy.

I thought to analyze why this was so, for there seemed little reason for my funk. I had completed a successful surgery, I had made the acquaintance of a beautiful young woman, I inhabited the castle of a lord, in a town where I held the respect of many. Why, then, did my mood lie as low as the clouds drifting above the church spire?

It was for some of these same reasons. I had met a winsome lass, but would not see her again for many days. And in Bampton I must resume the search for a murderer. Would I yet be respected should I fail? Many might wish me no success, for Henry atte Bridge had few friends. Perhaps the town would admire me more should I fail.

And if Henry atte Bridge slew Alan the Beadle, why did he do so? Leaving Bampton had meant leaving this puzzle also. But now it was approaching, with the town.

I am distressed to admit that no solution to any of these riddles occurred to me in the following days. 'Twas a Friday that I rode from Oxford home to Bampton. I busied myself about Lord Gilbert's work on Saturday, and called for hot water in the evening to bathe and prepare myself for Whitsunday.

Chapter 12

Many who approached St Beornwald's Church on Sunday morning wore red – if they owned a garment of that color – in honor of the day. I do not possess garb of red and so could not play the peacock.

As customary, few attended matins, but the village filled the church for the mass. Sunday dawned as cloudy and cool as the previous day had ended, though it was the first day of June. But during the service, when Father Simon kissed the pax-board and sent it to the congregation, a flash of sunlight illuminated the church's south windows. By the time Father Thomas shared the holy loaf the sun flooded the church with brilliant light much as the gospel of our Lord must have filled the Holy City on that day men preached His salvation to all, each in his own tongue.

The appearance of the sun raised my spirits. Why should this be so? Nothing about me or my situation was changed. But a June day should be washed in sunlight. When 'tis cloudy in February men are not disposed to complain for they expect it so. But June? If the sun shines not in June when may a man expect it to do so?

All who left the church that day must have been affected as I was, for there was a joyful babble of voices as villagers dispersed through the churchyard and lych gate. It is well the sun could lift their mood, for it is unlikely their dinner this day would do so. Most families have by June long since consumed the provisions they laid by in the autumn. And the next harvest was yet some months to come.

I could not forebear to halt on the bridge and watch the waters of Shill Brook pass under my feet. Dinner at the castle was an hour away, the sun was warm on my back, and the splashing of the stream over the mill dam was like music.

While I leaned upon a bridge timber the miller and his wife approached. The calm which had submerged my soul like a stone in the brook vanished. My eyes went to the stiffened linen on his arm and the sling which supported it. That vision brought with it a flood of memories. Memories of Holy Week, and the unholy events of those days. From those thoughts my mind had to travel but a short way to fasten upon my unmet obligations.

The miller and his wife greeted me, unaware of the effect their presence had upon my mood. "When will you remove this?" the miller asked, lifting his arm to me as he spoke.

"'Tis near time enough... You have no aches to distress you?"

"Nay," Andrew smiled. "Not these many weeks. 'Twas hurtful at first, mind you, but no longer. Itches, though."

I counted back the weeks. "Thursday will be eight weeks... long enough, I think."

The miller sighed with satisfaction. His wife also appeared pleased. No doubt she had seen her labors increase because of he husband's affliction.

The stout couple bid me good day and moved on up the bank toward the mill and their cottage. I turned back to the stream, but as I did so I heard rapid footsteps on the planks behind me. The sound intruded upon my thoughts because most who crossed the bridge that day did so with leisurely pace. I peered over my shoulder to see who it was who walked with such hasty determination. 'Twas Emma, widow of Henry atte Bridge, who thumped her way across the boards. If she saw or recognized me she gave no sign.

The woman marched across the bridge and to my astonishment turned from the road to follow the miller and his wife up the muddy path which led along the brook to the mill. I wondered what business she could have at the mill on Sunday, but my curiosity gradually faded under the calming influence of the stream's bubbling flow.

I soon pulled myself from the bridge. How would it look for Lord Gilbert's chief officer in Bampton to spend his time gazing vaguely into Shill Brook?

I was but a few steps along Mill Street from the bridge when the sound of angry voices reached my ears. I could not distinguish the words, but a male and a female were alternating in a shouting match and it was surely a wrathful exchange. I paused and looked toward the mill, for the tumult came from the open cottage door.

As I stared at the cottage I saw the miller's wife peer from the door, as if to see if any had heard the altercation. Her eyes fastened upon me and she quickly withdrew. An instant later the house became silent. Shrill voices were no more. The excitement now past, I continued to the castle and my dinner.

The gatehouse of Bampton Castle faces west. The town is to the east of the castle, and Mill Street passes along the south curtain wall. I had completed the passage along the south wall and turned north to the gatehouse when I glanced one last time toward the mill. It was well I did.

I saw Emma atte Bridge stalk from the mill, cross Mill Street, and disappear down the lane to the Weald and her hut. Over a shoulder she had slung a sack. She had not entered the mill with any sack. Why she should leave with one, on a day the mill wheel did not turn, I could not guess. Such behavior did seem odd. I thought on it as I passed through the gatehouse on my way to dinner.

The meal drove further contemplation of Emma atte Bridge and her sack from my thoughts. The event did not return to mind until Thursday, when I set out for the mill to remove Andrew's cast.

The week after Whitsunday is peculiar, of course, divided as it is between solemnity and frivolity. Wednesday, Friday and Saturday are Ember Days, when men are to spend the hours in fasting and prayer, contemplating the health of their soul. But Monday, Tuesday and Thursday are days of frolic and feasting. Lord Gilbert would have no work done this week.

The sluice gate was not open on Thursday, nor did the mill wheel turn, for the miller meant to enjoy a day free from labor, with his arm newly freed from the embrace of stiffened linen. The door of the miller's cottage was open to the June sun. Andrew sat on a bench just inside his door, enjoying the warmth, and saw me approach. He stood as I walked up the path from Mill Street.

"If you will draw that bench out, we may enjoy the sun and I will have good light to see my work," I said by way of greeting.

The miller grunted and with his good arm pulled on the bench until it bounced over the threshold and wobbled on the uneven ground before the cottage door. Andrew adjusted it until it was stable while I unslung my pouch from a shoulder and drew from it a set of tongs with which to nip off chunks of the plaster until the miller's arm was free.

We sat facing each other at opposite ends of the bench and I set to work. The image of Emma stalking from the mill with her sack had been in my mind since I approached the place, so I spoke of it.

"You had words with Emma atte Bridge on Whitsunday."

Andrew made no reply, but stared at his arm, as if his concentration was essential to the work. I decided to make a reply easier for him.

"From my experience with her, 'tis no great difficulty to begin a dispute with Emma."

The miller smiled thinly. "Aye. She can be quarrelsome."

"As was Henry," I replied. "I wonder, did two like souls find each other, or did the one make the other so?"

"What difference?" Andrew grimaced.

"Aye," I agreed. "We who live with such must deal with the effect, regardless the cause."

The miller made no reply, but watched warily as my tongs chewed through the remainder of his plaster. I was near finished with the work and so could wait no longer for the miller to explain his dispute with the widow atte

Bridge. I had given him opportunity to defend himself and belittle Emma, but he refused the offer.

"I saw her leave the mill with a sack."

Still the miller made no reply, but continued to study his arm as the tongs bit through the last of the stiffened linen. When the last of the plaster fell away Andrew flexed his arm, then looked at me and smiled.

"Good as ever?" I asked.

"Aye, so 'tis."

"The sack Emma carried... 'twas meal she was owed?"

The miller's smile faded. "She thought so."

"It was not so?"

"Nay," he said with some vehemence. "Claimed Henry'd brought barley to be ground and had not received 'is return."

"'Tis an odd time of year to bring barley to the mill."

"Aye," Andrew hesitated, as if he would say more, but thought better of it.

"Did Henry do so... bring barley to the mill? Or was she mistaken?"

"She, uh, was mistaken."

"I wonder that Henry would tell her so. Surely she would learn it was not so, did he yet live."

"Aye... but he does not."

"So 'twas your word 'gainst that of a dead man?"

"Aye. An' 'tis not well to speak ill of the dead."

"Even one like Henry atte Bridge?"

"'Specially 'Enry. Spirits lurk about to do evil to them as speak ill of the dead."

"So you gave up the meal to preserve peace with Emma?"

"I did. From my own store I gave her a peck."

"And she was satisfied?"

"Aye."

From the town, across Shill Brook, we heard the sound of pipes, drums, and laughter. Dancers were forming in the marketplace. Moments later the miller's wife and son appeared in the door, peering first at me, then across the brook to the east and the town. They wished to be off to join the merriment. So did I.

I trailed the miller and his family up Bridge Street. Most of the town was already gathered in the marketplace, either to join the dancing or encourage participants.

I am not given to noisy exhibitions, so my cheering was less exuberant than most. Nevertheless, I cheer better than I dance, so my weak exhortation must suffice. Were I to dance the assembly would collapse in mirth at what might appear to be a disjointed scarecrow suddenly granted life.

I stood at the rear of the mob of onlookers, able to see over the crowd, as my height is greater than most. I saw young Will Shillside cavorting gracefully amongst the dancers. Just opposite my place I watched Alice atte Bridge squeeze to the front of the throng. Her eyes fastened upon young Shillside and sparkled with pleasure at the exhibition. Well, yes, I suppose I was too far away to see sparkling eyes, but from her countenance it is fair to say her eyes must have twinkled at least a little.

I leaned back against the house which stands where Bell Lane joins the Broad Street, content to observe rather than join those who cavorted in the street. I was surprised to see Edmund the smith press through the throng and join the dancers. I had thought him a stolid, humorless sort, but he pranced with abandon, and gracefully, also. I was amazed that a man of his bulk could move so pleasingly.

Edmund's dancing did not hold my interest for long. After observing him circle the marketplace my eyes drifted to the crowd of onlookers. Among these I saw Philip the baker and his wife. They did not stand together. Philip was but a few paces to my left. His wife was near Alice, opposite my place. Her eyes were fixed on the dancers and her face glowed with admiration. Well, it glowed with something.

I looked from Alice to Margery, the baker's wife, and saw the same expression on both faces. Alice's attention was yet fixed upon Will Shillside. What, or who, I wondered, put the color into Margery's cheeks?

Her eyes followed the dancers and my eyes followed hers until they rested upon the sweating, twirling form of Edmund the smith. Sweat ran in rivulets from Edmund's forehead and cheeks and left glistening streaks through the soot on his unwashed face.

The dancers tended to twirl as they cavorted about the marketplace, so each participant passed my place several times. Their exertions caused their brows to flow with sweat, and perspiration soon stained kirtles and cotehardies. The moisture brought with it disagreeable odors when some dancers passed my place. Among the most repulsive was Edmund, who, I think, considered bathing a waste of good water. As he whirled past my wall I noticed others wrinkle noses in distaste and exchange glances. But his smell seemed to cause no annoyance to Margery. She smiled warmly at the blacksmith each time he passed her place. This seemed to encourage the fellow. He spun so enthusiastically I thought he might lose his equilibrium and stumble into the crowd.

He did not, but when the pipers ended the tune he swayed some on his feet, dripping and panting. Then, unaware that I watched, he turned to Margery and grinned, then walked slowly past my place. Philip stood a few paces to my left. As Edmund passed the baker he turned, faced him and smirked, then continued across the marketplace toward his forge. The throng parted to allow Edmund to pass, their noses no doubt warning of his approach.

Onlookers to the dance began to drift away when the musicians showed no intent to resume their tooting and banging, and tired dancers wandered off to their homes and a mug of ale.

Through the thinning throng I saw, across the marketplace, the frowning face of Ralph Dodwell. The vicar's arms were folded tightly across his robe. He did not, I think, approve of the frivolity he had witnessed. As I watched he unclenched his arms and stalked off toward the church and his vicarage.

The glances exchanged between the blacksmith,

the baker, and the baker's wife convinced me there was mischief here. The baker's wounded neck was further evidence. If this triangle became known in the town – and who could say 'twas not already – inhabitants would chose sides in the affair and much disquiet would follow. This would displease Lord Gilbert when he learned of it. I saw it as my duty to prevent such an uproar. I could see but one way to do that.

When I chose the profession of surgeon I did not foresee myself involved in the secret passions of potential patients. Even when Lord Gilbert invited me to serve as bailiff the thought that I might find myself embroiled in illicit lust did not occur to me. But now I found myself in such a place. There are many paths in life which, when chosen, seem broad, smooth, and bright. But after we have traveled down them too far to turn back they become dark, rough and twisted. We are left with no choice but to continue, to make our way as best we can through the snarls and hope for a better journey when we reach the other side of the tangle.

Of the two men, baker and smith, I thought the baker most likely to share the truth if pressed. No man likes to admit he has been cuckolded, but even less would he admit to adultery. And the blacksmith was of more unyielding character than the baker.

So I followed Philip to the bakery, and shouted for him to attend me as he was about to follow his wife through the shop door. Philip glanced at me and frowned, as did Margery, but I paid no heed to their dark looks. I invited Philip to walk with me and without awaiting an answer set off down High Street toward Bushey Row. I was sure the baker would follow. He did. When a lord's bailiff makes a request, 'tis much like a command. May God forgive me my pride, but I enjoy such moments. 'Tis well such times occur, else the onerous duties of a bailiff would overwhelm me.

I slowed my pace as we reached Catte Street so Philip could catch up. He did so at Bushey Row, where I stopped and turned to face him.

"How long," I challenged him, "has your wife betrayed you with Edmund Smith?"

"Betrayed me?"

I thought from his reply and the flash in his eye that the baker might disavow my claim. Indeed, I believe the thought crossed his mind. But denial quickly faded from Philip's face and his eyes dropped to study the mud at our feet.

"Aye... 'tis plain enough."

"It is?" the baker begged. "'Tis known in the town?"

"If not, 'twill soon be, unless the business ends. How long," I asked again, "has this gone on?"

"Near two years, I think," Philip muttered.

"You are uncertain?"

"Aye."

"And this is why you attacked Edmund with his hammer?"

The baker fingered the scar on his neck and mumbled assent.

"Why now? Why did you not confront him when you first suspected?"

The baker looked away, as if to study the forest which lay east toward St Andrew's Chapel. "I... I feared 'twould do no good. Edmund is a strong man. I could not threaten him, nor could I make his deeds known. The town would laugh at me before 'twould censure him."

"So you did nothing?"

"Aye... well, not nothin', like."

"Oh?"

"I thought, was I a better husband Margery might lose interest in Edmund."

"This was not so?"

"Nay." He spat the word. "The more I looked to please her, the more she scorned me. I should have beat her... but I thought that would drive her from me. I see now she thinks me weak."

"You will not beat her now?"

The baker studied the forest again before he answered. "She knows I must think of it. She told me while I lay in bed with my wound that Edmund would defend her and do worse to me should I raise my hand to her."

I was in no way competent to advise any man regarding his wife. We stood silent for a moment, poking toes into the mud, then the baker spoke again. "What will you do?"

I hesitated. Neither Oxford nor Paris had trained me to deal with such a puzzle. But as we faced each other in the road a plan took shape in my mind.

"Return to your wife, and tell her I know all. Tell her that if she sees Edmund again I will fine him for leirwite and raise his rent so high he must leave Bampton. The castle smith can meet town needs 'til another smith be found. Say nothing more to her. If she rants and storms, just smile and go about your business."

"And if she sneaks away to Edmund again?"

"You must tell me straight away."

The baker turned to go, and as he walked away it seemed to me his back was straighter, his shoulders firmer, his head higher. Well, I thought, 'twill be diverting to see how Margery takes the news.

It was my purpose to go straight to Edmund's forge and make demands of him for his future behavior. But as I watched Philip stride away the rotund figure of John Kellet approached down the path from St Andrew's Chapel.

As the priest neared I saw his eyes flick from me to the departing baker and back. His brow seemed creased in worry but when he was close enough to speak he greeted me warmly and his visage cleared.

"Good day, Master Hugh."

Kellet stopped in the path as he greeted me. No doubt he was puzzled as to why the baker and I had enjoyed a conversation while standing in the road far from either the castle or the bakery. I felt no necessity to enlighten him.

"Good day."

The fat priest glanced again over my shoulder at the

departing baker, peered at the sky, then spoke again. "A good day for a man to be free of his labors."

"Aye; any day will serve for that purpose."

"Hah… truly."

I did not intend to startle the fellow, but my next words surely did. Why, I did not then know. "Your skill at archery is great, for one who must see little practice."

Kellet's hands, folded across his belly, twitched, and his head jerked as if he had been slapped. Quickly as these motions appeared, they were gone. But I wondered why complimenting his talent would cause the priest to react so. Perhaps he worried that word of his exhibition had reached the vicars of St Beornwald's Church and put his position in jeopardy.

"'Tis not meet for one who has a vocation to disport himself with arms, so Father Ralph has said."

"There are bishops," I reminded him, "who mount chargers and go to war."

"Aye, well enough for bishops," Kellet grimaced.

"But you must obey Father Ralph or lose your living, eh?"

"Aye," the priest sighed.

During this brief conversation Kellet's eyes continued to dart from me to Philip's retreating back. I wondered what the priest found so compelling about the baker. My next thought provided the answer: the confessional.

I turned and stared in the direction of Kellet's gaze. Philip was at the moment disappearing past the curve of the High Street toward his shop. "A sad tale, that," I sighed, and watched intently from the corner of my eye to see if my words brought a response from the priest.

"The baker?" Kellet asked. "Is he ill? Does his business go badly?"

If the priest dissembled, he did so skillfully. I detected no hint that he knew of Philip's true adversity. Perhaps the baker and his wife confessed their sins at St Beornwald's confessional and Kellet knew nothing.

"Nay. 'Tis another matter vexes him."

The priest stared at me, and looked perplexed when

I explained no more but rather turned to make my way back to the castle. My stomach told me 'twas near time for dinner. As Kellet was headed in the same direction he fell in beside me and was my companion until we came to Broad Street. There he turned aside to the blacksmith's forge. We parted with wordless gestures.

It had been my intention to visit Edmund myself, but I had no wish to wait my turn to speak to him. I could just as well return after dinner. And perhaps my demands of the smith might seem more reasonable to him did I voice them on a full stomach.

Shill Brook beckoned to me as I crossed it on the bridge. I stopped and leaned over the rail to watch the flowing stream. No trout appeared this time. Without the attraction of a fish my eyes turned back to the town where I saw in the distance John Kellet and Edmund the smith in close conversation.

Something about their posture convinced me that the discussion was antagonistic. I lost interest in the brook and watched the two men. The smith stood with his left side to me, so I did not see him cock his right fist or deliver the blow. But the result was plain enough, even from 200 paces distant.

The priest grasped at his belly and dropped to his knees, then fell forward into the dirt, face first, his hands grasping at his stomach. As I watched Kellet tried to lift his face from the road, but no sooner got to his knees than Edmund dropped his strong right fist on the back of the priest's skull and he fell headlong again.

Kellet rolled about in the dirt and mud of the road, which, given his shape, was not difficult for him to do. Edmund stood immobile over him as Kellet alternately clawed at the ground and grabbed at his gut. The priest's thrashing about gradually subsided to more measured motions and he rose again to hands and knees. He remained, swaying, in this position for some time, as if he expected Edmund to thump him across the skull again.

Another blow did not fall. Instead the smith looked up the High Street as if to see if his blows were observed.

He saw me gazing dumbly from the bridge, shrugged, and disappeared into the smithy, leaving John Kellet to stagger to his feet.

The priest lurched to a vertical position, then brushed briefly at his robe and stumbled off down the High Street to the east and his chapel. I had two subjects now to discuss with the smith. It would not be a pleasant interview. My gut was tense, whether from hunger or sympathy for the priest and the blow which dropped him, I know not. I turned from the bridge and walked to the castle and my meal.

I do not remember much about the dinner which followed. My mind was busy with other things. I ate slowly, I remember, as if enjoying a last meal. But when all others who dined at Lord Gilbert Talbot's expense were sated and gone, and the valets drummed their fingers against the stones on which they leaned, I could hesitate no longer. I left the table.

I approached Edmund's forge with much apprehension. I wondered what issue between the smith and John Kellet had caused Edmund to strike the priest, and whether my questions might provoke a similar result. I prayed that the smith would remember my office and restrain himself from attacking Lord Gilbert's bailiff. He did, barely.

The smith, like others in the town and kingdom, did not work this day. His fire was banked. No smoke issued from his chimney. I found him in the dim interior of the smithy, shoving a maslin loaf into his mouth with grimy fingers. Across his broad forehead and cheeks the streaks which the sweat of his dancing had washed clean were yet visible. He looked up at me from his bench, but said nothing and continued to munch his loaf.

"You had a disagreement with John Kellet this day," I said by way of greeting.

Edmund continued to chew, and through a mouthful of bread replied, "Not a disagreement, exactly."

"Oh? What then was it, exactly, which I witnessed?"

The smith tore off another chunk of bread, stuffed

it into his mouth, and only then answered my question. "More an understandin', like."

"What is it then that you and Father John now understand?"

"It's personal, like," Edmund replied, and wiped his mouth with the back of a ham-like fist.

"When personal understandings lead to blows delivered on town streets the, uh, understanding is no longer confidential. And you will surely be reported to the vicars of St Beornwald's Church. No man can expect to assault a priest without censure."

The smith finished the last of his loaf, and stood while he chewed it. His hands, no longer occupied, he clenched and relaxed as they hung from his broad shoulders. Perhaps he intended I witness this, or perhaps it was involuntary. Edmund stood before his bench for a moment, then walked toward me and did not stop until he was close enough that I could smell his breath. The maslin loaf had done little to sweeten that emanation. What charms he held for the baker's wife I cannot guess, but neither his cleanliness nor his fragrance, I think, were part of the attraction.

He stopped his advance inches from me. I could not decide at that moment if I wished to be Hugh de Singleton, surgeon, or Hugh, Lord Gilbert's bailiff. Hugh the surgeon would retreat. Lord Gilbert's bailiff would not be intimidated. I took a deep breath, which Edmund probably noted, nearly choked on the odor, and stood my ground.

The smith was brawny but short. His attempt at intimidation failed in part because when his feet stopped he was staring from inches away at my collar, while I looked down on his greasy, thinning hair. It is always best to be atop the castle wall, looking down on the attacker.

"My doins' wi' t'priest is private," Edmund repeated in a soft voice which nevertheless carried a threat.

"Not when you strike him in the public streets... 'tis no longer private. If he will, he may bring a charge against you at hallmote, or lodge a complaint with the bishop, whom he serves. I saw all, and would be his witness."

A hint of a smile crossed the smith's lips. "He'll make no charge," he assured me.

"It seems no man will make a charge against you. You near slice a man's head off, and thump another in the street, yet neither man will assert their right against you in manor court. I wonder why this can be?"

The smith shrugged but provided no other answer. He left it to me to continue the conversation. Edmund must have disliked staring at my collarbone, for as I spoke he backed away a step. It was a small victory.

"I have learned a thing which may disturb the serenity of the town," I said softly. "Lord Gilbert would be distressed should he return and find it so."

"What has this to do with me?" Edmund challenged.

"Much, as you well know."

Before the smith could object I continued, "You are not to see Margery, the baker's wife, again. If I find that you have done so I will levy leirwite against you. Twelve pence, I think. And I will double... no, triple your rent."

Edmund was not intimidated.

"Bah, I care little for your threats. The town needs a smith. Where will you find another if you force me out?"

"The castle smith will deal with town business 'til we can replace you."

Edmund's eyes fell to study the clinkers at his feet. He had not considered this, I think.

"There be other towns happy to find a smith," he replied. "You cannot harm me by drivin' me off."

"I have no wish to do you harm. I will act only to preserve the peace on Lord Gilbert's manor of Bampton... as I am bound to do. If you see Margery again you will be free to seek another town. After you pay the fine for leirwite."

As I spoke I moved closer to the smith, so he was again forced to either stare at my neck or look up to my face. I braced myself against the odor and held my ground. I hope Lord Gilbert will appreciate the sacrifices I make to preserve good order on this manor.

Edmund shrugged and stepped back again. Another success. "Was gettin' too costly, anyway," he muttered, then turned to his cold forge.

I did not know what may have been costly about the smith's dealings with the baker's wife. She demanded presents, I assumed.

"You will heed this warning, then?"

"Aye," Edmund growled to the back wall of his smithy. As he spoke he grasped his hammer in what seemed a perfunctory gesture. I decided that so long as I had his acquiescence I would not press further a man with an iron hammer in his strong right hand. I turned to leave, but before I departed the cinder-coated toft I spoke once more. I could not resist nailing down a triumph.

"My eyes and ears will be open to discover if you keep this bargain," I said in my sternest voice, several paces now from Edmund and his hammer.

I suppose Edmund heard, but he gave no sign. He continued to stroke the hammer handle while he stared at the blank back wall of the smithy. I left him there.

If I could not learn the reason for John Kellet's bellyache from Edmund, I thought I might do so from the priest, so I set off from the smithy toward St Andrew's Chapel.

Trees along the way were in the full bloom of June. Brilliant shades of green filled the space between fields and sky. I wonder why God chose to color his leafy creation green when it is living, and red and gold when dying? Were I God I would have done it the other way round.

There is much about this world which would be different were it created by men. And most men think did they have the job, they could make a better world than the one we possess. But when I see the muddle men have made of the world they are given, it seems unlikely to me that, with the opportunity, they could create a better.

I resolved to be content with green summer foliage. Perhaps in heaven there will be time enough in eternity for God to take questions. There are many things I would ask of Him, not just His choice of color for a leaf.

These maunderings so occupied me that I was upon St Andrew's Chapel before I had time to think of questions I might ask John Kellet. I need not have concerned myself with this, for the priest's condition, when I found him, brought with it its own questions.

Chapter 13

The chapel door was ajar. I pushed it open on squealing hinges and stepped into the structure, waiting there until my eyes became accustomed to the gloom. The chapel is ancient, and its windows few and small, from a time when glass was rare and more dear than even now it is. And those few, narrow panes were coated in dust and grime, so little light entered even where it might. 'Tis an insult to our Lord, I think, to allow his house to decay so.

My eyes adjusted to the shadows as these thoughts swept through my mind. The priest wore black, an excellent camouflage in such a place, so when I first scanned the room I did not see him. Not until I studied more closely the tower steps – an especially dark corner of the chapel – did I see the man sitting on the lower step, his arms across his belly, slowly rocking to and fro.

The priest was so lost in his own misery that he had not noticed my entry. The opening door had permitted a shaft of light to penetrate the chapel, but the priest's eyes were closed. He muttered to himself as he swayed on the step.

It is, I know, improper to intrude on a man's thoughts at such a time. But had I not done so I might have been much longer at unraveling the tangled deaths of Alan the beadle and Henry atte Bridge.

Kellet's complaints covered the sound of my entry and approach, so that I stood quite close to the man and heard his words clearly. "Damn him... he'll pay. An' the others, too. Damn him. Henry got hinges... I'll have more'n that. Damn him... he'll pay... a penny... no, tuppence a month or I'll see that all know."

"All know what?" I asked.

The priest jerked as if Edmund had boxed his ears. His head snapped back, his eyes opened wide with fear, and he leaped to his feet – a move which surprised me, given the size and apparent affliction of his belly.

The beam of light from the open door was behind me. My face was in shadow, my form silhouetted against the light. I believe the priest thought for a moment that the blacksmith had followed him to the chapel and overheard his groaning threats. But my form is nothing like that of Edmund, which Kellet quickly noted. His hands had flown up to protect his paunch, but fell when he realized he was not in danger of another blow.

"Who... who is't?" he stammered.

"'Tis Hugh. I congratulate you, for having the forethought to prepare sufficient padding against this day."

"Padding?"

"I saw you suffer Edmund's blow. Will you complain of him to the bishop? Or present a charge at hallmote? I am your witness, whichever you choose."

"I, uh, am undecided," the priest whispered.

"What was it caused Edmund to strike you? I saw from a distance your conversation with him, and then the blow."

"Uh... 'tis a private matter."

"Hmmm. Edmund said much the same."

"You spoke to him?" the priest asked quickly, with, I thought, some alarm in his voice.

"Aye. He said little. Said you and he had an 'understanding.' I fail to understand an understanding sealed with a blow."

"A private matter," the priest asserted again. "Uh... from the confessional."

"Edmund confesses at the chapel?" I asked with, I suspect, some incredulity in my voice.

"He did... but no longer, I think," Kellet spoke somewhat ruefully, and rubbed his bruised gut as he did so.

"So you will let this attack pass?"

"Aye. Scripture demands of us to turn the other cheek," the priest said with a sigh. He sat, clumsily, again on the steps leading to the tower room. Indeed, we have two cheeks to offer for blows, but only one belly. What must a man offer next when struck there? I am no philosopher, nor theologian. I let the thought pass.

I was unwilling to leave the chapel with such incomplete knowledge of things happening in my bailiwick. "The confessional, you say? Why would words spoken in confidence lead to blows on the street?" I wondered aloud.

The priest did not answer.

"Did you demand of him a penance too harsh?" I thought, given what I had learned of Kellet and his practice, that this was unlikely. But I saw no other possibility, at the moment.

"Aye," the priest muttered. "'Twas much as you say."

Kellet stood to his feet and spoke. "I can say no more." And with those words he turned and lumbered up the darkening stairway to his tower chamber. I watched him disappear into the gloom and heard the chamber door creak open, then close with the drop of a latch.

It was pleasant to re-enter the brightness and warmth of a sunny June afternoon after the shadows of the decaying chapel. But the brilliance of the day did nothing to enlighten me regarding what I had seen this day, or what John Kellet might have learned or assigned at the confessional.

I walked slowly toward Bampton, partly because my thoughts were occupied, partly because I had no other pressing business, and partly because I enjoyed the warmth of the lowering sun in my face. The day was of the type for which June is justly admired. If a man wished to be warm he had but to stand or work in the sun and his desire would be met. Did he wish to cool himself he might seek a tree or shady wall and the breeze would accomplish the task.

Lord Gilbert knew nothing of the deaths of Alan the beadle and Henry atte Bridge – unless some whispered gossip had traveled past the marcher country all the way to Pembroke. I had thought to await his return to Bampton to tell him of these events. It was my hope that I would then also be able to present him with the conclusion to the business. As I ate my supper that day I concluded that no such resolution was in view.

I entered my chamber, set a sheet of Robert Caxton's parchment on my table, and with quill in hand composed a letter to Lord Gilbert in which I described events in Bampton since Holy Week.

Doing so was a rewarding experience. The effort to reduce the incidents so that the report could be written on but one sheet of parchment focused my mind wonderfully. It was necessary to dispense with all evidences not material to discovering the truth of things, else the tale would be too long.

The long summer twilight was near gone when I set down my quill, folded and addressed the message to Lord Gilbert Talbot at his castle at Pembroke, and sealed it with a drop of sealing wax and Lord Gilbert's crested seal from my cupboard. I would dispatch two grooms to carry the missive to Pembroke tomorrow. Lord Gilbert might require more men to assist his move to Bampton after Lammas Day. The fellows could remain at Pembroke until then.

My bed beckoned, but so did the puzzle of Alan and Henry. I knew that should I attempt sleep, my mind would churn over the thoughts I had distilled in the letter to Lord Gilbert. Better I should reflect on these things while alert and vertical. I departed my chamber and crossed the castle yard to the steps beside the gatehouse which led to the parapet. Wilfred watched me approach and tugged a forelock.

The night was near full dark. Only a faint glow in the northwest sky silhouetted the forest beyond the Ladywell. This glow would soon reappear to the northeast, for we approached the shortest night of the year.

In my circumnavigation of the parapet I lingered above the addition to the marshalsea. The new stables were below me, the new-thatched roof glowing dimly in the starlight.

I wonder if God intervened to halt my steps above the marshalsea. Certainly, had I maintained a steady pace round the castle wall, I would have been walking north along the east wall, rather than south atop the west wall, when a dark figure strode purposefully to the west on Mill Street.

I saw the shadowed form hastening along the road but I would likely not have noticed even that, but the walker carried a pale sack over a shoulder. It was the bouncing movement of the sack in the starlight which caught my eye. Only after I focused on that did I see the obscure form of a walker disappearing against the black rim of Lord Gilbert's forest to the west.

I was just past the gatehouse, beginning a second circuit of the castle wall, when I spied this hurrying shadow. I hurried to retrace my steps, ran down the stairs to the gatehouse, and awakened Wilfred, who was now snoring in his chamber behind the portcullis.

The porter reacted hesitantly to my command, for when the gate was closed and the portcullis down for the night they generally stayed that way until dawn. Some time passed before I was able to shout the cobwebs from Wilfred's mind and convince him that he must draw the portcullis and open the gate for me.

By the time he accomplished these tasks and I stumbled through the night to Mill Street, the walker had disappeared into the shadows where the path to Alvescot bent into the forest. There was nothing to be seen beneath the oaks and beeches of the wood.

I assumed some man of the town was setting out to lay snares, or check those already placed, in hope of one of Lord Gilbert's coneys for his dinner. The man had escaped John Prudhomme's notice and it seemed had escaped me as well, for in the time it took me to get from the castle parapet to the street before the castle, the fellow had disappeared.

I set off in pursuit. Had I been older and wiser, I would have returned to my bed and told the beadle to watch for the man. Surely he would repeat the behavior. But I was intent on the chase. My purpose was to make haste so as to catch up to my quarry, but to do so quietly, so when I found him I might see what he was about without myself being observed. I was not successful.

The sleeping huts of Alvescot eventually materialized in the night, now dimly lit by the light of a waning moon. But there was no sign of him I pursued. I had missed him on the road. I assumed his goal was some place in field or forest between the village and Bampton, not Alvescot itself. But I decided to make one circuit of the village to learn if I might be mistaken and there be some hut where perhaps the glow of a cresset through the skin of a window or crack in closed shutters might indicate my quarry's destination. There was no reason to fear discovery from beadle or hayward as Alvescot was too small, especially since the great dying, to employ either.

I felt no need for stealth, which was a mistake, but walked quietly through the village nevertheless. I had just passed the church and lych gate, opposite Gerard the verderer's hut, when a scraping sound from the gate caught my attention. The gate lay ten paces or so behind me. I turned to investigate the source of the sound. The night was still, so what I heard could not have been the wind moving an unlatched gate on rusted hinges.

The lych gate was indeed securely latched. I leaned over the gate to peer into the churchyard. Another blunder. In so doing I presented my head as a target, much like a man who stretches his neck on the block to await the axe.

I detected movement from the corner of my eye but had no time to parry the blow which followed. I saw a tenebrous shape rise from a crouch behind the churchyard wall and with one motion bring a club down toward my head. All the stars and planets in their heavenly orbs flashed before my eyes. Then, inexplicably, they went dark.

When I awoke the sky to the east above the church

tower was pale with approaching dawn. I was, I am sure, also pale, for a different reason. My head throbbed, my eyes refused to focus, and I felt a great lump on my skull just above my left ear. It is good that I follow the fashion much approved by young men of wrapping a long liripipe about my head. The layers of wool softened the blow somewhat, else I might have died there by the churchyard.

I managed to bring myself upright so much as to prop my back against the wall, at the base of which I had evidently spent the night. The cause of my headache lay beside me in the grass: a length of pollarded ash as long as a man is tall. Whoever laid this pole across my head had dropped it when it had served his purpose. I dragged the shaft across my knees and tried to inspect it but my eyes refused to converge. But 'twas light enough that I recognized where I had seen others like it. A stack of similar, longer poles lay across the street in Gerard's toft, awaiting use as rafters for huts which might never be built for the decline in population after the plague, which has struck twice in thirteen years.

The pole had been cut several years earlier, I think, and was well dried and tough; much tougher than my skull, for the wood was unmarked whereas the same could not be said for my scalp.

I used the club for a crutch and, with both hands fixed to it, lifted myself to my feet. Doing so made the world sway before me, but with the stick I regained my balance and staggered off from Alvescot toward Bampton and the relief I might find in my store of soothing herbs.

Dawn was but a promise in the glow above the treetops, and the path was rutted. I stumbled and fell twice, and would have done so many more times had not the pole which was laid across my skull now served to keep me aright.

I met no man on the road to Bampton. The hour was early, and before the Angelus Bell few had yet crawled from their beds. But the sun was up beyond the spire of St Beornwald's Church when the castle and town came into view. The walk in crisp morning air had restored my senses, so that I was able to approach the castle gatehouse with a surer step than when I began the journey at Alvescot.

The pole which laid me low having served its purpose, I was about to discard it against the castle wall when it occurred to my addled brain that a close inspection in good light might yield some clue as to who had attacked me and why. It might have, but did not.

Wilfred had the gate open and portcullis up. I stiffened my back and straightened my stride and passed through the gatehouse and castle yard with no man questioning a weaving path or halting gait.

I would be false, however, did I not admit to relief when I entered the hall and stood before my chamber door. I leaned the pole against the stones and was about to push open the door – a task which required two hands, for the hall was yet dim in the dawn light and my vision took that moment to again set all about me in a whirl – when I heard footsteps behind me in the hall.

I turned, too quickly. The movement, combined with lightheadedness, caused me to lose my balance. I staggered against the door, which provided no support but swung open. I ungracefully fell back into my chamber. For the next few days it was not only my head which was sore. My rump met the hard stone flags. I am of slender build. I had not John Kellet's foresight to prepare an adequate cushion for such a tumble.

'Twas Alice atte Bridge, with a mug of ale and a loaf fresh from the castle oven, whose approach caused my clumsy fall.

"Oh!" the girl exclaimed. She set the platter on the flags of the hall and rushed to my aid.

I had set the pole leaning against the wall beside my door. But in my harried state I had set it slightly askew. As the girl knelt to assist me the pole slid from its place against the wall and fell through the open door. I had turned my head toward Alice, so did not see it coming. The club gave me a solid smack across my right ear before clattering off on the flagging. I was become symmetrical. Within the hour another lump, smaller than the first, appeared on my skull above the right ear to balance the bulge behind my left.

Alice assisted me to my feet. She had nearly to do so a second time, for in some heat I kicked at the offending pole. Another error. I was unsteady upon my feet and nearly found the flags again.

The girl propelled me to my bench, uttering solicitudes the while. I suspect she thought me drunk. It was just as well she not know the real reason for my condition. I sat gratefully upon the bench, and gathered my wits while Alice gathered my breakfast. My stomach rebelled at the sight of the loaf, but I needed the ale. I thanked the girl for her aid and bid her notify Thomas that I was unwell and wished not to be disturbed.

When she was gone and the door shut behind her I made my way to my cupboard. I found my pouch of hemp seeds and another of lettuce and mixed a double measure of each into the ale. My gut was not pleased to receive this physic. I feared the first swallow might be rejected. But not so. I drank the remaining mixture cautiously, then found my bed. When I awoke my stomach was growling with hunger and my chamber window was pale in the evening twilight.

My head throbbed, but my step was steady as I made my way to the kitchen. The cook had learned that I was unwell and had the foresight to prepare a basket should I desire a meal. But as this was Friday, and Ember Day, the basket held but a piece of fish and a small loaf of maslin. Alice was completing her duties in the kitchen and pointed me to my dinner. I wonder was it the cook who was so considerate, or Alice? I took the basket to my chamber and ate by candlelight.

I was not sleepy, though 'twas now dark and my stomach was full. My mind was occupied with considering who might have attacked me, and why, while my fingers and mouth were busy at supper.

If my quarry the night before was poaching Lord Gilbert's coneys, it seemed to me likely that he would be at the business this night also, visiting his snares before some fox might rob him of his catch. As I had slept the day through and my head was yet knobby and sore I thought it probable that I would lay sleepless in my bed. I might as well spend a sleepless night watching the road for a poacher. Who, I assumed, was he who had whacked me across the head.

I roused Wilfred from his bed, and when he had opened the gate and raised the portcullis I made my way to Mill Street. The slender moon would rise even later this night, so I walked in darkness between fields of oats and peas.

My way became even more obscure, the night around me even blacker, when I came to the edge of the forest. If a man followed me this night I should never see him, even did he carry a pale sack over a shoulder. But there was advantage in this. I wore a dark cotehardie and grey chauces. I would also be invisible.

I crept carefully to the side of the road and felt before me as a blind man for obstacles which might trip me. I had no wish to fall on my bruised head. Only a few feet from the road I found a stump. Against the black background of the wood I could not be seen though I was but three or four paces from the verge. A man in the road would be nearly invisible to me, as well, but my advantage was my silence. A poacher, no matter how dark the night or hushed his step, could be heard as he approached. I would be silent upon my stump.

The waning moon rose over the town well past midnight. From my perch on the rotting stump I had a clear view of Mill Street from the castle until it entered the forest. In the darkness of the wood I was sure I was yet invisible. This lunar advantage gave me great satisfaction, but it was the only satisfaction I would have that night. Sitting on a cold, jagged stump provided little gratification and the only living thing I saw was an owl which swooped soundlessly from a tree to capture a mouse at the edge of a field of oats adjacent to the forest. Well, I think it was a mouse.

I watched the sky behind St Beornwald's spire

lighten for the second day in a row. It is pleasing to watch a new day begin, to hear birds twitter as they awaken and begin the business of seeking sustenance. Of course, it is also pleasing to lay in a warm bed in the coldest part of the night, as dawn glows golden in the east. This dawn would have been more profitably spent in bed.

I rose from the stump, stretched my stiffened limbs, and set off for the castle and breakfast. Smoke ascended from the kitchen oven into the still morning air, and a warm loaf awaited me there. As this day was also Ember Day the loaf would not be wheaten, but coarse maslin of barley and rye. I took the loaf and a mug of ale to my chamber and pondered my ignorance while I ate.

The catalog of things I did not know seemed to grow more rapidly than the list of things I did know. Why did Henry atte Bridge kill Alan the beadle, if indeed he did?

Why was Henry struck down in the forest, and who did the deed? Why did John Kellet receive blows from Edmund Smith, and why was the smith so sure the priest would not complain of him? Who struck me down in the Alvescot churchyard? And was the assailant the same man I saw walking the road in the dark? If so, was he indeed a poacher, or did some other interest put him on the road at midnight?

I decided to cease my nocturnal ways, but I wished for some eyes to be alert should a man with a pale sack make another late appearance on Mill Street. I left the castle and walked to Rosemary Lane and the house of John Prudhomme. I found it convenient to walk slowly. A rapid pace caused my head to throb at every step. For all his late-night obligation to see the streets clear, Prudhomme was awake and bright when he answered my knock on his door. I told him of sighting a man with a sack late at night on Mill Street, and of my failed attempt to apprehend this poacher. I charged him to be vigilant in his duty and to report to me any man out past curfew, whether he carried a sack or not.

John pledged that he would do so, and seemed wounded that a miscreant had escaped him. But I assured the new beadle that I attached no blame to him. The poacher, if such he was, had waited past midnight to be sure that even the beadle had entered his house and shut the door behind him.

"You think the fellow may set snares in other places?" John asked. "Perhaps while you lay in wait for him to the west he inspected traps some other place. To the north, along the road to Burford, there is much wasteland growing up from meadow. A good place for coneys, I think."

"Aye, and in truth Lord Gilbert will not miss a few, be they taken to the west or the north. But 'tis my duty, and yours also, to apprehend a poacher if I can. He who would snare a coney today may grow bold and take a deer tomorrow."

"I will attend this duty tonight," the beadle promised.

"Be watchful," I warned him. "I trailed the man to Alvescot, where he – or some other, I cannot know – lay in wait for me behind the churchyard wall. When I investigated a sound I heard from the lych gate I was thumped across my head for my curiosity." I rubbed the swollen side of my skull. Gently. "The blow left me sleeping the night away at the base of the churchyard wall, and I will have a headache for another day or two. See that you are more wary than I."

John peered quizzically at the side of my head. And then at the other. "I see the lump the fellow left you… but there is another, on t'other side."

"Aye," I muttered. I did not wish to tell him how I came to be so balanced. Rather, I tugged my hood down to obscure my misshapen skull, bid John good day, and set off for the castle.

Three days later, a Tuesday morning, John Prudhomme asked for me at the castle gatehouse. Wilfred came to fetch me as I swallowed the last of my morning loaf. The beadle waited at the gate with, I thought, some impatience. His eyes darted from the castle forecourt to the gatehouse to the meadow beyond Mill Street. And he shifted from one foot to the other as I approached, as if he stood on Edmund's coals.

When Wilfred told me who it was that sought me, my first thought was that John had discovered who it was who had taken to the roads at night and smitten me across the head. This was not so, but he did indeed have news of the business.

The beadle tilted his head as I drew near in a gesture that requested me to follow. He then turned and walked slowly from the gatehouse toward Mill Street. I caught up to him halfway between the street and gatehouse.

"You have news, John?"

"Aye," he said without breaking stride.

Whatever he wished me to know, he wanted it known to no other. The beadle eventually stopped and turned to face me well away from any ears on either the street or at the castle gatehouse.

"I watched the street, like you wanted. Saw nothin'. But last night, I was 'bout to end my rounds an' come as far as the bridge when I saw somethin' movin' in the Weald. Not my business, what goes on there, 'course, but it caught me eye, see."

I nodded as Prudhomme interrupted his tale to peer about for any who might stroll close enough to overhear his words. Whatever tale he wished to tell, it was for me alone. I said nothing and waited for him to continue.

"'Twas like you said 'twould be," John said when he was satisfied that we were unobserved and unheard. After all, should any be watching, why would they be surprised that the beadle should be in conversation with the bailiff? Unless they thought themselves the subject of the discussion. I took John's arm and propelled him toward the gatehouse.

"We will continue this conversation in my chamber," I said. Perhaps I was overly cautious. A blow on the head will do that to a man.

When the door latched behind us John continued his tale. "I seen somethin' light in the moonlight. Was well past midnight an' the moon is past last quarter, but I seen the sack you said t'watch for. 'Course I din't know then 'twas a sack. Just saw somethin' movin'."

"In the Weald, you say?"

"Aye. But while I watched whoso was carryin' the sack moved across the meadow an' into Lord Gilbert's wood."

"They avoided the road?"

"Aye, they did."

That might explain why I saw no man while I lay in wait all night at the edge of the wood. If this poacher had ventured to do more of his work that night, and if he avoided the road, he would have entered the forest south of where I sat in wait on the stump.

"Can you show me the place where you saw the fellow enter the forest?"

"Close, like... 'twas too dark to see for sure."

"What then? Did the fellow eventually come out to the road?"

"Nay. Least, not so far as I could tell. I went west on Mill Street's far as the wood. Saw nor heard nothin'. Dark in the wood, nights, now w'the leaves full out an' all."

"You do not know who it was who cut 'cross the meadow and made for the forest?"

"Nay."

"And that is why you are so apprehensive to tell me of this?"

"Aye. Was the fellow to see us or hear me speak, he might think I knew of him an' his business."

"And one beadle is dead these past three months for probing some nocturnal matter."

"Eh?"

"At night... Alan died at night."

"Oh, aye."

"Well, I do not blame you for your worry. I will look into the matter myself. How far south of Mill Street did the man enter the wood?"

The beadle scratched his head and looked to the ceiling beams before he spoke. "More'n a hundred paces... perhaps even 200, but no more'n that."

"Very well. Be off home, then. I will wait 'til afternoon to visit the wood, so if any man saw us in conversation he will have lost interest when I do not immediately seek a sign in meadow or wood."

Chapter 14

The sun was dropping toward the treetops to the west of the castle when I decided I must wait no longer to investigate the beadle's discovery. I had found much other business to occupy me after dinner. When I consider this now I understand that it was fear of being knocked again on the head which caused me to hesitate, not any desire for stealth. Had you received the blow I took at Alvescot Church, you would be cautious also.

My eyes fell upon the ash pole which had been dropped against my skull as I left my chamber. I had propped it in a corner after it fell against me. Perhaps the staff might this time serve to defend me and so make amends for its previous usage. I took the cudgel with me and set out for the gatehouse.

I watched carefully, when I reached Mill Street, to see if any man observed me set off to the west toward the wood. Two men walked from the mill and turned east to cross Shill Brook. They paid me no heed. In the Weald I saw Emma atte Bridge at work in her toft. If she saw me she gave no sign.

Reassured that I attracted no attention, I strode west and soon entered Lord Gilbert's forest. I counted 200 paces, then turned from the road. The forest here had not been coppiced for many years. Giant old oak and beech trees sought the sky. They would be worth a small fortune for long beams, did anyone want to build. But since the plague, few did. Their leafy branches so completely blocked the sun that few green things grew on the forest floor. No hawthorn or nettles impeded my way as I counted another hundred paces to the south.

I stopped often while I counted my steps. If a poacher

set snares this way I might hear a captured animal as it struggled to free itself. And if I was observed and followed, I might hear a stalker as leaves rustled and twigs snapped under his feet. No, I was not being over cautious. There really was a man who intended me harm. The shrinking lump on my head was proof of that.

A goldfinch twittered in the branches above me. A squirrel dug through rotting leaves for his supper. The breeze set leaves to shimmering and branches to rubbing against each other. I saw the sights and heard the sounds of the forest. And so delightful were they, I came near to forgetting my mission. It would be a poorer world were there no goldfinches singing or squirrels playing in it. In my prayers I do not recall ever thanking God for either birds or squirrels. I must amend my ways and my prayers.

When I had counted 100 paces from the Alvescot road I leaned against an oak to listen and observe my place. I might have been the only man in the shire, for no sound made by man came to my ears. And no sight foreign to a forest fell to my eyes.

I crept another ten paces, found another tree to hide me, and again watched and listened. Nothing, but for birds and the occasional squirrel. Did a man wish to set snares for squirrels, which is allowed, he should surely find success. Although I thought it unlikely such a hunter would require a sack across his shoulder to carry home his prize.

The ground I walked sloped gently down from the road. Each step took me closer to a tangle of ivy and marsh grass which grew about a bog where the forest ended. No man would try to push his way through such a place. The verge of such a marsh would be an excellent place to lay a snare. I became more cautious and observant as I approached this boggy place.

I found no snares, but the track of a man's passing was visible to an alert observer. There had been no rain for several days, so last year's fallen leaves should be dry atop the forest floor. But where the firm ground of the forest began to give way to the soft muck of the marsh I found a place where wet, rotting leaves had been kicked up above the drying surface leaves.

A few steps to the west I found another such place. These overturned bunches of leaves did not create a regular track, but were intermittent. It appeared that some man had stumbled or otherwise tripped while making his way through the forest. The fellow must have been unsteady on his feet. Or perhaps he traveled at night across the uneven ground.

The broken trail of disturbed leaves crossed my path. I thought I knew, should I turn to my left, where the track would enter the forest. I walked that way to assure myself of my supposition. My guess was correct. Nearly 200 paces east of the bog the trail of disturbed leaves ended at a hedgerow to the west of a pasture. The road to Alvescot formed the north boundary of this meadow. Across it to the northeast I saw the castle.

The stacked stones of the meadow wall were overgrown with nettles and hawthorne. I saw clearly where someone had torn nettles away from the wall so he might climb over without earning a stinging rebuke.

The field before me was fallow this year. A flock of sheep munched the grass midway across the clearing, turning grass into wool and manuring the ground for the wheat and barley strips John Holcutt would see planted there next year.

Across the meadow another hedgerow formed its eastern margin. I saw near this wall the remains of the blind where the reeve, the archers and I had looked on this meadow for the return of a wolf. Beyond this far hedgerow lay the huts of the bishop's men in the Weald.

While I studied the wall, nettles, meadow and sheep, another studied me. I looked up from examining the torn nettles and saw, 200 paces and more to the east, Emma atte Bridge staring over the far hedgerow in my direction from her toft. The hedgerow before me was waist high. Unless her vision failed she could identify me as clearly as I could her. I did not think this important at the time.

The woman went back to her work and I turned from the hedgerow to retrace my steps and follow the trail I had discovered. The occasional patches of disturbed leaves compassed the swamp around its north edge, then, to the west of the low ground it entered again into the higher ground of the forest.

I followed the trail through the wood, but not easily. I lost it several times and only found the path again by circling the last upturned leaves I had found. My search was made some easier because the nocturnal hiker I trailed had gone unfailingly west in a course which only gradually, after nearly half a mile, began to curve north. An hour later the track led me to the road to Alvescot, less than a mile from the village.

I stopped often while I followed the path through the forest, but heard no struggling animal nor saw any snare. Whoever had used this way through the wood wished only to be through to the other side. He had no other business which brought him here. And he had not been through the wood by this path often, for his route was not well trodden, but on the contrary, seemed used but rarely.

I could see no reason to return to Bampton through the forest. And there was no point in walking on to Alvescot. I was sure that whoso made the track I had followed through the wood was the same man who had traveled Mill Street toward Alvescot five days before. And likely was the same man who had bashed my head at the Alvescot churchyard.

If my quarry was a poacher, he did his work somewhere beyond Alvescot. The man had passed many likely places to set snares. Perhaps he had done so, and laid them so cleverly that I did not find them. But I did not think this could be so. Why set snares about a marsh, then continue through the forest to the road? It seemed to me a poacher would set his traps, then return through the wood the way he had come. No, this fellow had business elsewhere, be it poaching, or, as I was beginning to suspect, some other pursuit in mind.

Lord Gilbert's forest lay within my bailiwick, but was no responsibility of John Prudhomme's. I resolved to investigate the woodland path and he who trod upon it on my own. I did not wish any other to know what I was about, for fear that gossip might make my work known and my prey cautious. More cautious than he was already. A man would not forsake a road for a forest track in the dark of night was he not already alert and wary.

A large old beech stood over the road near the place where the path joined the road to Alvescot. I marked it so I might find the place on a dark night, then made my way back to Bampton in time for my supper. Unobserved, so far as I knew, but for Emma atte Bridge.

Wilfred was not known for loquacity but I did not want even the porter to know that I left the castle this night. A man will not tell what he does not know. A length of rope over the castle wall had served well. I resolved to use the method again.

When the castle was dark and quiet I stole to the marshalsea for rope, then silently mounted the steps to the parapet. There would be little moon this night, and that would not rise 'til near dawn. The north wall would be especially dark this night. My grey chauces and brown cotehardie would be invisible even if any who spent the night at the Ladywell chose that moment to awaken and examine the castle.

I knotted the rope every foot or so to aid my return, tied one end to a merlon, and tossed the other end to the ground. Moments later my feet also found the thin grass at the base of the north wall.

As there was yet no moon above the town rooftops, I saw no need to stumble my way across field and meadow to the forest. I could barely see Mill Street myself when I stood upon it at the southwest corner of the castle. No man, even if he knew I walked the road, could see me more than ten paces away. Of course, if another man traveled the road I should not see him, either. I walked silently, stopping every few paces to listen. My ears are good. Perhaps, if another man chose to be about on the road this night, I might hear him before he heard me. I wished I had remembered to bring with me the club, just in case.

The road through the forest was so dark I occasionally lost my way and stumbled against foliage growing at the verge. I was sure no man would attempt the wooded path I had found on such a night. Not until the waning moon rose to add some light to the tenebrous thickets near the bog.

Stars provided my only light. It was barely enough to locate the great beech I marked to fix the place where the forest path found the road. I settled myself into a cleft between two large roots. This location faced the road and its junction with the path. The seat had but one flaw. 'Twas too comfortable. I had no trouble staying awake when seated on a stump. But now I found myself drifting to sleep. Only when my nodding head with its symmetrical lumps met the smooth bark of the tree was I jolted awake.

This occurred several times before the thin light of a crescent moon brought some feeble illumination to the road which stretched across my sight. The soil of the road was lighter in color than the forest around it. A man walking upon it would produce a shadow against the lighter background. A shadow which would move. In the northeast, a predawn glow added to the light to illuminate the road.

If a man chose to walk this night the forest path I had found, I thought it reasonable to expect that he would wait until the moon could light his way. I found no difficulty in remaining alert for the remainder of the night, for I expected a poacher to step from the forest to the road at any moment. But no shadow moved past me on the way. The eastern sky grew light through the entwined branches of the trees when I finally rose from my seat, stretched, brushed off my chauces, and set off for the castle. The night was a failure.

The pale golden glow in the eastern sky lighted my way through the wood and across the meadowland west of town and castle. Where the road left the forest a gentle breeze caused me to shiver on my way. I had become stiff with cold, sitting at the base of the beech, but there had been no wind there in the forest to compound my discomfort.

I was near the castle wall when the gentle morning wind brought to my nose the welcome smell of roasting meat. It was early for the cook to be at his work in the castle kitchen, and he would not yet be roasting meat for the castle dinner. He would first be about baking loaves for the day when he did rise from his bed. But I smelled meat, not bread. And the breeze blew wrong to bring the scent of roasting meat to me from the castle kitchen. The wind came from the southeast; from the huts in the Weald.

It was my goal to climb the rope I had left tied to the merlon in the north-wall parapet before men rose to greet the new day. But this new scent asked too many questions which needed answers. I determined to seek them quickly, before daylight would make visible my climb up the castle wall.

I walked swiftly from Mill Street down the lane toward the Weald huts. In the twilight of early dawn I saw smoke from the eve vents of two huts, those of Thomas atte Bridge and the widow Emma. The inhabitants of these two dwellings were about their business early, and I knew why.

Few others in the Weald or elsewhere would have meat to roast in June. The flesh from autumn's slaughtered hog or goat was long since consumed in most men's homes. These two houses wished to roast their meat when no other would take note. I was convinced again I dealt with a poacher, and now knew who the man was. Although why Thomas atte Bridge would share with his sister-in-law I did not know. In truth, the question did not then occur to me.

I hurried back to Mill Street, hastened to the castle and climbed my rope ladder as the morning sun illuminated the cross atop the spire of St Beornwald's Church. From atop the wall I saw an old man praying at the Ladywell. His back was to me. I drew the rope from around the merlon, tucked it beneath my cotehardie, and stole down the parapet steps and across the inner yard to the great hall and my chamber.

Wisps of smoke from the kitchen chimney told me that the cook was risen from his bed and at his work. But he and his assistant were busy with oven and loaves. No face appeared at the kitchen door to observe my return.

I went to my bed, intending to rest for an hour or two, but found sleep elusive. I thought I now knew the poacher's identity. But how to catch him at his work? And Emma atte Bridge had seen me across the meadow from her toft. The thought troubled me. The Angelus Bell intruded upon my contemplation before I could fall to sleep.

I awoke a short time later but little refreshed and no nearer a plan to apprehend either Thomas atte Bridge or his brother's slayer. I awoke confused, weary, and feeling quite incompetent.

I had no wish to sit again all night in the forest awaiting Thomas atte Bridge. If it was fresh meat being roasted which I smelled this morning, then the fellow had eluded me in the night. Or perhaps 'twas meat he took earlier, and he had not been abroad in the night at all while I waited, cold and stiff, between the roots of the old beech.

If I took my place this night at the root of the beech it might be that Thomas would choose not to appear, or perhaps take another way. Could he be warned that I had found his path? And he had meat to roast. He would need no more for several days, perhaps.

I had no desire to spend another cold, uncomfortable night in the forest. I knew a better way.

I called at the kitchen for my morning loaf and ale. Did the cook look askance at me, or was it my imagination? I ate hurriedly in my chamber. I had a plan, and was impatient to set it in motion.

Wilfred tugged a forelock as I passed the gatehouse. I set my feet toward Alvescot and shortly after passed the beech where I had spent an unprofitable night. Did my scheme succeed, I would not need to visit the place again.

The door to Gerard the verderer's hut lay open to the warm June sun, but the forester was not there. He was, his wife explained, at work in the forest north of town with his sons and brothers.

I was but a few steps from the village on the road north to Shilton when I heard axes ringing through the forest to the west of the road. I picked my way through the wood and found the verderer sitting on a rotting stump from which place he directed the felling of a medium-sized ash. This was the second tree to fall this day. A few paces beyond lay another ash, already down.

Gerard stood when he saw me approach, and greeted me warmly, as a man might to one who had saved his life. He had no sooner spoke words of greeting than the second ash began its plunge to the forest floor. I waited until the crashing and splintering of branches was complete to reply.

"Good day... Are you well?"

"Aye, well as may be."

"The weakness on your left side – it troubles you as before?"

"Aye. No change there. Won't ever be, I think."

"There is a matter regarding Lord Gilbert's forest I must discuss with you. Pray, return to your seat."

I motioned to the stump. Gerard's sons and brothers ignored me and went to trimming branches from the fallen trees. Gerard saw me watching the work. Perhaps he worried that I might accuse him of abusing Lord Gilbert's forest. He explained what he was about.

"'Tis a wondrous thing, is a tree. These two will provide timber should Lord Gilbert need more, an' t'branches will warm him in t'castle an' us in our huts next autumn. From t'stumps coppiced shoots will soon rise. In a few months they'll be large enough for arrows. T'Frenchies will want war again soon enough. 'Twill be well to have shafts ready. An' we allow some of t'coppiced poles to grow, they'll make anything from rafters to plow hafts."

"Aye," I agreed. "God designed well a world for men to prosper in. And he did well to provide Lord Gilbert with a verderer who knows his business."

The old man beamed.

"Can't work as once," Gerard admitted, "but know as what's needful an' can see others do it. Trainin' Richard," he nodded toward his older son, "to take me place when I'm gone."

"Unless you allow some tree to drop on you again, you should live for many years."

The forester removed his cap and rubbed his head absently. The scar I made when I repaired his broken skull was visible through his wispy, thinning hair. "Keep me distance, now," he assured me. "But you'd not come 'ere to discuss me 'ead."

"Nay. I have other business. There is, I am sure, a poacher at work in Lord Gilbert's forest."

Gerard's eyes grew wide. He lifted his hands to protest, the right hand higher than the left. He thought I was about to accuse him of malfeasance, for it is a verderer's business to seek out those who violate forest law.

"I do not charge you with incompetence," I said, before he could protest. "But I will have you and your sons patrol the forest carefully. You have seen no sign of snares, or the taking of a deer?"

"Nay. Don't get through t'woods so easy meself anymore, but the others," he nodded toward his sons and brothers, "go 'bout regular, like. They'd tell me straight away did any poacher leave sign in t'woods."

"Require of them special vigilance, for there is surely a poacher at work. But I must have evidence before I can charge the man at hallmote."

"You know who the fellow is?"

"Aye, I think so. But I cannot charge him with the little I presently know."

Gerard took personally the idea of a poacher loose

in the forest. It was his responsibility more than mine to apprehend such a miscreant. That I had learned of activity in his forest of which he knew nothing was a blow to his pride. I knew he would be diligent in seeking the evidence I needed.

My head was aching again when I completed the return journey to the castle. Valets were preparing the hall for dinner, for which I had little appetite. I went to my chamber and mixed a draught of ground willow bark and hemp seeds in a mug of ale.

Dinner this day included a first remove of coney pie, as if the cook wished to mock my inability. I could not prove a poacher. I could not find a murderer. I could not find a wolf, was there a wolf to find. Nor could I find a reason why Henry atte Bridge would slay Alan the beadle. But he did. Of this I was certain. 'Twas the only sure thing in my life. Aye, I could not find a wife, either.

I mixed no lettuce in my ale, but the willow bark and hemp seeds, my lack of sleep, and food in my belly all combined. I went to my chamber thinking to rest briefly. I did not awaken until I heard through my closed door valets once again setting tables on trestles for supper.

I arose from my bed much refreshed. And for this meal there was a pike and roasted capon. No venison. No rabbit. My appetite returned.

My afternoon sleep was so deep I thought it might rob me of slumber that night. Not so. I climbed to the parapet and walked the castle wall 'til Venus appeared over the treetops to the west. Below me the marshalsea enlargement proceeded well. The new stables would be complete when Lord Gilbert returned to take up residence. But little else was well. Failure gnawed at me. I descended the steps to the inner yard, watched as Wilfred barred the gate and cranked down the portcullis, then went to my chamber.

I was sure that my heavy thoughts, combined with a long nap that day, would deny me rest. But perhaps the hemp and willow bark were yet effective. I slept soundly until from the church spire I heard the Angelus Bell announce the arrival of the feast day of Corpus Christi.

The procession began at St Beornwald's Church at the third hour. Thomas de Bowlegh, by virtue of his age and tenure at St Beornwald's, led the vicars, clerks and townsmen. He held the consecrated loaf high and set off down Church View Street for the marketplace. This could not have been an easy task for a man of his years. Try walking about for an hour with both hands held high above your head.

I followed, as was my duty. A duty both to God and to Lord Gilbert. It is right and proper to honor the Son of God for deigning to become a man and dwell among us. And Lord Gilbert's representative must set an example.

But as I marched my mind returned to a day when as a student I attended a lecture given by Master John Wyclif. He remarked that no pope or bishop ever thought to assert that the host became human flesh as of our Lord until the Lateran Council a century and a half past. Nor did the church require a spoken confession of sins to a priest before that council. But that is another matter.

Master John was no Donatist, however. He did not teach that a sacrament was vain was it administered by a sinful priest. Rather, Master John teaches that the sacrament is from the hand of God Himself, not from any "cursed man." This may not be Donatism, but is enough to raise the ire of bishops. If a sacrament is from God, what need of the intermediary hand of a man? And if it be not the blessing of a priest which turns bread to flesh, what does? Nothing, I believe Master John would reply. I am inclined to agree with him. Do not tell the bishops.

A band of players new arrived for the feast day had set up a stage at the eastern edge of the marketplace. After dinner I wandered back to the town to watch the drama. 'Twas a portrayal of the life of Christ, first presented, I was told, many years ago at York, before the great cathedral there. I thought the performance appropriate to the day.

The players recounted a story I knew well. I found myself watching the crowd of onlookers more than the stage. There was as much drama there as any actor could produce. They cheered Christ when he healed the lame, and hissed Pilate for his crime.

They wept with Mary as our Lord was nailed to the cross, and roared as the stone rolled magically from the tomb and our risen Lord departed his sepulcher. The actors gave a good performance. The residents of Bampton were magnificent.

When the play was done and the crowd dispersed I made my way to Rosemary Lane and the home of John Prudhomme. I found the beadle in his toft, tending his onions and turnips. He stood and stretched when he saw me approach.

"Master Hugh... have you news of a poacher?"

"Aye, I think so. But I will need more evidence before I can charge him at hallmote."

"And you wish me to provide it?" the beadle grinned.

"Aye."

"Who is the man?"

"Thomas atte Bridge. Do you know him?"

"Him of the Weald? His brother slain in the forest?"

"The same."

"Them of the Weald are the bishop's men."

"Aye. But if he takes Lord Gilbert's game he'll face Lord Gilbert's justice."

"You want me to watch the Weald as well as town after curfew?"

"Aye. Thomas atte Bridge lives in the second hut on the west side of the lane. It can be easily seen from the bridge across Shill Brook. But so will you, should you watch from the bridge. Best make your way down the stream and watch from the opposite bank. You'll be lost in the thickets there."

"An' among t'nettles, too," the beadle grimaced.

"It will be worth a few stings to you if you help me prove the fellow's guilt."

"And what if I prove his innocence?"

"Small chance of that, I think, for early yesterday

morn, while you and others of the town lay yet in your beds, I followed the scent of roasting meat to his hut."

John nodded in agreement. "Where would he find flesh to roast this season?"

"Aye. And the man you saw crossed the meadow from the Weald into the west wood."

"He did," the beadle confirmed.

"If we are alert, and do not give Thomas cause to suspect we know of his work, we will have him."

"Be he the man who attacked you at Alvescot Churchyard, he is surely on guard already. Else why cross the meadow and lose himself in the wood rather than make his way along the road?"

"Aye, he is some worried already. But not so much that he has lost his taste for Lord Gilbert's game, I think. And this is why we shall catch him. It may be difficult to begin a transgression. But even more difficult to abandon a sin and the reward it brings."

"Aye," John smiled. "If I knew of a way to put a haunch of venison on my table this eve I should be loath to give up the deed what put it there."

"Just so. Greed has damaged many men, lords and commons. It will, soon or late, betray Thomas atte Bridge, I think.

"You need not be much entangled in this business," I continued, "beyond observing who is about at night. Should you see Thomas atte Bridge – or any other man – set out for Alvescot and the forest to the west, send your wife next day to Wilfred, the porter. She must tell him to give me a message. She should say you are ill and cannot leave your bed to watch and warn. I will leave the castle at curfew to take your place and meet you here, before your house, to hear what you have seen."

I am not a superstitious man, but the next day was Friday, the thirteenth day of June. I had no wish to test fate, so abjured the oaken arms of the tree along the Alvescot road where I had spent a fruitless night.

I hoped each day to receive from Wilfred the message that John Prudhomme was ill. Three days later, Monday afternoon, Wilfred stopped me as I passed the gatehouse and told me the beadle was too ill to perform his duty that evening.

"Hmmm... I will see to it myself, be his illness brief. You must open the gate and portcullis for me at midnight, when I return."

Venus again hung over the forest, a dot of light in the darkening sunset, when I bid Wilfred good eve and set out with the ash pole for Mill Street and the town. I did not expect to need the club, but preparation is a great part of any victory. And if curious eyes should see me cross Shill Brook, they would see also the pole and be assured I had armed myself for watch and warn. They would not think a staff necessary for consulting with John Prudhomme.

I found the beadle sitting on a bench at his door. In the dark I nearly missed him, for what little light came from the new crescent moon and fading twilight left the front of his house in shadow.

"You have news for me?" I asked as the beadle stood.

"Aye... but not as you'd expect, I guess."

"What, then?"

"Last night, when I was near finished with me rounds, I did as you said an' walked along t'bank of Shill Brook 'til I was near opposite the hut you spoke of. 'Twas third night I did so."

"And are there nettles there?"

"Aye," he said ruefully, "there are."

"What else did you find?"

"As you thought, Thomas atte Bridge left his hut last night when all was silent an' dark."

"And stole across the meadow to his path through the wood to the road and Alvescot," I completed the beadle's tale.

"Nay... went t'other way."

"What other way?" I asked, puzzled.

"Crossed the bridge an' went through town, quiet like. Moved from one shadow to the next. 'Twas dark last night; no moon."

"And did he carry with him a sack?"

"Aye, he did. But odd thing is, 'twasn't empty. Was a lump in the bottom."

"He did not carry the sack to fetch game, but took something with him from his hut?"

"Aye, so it appeared."

"Where did he take this stuff in his sack?"

"Went through town on the High Street an' up Bushey Row to the lane what leads to St Andrew's Chapel."

"Did you follow?"

"Aye. Had t'duck into bushes more'n once when I thought he stopped and turned t'listen, to see if he was followed."

"You think he knew he was seen?"

"Nay."

"So in the sack he must have carried cords and sticks for new snares," I guessed. "Did he go into the wood behind the chapel to lay them?"

"Nay. Don't know what he could've been about. Didn't leave road 'til he was past t'wood, then went through the gate an' into t'chapel yard."

This was a new and unforeseen thing. Then I remembered that an earlier beadle had gone down this same path some months before. And that man was surely slain by the brother of the man who now walked the lane late at night. Did they travel to the same place? For the same purpose?

"Did Thomas enter the chapel?"

"Aye, think so. Didn't get close enough t'see, but heard hinges squeal."

"Was he long in the chapel?"

"Nay. I thought as how he was in t'chapel I'd hurry to t'yard an' hide behind t'wall. Maybe I'd hear 'im speak to priest. But he was out near as soon as he was in."

"And where did he then go?"

"Back to town, same way as he come. Only thing is, I think t'sack was empty. Wasn't enough light to see well, But t'sack is light-colored, like, so if there's a lump in the bottom a man can see."

"So on his way to the chapel Thomas carried a sack with something in it, but 'twas empty when he went to his home?"

"Aye. Went straight to the Weald an' 'is own hut an' shut the door. I watched from near the bridge for a while, but he must've gone to 'is bed. Never saw 'im again."

"You have done well… although I admit I have no guess what it is you have discovered."

The beadle's thoughts must have paralleled my own. His next words spoke his suspicion and worry. "Alan was found along t'road to chapel. Did he follow another man with a sack that night, you think?"

"I thought 'twas a beast which drew him from town, when he was first found. But 'twas not. I will tell you a thing which you must tell no other, not even your wife. Not yet. Henry atte Bridge slew Alan."

"You are sure of this?" John replied with surprise. Even in the dim starlight I saw his eyebrows rise.

"Aye. And now Henry's brother travels the same lane in the dark of night, and the new beadle sees and follows."

"Would Thomas do to me as Henry did to Alan?"

"He might, did he know what you have seen."

"So I must speak of this to no one, not even my wife," John whispered.

"Aye, until I can sort out this business you must appear ignorant of all we have spoken of this night."

"I am no scholar," John chuckled. "Seeming ignorant is a thing I can do well. God has granted me the skill."

"Do not seek to learn more of Thomas atte Bridge. Complete your rounds tomorrow night as if all was as should be. We must not give Thomas cause to suspect us. I will devise some way to learn what the fellow is about."

Chapter 15

I rose next morning at dawn and ate my breakfast loaf before the Angelus Bell tolled the beginning of the new day. I had notified the marshalsea that I would need Bruce this day early. He was saddled and waiting when I reached the stables. I tossed a pouch of herbs and surgical implements across his rump and led the old horse across the castle yard to the gatehouse, where Wilfred was about the business of cranking up the portcullis and swinging open the gate as I approached.

I had looked forward to this day for more than a fortnight. Even a man of little wit will understand why this was so. I never before appreciated how slow Bruce's ambling gait really was. My purpose was to remove the stitches I had used to seam Robert Caxton's back. But Bruce would not have seemed so plodding had I not another goal: a meal prepared by and in company with a beautiful lass.

It was well that I had business this day and so could not act on what I learned the night before from John Prudhomme. Bruce's languorous pace gave opportunity to consider options at leisure as I watched the Oxfordshire countryside pass by. Could there be a greener and more pleasant place for a man to live his days? 'Tis not meet to be boastful of such a thing, for God could have set me in a desert, was that His wish. But He did not. For that I must remember to thank Him each day.

In frustration I finally clucked to the old horse and gave him my heels in his ribs. Bruce responded. He broke into a lumbering gallop and I found myself bouncing from the saddle at frequent and regular intervals. How

Lord Gilbert, clad in armor, stayed atop Bruce during a charge I know not.

I tugged at the reins and Bruce slowed to his normal ambling walk. We had covered barely a hundred paces at a gallop. Had I allowed Bruce to continue, I would have arrived at Oxford so jostled and out of joint, I would have been of no use to Robert Caxton and his daughter would have thought me a cretin. I have new regard for knights who gallop into battle on ponderous destriers.

Before Bruce clattered across the Oxpens Road Bridge I was convinced I knew what was in Thomas atte Bridge's sack. The man was a poacher, I was certain of that. And certainly wrong, as I would soon learn.

In the sack which he used to retrieve his booty from the forest he had taken a rabbit or joint of venison to John Kellet. Why he should do so I could not guess. And did his brother, Henry, embark on a similar mission to St Andrew's Chapel the night Alan the beadle followed him and was slain? Would a man kill to preserve the secret of a gift? He might, was the gift unlawful. Did the priest of St Andrew's Chapel know the source of the bounty? How could he not, delivered after curfew as it was, when all virtuous men should be abed?

I left Bruce with the stableboy at the Stag and Hounds and set out through the mid-day throng for Holywell Street and Robert Caxton's shop. Both door and shutters were open this fine day. Kate greeted me. Her father, she said, was preparing ink in the work room.

The stationer overheard our conversation, for he appeared immediately at the door which separated the two rooms. He raised an ink-stained hand in greeting. "Ah, Master Hugh, we have been expecting you," Caxton said, and glanced to his daughter. "Kate has been preparing since yesterday."

I regarded the girl, and was rewarded with a smile. And a faint blush, do I not mistake me.

The stationer's wound was well healed, and he was strong enough that he, not Kate, helped me haul his ink-stained table into the toft. The day was much warmer than when last I visited the toft, and Caxton had not the same worries he had when last he removed his cotehardie and kirtle in this place. He did not shiver, but lay willingly upon the table for me to begin my work.

The seam along his rib was red, but showed no sign of putrescence. I asked him had it ever done so.

"Nay... but for t'first days."

"And you feel no pain, as before?"

"'Tis stiff, when I bend to put on a shoe, but not so as 'twas."

I carefully sliced each stitch and pulled the severed silk from the skin. A few small dots of blood appeared where the threads had been pulled free. I asked Kate for a clean cloth, and wiped away the traces of blood. No more followed.

Caxton stood and stretched, then dressed, and together we dragged the table back to its place in the work room. Kate waited there with a white linen cloth which she proceeded to lay upon the table. Having done so, she transformed it into a dinner table. She then ushered me and her father from the room to the front of the shop. We were told that our meal would be ready shortly.

We had already discussed the stationer's healing wound. No new depths of that subject remained to be plumbed. The weather was fine, and had been so for many days. Foul weather makes a better subject for conversation than fair when other topics fail. Caxton and I sat on facing benches in a shop empty of customers and waited in awkward silence to be called to our dinner.

The subject uppermost in both our minds was not the impending meal, but the future of the girl who prepared it. The stationer no doubt wondered of each new man in his daughter's life if he would become the father of his grandchildren. For my part I thought on how I might arrange to visit the shop now that my surgical skill was no longer needed. I could return for more ink and parchment. But I should seem foolish were I to ride from Bampton for one more gathering every week or two.

Perhaps it is the way of a young man who would court a maid – to appear foolish.

Caxton finally broke the awkward silence. "Is all well on Lord Gilbert's manor at Bampton?"

'Twas a question which could be answered with one word – either "Yes," or "No." But such an answer would not serve, for then silence would again settle over us like an autumn fog, with no rising sun in view to dissipate the cloud. The stationer was not so interested in affairs at Bampton as he was in ending the uncomfortable tranquility which enveloped the room.

"Some things are well, others not," I replied "Planting has gone well. There was enough rain, but not so much to interfere with plowing or rot the seed."

Caxton did not respond for a moment, then asked, "And what has not gone well?"

I sketched for the man a brief outline of two mysteries which were given to me to solve: the murders of Alan and Henry.

"So the death of the beadle was in your bailiwick, and you have solved that?"

"Aye... so I believe."

"And the other man was a bishop's tenant, but you are asked to find his slayer as well?"

"Aye. The death is only partly in my bailiwick. The dead man was the Bishop of Exeter's man, but he died in Lord Gilbert's forest to the north of town."

"And now you must deal with a poacher as well," Caxton commiserated. "I must remember to thank God in my prayers that I am but a purveyor of ink and parchment and books. Yours is not work I would seek."

Kate appeared at the door to the work room and announced that our meal was ready. There were but two places set at the table. The girl would not eat with her father and me, but rather scurried about serving us. I protested but she would not hear, and bade me sit. I did. 'Twas not the last time I would find it prudent to obey her.

Later, when I thought of the meal while swaying

atop Bruce on my return to Bampton, I realized that the home probably possessed but two wooden trenchers, two pewter cups, and two each of dinner knives and silver spoons. Two of each would serve father and daughter. I am often mortified at how slow I am to understand such things. 'Tis well I did not press the girl, but obediently took my seat.

In an iron pot hung over the fire Kate had baked a game pie, of chicken and rabbit, I believe. I have never eaten a better, and of this dish I ate enough that its quality was no mystery to me. There were also herb fritters fried in oil, and to finish the meal a cherry pottage, for which my groaning belly could barely find room. Cherries were a month from ripening. This pottage was made from fruit carefully dried and preserved for a year. I knew the trouble and expense which were ingredients of the dish.

Kate watched me eat with, I think, much satisfaction, nor did she allow my cup to go dry, but poured more ale each time I raised it to my lips.

When I was finished I thanked Kate much for the meal. This was necessary for good manners only, for surely she saw from my enthusiastic attack on the game pie that I approved her kitchen skills.

As her father and I finished our cherry pottage we heard footsteps enter the shop. Caxton heaved himself to his feet with an overfed groan and passed through the door to serve his customer. I was left alone with Kate.

Speaking the proper words to a lass is an art, not a skill. A skill may be taught. There is no course in the trivium or quadrivium to teach a man such competence. And if there was, who would teach it? Some bachelor scholar? I suppose 'twould not be the first time a master taught what he had learned from a book rather than from his own experience.

An art is a talent from God, which a man may surely improve with practice and effort. God did not choose to bless me with this craft, nor did I find occasion to practice what little talent He did give. I could set Lady Joan Talbot's broken wrist with skills I learned in study at Paris, but my conversation with the lady was clumsy. Had it been otherwise the outcome would have been no different. Our stations were too far apart. Sometimes even a God-given art may be insufficient.

Robert Caxton left the room and there followed a silence more awkward than I had experienced in the shop. Kate busied herself at the cupboard while I considered whether or not to belch – to show my appreciation for the meal and to break the uneasy silence. I decided against it. This was good, for at that moment Kate came to my aid. She would do so many times, but this I could not at the moment know.

"Do you return to Bampton today?" she asked.

"No. 'Tis a long journey for an old horse." I did not add, but could have, that it is also a long journey for a rump unaccustomed to a saddle. "And I have other business in Oxford. I have a matter to discuss with Master Wyclif."

It had occurred to me that the scholar might have an opinion regarding Thomas atte Bridge's nocturnal visit to St Andrew's Chapel. "There are empty rooms at New Canterbury Hall, where he is warden. He will permit me to stay in one this night, or I mistake me."

"I have heard of Master Wyclif," Kate replied. "He is, uh, capable of some controversy."

"Aye. There are those who do not appreciate all he teaches," I agreed.

Kate is not a timid girl. "And you?" she asked. "Are you among them? Surely not," she answered her own question, "else you would not seek him."

"You observe rightly. Master John is a scholar of great wit and insight."

"Is it his wit or his insight which leads to dispute?"

"Ah… some men are contentious not because of what they say, but the way they say it. Their words are sharp. They take pleasure in wounding an opponent."

"And does this describe Master John?"

"Not so," I replied firmly. More firmly than was merited, I fear. Kate shifted her weight back on her feet, her eyes opened wide.

"Master John," I continued (softly, for I recognized my error), "is gentle with most who challenge him. He is mild with those of little learning, or who have been misled. But he can be hard on men who hold foolish views when they have the learning and opportunity to know better."

"Oh," Kate nodded. The corners of her mouth lifted in a hint of a smile. "Who are these who should know better?"

I did not immediately reply. The conversation had drifted to deep waters. But Kate plunged ahead. "I hear students speak of such things from time to time."

"And what do they say?"

Kate smiled again. "It seems the pope and his bishops are not among Master John's favorite people."

It was my turn to display a sardonic smile. "He is known to criticize churchmen from time to time. What do your customers think of this?"

"Oh, he is a favorite among students who do business with my father."

"As when I was a student," I concurred. "The young seem always willing to smash the temple idols."

"And so they should," Kate replied with some vehemence. "Be it temple, cathedral, or chapel, an idol has no place."

"What idols seem most in danger these days... from the wrath of Master John's young charges?"

The girl screwed her lovely face into a mask of concentration. "Most likely they will decry the riches of pope and bishops. I heard one tell another that your Master Wyclif has said that a poor man need not contribute to the keep of a priest wealthier than he."

"Not a new thought with Master John," I agreed. "He said much the same thing five years ago."

"He has worked no great change," Kate observed. "I have not heard of the pope pleading poverty."

"Have you not? But he must be poor; he is always in need of money."

"True," Kate smiled again. "They say the king's brother is Master Wyclif's champion at court."

"Aye. Prince John seeks to avoid sending funds to a pope in Avignon who is little more than a puppet of the French."

"Master Wyclif's theology is useful for statecraft?" Kate concluded.

"Aye. Today. What may be tomorrow or next year no man can know."

"He may fall from favor?"

"He may... when he is useful no more."

"When will that be?"

"When we no longer quarrel with the French, and the pope is no longer at Avignon, I think."

"Ah," Kate laughed. "Then Master Wyclif will find friends at court for many years."

"You know much of the affairs of kings and ministers."

"I do but keep my ears open and my mouth closed," Kate replied. "So those who have opinions speak them before me, thinking I am witless and will understand nothing. 'Tis common for students to think so... of a lass."

"Not all young men are so disposed. My mother was a wise woman. My father sought her advice often, and I and my brothers saw."

"And did she offer counsel even when he did not ask?"

"That, too. But she was no termagant."

"How many brothers have you?"

Our conversation, which began with hesitancy, flowed from politics to family. I learned that her mother had died when Kate was five years old. She had but little memory of her. Her mother and the child had died at the birth of a younger brother. Her grandfather was a stationer in Cambridge, and rather than wait to inherit the shop there, her father had decided to remove to Oxford and open his own business. He had talked to Baliol scholars and knew the crusty reputation which Aelfred had built for himself.

I told Kate of growing up the youngest of four sons

at the manor of Little Singleton, in Lancashire. I told her of netting eels from the Wyre, and watching plague strike my family. I told her of the return of plague four years past, and how the disease had provided the book which sent me to Paris and gave me a profession.

"And now you have a murderer and a poacher to apprehend," Kate added. "I heard your conversation with father while I prepared dinner."

I was reminded that, while I was sated, Kate had taken no dinner, but served me and her father. I was reluctant to leave, but if I was to present to Master John the matter of Thomas atte Bridge and his nocturnal visit to John Kellet, I must be away. And my departure would allow Kate to take some of the meal she had prepared but so far not enjoyed.

Robert Caxton's customer was no longer present. I found the stationer reading at his desk when I passed through the door from the work room. He had surely overheard the conversation between his daughter and me, but had chosen to take no part in it.

There followed many thanks: I to Kate and her father for the meal, they to me for treating Caxton's wounded back. As I took the shop door latch in hand I turned to ask if I might call when next I was in Oxford. Of course, a man may call at a place of business any time he will without asking, and be welcome for his trade. But I wanted both father and daughter to know that business would not be my reason – at least, not my only reason – to visit Holywell Street when next I traveled to Oxford. These words I did not have opportunity to say. Kate spoke first.

"Master Hugh," she said softly, as I turned from the door, "I will take it amiss should you visit Oxford some future day and do not call."

Behind Kate, over her shoulder, I saw her father nod agreement. I promised that I would be obedient to the girl's command, said a last farewell, and set off down Holywell Street with a heavy stomach and light heart.

Oxford's streets were crowded. Black-gowned students, set free from study until the new term, elbowed each other through streets and lanes. Late buyers patronized shops before closing. I was become accustomed to the bucolic life of Bampton, but plunging into the noise and smells of Oxford's streets brought pleasant memories; memories of days when as a student I was concerned only with books and studies and enjoying the life of a fledgling scholar. Days when I had no murders to concern me or poachers to apprehend.

The porter at New Canterbury Hall recognized me. I was admitted with a smile and a tug of his forelock. He had no great esteem for me, I am sure. But I was a friend of the warden. That made me a man of consequence. If a man cannot achieve fame of his own merit, the next most rewarding thing is to be recognized as a friend of the famous and powerful. As if renown might slough off with recognition.

Master John's life turned about study and teaching. Since classes for the term were ended, I thought I might find him in his chamber bent over some tome. So he was.

I saw him through the small window which looked out from his room to the cloister. If he noted my shadow pass he did not think it important enough to raise his eyes from his book. I knocked on the door and eventually heard his bench scrape back from the table across the stone flags. Eventually. I was interrupting Master John while he was engrossed in some deep study, a thing no man should do lightly. I prayed he would forgive me.

He did. "Ah... Hugh... I was about to take supper. Have you eaten? Come in, come in."

Wyclif placed a leather strap between the pages of his book to mark his place, drew up a second bench, and invited me to sit.

"The kitchen will serve soon. A bell will announce supper. Meanwhile, what have you learned of your mysterious deaths in Bampton?"

I had barely opened my mouth when a tinny bell sounded from across the cloister. "Ah, the cook is ready," Wyclif said with some sorrow. "We will take our meal, then you will tell me the tale... you will lodge in the college this night, will you not?"

This was an offer I had hoped for. I readily agreed, and we set off across the cloister for a supper of barley pottage and wheaten bread. Not that I was hungry. But I was of an age wherein I could eat 'til bloated, then consume another meal an hour later. And soup is not a filling dish.

'Twas twilight when I returned with Master John to his lodgings. He lit a cresset to ward off the night and begged me tell him of Bampton and its mysteries.

I admitted that I was no closer to solving the death of Henry atte Bridge than when I was last in Oxford. Then I told him of Thomas atte Bridge and his late visit to St Andrew's Chapel. Master John caught the parallel with Alan the beadle's death along the road to the chapel and Henry atte Bridge's role in it.

"Tell me, then," the scholar inquired, "what is it happened the night your beadle was slain?"

"'Tis my belief Alan had seen Henry atte Bridge travel the road to St Andrew's Chapel before the night he was slain. But he was not careful in his pursuit. Henry knew he was discovered, and lay in wait for Alan another night, and slew him."

"How was this done?" Master John asked, pulling on his beard.

"I believe Henry hid in the shadow of the hedgerow until Alan was upon him. Then, who can know? Perhaps atte Bridge took a rock from the hedgerow wall and delivered a blow to the beadle's head as he passed. Or, mayhap there was a struggle, and Henry got hold of Alan's cudgel and beat him across the head with it. Whatever the source of the blow, it killed Alan. But Henry had planned another stroke."

"The wooden block with nails?" Wyclif guessed.

"Aye. He slashed Alan's face and arms and neck so 'twould seem some beast had set upon him there in the lane."

"But you suspected even when the beadle was first found that this was not so?"

"Aye. There was not enough blood. Living men bleed much when slashed across the neck. Bampton's baker was so attacked some days later and nearly lost his life."

"You saved him?"

"I did. A dead man bleeds little, and Alan did not bleed. 'Twas the blow which killed him, not the wounds."

"And what of the wolf? You heard it howl, did you not?"

"I heard something howl."

"Not a wolf? Or some other beast?"

"Nay. A man, I think."

"A man? Ah… I see. This same Henry atte Bridge, you think?"

"Aye. He knew we suspected a beast in Alan's death. 'Twas what he intended."

"So he thought to confirm your suspicion?"

"He did, and nearly succeeded."

"Think you, when he died, he suspected you knew 'twas no wolf attacked the beadle?"

"He knew I went north that day. He saw me pass the new tithe barn as he worked. He surely guessed what I was about, else he would not have set upon me in the road when I returned."

"But perhaps," Wyclif wondered aloud, "'twas only shoes he thought you would find out."

"Would a man strike down another to protect his misgotten shoes?"

"Ah, I take your point. Was it proved the shoes belonged to the beadle, he could still protest innocence of the death, and who could say otherwise? The fellow surely thought you disbelieved a wolf had done the harm."

"Aye. He feared I saw then what I do not see now… or see but through a fog."

The scholar was silent for a moment.

"There was an accomplice," he asserted. "Why else a man waiting while you were attacked on the road?"

"An accomplice who aided in the murder of the

beadle, or who knew of the deed when 'twas done and past?"

"What matter?" Wyclif replied. "What matters is what the man did with his knowledge... and perhaps what he yet does."

"He struck down Henry atte Bridge when Henry failed to kill me, for fear I would know who fell upon me, and when I might confront Henry he would entangle this other, whoso he may be, in the business."

"Just so," Wyclif nodded, his beard bouncing against his robe.

"The dead lamb; we watched over it two nights and saw nothing."

"The fellow atte Bridge again, you think?"

"'Twould make a kind of sense. He wished to put suspicion on a wolf, not a man. And when the hounds were put to the dead animal they knew what we did not... they scented a man, not a beast."

"The fellow would have used the block to tear the lamb's throat, then slice off a joint for himself to make it seem a wolf had dined," the scholar mused.

"And I was taken in. What a simpleton I am!"

"Nay, Hugh. Do not berate yourself so. We must all make judgment with the facts we have."

"But I had facts I did not read aright."

"You chose the simplest interpretation of the evidence at hand. This is always best."

"Is it so?"

"Aye." Wyclif reached for my arm. "'Tis not good for a man to seek complexity and falsehood where none may be. If the plainest answer prove mistaken, as now seems, time enough then to seek knots to untangle."

"And there are knots yet," I agreed.

"You think all these strange events be related?"

"I thought not. I sought the simplest explanation, as you advise."

"But such does not serve, eh?"

"Too many knots. Who set out for Alvescot with a sack over his shoulder? Was it Thomas atte Bridge? He carried a sack to St Andrew's Chapel. And who struck me down at Alvescot Church? The same man who carried the sack? Thomas atte Bridge? Or perhaps the man who put an arrow into Henry atte Bridge's back? And there are other knots in Bampton yet to be unraveled, of which you know not."

"Such a town! I am pleased I live in a quiet, gentle place."

"Oxford? Where scholars dispute even a comma in the scriptures."

"Aye, we dispute. But we do not go about clubbing one another across the skull or tearing out men's throats."

"Hah... I remember my first year at Baliol and the St Scholastica Day Riot."

"Hmm. You have a point. But that was about an important matter... so the students thought. The price of watered ale... or was it wine?"

"What are these other knots which bind your town?" Wyclif continued.

I told him of the baker, the baker's wife, the smith, and John Kellet. I told him of finding Kellet at the chapel after Edmund had struck him, and his words when he thought no man heard: "Henry got hinges... I'll have more'n that. A penny, no, tuppence a month or I'll see that all know."

The scholar's brows lifted and furrowed as I told of these events. "I wonder what it is that your priest may tell to all men? And why his silence may be worth tuppence each month to the smith?"

"I think he knows of Margery's infidelity, and Edmund cuckolding the baker."

"I wonder how he would know this... the confessional, you think? If so, 'tis a grievous sin to tell of it. And what of the hinges? Was it Henry atte Bridge he spoke of?"

"Aye. I did not tell you of the nails which Henry used to slash Alan's throat. They came from a set of hinges Edmund made for Henry's door."

"Iron hinges for a cotter's door?"

"Aye. The priest's words are telling, are they not? I

think Henry got his hinges without payment."

Wyclif scratched his scalp for a moment. "Which means, perhaps, that Henry knew of the smith and the baker's wife also... else why a gift from the smith, if not to purchase silence?"

"These are my thoughts," I agreed. "But how would atte Bridge know of the liaison, and how would the priest know what Edmund had paid for Henry's silence?"

"Ah, we have many questions this night and few answers. But take heart, Hugh, for the questions have become wiser than those we might have asked a month ago."

"Aye. But the wisdom has come in part through a stroke against my head. I have enough wisdom if that be how I must gain more."

Wyclif rose from his bench and went to a chest in a shadowy corner of his chamber. The lid creaked open and I watched him fumble about in the dim depths of the box. 'Twas too dark to see what the scholar did there, but soon I heard an exclamation of success and saw him stand and turn from the chest. He held some object to him, but 'twas too dark to see then what it was.

It was a dagger. Wyclif laid it on the table before me.

"You have found dangerous work," the scholar commented, "but I see only a dinner knife in your belt."

I was surprised that an Oxford master should own such a weapon. Wyclif must have seen this in my eyes, for he explained how he came by the dagger.

"I found this in a gutter outside Baliol College one morning during the St Scholastica Riot. I have kept it since, not for my own need, but so long as it lay in my chest it could do no harm. Now I think it time to put it to use."

"But what of scripture? We are commanded not to kill."

"Nay, Hugh, 'tis a mistranslation. God's word tells us not to do murder. Is there not a difference between murder and killing?"

"Aye... I suppose. But are we not to turn the other cheek?"

"We are, when another insults us with a slap. But when some miscreant would carve flesh from my cheek or another man's with his blade, I think our Lord would not require me to permit the fellow to do so. If murder is evil, as it is, it is a man's duty to stop it when he can... even when the murder be his own."

I took the dagger and slid it under my belt.

Wyclif gazed at his dark window. "We must sleep on these things and talk more in the morning. Perhaps God will grant a dream to resolve these matters."

He did not. Oh, He granted a dream, true enough. But not of Bampton and poachers and murderers. 'Twas of Kate Caxton I dreamt. And a delightful vision it was. No wonder. So when Master John asked me in the morning if some new insight had come to me in the night, I replied truthfully that I was as confused as before. It was well he did not ask of my dreams. I would have had to lie. What I dreamed was not such that it could be told a scholar.

We broke our fast with loaves hot from the kitchen and ale. The ale was not fresh, and near sour. Rather like my mood. For this Master John apologized. For the ale, I mean, not my mood.

"Fare you well, Hugh. When you have solved these mysteries I would hear of it."

"You may credit too much, Master John. You assume I will find a murderer and a poacher."

"I am a man of faith. What is it the Holy Scripture says of faith? 'Tis 'the substance of things hoped for, the evidence of things not seen.'"

"Aye, well, there is much I do not see and therefore must hope for."

"Because there is evidence not yet seen does not mean you will never see it. As the apostle wrote, 'now we see through a glass darkly, but then, face to face.'"

"The glass is surely dark. That much is true."

"Be of good cheer, Hugh. You are too solemn. You think too much of failure. Look rather at your success. All men fail on occasion. 'Tis our nature. Only the Lord Christ was perfect in all things. And consider that what seems failure this day may become success tomorrow or next day. You were much perplexed about the bones found in the castle cesspit, were you not?"

"Aye."

"But time and wit found the answer."

"And perhaps the grace of God, who looked on my feeble effort and chose to lead me through the maze."

"He does that, when we ask. Even, betimes, when we do not think to ask."

The scholar's words brought to mind the times I sought guidance. I nodded agreement. It is difficult to disagree with Master John.

"So before you are off to Bampton let us beseech God to grant you wisdom and success in this business."

Perhaps I expected a scholar's prayer to be filled with flowery language and erudite references. Master John spoke as if a third man sat with us in his chamber. A friend. A friend with authority, to be sure, but a beloved companion, rather than a great lord at whose feet we must tremble.

Wyclif's prayer requested two things: that God would grant me wisdom to find truth, and courage to do truth. What more does any man need? A man may want much more than these. I want more. But my needs and my wants, Master John saw, were different matters.

I breathed "Amen" along with Master John when he finished his petition. And silently added a request for one of my wants: a good wife. I admit it; this request accompanied an image in my mind's eye of Kate Caxton. A year before the image would have been Lady Joan Talbot. I was startled to consider that Lady Joan had not entered my thoughts for many weeks. Since near the time I met Kate.

How many other young men, I wonder, have breathed a similar prayer with the stationer's daughter in mind? They cannot all be answered. Well, yes, they will be; but the answer for most will be "No." Will my plea be among those? It surely was when I made similar appeal to God regarding Lady Joan.

A want? No, a need. God himself decreed that it is not good for a man to live alone and so made a helpmeet for him. I must adjust my thinking and my prayers and request our Lord that he provide for my need, not merely for my desire.

Chapter 16

Bruce neighed and stamped his great hooves when I approached his stall behind the Stag and Hounds. At home in Bampton the old horse was put out to grass in the west meadow most days. No doubt he found his stay in Oxford boring; the day spent staring at stable walls of wattle and daub.

Bruce's iron-clad hooves echoed loudly as we clattered across the Oxpens Road Bridge. In the water meadow to the west of the river teams of men moved across the field, scythes swinging rhythmically as they worked at hay-making. Behind the men women and older children followed, raking and turning the new-cut hay so it would dry evenly. This was a good year for hay-making. There would be fodder for beasts next winter, so long as the rains did not rot the hay on the ground before it could be dried and stacked.

This scene was repeated at Aston. There the meadows were cut and the scythe work near done for the day when Bruce ambled past. Villeins were stacking hay on their scythes to carry off for their own animals. A curious custom, unknown in Lancashire, from whence I come. Here in the south of England a man may carry off so much of the lord's hay as he may stack on his scythe when the day's work is done. But if the scythe or hay touch the ground the hay be forfeit. I watched Lord Doilly's reeve as he watched to see no hay grazed the ground. Some men staggered from the meadow with truly astonishing mounds of hay heaped upon their scythes.

As I completed my journey I shifted in the saddle so as to bring a different portion of my rump in contact with the hard leather. The movement brought the point of the dagger in contact with my leg. 'Twas too dark when Master John gave it to me to see it well, and I'd not taken time to examine it in the morning. I did so as Bruce shuffled the last short distance from Aston to Bampton.

The blade was well kept and sharp, and near as long as my forearm from elbow to wrist. No jewels ornamented the hilt. This was not a rich gentleman's weapon. But a coil of bronze wire circled the haft. This was decorative more than useful. The weapon was perhaps the property of some merchant's son. It suited my station and need. I slid it back under my belt, came near to pricking my thigh, and resolved to see the castle harness-maker about a sheath for the weapon.

The spire of the Church of St Beornwald is visible even before one reaches Aston. I enjoy my travels, especially when a conversation with Master John Wyclif – or Kate Caxton – is the purpose. But each time I approach Bampton and see that stolid spire I am reminded of what a pleasant place it is.

Ah, you say, but what of murderers and poachers and those who attack a man in the night? I suppose most towns have their miscreants. Else the king would need no sheriffs and lords no bailiffs. Bampton has its share of good men, as well. Hubert Shillside, John Prudhomme, John Holcutt, and Lord Gilbert himself. And good women, too: Matilda, Alan's widow, the child Alice, and until she became the Lady de Burgh, Lady Joan, who once mended the torn hem of my cloak, unhindered by her station – though her brother, I think, thought it unseemly.

I was – as had become my custom – late for dinner. Bruce covered the ground at a contented, ambling pace. So long as the old horse reached Bampton Castle in time for his own bucket of oats he was unconcerned regarding my growling belly.

I took from the kitchen a loaf and a cold capon and ate in my chamber while I considered paths I could follow which might lead to a resolution of my perplexity.

Two issues vexed me: who murdered Henry atte Bridge in the north wood, and who was poaching Lord Gilbert's game?

I decided that day to attend the poaching business first. I thought 'twould be easiest to solve. What I did not know then was that the discovery of a poacher would lead to discovery of a murderer. Had I sought first a murderer I might never have found either a killer or a poacher.

Although I wore the dagger at my hip, the steel seemed rather to strengthen my backbone. I went to my chamber the evening of the next day resolved to spend the night behind the broken-down church wall at St Andrew's Chapel. I would learn who approached the chapel so late at night, why he did so, and what was in his sack.

I was become accustomed to slipping over the castle wall at night. I worried that this familiarity might cause me to grow careless, so crept slowly through the shadows 'til I reached the place along the north wall I favored for the purpose.

I wore brown chauces and a dark grey cotehardie, to blend with the night. But I worried that face and hands might give me away when the moon rose, so applied a thick dusting of ashes from my fireplace to the offending skin. I was satisfied with the result.

I adjusted the dagger in my belt, secure in its new sheath, dropped the cudgel from the wall, then followed it down the rope. Once on the ground I sat at the base of the wall to watch and listen for movement. I neither saw nor heard anything but what is common to a summer evening. I paid special attention to the Ladywell. If any supplicant was there he was silent and took no notice of me.

No one, not even John Prudhomme, must know I was about this night. I avoided the town and circled to the north. This doubled the length of my journey, for the castle is on the west edge of Bampton, while St Andrew's Chapel lies near half a mile to the east of the town.

I stole across the meadow between the castle and the Ladywell, then made my way along a hedgerow north of the millpond until I came to Shill Brook. I removed my boots, waded the stream, and stumbled across a fallow field to the west of the Church of St Beornwald. The night was so dark I nearly missed Laundell's Lane, but this reassured me. If I could not see what I knew to be present, it seemed unlikely another would see what he did not expect – me.

Laundell's Lane is the northern boundary of the town. I was somewhat concerned about crossing the north road, so held back in the shadow of a hedge until I was sure no man was about. Across the road there was but a path which led east to the fields and crossed the north end of Bushey Row. I followed this track until past Bushey Row, then stumbled diagonally across a field of strips planted to barley. At the southeast corner of this field lay the small copse which formed the western shelter to St Andrew's Chapel.

This grove was thick with scrub and roots. I stumbled and tripped often as I groped through it. I could not be seen, but I was worried that, for all my caution, I might be heard. Dry twigs cracked under my feet and once I fell to my knees with feet entangled in ground ivy.

With much relief I saw the dilapidated churchyard wall appear from the shadows of the wood. The wall was not high. Crossing it was easy. There were, however, nettles growing up about the stones. I could not see them, but I surely felt them.

The parish about St Andrew's Chapel is poor. Few who worship there can afford a stone to mark a family grave. So there were few grave markers to hide behind as I crept across the churchyard. Only an occasional wooden plank, not yet rotted to mold, stood upright in the soil.

I crossed the churchyard to the gate and sat beside it, my back to the wall. The moon began to glimmer through the trees to the south of the chapel, but I sat in darkness in the shadow of the wall. No man could enter without my knowledge, for he would be on a moonlit path, and the rusted iron hinges would squeal a warning.

I know not how long I sat, cold on the damp ground, awaiting one who never came. I believe I dozed once or twice, but no man tried the gate.

The moon was well to the west when I stood, stretched, and crept across the churchyard to the broken-down place in the wall where I had entered. My stinging palms reminded me to this time avoid the nettles.

I took the same route back to the castle I had followed four hours earlier on my way to the chapel. I was careful not to be seen; not because of any violation of curfew. I am Lord Gilbert's bailiff. I may go where I wish, when I wish. Any who saw me might be curious, but I cared little for that. I did not want an observer because, was I seen, soon gossip would mean that many would know that Master Hugh was prowling about at night. Miscreants would then stay abed and await a more favorable time to work their evil. Or they would set out to ambush me while I thought to lie in wait for them. Neither of these was an outcome to be desired.

The next two nights – well, parts of the next two nights – I spent sitting against the crumbling south wall of St Andrew's Chapel churchyard. Midway through the third night I heard a distant creaking sound and my heart did handsprings. I looked up from my seat on the grass and watched the gate, expecting to see it swing open. It did not move, but the creaking continued.

My senses were alert. I had one hand on my cudgel and the other on the dagger, ready to leap to my feet and challenge whoever moved about in the night. Then I saw the light. A single flame, from candle or cresset, moved from the chapel porch and the rotund shadow carrying it moved across the churchyard to the north. It was John Kellet.

I heard another distant squawk of wood against wood as a door was opened. The flame disappeared. I remembered. The chapel privy was along the north wall of the churchyard, just outside the consecrated ground. A few moments later another squeal and the reappearance of the flame indicated that Kellet had completed his nocturnal business. I watched the flickering flame float toward me across the churchyard, then disappear into the porch. A squeal and thud told me that the priest had reentered the chapel. I remained against the wall until I was sure the slovenly priest was snoring in his bed, then set out for the castle.

After three nights propped against a churchyard wall I was tempted to end the practice. The fourth night was Sunday eve. Surely a poacher, or whoever sought John Kellet of a midnight, would not do his work on our Lord's Day? And it was raining. Not hard, more like a drizzle. But enough that I would soon be cold and soaked, even should I wear a cloak.

These were good reasons to stay in my bed this night, but I did not. I took rope, club and dagger, wrapped my cloak about me, and made my way again to the castle wall. I had given up brushing ashes on face and hands. 'Twas too difficult to remove the next day. I should have continued the practice.

For three nights I had walked the same path from castle to chapel. This night I varied my route, especially where I must cross the barley strips. The tenants whose fields these were might soon notice the flattened stalks and wonder how the crop came to be damaged.

I set out as soon as darkness enveloped the ground, but while the northwestern sky was yet pale beyond the trees. Even so, 'twas near midnight, I think, before I arrived at the chapel, this night being among the shortest of the year.

The grass along the wall was thick and wet with rain. I had sat three nights in the same place, near the gate. Perhaps, if John Kellet was observant, he might wonder why grass in his churchyard was beaten down at but one place along the wall. I crossed the churchyard path and sat against the wall at another place.

I had not long to sit in wet grass this night. Clouds began to break and stars appeared through fissures in the overcast. And then the waning moon appeared to the east. The grey stones of the chapel's east wall seemed to reflect the moon and stars. I sat in shadow, there by the south wall, but my hands glowed whitely in reflected moonlight.

A snapping twig caused my heart to leap and hairs

to stand erect upon the back of my neck. A moment later I heard footsteps on the road beyond the wall.

Moonlight, filtered through the trees to the south of the chapel, provided enough illumination that I saw a shadow fall across the gate. An instant later it swung open, quietly, on wet hinges. A dark figure, pale sack slung over a shoulder, passed the open gate and crept along the path to the chapel. The sack was white in the moonlight against the intruder's dark cloak. A small, round lump swelled the bottom of the sack.

A stray cloud left behind by the departing rain obscured the moon as the figure reached the shadows of the porch. I heard a soft rapping on the door, and rose from my place along the wall to follow the sound.

I was between gate and porch when the moon reappeared from behind the passing cloud. Without the ashes to disguise me, my pale hands and face would surely have been visible, did any man look in my direction. To my sorrow, a man did.

I must stop prowling about of night-time and seek rogues in daylight. Darkness is not kind to those who seek justice, but is rather an ally of those who do wrong. I crept to the porch and pressed against it, then peered around the corner to see the entrance. The night was suddenly illuminated. A thousand stars flashed before my eyes and I fell, numbed, to my knees. Just as the swirling of comets and stars seemed to cease they began again, accompanied by a sharp pain across my skull. The world went black.

Once again fashion saved me. The liripipe coiled about my head softened the blows. I awoke I know not how long after the two strokes laid me in the grass beside the porch. I heard the soft muttering of voices but had not at first enough wit to understand what they said. My head throbbed, but the cold, wet ground soon brought me to my senses. I heard John Kellet speak.

"You've killed 'im."

"Aye... let's hope," another said. I did not know the voice.

"You'll hang."

"Maybe."

"What'll you do with 'im?" Kellet asked.

"What'll I do with 'im? You're in this business, too."

"Aye... but I'll not hang."

The other man spat. "You'll lose yer livin'."

"Maybe. But Father Ralph'll not see me starve. Send me to some monastery t'be a lay brother; maybe make me go on pilgrimage. Always wanted t'see Canterbury, anyway," he chuckled.

"I'll drag 'im to the wood there beyond the wall, an' get a spade. I can have 'im buried and leaves strawed across grave afore dawn."

"Best be sure 'e's dead," Kellet replied.

I held my breath as a dark form bent over me. I thought to use the dagger against the man, but was unsure if my condition would permit a quick and accurate thrust. The man's stinking breath near caused me to choke but I smothered the impulse. A hand went roughly to my neck to seek a pulse. My right hand lay by my side. I made ready to seize the dagger, but the fellow knew not where to seek an artery and so a moment later stood and spoke to the priest.

"Ain't breathin'. 'E's dead. Whacked 'im 'cross the head hard enough. Shouldda hit 'im second time at Alvescot, when I had the chance."

"Live an' learn," Kellet chuckled.

"'Ere... grab 'is feet an' 'elp me get 'im over the wall."

I was taken up, dragged across the wet grass of the chapel yard to the west wall, hoisted to the top, and dumped over into a pile of nettles. 'Twas my life depended on my silence, so I did not cry out. Had I done so the nettles would not have stung the less.

"I'm off then, for me spade," a muted voice came from across the wall. "See you be here t'help when I return."

I heard the chapel door creak open, then close. I must not be here when the man returned. At least, not alone.

I had walked this grove so often in the dark, I felt at home in it. I rose, head throbbing, to my knees and listened, should the fellow think better of his plan and return. The night was silent. So was I as I wobbled to my feet and staggered through the wood to the barley fields beyond.

A plan formed in my scrambled mind as I stumbled from the shadows of the trees into the moonlit field. I hastened straight west across the wet field. Was a man to study the field he would see my dark form against the barley. But I did not seek to travel the path for fear my attacker might also be on the track, returning with his shovel. And the barley field was the most direct route to Rosemary Lane and John Prudhomme.

I did not wish to rouse John's neighbors from their beds, so rapped but gently on the beadle's door. My effort was like much else in life: too little will not serve, and too much may cause unwanted consequence. I knocked several times upon the door, each time more firmly than the last, before I heard from beyond the planks a muttered oath, then a question: "Who disturbs the night?"

"'Tis Hugh... open your door. There is mischief about."

John swung open the door in response and squinted at me.

"Clothe and arm yourself. Hurry. I will explain when we are off. And bring a length of rope, if you have it."

The beadle did not question my charge, but disappeared into the blackness of his house. I heard him speak to his wife and stumble about in the dark. Then he reappeared, shod, cudgel in one hand and a coil of rope in the other.

I explained our mission as I led him across the barley strips. "'Tis Thomas atte Bridge," John concluded when I had finished my tale.

"I could not see a face, nor identify the voice, but I think you speak true."

"And he spoke of poaching?"

"Nay. But 'twas a rabbit filled his sack, I think."

"But why give it to John Kellet?" the beadle puzzled.

"There is payment, or obligation, in this or I am mistaken. But what is owed and why I cannot guess."

John walked on my right hand as we hastened across the field. This was fortunate, for when we were nearly to the grove at its eastern edge the moon, which had been briefly obscured, reappeared from behind a scudding cloud. In its light a movement caught my eye. I grasped the beadle's arm, pulled him to the ground, and whispered, "Shhh."

I pointed to the south, toward the path from town to chapel, and together we cautiously raised our heads above the barley stalks. Another cloud chose that moment to obscure the moon, but before it did we saw a figure hastening along the lane toward the chapel. The moonlight was not bright enough to see, but I was sure there was an implement thrown over the fellow's shoulder. Such a tool might be a formidable weapon. I whispered a warning to John and bade him rise and follow me into the wood.

The clearing sky which followed the rain now began to thicken. Clouds hid the moon. It was well I had penetrated this grove in darkness many times, else I might have got turned round. But I found the west wall of the churchyard with no difficulty and drew John to his knees beside me behind the smooth skin of a beech.

"'Twas just there," I pointed, "aside the wall, where they left me for dead."

"Shall we await them here," the beadle whispered, "or have them in the churchyard?"

"Here, I think. We will have the black wood behind us, and I should like to hear what they say when they find me gone. Perhaps we will learn more."

We did.

We heard voices approach beyond the wall and shortly two shadowed forms appeared. I heard one warn the other of nettles, and after some indecision and prodding at the overgrown wall they found a place to their liking and clambered over. But not without a curse from a sting or two. It served John Kellet right. He should have taken better care of his chapel.

The two figures stood silent for a moment. I thought I could see their heads twisting as they examined the forest floor for the body they had left there. I could see this because the northeast sky was beginning to lighten with an early summer dawn.

"Where away was it you dropped him?" I heard Kellet ask.

"Here," came the puzzled reply, "or nearabouts."

"Well, it must be nearabouts. 'Tis not here... unless some beast," Kellet chuckled, "has dragged him off already."

"Ha," the other replied. "The king should employ you for his jester. You go that way, an' I'll go t'other. 'E's 'ere some'eres. Sing out when you find 'im."

The two shadows separated, Kellet to the south, the other to the north. John and I waited behind the beech as the dim figures poked through the grove along the wall until both were lost to sight and all that could be known of their search was the sound of it.

Eventually even that evidence faded, but soon enough returned. Each man had reached an end to the wall, found nothing, and retraced his steps. I heard much consternation in Kellet's voice when he spoke.

"I found no corpse... nor did you, I think. I heard nothing from you."

"'E's 'ere... got to be. 'Twas not three paces from this place where I shoved 'im over wall."

The words spoke surety, but the tone of voice spoke incredulity. A thought occurred to me that if my disappearance was incredible, my reappearance might be also. I touched Prudhomme's arm by way of warning, then moaned softly.

The effect was sudden and gratifying. From my refuge behind the beech tree I watched two shadows stumble quickly toward the wall.

"You said 'e was dead," the priest hissed. "He's crawled off somewhere."

"'E was dead," came a shaky reply.

I moaned again, a little more loudly this time.

"An' corpses cry out like that?" Kellet snorted.

I decided that more than a groan might be called for. I whispered, but loudly enough to be heard: "I will be avenged... who is't troubles my grave?"

Two shadows plunged, heedless of the nettles, over the wall and back to the openness and safety of the chapel yard. I saw John's teeth as he grinned at the performance. I motioned him to follow, then left the shadow of the tree and approached the wall in a crouch.

"Stay behind," I whispered, "so you are not seen. Stand beside me upon my signal."

Kellet and his visitor had slowed their race to escape the wood and were backing slowly across the chapel yard, eyes fixed on the wall and the dark copse beyond. I wish there had been more light. I should like to have seen their eyes when I stood at the wall and appeared, an apparition, as they thought, from the dead.

I moaned once more. The effect had been salubrious before, so I tried it again. The result was remarkably similar. The two men stood agape, too startled to run.

"I will be avenged," I said again. "And Alan, too." I pulled John to his feet beside me.

'Twas too dark for us to be identified. They might assume my identity – or that of my specter – at the wall, but they could not see to be sure. They could surely not see that the apparition beside me was the new beadle, not the old.

"You know we cannot pursue you on to consecrated ground," I hissed loudly. "But we will be avenged." John stood beside me, nodding vigorously, so that even in the dark his agreement might be seen.

"'Twasn't me," Kellet squealed.

"Shut up," the other cried.

"Why? They're spirits. They'll know who 'twas who did for 'em."

"Then no need to tell 'em."

"They won't know I had naught to do with it. 'Twas

Henry killed Alan," the priest blurted.

"And now he lies in his grave," I murmured. "As you will soon, Thomas atte Bridge."

"No," the man stammered, and I knew the beadle was right. It was Thomas there with the priest. I saw his shape take a step away from me and the wall. "You will not take me... you cannot enter here."

"True," I said softly, "I cannot enter. And you, you cannot leave... else I will have you."

Atte Bridge took another step back. Kellet turned from me to his companion and back again. I spoke next to the priest.

"A priest who profits from poaching. Lord Gilbert will find you out, even so I am gone and may not tell him so."

It was Kellet's turn to take a step back from the wall.

"'At's right," Thomas quaked. "'Twas 'im gained from all."

I believe it was about that moment that Kellet realized he might deal not with specters but with flesh and blood. "Be silent, you fool," the priest demanded.

"Nay... I'll not bear the wrath o' spirits alone when 'twas you planned all."

"The wrath of spirits," I murmured, "is much to be feared. But best fear this priest. When we come for you we may find you among us already."

I saw atte Bridge turn to Kellet, and realized that the churchyard was not so dark as had been. Dawn was beginning to lighten the sky to the east of the chapel.

"What... what does 'e mean?" Thomas asked the priest.

My next words were a gamble, but one with small risk. "Tell Thomas," I whispered loudly, "what happened to his brother."

The priest made no answer.

"What 'appened to me brother?" Thomas asked.

"Tell him," I sighed. "You know well."

"Who killed 'Enry? You know an' 'aven't told me?"

"He cannot tell," I hissed.

"Aye," Kellet agreed. "I cannot tell, for I know not who killed 'im."

"A lie," I charged. "You cannot tell for to do so would be to indict yourself."

"You...?" Thomas exclaimed.

"Nay... he lies," the priest cried.

"Spirits do not lie," atte Bridge declared.

"Be silent," Kellet shouted. "These are not spirits."

He said no more, for Thomas delivered a blow from his right fist which knocked the corpulent priest to his well-padded rump. He then set about pummeling Kellet about the head so that John and I were able to leap the wall and approach before Thomas knew we were upon him. The beadle was a step behind me, so I did not see him cock his cudgel. But I heard the club as it passed my ear and landed solidly upon Thomas atte Bridge's head. He fell across the priest's prone form, and both lay silent and unmoving at our feet.

"Well done," I complimented John. He, meanwhile, had drawn the club back for another blow, should it be necessary. 'Twas not.

The rotund priest struggled to draw himself from under the comatose cotter. I thought he intended to run, but then he saw the cocked club in the beadle's hands and thought of a better escape.

"I am the bishop's man. You have no bailiwick here," he cried.

"True enough. But when Lord Gilbert learns of this he will have a word with Thomas de Bowlegh. And Henry atte Bridge died in Lord Gilbert's forest." I stepped closer to the quaking priest. "That is my bailiwick."

"Then you must seek Henry's killer," Kellet stammered.

"I have... and found him."

"Have you proofs?"

The priest had me. I was sure 'twas he who lay in ambush with Henry atte Bridge that evening, awaiting my return from Witney. I knew it was he to whom Henry had cried, "He lives." And I knew the arrows Kellet had intended for me, should I return while 'twas still light enough for their use, had been turned on his companion. The priest surely feared then that I would know 'twas Henry atte Bridge who attacked me, and when pressed, Henry would confess the truth and tell of Kellet's role in the blackmail which existed in the town, which none had suspected. I suspected all this, but the priest spoke true. I could not prove it.

It was grown light enough that when Thomas atte Bridge twitched at our feet the movement caught our eyes. The beadle had wrapped the rope about his waist and tied it there. I told him to undo it and tie Thomas' hands behind his back with it and take the fellow to the castle. The cell there had not been used since I came to the town two years before. It would have an inhabitant now.

I demanded of John Kellet that he accompany me to Thomas de Bowlegh's vicarage. This he was reluctant to do. The priest turned from me to return to the chapel. His cowl presented the most convenient handle to prevent this. I grasped it and twisted the wool tight about his thick neck.

"The sack," I demanded. "Where is it?"

"S... s... sack?" he spluttered.

"The one Thomas brought this night. Where is it?" I twisted the cowl tighter.

"The porch," Kellet gasped.

I shoved him before me toward the porch and he pointed out the corner where it lay. I released my hold on Kellet's cowl, withdrew the sack from its shadowed corner, and emptied it. In the morning light a haunch of venison – no coney – fell out onto the grass of the churchyard.

"Did Thomas set snares for this, or is he accomplished with a bow and arrows... as you are?"

The priest did not reply. I returned the venison to the sack and motioned Kellet to the gate. Perhaps he feared I might again attempt to strangle him. He set out promptly.

The spire of St Beornwald's Church glowed golden in the rising sun as we approached Bampton. Most of this journey was accomplished in silence, but for the wheezing of the fat priest. But as we came to Bushey Row a question occurred to me.

"What business had Thomas in Alvescot that he would knock me in the head and wish me dead rather than have me know of it?"

Kellet made no reply. He was unaccustomed, I think, to walking so fast. His only sound was to gasp for breath.

"I thought I trailed a poacher," I continued, "but it seems odd to me that Thomas went to the town rather than the forest around it. 'Twas near midnight."

Kellet held his silence. This one-sided conversation was becoming tiresome. "Poachers do business in the forest, not in a village. What business had Thomas at midnight in Alvescot?"

"Ask 'im," the priest wheezed.

"I will. Just thought you might want to provide your version of this tale before I hear from Thomas. A few days in the castle dungeon before I question him will surely loosen his tongue."

"You'd believe a cotter before a man in holy orders?"

"Depends upon the cotter and the parson. The more I learn of you and Thomas the less likely I am to believe anything either of you say. But I suppose I shall be able to ferret out something like the truth of it."

"And if I choose to say nothing?"

"Well," I thought on this for a moment, "you've already said much... back in the chapel yard. Lord Gilbert will return from Pembroke soon. Perhaps he will get some truth from you if I fail."

"I am the bishop's man. I do not fear Lord Gilbert."

"You think the Bishop of Exeter will defend you and cross Lord Gilbert? Lord Gilbert has powers to make life unpleasant even for a bishop. What influence have you?"

This was a new and unwelcome thought for the priest. He walked on silently. I thought the contemplation would do him good.

There were few townsmen about so early, but those who were at their business glanced at the priest and me with curiosity in their eyes. A townsman might be out of his bed and at his work before the Angelus Bell, but it was unlikely Lord Gilbert's bailiff and the priest of St Andrew's Chapel would be. Unless some unusual circumstance had occurred. The commons are not so doltish as churchmen and gentlemen may believe. Those who watched as Kellet and I strode down the Broad Street to Church Street knew something was amiss.

Thomas de Bowlegh's cook was at his work. A column of smoke rose from the vicarage chimney into the still air of dawn. So Kellet and I did not wait long after I rapped upon the vicarage door before the vicar's yawning servant drew it open.

We were invited to warm ourselves before the fire while the servant went to wake his master. He hesitated when I asked him to do this. Some men awaken bright for the new day. Others are cranks until the sun is high and they have broken their fast. Thomas de Bowlegh is among the latter, as the servant well knew, and Kellet and I were about to learn.

I heard the vicar's feet fall heavily upon the steps leading down from his room. A warning that an unhappy man was about to appear. Amazing how a man's feet can echo his disposition. I have ever since that day sought to avoid discourse with Thomas de Bowlegh until after the third hour.

The fire and east window combined to provide enough light that the vicar could identify his interlopers. He took a step into the room, glared first at John Kellet, then at me, and said, "Well?"

"No," I replied. "I am not well. I took two blows across my skull this night, and was dumped in a bed of nettles. In your service." I can be as churlish as any other. Especially with two tender lumps above my ear and a foul headache.

The vicar's eyes, drawn near closed in a frown, opened wide at my words. Two benches sat either side of the blaze. I shoved Kellet toward one and motioned the vicar toward the other.

"Sit," I commanded, "and I will tell you who murdered Alan the beadle and Henry atte Bridge."

"The same man slew both?" de Bowlegh gasped.

"Nay. But the deaths are tied. This priest," I nodded toward Kellet, "was in league to do evil with Henry atte Bridge. When he saw that I lived and might identify Henry as my attacker on the road to Witney, he put an arrow into Henry's back to silence him."

"Arrow?" the vicar frowned. "I thought 'twas a dagger struck down the fellow. You said as much."

"'Twas my error. I found an arrowhead embedded in Henry's back when I examined him more closely. 'Twas this priest who drew the bow."

"Not so," Kellet exploded. "He cannot prove so."

This charge and the priest's denial so startled de Bowlegh that he did not think to ask when the inspection took place which brought forth an arrowhead from Henry atte Bridge's hairy back. The question seemed not to occur to him, for he never asked it of me. So I never told him. 'Tis not only sleeping dogs that are best left to lie.

"Henry atte Bridge and this parson wished me dead, for they feared what I might discover about the death of Alan the beadle."

Thomas de Bowlegh wore yet a frown, but not because of an early departure from his bed, I think. He was puzzled.

"Alan followed Henry one night as the cotter made his way from the town to St Andrew's Chapel. Perhaps Alan had followed him in this journey before. But on this night Henry lay in wait, smashed Alan's head with a rock from the hedgerow, then tore the beadle's neck with a nail-studded block so we who found Alan might think his death the work of a wolf. But Henry was greedy. He took the shoes from Alan's corpse and 'twas the shoes which betrayed his deed to me."

"And this is why he fell upon you on the road?"

"Aye."

"But what has Father John to do with this?" de Bowlegh asked, nodding toward the priest.

"He and Henry were in league. I do not yet know why, nor how, but poaching had to do with it. Henry took venison to this priest. It must have been payment, but for what I do not yet know."

"'Twas a gift," Kellet muttered. "I thought 'twas... a goat... or a leg of mutton Henry brought."

"And why would he do so?" de Bowlegh asked, disbelieving.

"We was friends... of old."

"And he could not give this gift in the day, but must do so at night, and kill a man to keep the gift secret?" the vicar scoffed.

"Now Henry's brother is in the same business," I continued. I picked up the sack and dumped its contents before de Bowlegh.

"Venison," he growled through pursed lips, "or I miss my guess. Surely no goat."

John Kellet, guilty or not, would be taken from my hands and tried before a church court. Thomas Becket had died to maintain that immunity. Right or wrong, I was not sorry to be rid of the fellow.

"I leave the priest to you. John Prudhomme has taken Thomas atte Bridge to the castle. I intend to let him sit in the dungeon for a day or two. He will be more likely to give the truth after a taste of life in a cell. I will call if I learn of the bargain between him and this... priest."

De Bowlegh and Kellet sat glaring at each other. I thought I knew which glare would prove most effective.

I was eager to know more of this affair which I had uncovered, but I was also thirsty, tired, hungry, and suffering a headache. I went straight to the castle kitchen for a loaf hot from the oven, not even pausing on the bridge over Shill Brook. I took a tankard of ale to my chamber and added a handful of ground willow bark and lettuce to the ale. This was effective, for I was asleep as soon as I went to my bed.

I left instructions to be awakened for dinner. I have

had enough of cold meat and bread taken in my chamber. This must have caused some puzzlement, for none of the castle grooms or valets knew I had been up awake all night. They would know the truth of it soon enough.

The trestle tables and benches awakened me as they were dragged across the great hall floor. So when Uctred rapped upon my door I was already alert. But when I stood from my bed I nearly fell back to it again. I was so dizzy I could not stand, but sought my bench and collapsed upon it. Perhaps it was the blows I had taken, or the willow bark and lettuce, which caused my unsteady legs. I was required to sit for a moment until my head cleared and I was able to stand again. Uctred continued thumping against the door, his exasperation at receiving no reply causing him to beat the oaken planks more and more vigorously until I finally found wit to call out that I would soon appear.

I stood cautiously, ready to resume my seat if need be. But my head did not whirl this time. I was nevertheless careful as I opened my door and made my way to my place at the table.

The meal was hot and tasty, and I was hungry, so I remember it well. Even a whack across the head will not harm my appetite for long. The first remove was a pike and roasted capons, and a pottage of peas and bacon. For the second remove there was a game pie of rabbit with onions and apples, and mushroom tarts. For the subtlety a pudding with Spanish almonds, dates, raisins and currants.

I rose, sated, from the table and ordered that a trencher be taken to Thomas atte Bridge in his cell. An old, stale crust, stained with the grease of a capon, so Thomas would know, there in his cell, what others consumed for their dinner. Of course, most cotters by this time of year lived on pottage and perhaps an egg. Meat and any other good thing from last year's slaughter and harvest was long since consumed, and the new harvest was a month and more away. If a villein or poor tenant could fill his belly with peas and barley pottage by St Swithin's Day he would think himself fortunate. But there had been roasted meat in the Weald only a fortnight before. Perhaps a part of the haunch of venison in Thomas' sack was yet in his hut, where, were he free, he might now be licking grease from his fingers rather than chewing a stale crust and considering what might have been.

I did not sleep well that night. Perhaps the long nap before dinner was responsible. Or perhaps the tender lumps on my head were the cause. They reminded me of their presence each time I turned upon my pillow. I never knew goose feathers could be so firm.

Chapter 17

The Bampton Castle dungeon is beneath the buttery. If wine is spilled on the planks above, the drippings might sweeten the place. But the west wall of the cell is the east wall of the castle cesspit. The stones of that foundation passed more of their contents, I think, than did the oaken boards of the buttery floor above. The stench was awful. Good. A man might be so eager to leave the place he might even tell the truth if it meant his release.

The door to the dungeon had no latch or lock. It was fixed on one side to the stones with three iron hinges pinned to the wall. To make the door secure it was held in place by two oaken beams which dropped into iron fixtures on either side of the door. These were also pinned to the stones. A small opening little larger than my fist permitted conversation through the door, and the passage of food and water.

Uctred accompanied me down the stone steps behind the kitchen. We each held a cresset, for although the new day dawned bright and golden, no windows or embrasures lit either the cell or the steps and passage leading to it. The stone walls of this corridor were cold and damp. Thomas, I decided, should be thankful he'd taken residence in this place in summer, rather than winter.

Thomas heard us approach. His face appeared at the opening in the door, expecting a crust for his breakfast, I think. He had a crust the day before, and would receive another after this day's dinner. With such he must be content. I had little sympathy for a man who thought he had slain me and would have buried me, unknown and ungrieved, in unconsecrated ground outside St Andrew's Chapel churchyard wall.

Uctred lifted the timbers which secured the door and swung it open on protesting hinges. Hinges always seem to squeal in protest when required to perform their appointed work. Like some men. Thomas atte Bridge glowered at me through the open door. I glowered back. I had been Lord Gilbert's bailiff for nearly two years. In that time I had learned the potency of a practiced scowl. I stepped through the open door and was gratified to see atte Bridge retreat and cast his eyes to the hard-packed earth at his feet. The opening skirmish in this battle was won.

"John Kellet," I began, "is in the hands of the vicars of St Beornwald's Church. No doubt the bishop's court will see to this business and I will be called to testify. Will you have me learn of your crimes from the priest, or will you tell me?"

Thomas stood silent before me, clenching and releasing his fists, considering his options, which were few. It must be a family inheritance, for Henry clenched his fists when pressed in much the same way.

"Ain't no poacher," he finally muttered.

"The venison in the sack you would have given to John Kellet was surely Lord Gilbert's deer. I think I followed you to Alvescot three weeks past, where you gave me a blow from behind the churchyard wall. You were seeing to your snares, I think."

"Never set no snares," Thomas replied. I watched the muscles of his jaw twitch as he spoke.

"You used bow and arrows? In the dark?" I found this dubious. The man I followed to Alvescot carried no bow.

"Never kilt none o' Lord Gilbert's deer, w'snare or arrows."

"Ah... but you do not deny whacking me across the head. And you would have made of me a corpse at St Andrew's Chapel. You had a haunch of venison there, and a sack. The same sack as at Alvescot, I'd guess. You wished me dead to hide something, but not poaching?" I scoffed.

Thomas had been inspecting his feet during this conversation. But now he looked up, first at me, then to the door, where Uctred stood frowning, then to the walls of his cell, and then back to me. He would have glowered again, I think, but to do so requires some confidence and his was melting away like an April snowfall. He was trapped, and he knew it.

"You and your brother took meat to John Kellet. And late at night, so none would know. Fair dealings may be done in the day. Only mischief need be done in the dark."

The logic of this remark seemed to strike home. Thomas looked down and studied the ground at his feet again.

"You sought to pay Kellet for some service, I think. A debt. To save his own skin he'll tell the bishop's men a tale to benefit him, not you. He will surely lay blame at your feet where he can. You will already be charged with poaching and venturing murder. What new indictment will come when John Kellet absolves himself of guilt?"

Atte Bridge did not respond for a moment. He was thinking, I assume. Thinking was an exercise Thomas atte Bridge tended to avoid. Doing so now was surely a new experience. Anything done for the first time will likely be done slowly. I gave him time to ponder his options. When he finally spoke several riddles were explained.

"'Twas Walter killed the deer. Not me."

"Walter?" I scratched my head, trying to match the name with a face. I did, to my vexation.

"The verderer's son?"

"Aye."

"Did Gerard know of this?"

"Nay… don't think so. I was always t'come late for my share."

"Your share? Why should Walter bestow his ill-got venison on you?"

Thomas stared again at the walls of his cell for a moment, wondering, I think, should he say more. I thought I could guess the answer, but better it come from Thomas than from me.

"Blackmailed 'im," he finally muttered.

"You learned of his poaching Lord Gilbert's deer? He who was to protect the forest against such a thing? How? Did you hear rumor and follow him about?"

More silence followed, and another question came to me: "And what had the curate to do with this that you would give him a portion of venison?"

"Confession," he whispered.

"Confession? You confessed this sin to Kellet and he demanded a share as penance?" I was incredulous.

"Nay," Thomas spat. "Might be as 'ow that's what 'e'll say, but 'twas 'is plan from t'first."

"Then what had confession to do with this?"

"Walter confessed to Kellet," Thomas admitted. "Walter didn't want to confess to the priest at Alvescot. Kellet an' Henry was old friends. The priest told me brother to blackmail Walter for some of the meat, an' they'd share. Henry went to Walter an' told 'im 'e knew of 'is poachin' Lord Gilbert's deer. Didn't tell 'im 'ow, 'course. Told 'im 'e'd seen 'im in the forest, huntin'. Told Walter 'e'd keep quiet 'bout it did Walter give 'im some of what 'e took."

"And some of Henry's portion went to Kellet?"

"Aye."

I took a moment to digest this. Kellet had violated his vows, breaking the seal of the confessional. Was blackmail a worse crime than this?

"When Henry died... what then?"

"Kellet come t'me. Told me what 'e an' Henry was about. I wondered 'ow Henry got so prosperous, like," Thomas muttered.

"He had iron hinges for his door, and an iron spade," I commented.

"Aye," Thomas mumbled.

"Henry blackmailed Edmund also?"

"Aye."

I knew what Edmund must have confessed to Kellet. No wonder then that the smith thought his dalliance with the baker's wife too costly. He had been paying a high price for Henry's silence.

"Have you sought goods of the smith?"

"Aye," he grimaced. "Threw me out, 'e did."

"His sin is known. He has no need to pay to keep it from me or any other. I saw Emma in dispute with Andrew Miller. Next day I saw her leave the mill with a sack. Did Henry blackmail the miller, also?"

"Aye. Andrew confessed givin' short weight."

Why a miller would think himself in danger should this news be about I do not know. All know millers do such a thing. Indeed, they consider such taking a part of their fee. Although Lord Gilbert is perhaps more strict about the conduct of his demesne tenants than most nobles. Andrew must have thought an occasional gift to Henry atte Bridge a small price to pay to keep the man silent.

While I thought on these things Thomas looked up and spoke. "Did John Kellet slay me brother?"

"He did."

"All 'cause o' them shoes?"

"Aye. Greed will destroy a man... eventually. Had Alan yet worn shoes when we found him in the hedgerow I might have been satisfied that a wolf caused the beadle's death. When Henry and John feared that I would seek out Henry and demand of him what he knew of Alan's death, they determined to waylay me along the north road. But your brother failed to kill me, so John Kellet killed him, rather than me, to silence him. So I believe."

"That fat priest should die," Thomas spat.

"For killing a man who would have killed me? As you would have. Two brothers much alike."

"But we didn't."

"Not for lack of effort or desire."

"What will t' bishop do with 'im?"

"The church executes no one. And I cannot prove he murdered your brother... nor can any man, I think."

"'E'll go free, then?"

"Not after what you've told me. The bishop's court will demand penance, and when he completes that, he'll be made a servant at some monastery, I'd guess."

Thomas turned from me to face the wall. I heard

him mutter imprecations against the church for allowing a murderer to escape hanging. Of course, he had escaped hanging only because he had not laid his cudgel a third time across my yet tender head. Or perhaps not. He might have got away with it. And surely Henry deserved hanging. But Thomas thought only of himself and the injuries done to him. He did not consider the wounds he gave others. But for the Spirit of God in some we are all much the same.

I turned to leave the cell. I had the knowledge I had come for. Uctred pulled the door closed behind me. As it slammed shut Thomas cried out.

"Wait... what will you do with me?"

"A jury of presentment will consider your crimes. You will be tried at hallmote, I think."

"You will leave me here 'til Michaelmas?" he shouted through the opening in the door.

"'Twas your choice to deal with a poacher and lay blows across my head. And you will have a companion soon enough."

Uctred dropped the beams through the iron fittings and across the door. A shadowed nose and eye pressed against the hole as we turned and climbed the steps to sunlight and fresh air.

I sent the porter's assistant to Alvescot with a message for Gerard that I wished to see him and his sons immediately. No one wishes to receive such a notice from a lord's bailiff. Gerard, whose conscience, so far as I knew, was unmarred, would be concerned. Walter would worry with each step which brought him to Bampton Castle. If he had a conscience. A little worry can be a good thing. Although in Walter's case worry before he poached Lord Gilbert's deer would have served better than worry after.

Gerard and his sons arrived just before dinner. I decided to let them wait while I took my meal, so directed the porter's assistant to assign them to an anteroom off the gatehouse until I should call for them. Another hour or so of apprehension would do Walter no harm.

Dinner this day was the usual three removes,

and more elaborate than many. The cook, I think, was practicing for Lord Gilbert's return to Bampton now little more than a fortnight away.

For the first remove there was Vyaund cyprys, boiled duck, and currant tarts. The second remove featured a roasted kid, stuffed partridge, and a custard. Grooms, of course, received of the second course only the custard. Since the Sumptuary Laws of 1363 they are permitted but one meal of meat or fish each day.

For the third remove there was fried pigeon and coney and for the subtlety a Lombardy custard. My belly was well filled and I was content with the world. Perhaps my interrogation of Walter Forester would have been sharper and more effective had I been hungry.

I found Richard and Walter yawning and scratching themselves on a bench in the gatehouse anteroom. Vermin, no doubt. Their father snored peacefully, propped against the opposite wall of the small room, on the other bench.

The verderer's sons leaped to their feet as I entered. Their bench banged off the wall behind them and awakened Gerard. The old man snorted, blinked, and stood also when his rheumy eyes fixed on my shadow in the doorway.

I stared silently from Gerard to his sons for several heartbeats. I wished them to know from the outset that their presence at the castle was about no ordinary business. I would allow them time to imagine what business it might be.

Gerard was puzzled. But his face betrayed no guilt. I was relieved. Had he seemed defensive or addressed me quickly on some trivial matter I would have suspected otherwise.

"You summoned us, an' 'ere we are," the old forester said. He was tottery from his nap, and swayed on his feet as he spoke. "Somethin' amiss w' the timbers?"

That explained the verderer's brow, which was beginning to fold into worry lines.

"Nay. They serve well. Lord Gilbert's new stables are nearly ready for his return. 'Tis another matter we must speak of."

But I did not speak of this other matter immediately. I waited, looking from father to sons. 'Twas Walter who looked away first. When he did so I felt ready to broach the matter at hand.

"Two days past a man of the Weald was found with a joint of venison in his sack."

"A poacher!" Gerard cried. "In my... I mean, Lord Gilbert's forest?"

"Aye. So 'twould seem."

"Who is the fellow?" Richard asked.

"He is called Thomas atte Bridge... but he claims he is not a poacher."

"How then did 'e come by venison?" Gerard fumed. Walter remained silent, looking from his father to me and back again.

"Blackmail. Claims he learned of the poacher's work and threatened to expose the man did he not share the spoil."

"Is this poacher known?" Gerard seethed.

"Aye, to me... and to you."

"Nay," the old man protested.

"Oh, he is not known to you as a poacher, but you do know of him."

"Who is't?" Richard demanded.

I was not required to answer. Walter bolted past me through the door and disappeared into the gatehouse. Gerard and Richard were too stunned to do anything but blink wide-eyed at me and each other, but I recovered my wits and shouted through the door for Wilfred to stop the fleeing Walter.

I was too late. I flung myself to the door but Richard arrived there first. Wilfred stood agape as we scrambled from the anteroom. I ran under the portcullis just in time to see Walter dodging through the castle forecourt and those who had business there.

I hesitated, but Richard did not. His flying feet raised puffs of dust as he pursued his brother. Gerard stumbled up beside me and we watched as Walter fled west on Mill Street toward the forest and Alvescot. I recovered my wits and shouted for Wilfred and his assistant to give chase also. Soon four men were pounding down Mill Street between meadow and plowland toward the wood. Walter disappeared into the forest with Richard but a few strides behind.

Gerard set off across the forecourt as rapidly as he could. His limp was pronounced when he hurried. Before Gerard reached Mill Street the sound of distant shouting and conflict came from the forest. At that moment Wilfred and his assistant vanished into the trees. And then the sound of struggle ceased. Silence filled the forecourt as those who had business there and at the castle looked from me to the forest and back. The only sound was Gerard's dragging left foot as he hobbled toward Mill Street.

As the verderer reached the street four figures emerged on the road from the wood. Richard had a firm grasp on his brother's right arm, which even from 300 or so paces I could see he had twisted high behind Walter's back. Wilfred marched along on Walter's left, one hand at the malefactor's collar, the other grasping his left arm. Wilfred's assistant strode behind the three. In his hands he carried a downed limb which he waved threateningly over Walter's bowed head.

Gerard approached his son and as I watched, without breaking his halting stride, he swung his right fist firmly against Walter's jaw. I could not hear the blow strike, but saw its result clear enough. The old verderer might have a weakness in his left arm, but there was no fault in his right hand. And many years of swinging axe and adze had toughened the man. Walter dropped to his knees like a poleaxed ox. Had not Wilfred and Richard held him aright I think the blow would have laid Walter face down in the road.

Richard released Walter's arm, leaving Wilfred to help Walter regain his feet. I was too far away to hear, but wild gesticulation indicated that Richard and his father were in animate conversation. I think Gerard would have thumped Walter again had not Richard placed himself between the two.

This lively discourse seemed eventually to cool. Gerard stomped off toward the castle and Richard once again took his brother's arm. Walter seemed sufficiently recovered to put a foot in front of another. Slowly the party set off for the castle in Gerard's wake. As they drew near I saw a trickle of blood at the corner of Walter's mouth. I wondered if the punishment meted to him at hallmote would equal that he would receive from his father.

Gerard was surely frantic that, because of his son, he would lose his place as Lord Gilbert's verderer. And perhaps he should have given better oversight to forest and family. But he had, so far as I knew, always done faithful service to Lord Gilbert. That would surely weigh in his favor. Lord Gilbert would return to Bampton in a fortnight. Gerard's future would be his decision, not mine.

Uctred and the porter's assistant dragged Walter off to join Thomas in his cell, while Gerard apologized noisily for his son's behavior. I thought the man might throw himself on the ground and kiss my feet, so voluble were his protests of innocence and regret.

I was eventually able to convince the verderer that I held no grudge against him or Richard. With somewhat dazed expressions on their faces, they went home.

Thomas and Walter enjoyed one another's company in the dungeon for two months, until Michaelmas. At hallmote they were fined six pence each for poaching Lord Gilbert's deer. There were, I feel certain, men on the jury who felt some sympathy for them, and who would, perhaps, have taken a deer or two themselves had they thought they might escape discovery.

But for Thomas' blows against my skull there was less sympathy. He was fined an additional six pence and required to provide another to pledge for him until it was paid. To me. So I received two pence for each lump on my head. Not a bargain I wish to repeat. And he was made to stand in the stocks at the edge of the marketplace for a day while children laughed at him and adolescents threw rubbish when they thought no one would see. And sometimes when others did see.

John Kellet lost his place at St Andrew's Chapel. 'Twas as I suspected: he was sent on pilgrimage, to Compostella, there to seek absolution. The bishop demanded of him that he leave the realm with no coin, and live as a mendicant while on pilgrimage. He has not yet returned. When he does he is to retire to the Priory of St Nicholas in Exeter, there to live out his days as servant to the Almoner. The pilgrimage to Spain is long and surely difficult. Perhaps he will not survive the journey. One who so betrays his vocation surely deserves whatever evil may befall him.

Thomas de Bowlegh has assured me that the Prior of St Nicholas is a stern man. Good. If the walk to Spain does not thin the fat priest, perhaps life in the priory will.

There is always the chance that King Edward will find cause for war with France. Kellet's skill with a bow may help him escape the priory. Then he might find himself in battle with the French. Perhaps some Genoese crossbowman will take aim at him. Between pilgrimage and war God will have many opportunities to do justice and take John Kellet from this world to the next for judgment. I pray he does so soon.

The day after hallmote I bid Lord Gilbert farewell, retrieved Bruce from the marshalsea, and set off for a visit to Oxford. I needed more parchments and a pot of ink. And I had promised Master John to tell him of the resolution of this tale when I might. But you may guess that above all I wished to see Kate Caxton again.

I might have enjoyed Bruce's languid gait had I not been in a fever to see the lass. Swineherds drove pigs into the autumn wood for pannaging as I passed. And wheat stubble, now the harvest was finished, was being gathered to mix with hay for winter fodder.

I berated myself as I rode that day that I had not found excuse to visit the stationer and his daughter sooner. Oxford was full to bursting with burghers' sons and bachelor lawyers. They would be drawn to Kate like the swineherd's hogs to acorns. A poor metaphor. Well, reader, you will grasp my meaning.

Bruce clattered across the Oxpens Road Bridge and the bustle and smells of Oxford returned to me. How is it that when I return to the town after some time away I am always pleased to do so? But after a few days, when I take leave and return to Bampton, I am likewise pleased to leave the clamor and odors behind.

I left Bruce at the Stag and Hounds and set off toward Holywell Street and Caxton's shop. Each step brought me closer to Kate, and also more apprehension of what I might find there. I reproved my lack of romantic effort and considered days in the summer now past when I might have found excuse to visit Oxford. I have often prayed that God would exert Himself and provide for me a good wife. Perhaps He had done so and left the conclusion of the task to me. As I strode down the curve of Holywell Street and the stationer's shop came into view I resolved to end my laxity – was I not too late.

The stationer looked up from his desk as I entered. I greeted him and asked of his injured back while casting about through the corners of my eyes for Kate. She was not present, and my heart sank.

Caxton was no fool. He saw that, while my greeting was for him, my interest lay elsewhere.

"Kate," he shouted through the door to the workroom. "Master Hugh has come."

I was much relieved. I heard the rustle of a long cotehardie from through the open door and a heartbeat later Kate appeared. She gave the appearance of having hurried from her task to the door, but once there remembered decorum and walked toward me with dignified mien. Actually, a heartbeat was quite a long time, for mine skipped several beats when she appeared. Neither of us spoke for a moment.

"Master Hugh," she exclaimed. "I thought you had forgot us."

"Ah, Miss Caxton, I have an excellent memory... and even had I not, it is unlikely I could forget you."

The girl blushed.

I saw from the corner of my eye Robert Caxton return to his desk and busy himself there. As Kate drew near she came between her father and me. I looked past her and was relieved to see a smile at the corner of his lips, rather than a scowl across his brow.

We made small talk for some time before I announced that I had come for parchment and a pot of ink.

"Do you return to Bampton this day?" Caxton asked.

"No. 'Tis too far to journey here and back in one day. Especially on a horse so old as mine. And I promised when last in Oxford to call on Master Wyclif and tell him of the resolution of events in Bampton."

"Then if you can return tomorrow I will have a fresh pot of ink prepared for you."

I promised to do so, and an awkward silence followed. Kate finally spoke.

"I must return to my work," she smiled. "But the task will be done tomorrow when you call."

She left the room and her father and I were left staring at each other. A moment of boldness came over me. Kate could do that to a man. "Sir, I would like to pay court to your daughter... if you approve."

"I do," he replied softly. "And so, I think, does Kate."

I bid the stationer good day, promised to return next day for parchment and ink, and set off for Canterbury Hall with light feet and lighter heart.

The porter remembered me and readily granted me the freedom of the college. Autumn days grew short. 'Twas dark enough that I could see a cresset glow from Wyclif's window as I approached his chamber. I rapped upon his door and, as before, heard a bench grate upon the flags. I expected to see a book open upon his desk, the flame lighting his study. But not so. Master John opened the door, saw 'twas me, turned to his barren table and spoke.

"Master Hugh... you are well met. I was about to send for you. They've stolen my books."

An extract from the forthcoming third chronicle

of Hugh de Singleton, surgeon

Chapter 1

I had never seen Master John Wyclif so afflicted. He was rarely found at such a loss when in disputation with other masters. He told me later, when I had returned them to him, that it was as onerous to plunder a bachelor scholar's books as it would be to steal another man's wife. I had, at the time, no way to assess the accuracy of that opinion, for I had no wife and few books.

But I had come to Oxford on that October day, Monday, the twentieth, in the year of our Lord 1365, to see what progress I might make to remedy my solitary estate. I left my horse at the stable behind the Stag and Hounds and went straightaway to Robert Caxton's shop, where the stationer's comely daughter, Kate, helped attract business from the bachelor scholars, masters, clerks, and lawyers who infest Oxford like fleas on a hound.

My pretended reason to visit Caxton's shop was to purchase a gathering of parchment and a fresh pot of ink. I needed these to conclude my record of the deaths of Alan the beadle and of Henry atte Bridge. Alan's corpse was found, three days before Good Friday, near to St Andrew's Chapel, to the east of Bampton. And Henry, who slew Alan, was found in a wood to the north of the town. As bailiff of Bampton castle it was my business to sort out these murders, which I did, but not before I was attacked on the road returning from Witney and twice clubbed about the head in nocturnal churchyards. Had I known such assaults lay in my future I might have rejected Lord Gilbert Talbot's offer to serve as his bailiff at Bampton Castle and remained but Hugh the surgeon, of Oxford High Street.

Kate promised to prepare a fresh pot of ink, which

I might have next day, and when she quit the shop to continue her duties in the workroom I spoke to her father. Robert Caxton surely knew the effect Kate had upon young men. He displayed no surprise when I asked leave to court his daughter.

I had feared raised eyebrows at best, and perhaps a refusal. I am but a surgeon, and bailiff to Lord Gilbert at his manor at Bampton. Surgeons own little prestige in Oxford, full of physicians as it is, and few honest men wish to see their daughter wed to a bailiff. There were surely sons of wealthy Oxford burghers, and young masters of the law, set on a path to wealth, who had eyes for the comely Kate. But Caxton nodded agreement when I requested his permission to pay court to his daughter. Perhaps my earlier service to mend his wounded back helped my suit.

I left the stationer's shop with both joy and apprehension. The joy you will understand, or would had you seen Kate and spent time in her presence. I was apprehensive because next day I must begin a thing for which I had no training and in which I had little experience. While at Balliol College I was too much absorbed in my set books to concern myself with the proper way to impress a lass, and none of those volumes dealt with the subject. Certainly the study of logic avoided the topic. Since then my duties as surgeon and bailiff allowed small opportunity to practice discourse with a maiden. And there are few females of my age and station in Bampton.

I made my way from Caxton's shop on Holywell Street to Catte Street and thence to the gate of Canterbury Hall, on Merton Street. As I walked I composed speeches in my mind with which I might impress Kate Caxton. I had forgotten most of these inventions by next day. 'Twas just as well.

Master John Wyclif, former Master of Balliol College and my teacher there, was newly appointed Warden of Canterbury Hall. Several months earlier, frustrated at my inability to discover who had slain Alan the beadle and Henry atte Bridge, I had called upon Master John to lament my ignorance and seek his wisdom. He provided encouragement, and an empty chamber in the Hall where I might stay the night, safe from the snores and vermin at the Stag and Hounds.

When I left him those months earlier he enjoined me to call when I was next in Oxford and tell him of the resolution of these mysteries. At the time of his request I was not sure there ever would be a resolution to the business.

But there was, and so I sought Master John to tell him of it, and seek again his charity and an empty cell for the night. The porter recognized me, and sent me to Master John's chamber. I expected to find him bent over a book, as was his usual posture when I called. But not so. He opened the door to my knock, recognized me, and turning to his barren table said, "Master Hugh ... they've stolen my books."

The greeting startled me. I peered over the scholar's shoulder as if I expected to see the miscreants and the plundered volumes. I saw Master John's table, and a cupboard where his books were kept. Both were bare. He turned to follow my gaze.

"Gone," he whispered. "All of them."

"Who?" I asked dumbly. Had Master John known that, he would have set after the thieves and recovered the books. Or sent the sheriff to do so.

"I know not," Wyclif replied. "I went to my supper three days past. When I returned the books were gone ... even the volume I left open on my table.

Master John is not a wealthy man. He has the living of Fillingham, and prebend of Aust, but these provide a thin subsistence for an Oxford master of arts at work on a degree in theology. The loss of books accumulated in a life of study would be a blow to any scholar, rich or poor.

"The porter saw no stranger enter or leave the Hall while we supped," Wyclif continued. "I went next day to the sheriff, but Sir John has other matters to mind."

"Sir John?"

"Aye. Roger de Cottesford is replaced. The new high sheriff is Sir John Trillowe."

"He offered no aid?"

"He sent a sergeant round to the stationers in the town, to see did any man come to them with books he offered to sell. Two I borrowed from Nicholas de Redyng. He will be sorry to learn they are lost."

"And the stationers ... they have been offered no books?"

"None of mine missing. And Sir John has no interest, I think, in pursuing my loss further."

The colleges have always wished to rule themselves, free of interference from the town and its government. No doubt the sheriff was minded to allow Canterbury Hall the freedom to apprehend its own thief, without his aid or interference.

"How many?"

"My books? Twenty ... and the two borrowed."

I performed some mental arithmetic. Master John read my thoughts.

"The books I borrowed from Master Nicholas ... one was Bede's Historia Ecclesiastica, worth near thirty shillings. One of mine was of paper, a cheap set book, but the others were of parchment and well-bound."

"Your loss is great, then. Twenty pounds or more."

"Aye," Wyclif sighed. "Four were of my own devising. Some might say they were worth little. But the others ... Aristotle, Grosseteste, Boethius, all gone."

Master John sighed again, and gazed about his chamber as if the stolen books were but misplaced, and with closer inspection of dark corners might yet be discovered.

"I am pleased to see you," Master John continued. "I had thought to send for you."

"For me?"

"Aye. I have hope that you will seek my stolen books and see them returned to me."

"Me? Surely the sheriff ..."

"Sir John is not interested in any crime for which the solution will not bring him a handsome fine. Rumor is he paid King Edward 60 pounds for the office. He will be about recouping his investment, not seeking stolen books. And you are skilled at solving mysteries," Wyclif continued. "You found who 'twas in Lord Gilbert's cesspit, and unless I mistake me you know by now who killed your beadle and the fellow found slain in the forest. Well, do you not?"

"Aye. 'Twas as I thought. Henry atte Bridge, found dead in the wood, slew Alan the beadle. Alan had followed him during the night as Henry took a haunch of venison poached from Lord Gilbert's forest, to the curate at St Andrew's Chapel."

"Venison? To a priest?"

"Aye. 'Tis a long story."

"I have nothing but time, and no books with which to fill it. Tell me."

So I told Master John of the scandal of the betrayed confessional of the priest at St Andrew's Chapel. And of the blackmail he plotted with Henry atte Bridge – and Henry's brother, Thomas – of those who confessed to poaching, adultery, and cheating at their business.

"I came to Oxford this day to buy more ink and parchment so I may write of these felonies while details remain fresh in my memory."

"And what stationer receives your custom?"

"Robert Caxton. 'Twas you who sent me first to Caxton's shop. You knew I would find more there than books, ink, and parchment."

"I did? Yes, I remember now telling you of the new stationer, come from Cambridge with his daughter ... ah, that is your meaning. I am slow of wit these days. I think of nothing but my books."

"You did not guess I might be interested in the stationer's daughter?"

"Nay," Wyclif grimaced. "I surprise myself for my lack of perception. You are a young man with two good eyes. The stationer's daughter ..."

"Kate," I said.

"Aye, Kate, is a winsome lass."

"She is. And this day I have gained her father's permission to seek her as my wife."

Master John's doleful expression brightened. The corners of his mouth and eyes lifted into a grin. "I congratulate you, Hugh."

"Do not be too quick to do so. I must woo and win her, and I fear for my ability."

"I have no competency in such matters. You are on your own. 'Tis your competency solving puzzles I seek."

"But I am already employed."

Master John's countenance fell. "I had not considered that," he admitted. "Lord Gilbert requires your service ... and pays well for it, I imagine."

"Aye. I am well able to afford a wife."

"But could not the town spare you for a week or two, 'til my books are found? Surely a surgeon ... never mind. You see how little I heed other men's troubles when I meet my own."

"Why should you be different from other men?" I asked.

"Why? Because my misplaced esteem tells me I must."

"What? Be unlike other men?"

"Aye. Do you not wish the same, Hugh? To be unlike the commons? They scratch when and where they itch and belch when and where they will and the letters on a page are as foreign to them as Malta."

"But ... I remember a lecture ..."

Wyclif grimaced.

"When you spoke of all men being the same when standing before God. No gentlemen, no villeins, all sinners."

"Hah; run through by my own pike. 'Tis true. I recite the same sermon each year, but though we be all sinners, and all equally in need of God's grace, all sins are not, on earth, equal, as they may be in God's eyes. Else all punishments would be the same, regardless of the crime."

"And what would be a fitting penalty for one who stole twenty books?"

Wyclif scowled again. "Twenty-two," he muttered.

"My thoughts change daily," he continued. "When I first discovered the offence I raged about the Hall threatening the thief with a noose."

"And now?"

Master John smiled grimly. "I have thought much on that. Was the thief a poor man needing to keep his children from starvation I might ask no penalty at all, so long as my books be returned. But if the miscreant be another scholar, with means to purchase his own books, I would see him fined heavily and driven from Oxford, and never permitted to study here again, or teach, be he a master. Both holy and secular wisdom," Wyclif mused, "teach that we must not do to another what we find objectionable when done to us. No man should hold a place at Oxford who denies both God and Aristotle."

"You think 'twas an Oxford man who has done this?"

Wyclif chewed upon a fingernail, then spoke. "Who else would want my books, or know their worth?"

"That, it seems to me, is the crux of the matter," I replied. "Some scholar wished to add to his library, or needed money, and saw your books as a way to raise funds."

As it happened, there was a third reason a man might wish to rob master John of his books, but that explanation for the theft did not occur to me 'til later.

"I am lost," Wyclif sighed. "I am a master with no books, and I see no way to retrieve them."

I felt guilty that, for all his aid given to me, I could offer no assistance to the scholar. I could but commiserate, cluck my tongue, and sit in his presence with a long face.

The autumn sun set behind the old Oxford Castle keep while we talked. Wyclif was about to speak again when a small bell sounded from across the courtyard.

"Supper," he explained, and invited me to follow him to the refectory.

Scholars at Canterbury hall are fed well, but simply. For this supper there were loaves of maslin – wheat and barley – cheese, a pease pottage flavored with bits of pork, and tankards of watered ale. I wondered at the pork, for some of the scholars were Benedictines. Students peered up from under lowered brows as we entered. They all knew of the theft, and, I considered later, suspected each other of complicity in the deed.

A watery autumn sun struggled to rise above the forest and water meadow east of Oxford when I awoke next morning. Wyclif bid me "fare well" with stooped shoulders and eyes dark from lack of sleep. I wished the scholar well, and expressed my prayer that his books be speedily recovered. Master John believes in prayer, but my promise to petition our Lord Christ on his behalf seemed to bring him small comfort. I think he would rather have my time and effort than my prayers. Or would have both. Prayers may be offered cheaply. They require little effort from men, and much from God. The Lord Christ has told us we may ask of Him what we will, but I suspect He would be pleased to see men set to their work, and call upon Him only when tasks be beyond them.

I thought on this as I walked through the awakening lanes of Oxford to Holywell Street and Robert Caxton's shop. Was it really my duty to Lord Gilbert which prevented me from seeking Wyclif's stolen books, or was I too slothful to do aught but pray for their return? I did not like the answer which came to me.

As I approached the stationer's shop I saw a tall young man standing before it, shifting his weight from one foot to the other. The fellow was no scholar. He wore a deep red cotehardie, cut short to show a good leg. His chauces were parti-colored, grey and black, and his cap ended in a long yellow liripipe coiled stylishly about his head. The color of his cap surprised me. All who visit London know that the whores of that city are required by law to wear yellow caps so respectable maidens and wives be left unmolested on the street. He was shod in fine leather, and the pointed toes of his shoes curled up in ungainly fashion.

The fellow seemed impatient; while I watched he strode purposefully past Caxton's shop, then reversed his steps and walked past in the opposite direction, toward my approach. I drew closer to the shop, so that at each turn I could see his face more clearly. His countenance and beard were dark, as were his eyes. The beard was neatly trimmed, and his eyes peered at my approach from above an impressive nose – although, unlike mine, his nose pointed straight out at the world, whereas mine turns to the dexter side. He seemed about my own age – twenty-five years or so. He was broad of shoulder and yet slender, but good living was beginning to produce a paunch.

I slowed my pace as I approached the shuttered shop. Caxton would open his business soon, and I assumed this dandy needed parchment, ink, or a book, although he did not seem the type to be much interested in words on a page. He was not.

I stood in the street, keeping the impatient coxcomb company, until Robert Caxton opened his shop door and pushed up his shutters to begin business for the day. The stationer looked from me to his other customer and I thought his eyes widened. I bowed to the other client and motioned him to precede me into the shop. He was there before me.

The morning sun was low in the south-east, and Caxton's shop is on the south side of Holywell Street, facing north. But dark as the shop was I could see that Kate was not within. He of the red cotehardie saw the same, and spoke before I could.

"Is mistress Kate at leisure?" he asked.

Caxton glanced at me, then answered. "Near so. Preparing a pot of ink in the workroom. Be done shortly."

"I'll wait," the fellow said with a smile. "'Tis a pleasant morning. And if Kate has no other concerns, I'd have her walk with me along the water meadow."

He might as well have swatted me over my skull with a ridge pole. My jaw went slack and I fear both Caxton and this unknown suitor got a fine view of my tonsils.

Robert Caxton was not so discomfited that he forgot manners. He introduced me to Sir Simon Trillowe. A knight. And of some relation to the new sheriff of Oxford, I guessed.

When he learned that I was but a surgeon and bailiff to Lord Gilbert Talbot, Sir Simon nodded briefly and turned away, his actions speaking what polite words could not: I was beneath his rank and unworthy of his consideration.

"We heard naught of you for many months, Master Hugh," Caxton remarked.

'Twas true. I had neglected pursuit of Kate Caxton while about Lord Gilbert's business in Bampton. And, to be true, I feared Kate might dismiss my suit should I press it. A man cannot be disappointed in love who does not seek it.

"No doubt a bailiff has much to occupy his time," the stationer continued.

Sir Simon surely thought that I was but a customer, not that I was in competition with him for the fair Kate. He would learn that soon enough.

The door to Caxton's workroom was open. Kate surely heard this exchange, which was a good thing. It gave her opportunity to compose herself. A moment later she entered the shop, carrying my pot of promised ink, and bestowed a tranquil smile upon both me and Sir Simon. I smiled in return, Trillowe did not. Perhaps he had guessed already that it was not ink I most wished to take from Caxton's shop.

"Mistress Kate," Sir Simon stepped toward her as she passed through the door. "'Tis a pleasant autumn morn ... there will be few more before winter. Perhaps we might walk the path along the Cherwell ... if your father can spare you for the morning."

With these words Trillowe turned to the stationer. Caxton shrugged a reply.

"Good." Sir Simon offered his arm and, with a brief smile and raised brows in my direction, Kate set the pot of ink on her father's table and took Trillowe's arm. They departed the shop wordlessly.

Caxton apparently thought some explanation in

order. "You didn't call through the summer. Kate thought you'd no interest. I told her last night you'd asked to pay court. But Sir Simon's been by a dozen times since Lammas Day ... others, too."

"Others?"

"Aye. My Kate does draw lads to the shop. None 'as asked me might they pay court, though. But for you."

"Not Sir Simon?"

"Nay. Second son of the sheriff, and a knight. He'll not ask leave of one like me to do aught."

"And Kate returns his interest?"

Caxton shrugged. "She's walked out with 'im three times now. A knight, mind you. An' son of the sheriff. Can't blame a lass for that."

"No," I agreed.

"Can't think how 'is father'd be pleased, though. A stationer's daughter! A scandal in Oxford castle when word gets out, as it surely has, by now," Caxton mused.

"Aye. What lands his father may hold will pass to his brother. The sheriff will want Sir Simon seeking a wife with lands of her own, surely."

I hoped that was so. But if a second or third son acts to displease his father it is difficult to correct him. How can a man disinherit a son who is due to receive little or nothing anyway? So if a son courting Kate Caxton displeased the sheriff of Oxford such offence might escape retribution. This thought did not bring me joy.